T0000097

"One of my all-time favorite historicals."

—*New York Times* bestselling author Maisey Yates

"*Bringing Down the Duke* is one of the best books I've ever read—absolutely adored it. Dunmore had me in tears, had me holding my breath . . . the emotion and passion made the book ache and sing."

—*New York Times* bestselling author Jane Porter

"Charming, sexy, and thoroughly transportive, this is historical romance done right." —*Publishers Weekly* (starred review)

"Funny, smart, and a fantastic read! *Bringing Down the Duke* is absolutely brilliant!"

—*New York Times* bestselling author Corinne Michaels

"Full of witty banter and swoonworthy moments. . . . A deliciously delightful romance." —*Woman's World*

"Dunmore's beautifully written debut perfectly balances history, sexual tension, romantic yearning, and the constant struggle smart women have in finding and maintaining their places and voices in life and love, with the added message that finding the right person brings true happiness and being with them is worth any price. A brilliant debut." —*Kirkus Reviews* (starred review)

"Chock-full of verve, history, and passion."

—*Library Journal* (starred review)

"Full of witty banter, rich historical detail, and a fantastic group of female friends, the first installment in Dunmore's League of Extraordinary Women series starts with fireworks as Annabelle and Montgomery try to find a path to happiness despite past mistakes and their vastly different places in society. Dunmore's strong debut is sure to earn her legions of fans." —*Booklist* (starred review)

"What an absolutely stunning, riveting, painfully gorgeous book! It's going straight to my keeper shelf, and I will be buying a copy the moment it comes out to reread again and again. It's not only the best historical romance I've read in a long, long time, it's one of the best books I've ever read! I adored it!"

—*USA Today* bestselling author Megan Crane

"Evie Dunmore has written a story we need right now—strong, smart, and passionate, featuring a heroine who won't settle for less than what she deserves and a swoony hero who learns to fight for what really matters. With her debut novel, Dunmore has instantly become a must-read for me."

—Lyssa Kay Adams, author of *The Bromance Book Club*

"*Bringing Down the Duke* is the best historical romance I've read all year. I was spellbound by this story of forbidden love between a spirited, clever suffragette heroine and her straitlaced duke, a man who proves that fire burns hottest when it's under ice. Evie Dunmore is a marvelous, fresh new voice in romance who is sure to go far. Don't miss her brilliant debut!"

—Anna Campbell, bestselling author of the Dashing Widows series

"With just the right blend of history and romance (and a healthy dash of pride from the British suffragists that would make Jane Austen proud), I was hooked on Annabelle and Sebastian's story from the very first page. I can't wait for the rest of the League of Extraordinary Women novels!"

—*USA Today* bestselling author Stephanie Thornton

"Evie Dunmore's *Bringing Down the Duke* delivers the best of two worlds—a steamy romance coupled with the heft of a meticulously researched historical novel. . . . Readers will be entranced watching Annabelle, a woman ahead of her time, bring the sexy duke to his knees."

—Renée Rosen, author of *Park Avenue Summer*

ALSO BY EVIE DUNMORE

Bringing Down the Duke

A Rogue
of
One's Own

EVIE DUNMORE

BERKLEY ROMANCE
New York

BERKLEY ROMANCE
Published by Berkley
An imprint of Penguin Random House LLC
penguinrandomhouse.com

Copyright © 2020 by Evie Dunmore
Readers Guide copyright © 2020 by Evie Dunmore
Excerpt copyright © 2020 by Evie Dunmore
Penguin Random House supports copyright. Copyright fuels creativity, encourages diverse voices,
promotes free speech, and creates a vibrant culture. Thank you for buying an authorized edition
of this book and for complying with copyright laws by not reproducing, scanning, or distributing
any part of it in any form without permission. You are supporting writers and allowing
Penguin Random House to continue to publish books for every reader.

BERKLEY and the BERKLEY & B colophon
are registered trademarks of Penguin Random House LLC.

The Library of Congress has cataloged the Jove trade paperback edition of this book as follows:

Names: Dunmore, Evie, author.
Title: A rogue of one's own / Evie Dunmore.
Description: First Edition. | New York : Jove, 2020. |
Series: A league of extraordinary women; 2
Identifiers: LCCN 2020004978 | ISBN 9781984805706 (trade paperback) |
ISBN 9781984805713 (ebook)
Subjects: GSAFD: Love stories.
Classification: LCC PR9110.9.D86 R64 2020 | DDC 823/.92—dc23
LC record available at https://lccn.loc.gov/2020004978

Jove trade paperback edition / September 2020
Berkley Romance trade paperback edition / March 2024

Printed in the United States of America
6th Printing

Book design by Laura K. Corless

To Brad and Judy,
the most genuinely good people
who always bring out the best in me.

A Rogue of One's Own

Chapter 1

Buckinghamshire, Summer 1865

Young ladies did not lie prone on the rug behind the library's chesterfield and play chess against themselves. They did not stuff their cheeks with boiled sweets before breakfast. Lucie knew this. But it was the summer holidays and the dullest of them yet: Tommy had come home from Eton a proper prig who wouldn't play with girls anymore; newly arrived cousin Cecily was the type of child who cried easily; and, at barely thirteen years of age, Lucie found she was too young to just decorously die of boredom. Her mother, on the other hand, would probably consider this quite a noble death. Then again, to the Countess of Wycliffe, most things were preferable over hoydenish behavior.

The smell of leather and dust was in her nose and the library was pleasantly silent. Morning sun pooled on the chessboard and made the white queen shine bright like a beacon. She was in peril—a rogue knight had set a trap, and Her Majesty could now choose to sacrifice herself to protect the king, or to let him fall. Lucie's fingers hovered over the polished ivory crown, indecisive.

Rapid footsteps echoed in the hallway.

Her mother's delicate heels—but Mother never ran?

The door flew open.

"How could you? How could you?"

Lucie froze. Her mother's voice was trembling with outrage.

The door slammed shut again and the floor shook from the force of it.

"In front of everyone, the whole ballroom—"

"Come now, must you carry on so?"

Her stomach felt hollow. It was her father, his tone coldly bored and cutting.

"Everyone knows, while I'm abed at home, oblivious!"

"Good Gad. Why Rochester's wife calls herself your friend is beyond me—she fills your ears with gossip and now look at you, raving like a madwoman. Why, I should have sent her away last night; it is rather like her erratic self to invite herself, to arrive late and unannounced—"

"She stays," snapped Mama. "She must stay—one honest person in a pit of snakes."

Her father laughed. "Lady Rochester, honest? Have you seen her son? What an odd little ginger fellow—I'd wager a thousand pounds he isn't even Rochester's spawn—"

"What about you, Wycliffe? How many have you spawned among your side pieces?"

"Now. This is below you, wife."

There was a pause, and it stretched and grew heavy like a lead blanket.

Lucie's heart was drumming against her ribs, hard and painful, the thuds so loud, they had to hear it.

A sob shattered the quiet and it hit her stomach like a punch. Her mother was crying.

"I beseech you, Thomas. What have I done wrong so you won't even grant me discretion?"

"Discretion—madam, your screeching can be heard from miles away!"

"I gave you Tommy," she said between sobs. "I nearly died giving you Tommy and yet you flaunt that . . . that person—in front of everyone."

"Saints, grant me patience—why am I shackled to such an over-emotional female?"

"I love you so, Thomas. Why, why can't you love me?"

A groan, fraught with impatience. "I love you well enough, wife, though your hysterics do make it a challenge."

"Why must it be so?" Mama keened. "Why am I not enough for you?"

"Because, my dear, I am a man. May I have some peace in my library now, please."

A hesitation; then, a gasp that sounded like surrender.

The thud of the heavy door falling shut once more came from a distance. A roar filled Lucie's ears. Her throat was clogged with boiled sweets; she'd have to breathe through her mouth. But he would hear her.

She could hold out. She would not breathe.

The *snick* of a lighter. Wycliffe had lit a cigarette. Floorboards creaked. Leather crunched. He had settled into his armchair.

Her lungs were burning, and her fingers were white as bone, alien and clawlike against the dizzying swirls of the rug.

Still she lay silent. King and queen blurred before her eyes.

She could hold out.

Black began edging her vision. It was as though she'd never breathe again.

Paper rustled. The earl was reading the morning news.

A mile from the library, deep in the cool green woods of Wycliffe Park, Tristan Ballentine, the second son of the Earl of Rochester, had just decided to spend all his future summers at Wycliffe Hall. He might have to befriend Tommy, Greatest Prig at Eton, to put this plan into practice, but the morning walks alone would be worth it. Unlike the estate of his family seat, where every shrub was pruned and accounted for, Wycliffe Park left nature to its own devices. Trees gnarled. Shrubbery sprawled. The air was sweet with the fragrance of forest flowers. And he had found a most suitable place for reading Wordsworth: a circular clearing at the end of a hollow way. A large standing stone loomed at its center.

Dew drenched his trouser legs as he circled the monolith. It looked suspiciously like a fairy stone, weathered and conical, planted here before all time. Of course, at twelve years of age, he was too old to believe in fairies and the like. His father had made this abundantly clear. Poetry, too, was forbidden in Ashdown Castle. Romantic lines ran counter to the Ballentine motto, "With Valor and Vigor." But here, who could find him? Who would see? His copy of Wordsworth and Coleridge's *Lyrical Ballads* was at the ready.

He shrugged out of his coat and spread it on the grass, then made to stretch himself out on his belly. The fine fabric of his trousers promptly grated like chain mail against the broken skin on his backside, making him hiss in pain. His father drove his lessons home with a cane. And yesterday, the earl had been overzealous, again. It was why Mama had grabbed him, Tristan, and he had grabbed his books, and they had taken off to visit her friend Lady Wycliffe for the summer.

He tried finding a comfortable position, shifting this way and that, then he gave up, unhooked his braces and began unbuttoning the fall of the pesky trousers. The next moment, the ground began to shake.

For a beat, he froze.

He snatched his coat and dove behind the standing stone just as a black horse thundered into view in the hollow-way. A magnificent animal, gleaming with sweat, foam flying from its bit. The kind of stallion kings and heroes rode. It scrambled to a sudden halt on the clearing, sending lumps of soil flying with plate-sized hooves.

He gasped with shocked surprise.

The rider was no king. No hero. The rider was not a man at all.

It was a girl.

She wore boots and breeches like a boy and rode astride, but there was no doubt she was a girl. A coolly shimmering fall of ice-blond hair streamed down her back and whirled round her like a silken veil when the horse pivoted.

He couldn't have moved had he tried. He was stunned, his gaze riveted to her face—was she real? Her face . . . was perfect. Delicate and heart-shaped, with fine, winged eyebrows and an obstinate, pointy little chin. *A fairy.*

But her cheeks were flushed an angry pink and her lips pressed into a line. She looked ready to ride into battle on the big black beast . . .

She made to slide from the saddle, and he shrank back behind the stone. He should show himself. His mouth went dry. What would he say? What did one say to someone so lovely and fierce?

Her boots hit the ground with a light thud. She muttered a few soft words to the stallion. Then nothing.

He craned his neck. The girl was gone. Quietly, he crept forward. When he rose to a crouch, he spotted her supine form in the grass, her slender arms flung wide.

He might have moved a little closer . . . closer, even. He straightened, peering down.

Her eyes were closed. Her lashes lay dark and straight against her pale cheeks. The gleaming strands of her hair fanned out around her head like rays of a white cold winter sun.

His heart was racing. A powerful ache welled from his core, an anxious urgency, a dread, of sorts—this was a rare, precious opportunity and he was woefully unprepared to grasp it. He had not known girls like her existed, outside the fairy books and the princesses of the Nordic sagas he had to read in secret . . .

An angry snort tore through the silence. The stallion was approaching, ears flat and teeth bared.

"Hell," Tristan said.

The girl's eyes snapped open. They stared at each other, her flat on her back, him looming.

She was on her feet like a shot. "You! You are trespassing."

She had looked petite, but they stood nearly eye to eye.

He felt his face freeze in a dim-witted grin. "No, I—"

Stormy gray eyes narrowed at him. "I know who you are. You are Lady Rochester's son."

He remembered to bow his head. Quite nicely, too. "Tristan Ballentine. Your servant."

"You were spying on me!"

"No. Yes. Well, a little," he admitted, for he had.

It was the worst moment to remember that the flap of his trousers was still half undone. Reflexively, he reached for the buttons, and the girl's gaze followed.

She gasped.

Next he knew, her hand flew up and pain exploded in his left cheek. He staggered back, disoriented and clutching his face. He half-expected his hand to come away smeared with red.

He looked from his palm at her face. "Now that was uncalled for."

A flicker of uncertainty, perhaps contrition, briefly cooled the blaze in her eyes. Then she raised her hand with renewed determination. "You have seen nothing yet," she snarled. "Leave me alone, you . . . little ginger."

His cheeks burned, and not from the slap. He knew he had barely grown an inch since his birthday, and yes, he worried the famous Ballentine height was eluding him. The runt, Marcus called him. His hand curled into a fist. If she were a boy, he'd deck her. But a gentleman never raised his hand to a girl, even if she made him want to howl. Marcus, now Marcus would have known how to handle this vicious pixie with aplomb. Tristan could only beat a hasty retreat, the slap still pulsing like fire on his cheekbone. The *Lyrical Ballads* lay forgotten in damp grass.

Chapter 2

London, 1880

Had she been born a man, none of this would be happening. She would not be left waiting in a musty antechamber, counting the labored tick-tocks of an old pendulum clock. The secretary wouldn't shoot suspicious glances at her from behind his primly organized little desk. She would not be here at all today—Mr. Barnes, editor and current owner of half of London Print, would have signed the contract last week. Instead, he was _encountering challenges_ in closing the deal. Naturally. There were things a woman could do just because she was a woman, such as fainting dead away over some minor chagrin, and there were things a woman could not do because she was a woman. Apparently, a woman did _not_ simply buy a fifty percent share of a publishing enterprise.

She let her head slump back against the dark wall paneling, belatedly remembering that she was wearing a hat when it crunched in protest.

She was so close. They had shaken hands on it; Barnes was eager to sell quickly and to relocate to India. As usual in her line of work, this was simply a matter of waiting. Unfortunately, patience was not a virtue she possessed.

Behind her drooping eyelids, her mind took an idle turn around London Print. From the outside, the publisher's headquarters had an appealing, modern look: a gray, sleek granite façade four stories high, located on one of London's increasingly expensive streets. Befitting for an enterprise whose two best-selling periodicals regularly reached over eighty thousand upper- and middle-class women every month. The office floors, however, were as dull as the publisher's editorial choices: desks too small, rooms too dim, and the obligatory side entrance for the only woman working here—Mr. Barnes's typewriting daughter—was a cobwebbed servants' staircase. If she were serious about keeping the place, the side entrance would be the first thing she'd dispose of.

The tinny sound of a bell made her eyes slit open.

The secretary had come to his feet. "Lady Lucinda, if you please."

Mr. Barnes approached in his usual hasty manner when she entered his office. He hung her hat and tweed jacket on an overburdened hat rack, then offered her tea as she took her seat at his desk, an offer she declined because she had a train back to Oxford to catch.

More covert glances, from the direction of Miss Barnes's typist desk in the left corner. Unnecessary, really, considering the young woman had seen her in the flesh before. She gave her a nod, and Miss Barnes quickly lowered her eyes to her typewriter. Hell's bells—she was a leader of the suffrage movement, not a criminal on the loose. Though granted, for many people, this amounted to one and the same.

Mr. Barnes eyed her warily, too. "It's the board," he said. "The board is currently trying to understand why you would be interested in taking over magazines such as the *Home Counties Weekly* and the *Discerning Ladies' Magazine*."

"Not taking over; co-owning," Lucie corrected, "and my reasons are the same as they always were: the magazines have an impressively wide reach, a broad readership, and still clear growth potential. Furthermore, your acquisition of the *Pocketful of Poems* line showed that London Print is able to branch out successfully into the book market. Everyone with an eye on publishing is interested, Mr. Barnes."

Most importantly, there were only two other shareholders, each one owning twenty-five percent of London Print respectively, both silent partners, one of them residing abroad. She'd have as good as nothing standing in the way of her editorial decision making.

"All this is quite true," Mr. Barnes said, "but the board was not aware until our last meeting that you were behind the Investment Consortium."

"I'm afraid I can't see how this affects our deal."

Mr. Barnes tugged at his necktie. His bald pate had the telltale shine of nervous perspiration. Invariably, she had this effect on people— making them nervous. *It's because you are very purposeful*, Hattie had explained to her; *perhaps you should smile more to frighten them less.*

Experimentally, she bared her teeth at Mr. Barnes.

He only looked more alarmed.

He made a production of taking off and folding up his glasses before finally meeting her eyes. "My lady. Allow me to be frank."

"Please," she said, relieved.

"You are rather active in politics," Mr. Barnes ventured.

"I'm a leader of the British suffragist movement."

"Indeed. And as such, surely you are aware you, erm, are a bit of a controversial figure. I believe a recent article in the *Times* called you exactly that."

"I believe the article used the words 'nefarious nag' and 'trouble-some termagant.'"

"Quite right," Mr. Barnes said awkwardly. "Naturally, the board is wondering why someone with the aim to overturn the present social order would have an interest in owning such wholesome mag-azines, never mind a line of romantic poetry."

"Why, it almost sounds as though the board fears I have ulterior motives, Mr. Barnes," she said mildly. "That I am not, in fact, keen on a good business opportunity, but shall start a revolution among respectable women through the *Home Counties Weekly*."

"Ha ha." Mr. Barnes laughed; clearly it was precisely what he feared. "Well, no," he then said, "you would lose readers by the droves."

"Quite right. Let us leave the revolutionary efforts to *The Female Citizen*, shall we not."

Mr. Barnes winced at the mention of the radical women's rights pamphlet. He recovered swiftly enough. "With all due respect, publishing requires a certain passion for the subject matter, an intimate knowledge of the readership. Both the *Discerning Ladies' Magazine* and *Home Counties Weekly* focus on issues relevant to the gently-bred woman."

"Which should pose no problem," Lucie said, "considering I am a gently-bred woman myself." *Unlike you, Mr. Barnes.*

The man looked genuinely confused. "But these magazines endeavor to promote healthy feminine pursuits . . . fashion . . . home-making . . . a warm, happy family life." He turned toward the corner where his daughter had ceased typing a while ago. "Do they not, Beatrix?"

"Yes, Father," Miss Barnes said at once; clearly she had hung on every word.

Lucie inclined her head. "Miss Barnes, do you read the *Home Counties Weekly* and the *Discerning Ladies' Magazine*?"

"Of course, my lady, every issue."

"And are you married?"

Miss Barnes's apple cheeks flushed a becoming pink. "No, my lady."

"Very wise." She turned back to Mr. Barnes. "Since Miss Barnes is a keen reader of both magazines, being a single woman evidently does not preclude an interest in *healthy* feminine pursuits."

Now he was clearly at a loss. "But the difference is, my daughter would be interested because she has the prospect of *having* all these things, and soon."

Ah.

Whereas she, Lucie, had no such prospects. *A home. A happy family life.* Her train of thought briefly derailed. Odd, because it shouldn't—what Barnes said was only true. She was not in possession of the attributes that enticed a man, such as the softly curving figure and gentle eyes of Miss Barnes, which promised all the domestic comforts a husband could wish for. No, she was a political activist and rapidly approaching the age of thirty. She was not just left on the shelf, she *was* the shelf, and there was not a single gentleman in England interested in her offerings. Admittedly, her offerings were meager. Her reception room hosted a printing press and her life revolved around the Cause and a demanding cat. There was no room for the attention-hungry presence of a male. Besides, her most prominent campaign was waging war against the Married Women's Property Act—the very reason why she was presently sitting in this chair and dealing with Mr. Barnes, in fact. Unless the act was amended or abolished altogether, she would lose her small trust fund to any future husband upon marriage, along with her name and legal personhood, and she would, quite literally, become a possession. Consequently, the right to vote, too, would move forever out of reach. Terribly enticing. No, what she wanted was a voice in London Print. And it seemed they were refusing to give it to her.

She loathed what she had to say next. But she hadn't personally cajoled a dozen well-heeled women into investing in this enterprise only to tell them she had failed shortly before the finish line. Was Barnes aware how near deuced impossible it was to find even ten women of means in Britain who could spend their money as they wished?

Her voice emerged coolly: "The Duchess of Montgomery is part of the Investment Consortium, as you may know."

Mr. Barnes gave a startled little leap in his chair. "Indeed."

She gave him a grave stare. "I will call on her soon to inform her of our progress. I'm afraid she will be . . . distressed to find that her investment was not deemed good enough."

And a distressed duchess meant a displeased duke. A powerful, displeased duke, whose reach extended all the way to India.

Mr. Barnes produced a large handkerchief from inside his jacket and dabbed at his forehead. "I shall present your, erm, arguments to the board," he said. "I'm confident it will adequately clarify all their questions."

"You do just that."

"I suggest we meet again at the beginning of next week."

"I shall see you Tuesday next, then, Mr. Barnes."

Oxford's spires and blue lead roofs were blurring into the fading sky when she exited the train station. The university's golden sandstone structures were still aglow with the warmth of the sun after it had set. Normally, the sight of the ancient city soothed whatever mood she brought back from London. The founding academic walls and halls had not changed much since the last crusade and were wound through the town center as indelibly as the slew of inane scholarly traditions was shot through Oxford's social fabric. There was a comforting permanency to it, the very reason why she had set up home here ten years ago. Of course, there were other reasons that had made the town an obvious choice: it was considerably more economical than London, and, while located blissfully far from the prying eyes of society, still close enough to Westminster by train. Sometimes, she was struck by fleeting regrets that the women's colleges had opened only as recently as last year, when she had been too old and certainly too notorious to enroll, but back in her day, she had at least succeeded in paying acclaimed university tutors for some private lessons to improve her algebra and Latin. But, above all, she had chosen Oxford because it was assuredly untouched by time. A simple walk through town had put things into perspective, akin to the vastness of the ocean: what was a girl's banishment from home in the face of these walls guarding seven hundred years of the finest human knowledge? Less than a mile east of her house on Norham Gardens, geniuses like Newton and Locke and Bentham had once been at work. On the rare occasions she felt whimsical, she imagined the long-gone brilliant minds surrounding her like grandfatherly ghosts, murmuring encouragement, because they, too, had once dedicated themselves to causes others had deemed nonsensical.

Tonight, the city failed to lift her spirits. A dark emotion was still crawling beneath her skin by the time she had arrived at her doorstep, and her legs were still itching for exhaustion. At this hour, she could hardly pay a social call to her friends, though Catriona was probably still at work on an ancient script in her father's apartment in St. John's. . . . She unlocked the front door instead. Lamenting about the spineless Barnes would not ease her restlessness. Now, a good long ride took care of twitchy limbs. But she hadn't seen her horse in the decade since she had left Wycliffe Hall and for all she knew the stallion was long dead. She wandered through her dimly lit corridor, wondering whether she should stop using her title. She had been a lady in name only for a while.

She nodded at Aunt Honoria there in her portrait on the wall when she crossed the reception room, then paused in the doorway to the drawing room. Her lips curved in a wry smile. No, this was not the residence of a noblewoman. The battered table at the center of the room was surrounded by mismatched chairs and covered in strategic maps, empty teacups, and a half-prepared suffragist newsletter. The sewing machine against the wall on the left was mainly employed for making banners and sashes. There was a dead plant the size of a man in the right-hand corner. Not a single invitation by a respectable family graced the mantelpiece above the fireplace; instead, the wall around it was plastered in yellowing newspaper clippings and the banner she had embroidered with her favorite quote by Mary Wollstonecraft: *I do not wish women to have power over men, but over themselves.*

Worst of all, this room had, on occasion, harbored prostitutes from the Oxford brothel, who had heard of her through word-of-mouth and sought assistance, and sometimes it received mortified, unmarried women with questions about contraceptive methods. She kept a box with contraceptives hidden in the innocent-looking cherry-wood cabinet. Not even her friends knew about this box or those visits, for while saving *fallen women* was currently very fashionable under Gladstone's government, she was not saving anyone; she assisted her visitors in the ways they saw fit, which was nothing short of scandalous. Yes, most ladies worth their salt would beat a hasty retreat from her home.

Small paws drummed on the floorboards as a streak of black shot toward her. Boudicca scrabbled up the outside of her skirt and settled heavily on her left shoulder.

"Good evening, puss." The sleek fur was comfortingly soft and warm against Lucie's cheek.

Boudicca bumped her nose against her forehead.

"Did you have a fine day?" Lucie cooed.

Another bump. She reached up and ran her hand over the cat from ears to rump. Satisfied, Boudicca plunged back to the floor and strutted to her corner by the fireplace, her tail with the distinct white tip straight up like an exclamation mark.

Lucie slid her satchel off her shoulder with a groan. She still had work to do, and she had to eat, for her stomach was distracting her with angry growls after a day without lunch or tea.

Mrs. Heath, long accustomed to her poor eating habits, had left a pot with cold stew on the kitchen stove. Today's newspaper sat waiting on the table next to a clean bowl.

She read while she ate, tutting at the politics headlines. In the matrimonial advertisement section, a farmer with two hundred pounds a year was looking for a woman in her forties who would care for his pigs and five children, in this order. She tutted at this especially. By the time she returned to her desk in the drawing room, fed and informed, night had fallen beyond the closed curtains of the bay windows.

Tonight, her highest stack of unfinished correspondence loomed in the women's education corner of her desk. She had just put pen to paper when the sound of laughter reached her. She glanced up with a frown. The high-pitched giggle belonged to Mabel, Lady Henley, a widow, fellow suffragist, and tenant of the adjacent half of her rented terrace house. This arrangement suited them well, as it gave a nod to the rule that no unmarried younger woman should live on her own. But it sounded quite as though Lady Henley was in front of her window, and knowing her there was only one reason why she would be tittering like a maiden. Sure enough, there followed the low, seductive hum of a male baritone.

Her pen scratched onward. More laughter. Her neighbor's shenanigans should not concern her. If brazen enough, a widow could discreetly take liberties no unwed woman would dare, and from what she had had to overhear through the shared walls of their house, Lady Henley dared it once in a while. Risky. Foolish, even. It could reflect badly on Lucie, too. But then, most *men* installed mistresses in plush apartments and took their pleasure whenever the mood struck, and everyone blithely pretended the practice did not exist. . . .

An excited feminine squeak rang through the closed curtains.

Lucie put down her pen. Widow or not, no woman was beyond scandal. And while Lady Henley was not enrolled at the university, she mingled with female Oxford students through the suffrage chapter, and thus, anything besmirching her reputation would also besmirch the women at Oxford, when they must comport themselves beyond reproach.

She rounded her desk and yanked back the curtains. Heads jerked toward her, and she leveled a cool stare.

Oh. By Hades, no.

The light from her room revealed, unsurprisingly, an excited Lady Henley. But the man . . . there was only one man in England with such masterfully high-cut cheekbones.

Without thinking, she pushed up the window.

"You," she ground out.

Chapter 3

Tristan, Lord Ballentine. Scoundrel, seducer, bane of her youth.

His cravat loosened, his hair ruffled as if attacked by amorous fingers, he looked every bit the man he was. Her heart gave an agitated thud. What was he doing at her doorstep?

His own emotions, if he felt any, did not show. He contemplated her with his usual bored indifference before the corner of his mouth turned up and he dipped his head. "The Lady Lucie. What a pleasant surprise."

"What. Are you doing here," she said flatly.

His teeth flashed. "Making merry conversation until a sourpuss opened a window."

She had not seen him in a year. He had returned from the war in Afghanistan six months ago; the newspapers had broadcast far and wide that he had been awarded the Victoria Cross for outstanding bravery on the battlefield. More interestingly, he had been given a seat in the House of Lords by appointment.

He was still a rogue. She knew he had bothered Annabelle at Montgomery's New Year's Eve ball. Now he was flaunting his seductive prowess in front of her window.

"I gather you two are acquainted?" Lady Henley slunk into the path of their locked gazes.

Lucie blinked at her. She had forgotten her ladyship was present.

"Lord Ballentine is an old friend of my brother's," she said.

"Oh. Lovely."

Lady Henley was pining for the man—before his very eyes. Of course, he would be used to it. From debutante to matron, women had made a sport of being at least a little bit in love with Lord Ballentine. One half adored him for his rare masculine beauty, his silky auburn hair and perfect jawline and indecently soft mouth. The other half was drawn to the promise of depravity lurking beneath his even features: the dissolute edge to these soft lips and the knowing glint in his eyes that whispered *Tell me your desires, your darkest ones, and none of it shall shock me.* There was a black magic about a beautiful man who was easily intrigued and impossible to shake. Lady Henley now appeared drunk on this sinister brand of charm and was tumbling toward Tristan's maw like a fly into a carnivorous plant.

Lucie gave her a pointed look. "Forgive my being forward, but it would be ill-advised to become more closely acquainted."

"Acquainted," Lady Henley said slowly.

"With his lordship." She gestured a circle around the now deceptively idly lounging nobleman.

Lady Henley's expression cooled. "How kind of you to advise me."

"I'm afraid you risk attracting attention."

"No one can see us. There's a shrub." The lady gestured at the sprawling rhododendron shielding them, her body already arching toward the viscount again.

Lucie's neck prickled with an unpleasant emotion. "It's still a rather unbecoming look for a suffragist."

Lady Henley, stubborn creature, wrinkled her nose. "It is? Say, was it not you who told us women should strive to own their aspirations and desires? Yes, you did say it."

"Did she now," drawled Ballentine, intrigued.

Lucie unlocked her jaw with some effort. "The context was

slightly, but significantly, different. Have we not had enough scandal threatening the women's colleges this year?"

Lady Henley made a pout. "Very well. I suppose the hour is quite late." She eyed Ballentine from beneath her lashes.

"I did advise you," Lucie said, and made to close the window. Or tried to. The window did not budge. She pulled harder. Still it stuck. Lady Henley tilted her head. His lordship was watching her efforts with growing interest.

Her head was hot. How could it be stuck? She gritted her teeth. Fires of Hades, the window would not move.

"Allow me," Tristan said, and stepped closer.

"I don't need—"

He spread his long fingers and settled his fingertips on the wooden frame. With a slow, steady glide, the window lowered and settled gently on the sill between them.

Her own face was reflected back at her, distorted, narrow-eyed, with her blade-straight hair gracelessly escaping her chignon.

On the other side of the glass, Ballentine's smugness gleamed like a beacon in the night.

She all but yanked the curtains shut.

"Do not mind her," came Lady Henley's muffled voice, "she's a spinster."

She spun around, her heart pounding as though she'd run a mile. What a silly, exaggerated physical reaction. No need to be emotional. But she would have to leave, unless she wished to witness Ballentine's exploits with Lady Henley through shared walls. She truly did not wish to witness it.

Attuned to her moods, Boudicca came strolling from her corner again, her eyes yellow in the gaslight. She butted Lucie's skirts until Lucie bent and stroked her. At the feel of the soft fur beneath her fingers, her pulse slowed.

She needn't worry about Lady Henley flinging herself into the river Isis over Ballentine as others had threatened before—she was no green girl. And Ballentine's reputation as a seducer preceded him; in fact, he was the last person to try and hide what he wanted. Calculation on his part, she suspected, as it encouraged scores of women to try and reform him with healing feminine love, and a good number of them made a noose for themselves out of their own ambition.

She gathered the inkwell, the blotter, the fountain pen, her notes. On her way to the door, she picked up a shawl, because there was always a draft in Lady Margaret Hall's library.

She all but bolted out the front door and skipped down the stairs, then paused to drag a breath deep into her lungs. The cool night air was a balm on her heated cheeks.

"Taking a walk, my lady?"

The silky voice wrapped around her from behind.

She turned slowly, her hands drawn into fists.

Tristan was leaning back against the windowsill, a lit cigarette between his fingers. Next to him, his walking cane was propped against the wall, the oversized amber pommel aglow like an evil eye in the shaft of lantern light.

"Why, that was quick." There was no trace of Lady Henley.

"Something happened to spoil the mood," he said, exhaling smoke through his nose.

"A pity."

"Not at all. It was quite entertaining."

He detached himself from the sill and approached, his tall frame throwing a long shadow toward her. A sensation fluttered low in her belly, like a hundred soft and frantic wings. Well, bother. During his absences, she forgot how imposing he was; whenever they crossed paths again, she became acutely aware of it.

She had first felt the flutter years ago when petitioning parliamentarians in a corridor in Westminster. Tristan had been about to embark on his first tour—by orders of his father, she'd assumed, for there wasn't a sliver of a soldier's discipline in him. But when he had unexpectedly appeared in front of her, a bolt of heat had shot through her body and rooted her to the spot. She had not yet put the lens in place that showed a bothersome carrot-head. Instead, she had been ambushed with a version of him everyone else was seeing: a face of chiseled symmetry. Wide shoulders. Slim hips. The famous Ballentine build, in a tightly tailored uniform. All the sudden, unbridled attractiveness had afflicted her with the unfamiliar urge to fuss with her hair. Humiliating. It was hardly beyond her to admire the aesthetics of a well-made man. But *him*? For six long summers, Tristan the boy had plagued her in her own home with leering stares and pranks—when she *loathed* pranks. Worse, he had endeared himself to her brother, her cousins, and her mother, until she had felt ever more out of place at the dining table. Judging by the outrageous headlines whenever he set foot on British soil between deployments, he had failed to improve.

He halted before her, too close, and she raised her chin. By some irony of fate, *she* had gained a bare inch in height since their first encounter in Wycliffe Park.

"You shouldn't idle on our doorstep," she told him.

"And you shouldn't traipse about alone at night."

On his right ear, his diamond earring glimmered coldly like a star.

Her lip curled. "Don't trouble yourself on my behalf."

She resumed walking.

"I rather wouldn't." He was next to her, needing only one stride where she took two. "However, I'm afraid I'm obliged to escort you."

"Truly, there is no need for gentlemanly overtures."

"A gentleman would insist on carrying your bag. You are lopsided."

He was, notably, not insisting to carry it.

And she was walking into the wrong direction, she realized, appalled. Blast. She could hardly turn back now; it would look as though she had been running from him, quite mindlessly, too.

"A lady's reputation is in greater jeopardy when she is in your company than when she's on her own after dark," she tried.

"Your faith in my notoriety overwhelms me."

"It certainly worked a charm on Lady Henley."

"Who?"

She sniffed. "Never mind." And, because it *did* irk her that he would endanger their household's reputation for nothing at all: "I suppose where the chase is the aim, names are but tedious details."

"I wouldn't know." He sounded bemused. "I never chase."

"What a worrying degree of self-delusion."

He tutted. "Have you not read your Darwin? The male flaunts himself, the female chooses, it has ever been thus. Beware the determinedly chasing male—he is hoping you won't notice his plumage is subpar."

"Whereas yours is of course superiorly large and iridescent."

"I assure you it is not iridescent," he said in a bland voice.

Annoyance crept hotly up her neck. "The ladies do not seem to mind."

"My dear," he murmured. "Do I detect jealousy?"

Her fingers tightened around the strap of her satchel. Could she make her wrong turn look deliberate? Unless she changed direction, she would end up in Oxford's town center.

"I think that is exactly what it is," Tristan said. "It would certainly explain your frequent sabotage of my liaisons."

"I know you find your own banter highly entertaining, but it is wasted on me tonight."

"I remember the one time with Lady Warwick."

Despite herself, a memory flashed, of two figures in a shadowed garden. He could have been no older than seventeen. "It was ghastly," she said. "She had just returned from her honeymoon."

"And was already bored witless."

"She must have been desperate indeed. It does not mean she deserved to be despoiled on a garden table."

"Despoiled? Good Lord."

He sounded vaguely affronted. Good. They were halfway down Parks Road, and she wished him gone.

"Who would have thought," she said, "the infamous rake remembers his liaisons."

"Oh, I don't," came his soft reply. "Only the ones who got away."

Who probably were very few.

She stopped in her tracks and faced him. "Was there anything in particular you wanted?"

His eyes glittered yellow in the streetlight, not unlike Boudicca's.

"It would not be too particular, I think," he then said, his voice low. Almost a purr.

She stared at him unblinking, down her nose, while her heart beat faster. He did this sometimes, say things in a manner that suggested he was picturing her alone with him, in a state of undress. She supposed it was how he spoke to all women: with the intent to seduce. To her, he did it to aggravate.

He made to speak, more inane commentary no doubt, but then appeared to have a change of mind. What he did say next could not have surprised her more: "I was in the process of leaving my card to meet with you when I met your neighbor."

Meet. With her. But why?

"The day after tomorrow in Blackwell's new café," he said when she didn't reply. "Unless you prefer another venue."

"What is the matter, Ballentine?"

"Rumor has it you are an expert on the British publishing industry, and I need your advice."

All of this alarmed her. "Who told you?"

He smiled. "Meet me and I shall tell you."

He was terribly tedious and it was difficult to read him in the dark of night.

"Even if I were inclined to meet you—and I am not—there must be dozens of gentlemen who could advise you."

"I have an interest in middle- and upper-class women readers. It seemed logical to approach a woman who knows the readership."

Her gaze narrowed at him. The man before her looked like Tristan, with his garish, crimson velvet coat and ostentatious amber cane. The words coming out of his mouth, however, were not like him, for she had never known him to be interested in anything in particular nor had she suspected him to be capable of much logic. Then again, he was interested in *female* readers, which was true to his character and worrying.

"Come now, Lucie." His voice had deepened to a warmer, richer tone. The kind that sank beneath a woman's skin and lulled her into committing stupidities.

"Let us meet," he said. "For old times' sake."

Tristan stood back and watched the turbulence roil behind Lucie's eyes, dark and billowing like storm clouds. Her elfin face was all pointy with chagrin as two mighty emotions pulled her this way and that: her curiosity, and her profound dislike of his person.

There had been a time, those summers of pleasure-pain at Wycliffe Hall, when he had lived for provoking a reaction, any reaction, in the unassailable Lady Lucinda Tedbury. His crimes had been petty, hardly worse than dipping her pale braids into ink—the one time he had touched her hair—or replacing her collection of first edition Wollstonecraft essays with filthy magazines.

Or letting himself be caught when kissing Lady Warwick on a garden table.

Anything to provoke a reaction.

And while he wasn't a scrawny boy anymore, greedy for scraps of her attention, it appeared she held some sway over him still. Nostalgia, no doubt. She was radiating annoyance and holding grudges, dating back to those summers. But she was here, living and breathing, the familiar, crisp notes of her lemon verbena soap reaching him through the smoke of his cigarette, and it made him feel warm beneath his coat.

"There is nothing in the old times to recommend you," she said cooly.

"Then I'm afraid I have to appeal to your charitable mind," he replied.

The moon stood high in the night sky, and in the diffuse light her hair shone like a polished silver coin. He remembered how it had felt between his fingers in those stolen seconds years ago, cool and sleek like finest silk . . . *And all that's best of dark and bright / Meet in her aspect and her eyes . . .*

He stilled. Felt frozen in the summer breeze. The line had all but ambushed him. Granted, it was just a staple line from Byron. But he hadn't heard poetry . . . in years. Interesting.

He gave a shake.

Matters were about to become interesting for another reason entirely. Lucie's real reasons for dabbling in publishing had not much to do with publishing at all—his instincts were rarely wrong on such matters. And if his suspicions proved correct, he'd be compelled to stop her.

"I shall be at Blackwell's at half past ten," he said. "The day after tomorrow. I hear the coffee is sufferable, and I would be delighted if you were to join me." He flicked the cigarette butt into the dark. "And my dear. I do believe the library lies the other way."

Chapter 4

The next day, Ashdown Castle

Dark, cool, void of sound—his father's office was a crypt. This impression was caused in part by heavy ebony furniture and finger-thick curtains, but mostly by the crypt keeper himself: surroundings dimmed and silence fell where the Earl of Rochester trod.

He was ensconced behind his desk when Tristan entered, against the backdrop of his most prized possessions: a vast tapestry displaying the Ballentine family tree since 1066, personally gifted to the House of Rochester by Henry VIII. Tradition. The family name. Royal favors. Everything Rochester valued most highly was embodied in this moldy piece of embroidered silk. If given the choice between saving a helpless babe or the tapestry from a fire, he wouldn't hesitate to let the infant burn. And whenever Rochester took a seat at his desk, the family tree's branches were sprawling out just so from behind his head, giving an impression of him growing leafy antlers. The first time Tristan had noticed this from his side of the desk, he had been eight years old, so naturally, he had burst out laughing. The next moment, he had been bleeding from a split lip, while Rochester had already been seated in his chair again. The back of his hand struck quick and sudden like a snake.

"Your mother is unwell," Rochester said. It was a complaint, not a concern.

"I'm sorry to hear it," Tristan said evenly.

"If you were, you would have called on her. You have not set foot in this house since your return."

He nodded. It had, of course, been Rochester's idea to enlist Tristan in Her Majesty's army and to send him to such far-flung places as the Hindu Kush. And he would have gladly left him there, had it not been for Marcus, infallible Marcus, breaking his neck.

"I shall go and see Mother after this." Whatever *this* was. His father hadn't yet disclosed the purpose of their meeting.

Rochester steepled his long, pale fingers, as he did when he came to the crux of a matter, and fixed him with a cold stare.

"You must get married."

Married.

The word turned over and over in his mind, as if it were a complex phrase in Pashtun or Dari and he was scrambling to gather its full meaning.

"Married," he repeated, his own voice sounding oddly distant.

"Yes, Tristan. You are to take a wife."

"Right now?"

"Don't be precious. You have three months. Three months to announce your engagement to an eligible female."

The first tendrils of cold outrage unfurled. A wife. He was in no position to commit himself to such a thing. Of course, since he had become the heir, matrimony had loomed on the future's horizon, but it kept melting into the distance as he drew closer. Much as he liked women, their softness, their scent, their wit, a woman in the position of wife was a different animal. There'd be demands and obligations. There'd be . . . little spawns in his own image. There'd be . . . expectations. A shudder raced up his spine.

"Why now?" His tone would have alarmed another man.

Rochester's gaze narrowed. "I see the military failed to cure your dire lack of attention. I shall lay it out for you: you are seven-and-twenty. You are the heir to the title, and since Marcus left his widow childless, you are the last direct heir in the Ballentine line. Your main duty now is to produce another heir. If you don't, four hundred years of Ballentine rule over the Rochester title come to an end and the Winterbournes move into our house. And you have been shirking your responsibilities for nearly a year."

"Then again, I was held up in India, trying to convalesce from potentially fatal bullet wounds."

Rochester shook his head. "You returned six months ago. And have you diligently courted potential brides? No, you have caused headlines implying the cuckolding of fellow peers and rumors alluding to . . . punishable offenses."

"I did?" He was genuinely intrigued.

Rochester's lips thinned. For a blink, he looked like the younger version of himself who used to take his time when selecting an instrument to mete out yet another punishment. For Tristan's fidgeting. Or for his fondness of poetry and pretty objects, or his "girlish" attachment to his pets. It had to grate on Rochester that his only instrument of control nowadays was the tight financial leash on which he kept his son. It had to lack the element of immediate gratification. And if all went according to plan, Rochester would soon lose his grip on the leash, too. Things had to go to plan because hell, he was not taking a wife now.

"I'm not in the habit of reading the gossip sheets," he said. "Consider me blissfully ignorant of any rumors pertaining to my person."

The earl slowly leaned forward in his chair. "You have been seen in an establishment."

"Entirely possible."

"With the Marquess of Doncaster's youngest son."

That surprised a chuckle from him. "The rumors are about Lord Arthur?"

The casual way he said it made Rochester go pale. Interesting.

Do not worry about Lord Arthur Seymour, Father—I let him watch while I shagged someone, but he hasn't been on the receiving end of it. The words were on the tip of his tongue.

"Trust society to manufacture something out of nothing," he said instead. "I doubt they dared to be explicit about it."

A muscle twitched under his father's left eye. "Enough for Doncaster to briefly contemplate a libel suit."

"Against whom? Either way, a patently silly idea. Every person in the British Isles would learn about sweet Arthur's inclinations."

"And possibly yours," Rochester snarled. "Mere whispers about such a thing are an impediment to your standing. An alliance with a lady of impeccable repute can redeem your reputation, but naturally, the fathers of such women are presently disinclined to hand them to someone like you—unless I laid out a fortune."

Tristan's jaw set in a hard line. "Keep your money. I'm in no need of a wife."

There was exactly one woman with whom he'd ever contemplated something beyond a fleeting association, and she was not on the marriage mart.

Rochester was not interested in any of those facts. "Under the circumstances, we need to move fast," he said.

Tristan shrugged. "Quite frankly, Cousin Winterbourne is welcome to all this." He gave a careless wave, vague enough to include the entire house of Rochester: a sort of careless vagueness bound to annoy his father.

Rochester's eyes were dark. "This is not a game, Tristan."

"Sir, have you considered I might not find a willing, eligible woman in three months' time, given my devilish reputation? Then again"—and this occurred to him now—"I suspect you have long selected an appropriate bride."

"Of course, I have. But the potential scandal induced her warden to hold off on signing the contract. You cannot humiliate the lady in question and her family by proposing to her as you are."

"Right—who is the lucky thing?"

Rochester shook his head. "And tempt you into committing some tomfoolery before matters are settled? No. For now, your task is simply to establish a rapport with relevant society matrons, and to dress and act like a man of your station. Start with taking out this . . . thing."

He flicked his fingers toward Tristan's right ear. Tristan had it pierced with a diamond stud. He *liked* the stud. He gave his father a cold stare and rose.

"I have survived the Siege of Sherpur and I walked to Kandahar while carrying a half-dead man on my back," he said. "My days have been steeped in more death, blood, and filth than I care to remember, so forgive me if the matter of lily-white wives and gossip rags strikes me as trivial."

He had nearly reached the door when the earl said: "If you wish for your mother to stay at Ashdown, I suggest you begin to see the gravity of these matters."

He froze. Several things were happening at once: heat and cold, the spike of his pulse, the roar of blood in his ears. Part of his mind was racing; another had gone deadly still.

He turned back with deliberate slowness. His body was still all too ready for combat: useful on enemy territory, but not when the territory came in the shape of a nobleman's study. *Kill or be killed* was but a figure of speech on British country estates, wasn't it?

"What does it have to do with Mother?" His soft voice was softer still.

Rochester's face was all shadows and hard angles. "As I said: she is unwell. She might be better cared for elsewhere."

Tristan's fist was white around the cane. "Be plain."

"There are places more suited for people with her moods—"

"Are we speaking of Bedlam?"

The earl tilted his head, his smile thin as if slashed with a knife. "Bedlam? No. There are private asylums that are quainter, more suited for her care."

Private asylums. The places where perfectly sane but inconvenient wives and daughters were still sometimes sent to die.

As he walked back to the desk, wariness flickered in Rochester's eyes—the bastard knew he had gone too far. He had done it anyway, so he must be feeling bloody emboldened.

"She's grieving," Tristan said, his gaze boring into his father's. "Her son is dead."

Another flicker of emotion. "So is mine," the earl then said, roughly.

On another day, in another life, he might have commiserated. "She does not belong in a mental institution. It would kill her, and you know it."

"Tristan, I can only accommodate so much irregularity in my household. You may decide whose it is going to be: yours, or hers."

It was an act of extortion, one to which he would have to bend, and every fiber of his body strained to eliminate the threat to his freedom there and then. He drew a breath deep into his body, and another, until the wrathful heat in his veins abated.

Rochester gave a nod and said, almost amicably: "I appeal to you to do your duty. Marry, make an heir and a few spares. You have three months to reestablish a tolerable reputation. Prove you are not altogether useless."

Useless. Another deep breath. Useless—Rochester's favorite insult. Everyone who was not serving the earl's plans in some capacity fell into this category, and yet, growing up, *useless* had always cut the deepest.

Well then. Visiting Mother in Ashdown's west wing had to wait.

By the time he was back in the carriage and speeding down the driveway, he had formed a conclusion why Rochester was using the countess to force him rather than, as usual, his bank account: first, he must have become aware that he, Tristan, was close to achieving a modicum of monetary independence. And second: the marriage business was serious, and Rochester rightly suspected that another cut to his allowance would not yield results. Marry a woman of Rochester's choosing, and have their children remind him of the earl for the rest of his days? Hardly. Hence, his father's blackmail, a life for a life, his or his mother's.

If he gave in, Rochester would turn his mother into the noose around his neck when it suited him for as long as she lived. It meant he needed a plan, too. He would send word to Delhi, to General Foster's residence—perhaps he would be inclined to house two English guests for a while and not ask questions. This would take time, damnation; letters took weeks to travel back and forth such distances. He could use the submarine cable to telegraph a message to Bombay, but the cables from there to New Delhi were often cut. Briefly, he toyed with the idea of setting off with an invalid into the unknown; to hell with Foster, to hell with plans. But this kind of impulsiveness had rarely served him well.

What was clear was that he needed to increase and secure his money supply a lot faster than expected. Lucie's face flashed before his eyes, and a fresh wave of resentment hit his gut. She was, unwittingly, on the cusp of crossing the plans he had made for his new, settled life in Britain. And as of fifteen minutes ago, her interference had become a threat.

He was looking out the carriage window, not seeing a thing, as Lucie kept barging into his thoughts. By the time he had reached the train station, he wondered whether a part of him, the one that had sometimes filled his long nights in the East with memories of her and unencumbered English summers, had been keen on being in the same country as her again.

His coach was empty, and the silence was blaring. He fished for the whiskey flask in his chest pocket. For a while, he would have to play along in Rochester's game to buy time. But first, he would get drunk.

Chapter 5

Lucie woke with a cat on her face and her toes cold as lumps of ice. "Blast it, Boudicca."

Boudicca jumped and landed on the floorboards with a thud.

"Your place is on my feet, as you well know."

Boudicca turned and was on her way down to the kitchen, because frankly, she was a cat, not a foot warmer. A lady might keep a pug for such services.

With a sigh, Lucie threw back the blanket and padded to the corner with the ceramic bowl and pitcher, trying to blink the remnants of sleep away. Her lids scraped like metal sponges against her eyeballs. She had finished working at the darkest hour.

A glance at the small mirror confirmed it: she looked haggard. A little ashen around the gills, too. Not unlike the women depicted on the cards tucked left and right into the mirror's frame. Valentine Vinegar cards, carefully curated from the avalanche of anonymous ill-wishes that poured through her letter box every February. Their little rhymes and verses all concluded the same: she was a blight on womanhood, would suffer a tragic life and then die alone. *She caught a poor cat and a bird, but she can't snare a man, so we've heard . . . to see you muzzled, fast and tight, would be for all a joyful sight . . .* Her favorite card showed a shrill-looking suffragist skewered on a pitchfork. The spinster's wiry hair was flying in every direction; her nose was red and crooked like a beak. She had a touch of witch to her. And everyone was secretly afraid of witches, were they not?

Her reflection gave a sardonic little smile. She felt not at all powerful this morning. She wished to creep back under the covers, clammy as they were.

Downstairs, Boudicca was yowling and causing a racket with her empty food bowl.

Resigned, Lucie slipped into her morning wrapper.

The white light of an early morning gleamed off the white kitchen wall tiles and polished wooden cabinets. It smelled of tea, and Mrs. Heath, marvel of a housekeeper, had already kindled the fire, toasted bread, and chiseled open a tin can of Alaskan salmon.

"You can thank Aunt Honoria for the money she left me, or else you would feed on whatever the cat meat man has on offer," she said to Boudicca while alternately spooning salmon chunks onto her own plate and into the cat bowl under the cat's watchful eye. "Or worse, you would be out hunting mice every day, like a regular cat. What have you to say to that, hm?"

Boudicca's white-tipped tail gave an unimpressed flick.

"Ungrateful mog. I could have left you in that basket. I could have put you back onto the street, easily."

You are bluffing, said Boudicca's green stare. *You were as lost as I was and in dire need of company.*

Possibly. Ten years ago, she had hurried out the door one morning and had nearly tripped over the tall wicker basket on the steps. The basket had contained a handful of mewing black fluff. That fluff had proceeded to ferociously attack Lucie's prodding finger, and she had decided to keep it. She had only just settled on Norham Gardens after her banishment from Wycliffe Hall, and well yes, she had been feeling terribly lonely. No one had ever come to make a claim on her new friend.

The clock in the reception room chimed seven thirty, and the tea still had not fully revived her. It was a bad day to be tired, considering the number of appointments in her diary: First, Lady Salisbury at the Randolph Hotel, where she would admit to a negligible delay in the purchasing of London Print. Then, a second breakfast with Annabelle, Hattie, and Catriona, also at the Randolph, where she would tell her friends that they might be in trouble.

And at half past ten, Lord Obnoxious occupied a slot.

Her stomach gave a little twist. Her fractured night was in part caused by their latest encounter. She had tossed and turned in her bed, unable to shake the sense of unease about their meeting. *For old times' sake*, he had said. The audacity. Their only history was one of antagonism. Even those days were long gone; they belonged to a different life of which nothing was left but oddly, occasionally, Ballentine himself. There were chance encounters at functions in London, and then there were the headlines and rumors which somehow always found a way to her. She'd rather not see him at all. But if he had even remotely nefarious plans regarding women and the publishing industry, she had to know.

Below the table, Boudicca yodeled bitterly, as though she had not been fed in days.

"Tyrant," said Lucie, and scraped the rest of the fish from her own plate into the bowl.

Lady Salisbury had taken a room at the Randolph under the name of "Mrs. Miller," which was ludicrous because the countess was so obviously an aristocrat in both manners and looks, no one would mistake her for a Mrs. Anything. But Lady Salisbury preferred to keep her involvement in the Cause *incognito*, as she called it, especially where this particular mission was concerned. She had still brought several women beyond Lucie's circle of acquaintances into the Investment Consortium and had donated a considerable sum herself. Having to disappoint her now grated.

The countess was seated in the drawing room on a French chaise longue, a black shawl around her shoulders and a dainty teacup in hand. She put the cup down and rose when Lucie entered, something she insisted on doing despite being well into her seventies and walking with a cane.

"Lady Lucinda, soon-to-be mistress of London Print," she exclaimed, her rounded cheeks crinkling with joyful anticipation.

Lucie pasted on a smile. "Not quite yet, I'm afraid."

Lady Salisbury's face fell. "Not yet? But the contract was to be drawn up days ago—here, have a seat. Will you have tea, or sherry?"

Sherry? The clock on the mantelpiece said it was nine o'clock in the morning.

"Tea, please."

She seated herself and Lady Salisbury poured and said: "Now. What is this 'not yet' nonsense?"

"Mr. Barnes is experiencing a delay in drawing up the papers. I should have the matter resolved by next week."

The countess was not fooled. Her shrewd blue eyes had the sharpness of those of a woman Lucie's age, and they narrowed knowingly. "They object to who you are and are giving you trouble."

"It is not out of the ordinary. We shall succeed."

"I would certainly welcome that," Lady Salisbury said mildly. "My Athena is raring to make herself useful."

Lady Athena was Lady Salisbury's niece and had her eyes on assisting with their coup. She was one of many of her station interested in applying herself to something, anything, outside the doily making in a drawing room.

"My regards to Lady Athena," said Lucie. "It shall be a matter of days."

Lady Salisbury shook her head. "Ghastly business, these games of politics."

"It could be worse. We could be using swords and pitchforks to win our liberty rather than pen and paper."

Though increasingly, the idea of charging ahead while brandishing a primitive weapon struck her as a more satisfying way of doing it.

Lady Salisbury regarded her pensively while she stirred her tea. "Have you perchance considered becoming a little more likable?" she asked. "Less brash, less radical, less unfashionable? It could make everything less controversial."

Lucie gave her a weak smile. How could she not have considered it? The suggestion was thrust upon her at frequent intervals.

"If fashionable clothes and pretty smiles wielded any significant influence, surely our bankers, dukes, and politicians would be strutting around impeccably dressed and grinning like Cheshire cats," she said. "But they don't."

"Ah, but then the weapons of men and women are not quite the same." Lady Salisbury's tone was well-meaning. "See, a woman overtly grasping for power is a most vulgar creature—it helps when she looks lovely while she does it. And it so confuses the demagogues."

"Ma'am, I'm afraid the idea that a woman is a person, whether married or not, is so inherently radical no matter which way I present it I shall be considered a nuisance."

More than a nuisance. An outright challenge, a threat. For if a woman was a person in her own right, one could conclude she was also in possession of a mind and a heart of her own, and thus had needs of her own. But the unwearyingly self-sacrificing good mother and wife must not have needs, or, as Patmore's perseveringly popular poem put it: *Man must be pleased; but him to please / Is woman's pleasure* . . .

"Ghastly business," the countess repeated, and shook her head. "I can tell it is taking a toll on you—you look awfully tired. Here, have a biscuit."

"I lost track of time while reading letters last night," Lucie said. "Or perhaps I am getting old." Now, this had slipped her lips unintended.

The countess drew back, her brows arching high. "Old, you! Do not say so, for it would mean I was practically dead and gone. No, dear, take it from a truly old woman: you are still of a good age. Certainly too young to have such lines between your brows. Say, do you have a special friend?"

Lucie's brows promptly pulled together. "I have three close friends. They are in residence here during term time, in the apartments on the first floor."

"Well, how lovely." Lady Salisbury took a delicate sip from her cup. "But what I meant is: have you a suitor in your life?"

Oh. She gave the countess a bemused look. "I do not."

"I see."

"I lead the campaign against the Married Women's Property Act—I doubt I could marry and remain credible."

Lady Salisbury gave a shrug. "Millicent Fawcett is married, and she is well-regarded by everyone in the movement."

"I suppose it helps that her husband was a suffragist long before they met," murmured Lucie. It was a little bewildering. In her current position, she was a rare creature—an independent woman. She had a modest but secure income, and yet she belonged neither to a father nor a husband. Usually, only widowhood gave a woman such freedom. Why would Lady Salisbury suggest she give this up?

"I was not speaking of quite such a formal arrangement in any case." Lady Salisbury leaned closer, a conspiring gleam dancing in her eyes. "I was speaking of a beau, as they called them in my time. A lover."

A lover?

She eyed the lady's cup with suspicion. Was the countess having the sherry for breakfast?

The lady chuckled. "My, what a look of consternation. Surely you must know there is joy to be had from a man, on occasion—it is vital to discern between the individual and the politics that be. And you are certainly *not* old; look, you are blushing at the mere mentioning of lovers."

Her cheeks did feel warm. This was verging on bawdy talk, and why, oh why was it Tristan's arrogantly bored countenance that had just sprung to mind?

Lady Salisbury reached across the table and patted Lucie's hand. "Never mind. Lonely are the brave, it's always been thus. I do hope we buy this publishing house. You must know that we are all putting our faith in you. You carry the torch for all those of us who can't."

"Right," Lucie said absently. "I shall do my very best."

"Lord knows I won't see the changes in my lifetime," Lady Salisbury said, "but I have high hopes for my Athena. And it is invigorating, having a cause. My lawyer still thinks I used the money for a new hat collection." She cackled with glee. "How many hats does the man think a woman needs?"

Hattie's apartment on the hotel's first floor was usually guarded by her protection officer, a Mr. Graves. Today, there were two of the kind lurking in the shadows, men pretending to be footmen, their faces notably bland. Of course. These days, Annabelle was being followed, too. One of several disadvantages of being married to a duke. She supposed they had to be grateful Montgomery permitted his new wife to continue her studies of the classics at all.

She crossed the thickly carpeted corridor on soundless feet, wondering about the silence greeting her. The open wing doors to the drawing room revealed a cozy tableau: the Venetian glass chandelier cast a glittering light over the low-legged tea table and the surrounding settees. The tiered platter for the scones and lemon tarts towered on the table and, astonishingly, there were some pastries left. Her friends were huddled close on the yellow settee with their heads, one red, one black, one brunette, stuck together over a periodical. Hence, the absence of chatter. One could hear the fire crackling softly on the grate. Above the fireplace hung the canvas emblazoned with their most pressing mission:

Amend the Married Women's Property Act

One of those ubiquitous portraits of an elderly gentleman in a powdered wig had had to make way for the canvas. The gent was now leaned against a sideboard, at the ready to be put back in place when Hattie's parents came to visit, because the wealthy banker family wouldn't approve of her activism. Hattie's live-in, chaperoning great-aunt was too shortsighted to take any notice. Presumably, Aunty was currently napping, allowing the young women to shamelessly over-stay the fifteen minutes of a social call.

What a curious place Oxford was, Lucie thought, watching her friends. Without much ado, the university had united on the same settee a banking heiress studying the fine arts, a Scottish lady work-ing as a research assistant for her professor father, and a vicar's daugh-ter, now a duchess, studying the classics.

"Goodness, Lucie, you spook us, just standing there." Hattie had glanced up and jumped to her feet, the red curls tumbling from her coiffure bouncing around her face.

"The contract has not been drawn up," she said quickly. Anna-belle and Catriona, who had also made to rise, sank back down onto the settee.

"It's you, isn't it," Annabelle said, her green gaze assessing as Lu-cie approached.

"Apparently." She sprawled unladylike on the velvet divan. "I un-derstand the board took notice of me being listed in the consortium's legal papers. Now they rightly suspect that I shall corrupt London Print, and they are advising Mr. Barnes not to sell us his shares."

Hattie stopped in the process of pouring her a tea, her round brown eyes rounder with worry.

"He hardly has to take their advice, has he?" she asked.

"He is a nervous man."

"So what shall we do?"

She gave a little shrug. "What we always do. We wait."

Catriona took off her glasses, her blue eyes serious. "Don't blame yourself," she said, her Scottish lilt more pronounced, which meant her emotions were heightened. "We considered all options—having you at the helm during this undertaking was the least worst option out of various bad options."

"Why, thanks," Lucie said wryly. In truth, since her last visit with Mr. Barnes, she secretly wondered whether the entire plan was perhaps a trifle harebrained. When she had first had the idea to acquire a publishing house to publish a suffrage report attacking the Married Women's Property Act, the idea had made terrific sense. After all, sometimes, one had to meet great challenges with equally great artillery. However, it had been easy to become lost in the tasks at hand, such as assembling an investment consortium under special constraints, and understanding the legal works, rather than think all possible consequences through to the end. Ruined reputations and plummeting goodwill toward the already largely unpopular suffrage movement were but a few of the risks. Easily ignored, when shares in a suitable publishing house had unexpectedly become available a month ago. But now, on the line between victory and unanticipated defeat at the very last moment, she felt the weight of the enormity of her plan. *I'm a little worried*, she wanted to tell her friends. *I'm worried I may have bitten off more than I can chew.* She would, of course, say no such thing. A dithering leader was about as useful as a wet blanket. Besides, the whole movement depended on women acting before they felt ready.

She turned to Annabelle. "I'm afraid I had to threaten Barnes with the wrath of the House of Montgomery. I know it is a delicate time to use your name in potentially scandalous activities, but I felt it was my last chance."

The Duke of Montgomery *was* a powerful man, but his social standing had suffered when he had married Annabelle a few months ago—the upper ten thousand had not taken kindly to his decision to take the daughter of a vicar for a wife, nor his switch of party affiliation. He had largely avoided society since.

"I don't believe it will do us harm," Annabelle said. "And by the time the report is published, we shall have wiped all traces of my involvement."

"You are too gracious."

Annabelle, very graciously, inclined her head. A jewel on her hairpin caught the light and sparked a rainbow in her mahogany hair. A remarkable thing about dukes? No scandal was ever large enough to bankrupt them.

Hattie, meanwhile, was piling scones and tarts onto her plate. "Does Lady Salisbury have any advice on the matter?"

Yes. That I go and take a lover so as to ease the frown lines on my brow.

"Only the usual," she said, "I should be less of me and more of a paragon to make the movement more likable." She reached for a scone, then proceeded to crumble it between her fingers. "It never ceases to puzzle me. I understand it's easily forgotten within our small, and, dare I say, enlightened, circle, but the truth remains: before the law, once we are married, we have the same rights as children and prisoners, namely none. And yet," she said, ignoring Hattie's reprimanding stare at the demolished scone, "and yet there are people who believe being fashionable and pleasant shall make a difference. I understand how being pleasant can keep the peace, but how will it win a war?"

Both Annabelle, well versed on the wars of antiquity, and Catriona, well versed on any topic, regarded her with mild amusement. Very well. She took a deep breath. She *was* feeling unusually flustered. There was the matter of uncertainty regarding London Print, and Tristan's appearance before her window the other night prowled circles at the back of her mind. Briefly, she considered telling her friends about her fast-approaching meeting at Blackwell's, but the truth was, Ballentine should not preoccupy her at all.

"What if there is some truth to the merits of likability," Hattie suggested. "Dripping water hollows the stone—Ovid said so, I believe."

Annabelle nodded. "He did."

"It only takes a thousand years, doesn't it," Lucie said dryly.

"While we proceed with the hollowing, we may as well look fashionable," Hattie said unperturbed. "If you wished to *try* Lady Salisbury's strategy, perhaps you could start with being seen at social events. In fact, we were just talking about Montgomery's house party." Her smile was dazzling. "Wouldn't it be fabulous if you joined us for once?"

Lucie blinked. "I haven't attended a house party since the incident with the Spanish ambassador and the fork."

"It appears to be high time, then. We could shop dresses together." Hattie nudged the periodical they had studied earlier across the table—a fashion magazine, depicting a woman in an impossibly narrow skirt and a tiny hat.

"Is it time yet for a house party," Lucie said quickly, "considering Montgomery's current position?"

"It may strike some as too soon," Annabelle admitted, "but the Prince of Wales invited himself to Claremont for some grouse hunting. We decided to make him the guest of honor at a house party."

"Isn't it terribly clever," Hattie said.

It was. With the Prince of Wales in attendance, not even Montgomery's opponents would decline the invitation; they'd send a son in their stead, perhaps, but every family of consequence would be represented. The prince himself was probably doing it to needle Her Majesty the queen, who was highly unamused by her son's libertine antics. Altogether, it could do wonders for Montgomery's rehabilitation.

"I thank you for the invitation," she told Annabelle. "But it strikes me as imprudent to have me among the guests if Montgomery wants to leave scandal behind."

Annabelle shook her head. "You are my friend. Frankly, I shall need my friends there. Everyone else is just vying to see a social-climbing upstart make a fool of herself."

Bother. She hadn't considered that Annabelle might require a helping hand.

Hattie gave her a coy look. "Wouldn't Annabelle's first Claremont house party be a worthy occasion for a visit to the modiste?"

As an artist and a romantic young woman, Hattie held strong opinions on colors, cuts, and compositions—and behind the girl's upturned nose and readily smiling mouth lurked a stubbornness vastly superior to Lucie's ability to patiently weather an argument.

"Hattie, I am not denying that fashion's allure is a weapon of sorts in a lady's hands. What I object to is the fact that it is the only weapon we may wield in public without suffering scrutiny . . ."

". . . and refusing to use it is a statement, I know, I know," Hattie said. "And I like to choose my weapons, and frumpiness is not one of them—how lucky you are to not have a mother who picks your gowns! The things you could wear!"

"I have plenty of dresses."

"Your dresses are fine," Hattie said unconvincingly. "But they are all . . . gray."

"They are."

"And they all . . . look the same."

"Because it saves me half an hour a day, not needing to think about assembling an outfit."

Besides, gray was a practical color for a woman whose daily activities invited dust and ink splats onto her garments. Garments she and Mrs. Heath had to painstakingly clean every Saturday. She caught Catriona's harangued gaze; no doubt she had been besieged by Hattie prior to her arrival. Heiress to a Scottish earldom or not, Catriona felt most comfortable wrapped in her old Clan Campbell tartan shawl, with her black hair in a plain bun and her nose buried in a Byzantine parchment. Poor Hattie.

It took not twenty seconds for the girl to throw up her hands. "Lemon yellow," she cried. "With your coloring, you should wear lemon yellow, perhaps for a morning dress. Mauve, and light blue and powder blue for an elegant walking dress, at most a soft dove gray, but never this dreary shade of slate. Cerise for a striking evening gown. Consider crimson for the most stunning entrance at a ball. No intricate patterns for you, but clean lines—I'd recommend adding touches of softness with plush textures instead. Truly, Lucie, I see such potential!"

"You overwhelm me, my dear."

"Be careful if you do go shopping with her," said Annabelle. "The last time I let her choose my gown, I found myself wearing magenta and scandalized the ballroom."

Hattie gave her a smug look. "And then a duke fell hopelessly in love with you and made you his duchess. Indeed, I'm a terrible friend."

A glance at the advancing hour on the tall pendulum clock made Lucie feel queasy. She put down her cup.

He should not preoccupy her, but she might as well come prepared.

"Hattie—"

"Yes?" Hattie's expression was immediately hopeful.

"I have a query about Lord Ballentine—"

Hattie raised a hand to her mouth in delighted shock. "*The* Lord Ballentine, rake extraordinaire?"

"The very same. He recently received the Victoria Cross."

"Yes?"

"What act of bravery did he commit? Do you know?"

This prompted a mildly offended look. "Of course. He ran toward danger instead of away from it."

"Every soldier does so."

Hattie shook no. "Apparently, he went above and beyond. I understand his battalion had become trapped against a rock face in an ambush, with only scarce cover, and his captain had been shot."

Annabelle's mouth turned downward. "How dreadful."

"Indeed—and worse, the men could not recover the captain because the place where he lay was still in a direct line of fire—and they knew they would soon be picked off one by one, too, as they could not quite determine where the attack came from."

Skepticism was written plain on Catriona's face. "How did Lord Ballentine escape the trap, then?"

Hattie's cheeks reddened. "Apparently, there was an element of chance. He had been trailing behind—there are rumors he was missing without leave." Her voice dropped to a hush. "He had been taking a bath in a nearby stream . . . now, this was not in the papers, but I heard Mrs. Heathecote-Gough say he was not even fully clothed when the incident occurred."

"Typical," muttered Lucie.

"Lord Ballentine, upon hearing the gunfire, very recklessly and in a state of undress, set out to locate the hidden source of the attack and approached the post from a dead angle. Then he proceeded to eliminate as many as he could with just a revolver until he ran out of bullets, and by then he was upon them and vanquished the rest of them in close combat—but then, when he tried to recover the captain, he was shot through the shoulder by an ambusher he had not effectively dispatched after all."

"So he was careless," Lucie said. "Also typical."

Hattie's eyes widened with disapproval. "He saved lives, Lucie. He shielded the captain with his own body while his comrades rallied and overwhelmed the shooter. Then he led them to safety through enemy territory while wounded. That said," she allowed, "he is still a rogue for bothering Annabelle at the winter ball."

"Definitely a rogue," Annabelle said darkly. "A hero and a pest, a man can be both."

"Then again, it did spur Montgomery on to declare his feelings," Hattie suggested.

"Of sorts," Annabelle said, and her cheeks turned rosy.

Lucie was still struggling with visions of a murderous, partially nude Tristan Ballentine when the pendulum clock whirred and announced with a bong that she must take her leave and meet the man.

Chapter 6

Early morning had transitioned into a warm midmorning with not a whisper of a breeze to cool her curiously overheated face. She arrived in front of Blackwell's bay windows feeling sticky and vaguely provoked by the sight of Ballentine's maroon coat. It shone like an errant chestnut in the summer sun, while the man himself looked pleasantly cool and collected. She had observed him awhile before he had noticed her, because he stood head and shoulders above the flow of pedestrians going past the bookshop while she was all but submerged in it.

The corner of his mouth tipped up when she halted in front of him.

He lifted his top hat. "My lady."

A sunbeam struck off his auburn hair as if it were polished copper. She was certain she'd heard a woman sigh in the crowd moving past.

"I have half an hour to spare," she said.

"That suits my schedule perfectly."

He was going back to London, she supposed. She swept up the three steps and into the bookstore, sending the bells above the door jingling erratically.

A dozen heads swiveled toward her in the dim heat: pale, bespectacled student faces. Eyes widened, possibly with recognition. Too many people in this town knew of her, or perhaps, they knew Tristan. Anyone would find it sensationally curious to see Lady Lucie Tedbury with the prize rake of London in tow. Quite literally. Tristan was looming behind her, standing too close after her abrupt standstill. His scent curled around her, warm and disturbingly familiar. She could have picked out of a line with her eyes closed.

She made for the narrow staircase.

The coffee room on the second floor was no larger than the shop below, fitting perhaps ten patrons on the few tables clustered around the cold fireplace. They were alone. On a hot day, except for the keen specimen downstairs, students were either abed or drunkenly floating down the river Cherwell in a punt. Tristan certainly knew how to pick a secluded place in plain sight.

By the time he pulled back a chair for her at the table next to the window, she was feeling prickly like a hedgehog. The face he was putting on was too harmless for her liking, not a leering stare or smirk in sight.

"Coffee," he said to the waiter who had bustled in with a fresh white tablecloth. "Milk and three sugars for the lady, black for me. Unless"—he glanced at her—"you take your coffee differently these days."

For a moment, she was tempted to say that she did. It appeared someone had spied on her during breakfast in her previous life at Wycliffe Hall.

"Milk and three sugars it is," she muttered.

The table was small. Observed from the outside, they were friends taking coffee, their knees in danger of touching beneath the tablecloth.

And this close, she noticed changes in Tristan's face that the dark had concealed during their encounter two days ago. Months after his return to England, his skin still had the honeyed hue of a man who had marched for miles under a foreign sun. There was a first hint of horizontal lines across his brow. Faint purple crescents were smudged beneath his eyes, as though he had slept little. None of it detracted from his beauty, but it gave him a harsher varnish. Something else was different, and it took her a moment to identify it as the absence of the diamond stud. Had she imagined it there on his ear a few nights ago? Was Ballentine not just growing older, but growing up? She could not help but wonder, then, what changes time had wrought upon her own appearance.

"You look lovely, Tedbury," he said smoothly, as though her thoughts had been written plain on her face. "May I compliment you on your well-preserved complexion?"

"I would rather you did not," she said. "In fact, before I discuss any matter with you at all, I must know: what were your designs on the Duchess of Montgomery at the New Year's Eve ball?"

He blinked at her slowly. "What?"

"Montgomery's New Year's ball. I heard you were trying to coax the duchess to accompany you outside after a dance."

"Ah. She was plain Miss . . . Country-Bumpkin, then, wasn't she."

"That's of no consequence to my question."

An emotion was brewing in the depth of his gaze. "If I were the type of man you evidently take me for, would I tell you the truth?"

"I would know if you were lying."

His smile was derisive. "I doubt it."

"Very well."

Before she could come to her feet to make good on her threat and leave, he braced his elbows on the table and leaned in close, a startling intensity flaring at the back of his eyes.

"I don't force my attentions on women," he said quietly. "I never have."

She had never seen him so annoyed, all languor gone. She was transfixed despite herself.

"Then why insist she accompany you outside?" she managed.

He gave a shrug. "I don't quite recall. I was likely bored. Perhaps I felt she was wasted as a wallflower, and that she required some assistance. Propriety is dreadfully pervasive among the middle classes—much to the detriment of their own enjoyment. It does not mean I would have taken liberties against her will."

"You arrogant cad—you claim you were doing her a favor."

"Well, we shall never know, shall we? Montgomery became a little territorial, seeing his future duchess on my arm, and I thought it wise to retreat before he ordered one of his minions to run me through on the ballroom parquet."

If he *was* lying, it was indeed impossible to tell. His eyes were a murky mélange of amber and green, and the more deeply she looked the fuzzier she felt. She realized she had leaned in close enough to feel his breath softly brush her cheek. Unbidden, her gaze strayed to his left cheekbone. Long ago in Wycliffe Park, it had borne a perfect imprint of her hand after she had slapped him, gripped by a terrible, angry sense of helplessness of which he had not been the cause. . . .

The waiter hurried back into the room and slowed abruptly at seeing their heads stuck together so intimately. Lucie drew back, allowing two steaming cups to be placed on the table.

She reached for her spoon and gave her coffee a superfluous stir. "What brings you to England in the first place?"

Tristan gave her a last assessing look, and then the rigidness in his shoulders eased and he leaned back into his chair. "I sold out."

"Already?"

He hadn't yet made the rank of captain, when he should have, after six years in the army. But then, if rumors could be trusted, his disobedience, which saw him frolicking in a river while his comrades were under fire, had been a reoccurring problem, and it was astonishing he hadn't been dishonorably discharged several times over.

He smiled in some mild amusement. "There is not much to be had after the Victoria Cross, Lucie."

Well. There was that. He *had* been awarded the highest military honor of the country. The Ballentine men always distinguished themselves on the battlefield; *With Valor and Vigor* was their family motto. His older brother, Marcus, had advanced rapidly through his naval career, until a riding accident had put a tragic end to it all.

She eyed Tristan's left hand, wrapped loosely around his coffee cup. The signet ring of the House of Rochester encircled his little finger, its ruby glistening like a fat dollop of blood. This was likely the real reason why he had sold out—as the last heir, he must not risk his life on front lines. His main responsibility now was to secure the family line and to quickly learn everything the previous Lord Ballentine had been taught from the cradle. It made her wonder: Had grief drawn the fine lines across his brow? Their mothers had been close friends once; perhaps they were friendly still. It would be within the bounds of etiquette to inquire after the well-being of Lady Rochester, or even his. However, inquiries of the kind might unexpectedly stir unwanted memories and sentiments. Besides, she was currently sharing a table with him because he was not up to any good. *A hero and a pest, a man can be both.* The reasons for their meeting, she suspected, were firmly inspired by the pest side of him.

"Now," she said. "Who told you I was an expert in the publishing industry?"

His lips quirked. "My lawyer. He insists on giving me a lecture on the state of the British economy every month. Apparently, we currently own over twenty percent of world trade, and you are busy buying publishing houses."

Tristan had a lawyer. Who would have thought.

She raised her chin. "And what sparked your sudden interest in women readers?"

He picked up his spoon. "Even more interesting is the question: what sparked yours?"

Her brows lowered. "What do you mean?"

He was toying with the spoon now, turning it back and forth as a child would, admiring his upside-down reflection. "It's an *interesting* match, isn't it," he said. "A woman with your views and ambitions, acquiring a majority stake in one of Britain's established women's magazine publishers. Such *wholesome* magazines, too."

She sat oddly frozen, like a rabbit unexpectedly stumbling upon a lethal predator.

What did he know?

Nothing. He knew nothing, and even if he did know something, it would be of no consequence to him.

He looked up from the spoon then, his eyes cold and intent.

She nearly recoiled. She had *felt* him inside her head for a beat, his gaze entering her as easily as light filtering through a cotton sheet. And she must have schooled her features a fraction too late, for there was a hint of a smile on Tristan's lips and it was not a friendly one.

She forced a cool smile of her own. "It's not unheard of to hold multiple interests. You see, I can both champion women's political rights and still be keen on a good business opportunity. In fact, the two go very well together—the suffrage movement is an expensive undertaking. It costs time, too, and presently, you are wasting mine."

He inclined his head. "Well then. If I were of a mind to publish a book," he said slowly, "should it be by Anonymous, or by a John Miller, or by Lord Ballentine?"

His hesitation gave her pause. "This is not a rhetorical question, is it," she then said. "You have already written the book."

He nodded. "The question is whether my name, or, rather, the reputation attached to it, would entice or deter the good women of Britain to purchase it. My instinct tells me they would throw their pin money at my works."

"You are asking whether women would purchase something not for its content or quality but because it was associated with your name?"

His brows rose at her incredulous tone. "Content and quality are excellent, but yes."

"That's preposterous. You are hardly enough of a rogue as to turn it into profit."

"Now, there's a challenge. But let us assume the book exists and is already profitably published, and what I have in mind is a new edition with the Ballentine name."

"Already published," she echoed, not liking the tickling sensation on her nape. "What sort of book is it, anyway? It's a war diary, isn't it?"

A look of surprise passed over his face. "No," he said. "It would be poetry."

"Poetry."

"Yes."

"War poetry?" she tried.

Again, a hesitation. "No," he said. "Romantic poetry."

Her gray gaze sharpened on him, pricking his skin like a blunted razor blade. Ironic, because he was truthful about the poetry and about his interest in her opinion—but she was right to suspect deviousness of sorts. Clever as a cat, Lucie. And quite incapable of deviousness herself, so despite all the battles she had fought, one could still call her naïve. He had just read her face like an open book—the hell did she want London Print solely for business reasons.

He picked up his coffee cup and drank without tasting the black brew. She had a habit of making things difficult for him. Undoubtedly, she made things difficult for herself, too. The two frown lines, rigidly upstanding between her slender brows, made his thumb twitch with the irrational desire to smooth them. She probably still thought she could take on the ills of humanity with her bare hands because she had justice on her side. To hold any such conviction was of course a source of endless frustration. Otherwise, he would have envied her the purity of her single-minded rage and determination. *She* would never wake in the morning and stare at the ceiling, wondering where to go this day.

"Romantic poetry," she said. Her tone was belittling, as though poetry held as much gravity as nursery rhymes. It could have crushed a wordsmith; poets were saddled with sensitive souls, after all, but, having successfully rid himself of both sensibilities and much of his soul, he just felt his male instincts stir, keen to pick up the gauntlet. A bad direction for his mind to take, in a public coffee room, as the scenario of vanquishing Lucie Tedbury inevitably ended with her in the nude, her fair skin flushed with desire and her tongue busy with something other than trying to cut him down to size. . . . Her eyes widened, and he realized he might have growled.

"Coffee," he said, clearing his throat. "Irritating stuff."

He'd never know her reply, for she became distracted by a small commotion behind his back.

He glanced over his shoulder.

Three young women were forming an excited, tittering cluster in the doorway to the tearoom. He had registered them earlier, when they had made their way upstairs amid giggles and hushed whispers. They must have dawdled in silence somewhere out of sight and had now decided to advance. Shopgirls, by the looks of it. Rosy cheeks all around. A little young to be out without a chaperone, even as a group. They tried to halfheartedly hide behind each other as he surveyed them.

"Good morning, lovelies," he said. "Can we be of assistance?"

Their enthusiasm rushed toward him like a breeze.

"Lord Ballentine."

They moved toward their table as one, bringing with them the scent of lily of the valley, until the most courageous of them stepped forward after her curtsy, her hands behind her back.

"We saw your lordship enter the bookshop . . ."

"Did you now."

Their sparkling eyes did not match their bashful tone. On her side of the table, Lucie's gaze had narrowed.

"We were hoping you would sign this for us," one of the girls said, a redhead. Her little nose was enticingly freckled. Lovely. Since Lucie was glowering a mere arm's length away, he was briefly tempted to provoke her and flirt, but then the redhead thrust something at him. A card. It was of the size of a Valentine card, he knew; he had seen a shipload's worth of them in his lifetime thanks to tireless legions of admirers. Except that the motif of this particular card was— himself. Someone had cut out his picture—the one in uniform, where he was staring valiantly into the middle distance—from a newspaper article about his Victoria Cross. Someone had glued it onto a card. And had added a lace frame. They had colored his eyes blue. And there was an illustration of a *dog*, a small, fluffy one that looked as though it would yap and bite ankles.

"It's . . ." He squinted. "It's—"

"It's a *Ballentine card*," said the girl who had addressed him first, setting off more giggling.

"I see," he said blandly. "How neat."

"Aren't they lovely?" one of them cooed.

"If only you could sign them, milord—it should make them even more precious than the others."

"There are . . . more?" he dared to ask.

Three heads nodded vigorously.

"They're all the rage," the redhead said. "There are a few other heroes the girls like to put on a card, but your lordship is by far the most popular. It costs two or more other heroes to trade, more if they have no lace frame."

"We wouldn't ever trade ours," the leader added hastily. "They're our good-luck charms."

He supposed it wasn't necessary to comprehend any of this.

His hand slipped inside his jacket and pulled a pen from the inner breast pocket.

He signed the card with the dog as the girls stood with bated breath, and two more equally absurd ones.

They disappeared in a chorus of sighs, leaving a delightful trail of spring flower fragrances behind.

He turned back to Lucie slowly.

An evil gleam was dancing in her eyes.

"Well," she said mildly.

"Well," he said darkly.

The corners of her mouth were twitching. "This should sufficiently answer your question. You see, I would have recommended you pursue the idea of the war diaries, but romantic poetry under your name might work very well indeed. You could, however, just set up a shop . . ." She lost the struggle. She burst out laughing, her small white teeth flashing.

"Here now—" he began.

". . . a shop," she wheezed, "and sell . . . *Ballentine* cards. Most lucrative. One for two!"

He should say something stern, but she was bewitchingly ill-mannered, laughing out loud in public. Unfortunately, the object of her glee was—him.

"Do not forget the lace frame, for highest value," she told him, and took her leave after a glance at her pocket watch, abandoning him to the company of her empty cup.

He finished his coffee seemingly unmoved, a wry smile on his lips, but her absence, compounded by the emptiness of the place, was palpable. The world quickened its pace again; the noise of the street below swelled, and he noted the room's décor. His mind, usually sprawling and contemplating several different things at once, became calm the more his surroundings exploded; it was the reason he was a good soldier when it counted, and why he felt a remarkable sense of focus and quiet in Lucie's presence, antagonistic force of nature that she was. An underrated feeling, quietness. If he had a conscience, he would probably regret having to wipe the laughter off her face so soon.

Chapter 7

The Great Western train from Oxford to Ashdown crept through the Cotswolds with remarkable slowness. Gently rolling hills were drifting past the window, so very civilized and English with their low peaks and quaint valleys and a lone gnarled oak tree here and there. How they paled in comparison to the emerald mountains of Afghanistan. England's colors appeared to have faded since his return, and everything outside London was *slow*: the service, people's minds, life. But renting his St. James apartment including seven staff had become too expensive the moment Rochester demanded he marry, and the family town house was out of the question. The walls there had eyes. The rooms he now rented off an old fellow student in Oxford's Logic Lane were cheap as well as located much closer to Ashdown. Of course, it meant his valet was grumbling over a multitude of new duties, and he was stuck in Oxford, where the tailor was mediocre, the food stodgy, and the debauchery tepid. Unacceptably dull, having to keep an eye on the accounts.

He ran his palm down the slippery-smooth silk of his waistcoat. He had thought of costly, well-made things often during his time abroad. Amid heat and weevils and gore, he had envisioned sleek fabrics that wouldn't make his whole body itch. The smell of fresh, clean bedding. Wine as rich and soft as velvet.

He would give it all up again before he bent to Rochester's will.

He could not, however, give up his mother quite so easily, could he. It was, in fact, a lamentable habit of his to think of his mother whenever an opportunity to break his bonds with Ashdown presented itself. The first time he had chosen not to leave, he had been sixteen and in possession of a handsome sum from selling erotic short stories to the other boys at Eton and to an illegal shop in Whitechapel, enough to pay for a steamer ticket to America and keep him in comfortable lodgings until he'd found employment. Neither taking employment nor living among raucous Americans had held any appeal, but Rochester and his whip had increasingly appealed less. But there was Mother. If he left, how would she fare? Marcus had never been cruel, but he had been Rochester's pet and had taken after him in disposition—he had no patience for eccentricity and moods. Neither did Tristan, in fairness, unless they were his own, but out of the three Ballentine men he was the one who felt protective rather than provoked when the countess did something silly. Such as locking herself away for a whole spring season to paint two mediocre Impressionist paintings a day, only to never touch a brush again after she had reemerged. The truth was, if one could not escape in a straightforward manner, because a man like Rochester had rules and all the money, one had to do it inwardly. By way of painting. Or writing. Or drinking and fucking, when one wasn't crawling through dust in the East.

He sprawled back into the plush train seat. He should be writing now, because Lucie was, of course, correct; his war diaries would sell well indeed. His notebook lay already spread open on the coach table, the blank page demanding he jot down a structure for the narrative, and possibly some thoughts on which events to include and which ones to erase from history. However, the trouble with words was that putting them onto paper was a bloody slog even at the height of inspiration. Presently, he wasn't inspired in the slightest. The war had not been his war, and he had no desire to tie himself to it more closely, now it was over. Granted, he had been made to fit the military boots by way of Rochester's diligent training and a few generations' worth of Ballentine vigor and valor rolling in his veins. And where chaos reigned, his impulsive decisions were superior to lengthy contemplations. Thus, he was occasionally compelled to do things the public loved. Covering his wounded captain with his own body rather than duck and run, for example. To make coin from it now left a cynical taste in his mouth, but damned if he wasn't going to be pragmatic and edit these diaries. Tomorrow.

The sandstone quadrangle of Ashdown Castle glowed golden like a honeycomb in the afternoon sun. Any unsuspecting visitor would be fooled by the inviting façade; it was a sinister place.

Rochester was in London today, some business or such in the House of Lords, but Jarvis, his father's thin-lipped butler-cum-spy, would try and sniff around his heels. And to reach the west wing, he had to walk past Marcus's life-sized portrait in the Great Hall, and it did funny things to him. Under his brother's fixed brown gaze, the signet ring grew heavy on his little finger, like a ball and chain, and his insides turned cold. He quickened his pace and felt Marcus's stare between his shoulder blades until he reached the grand staircase.

He entered his mother's bedchamber after a quick rap on the door. For a moment, he stood disoriented. The chamber was steeped in nightlike darkness. There was no sound. Had he not known better, he'd have thought the bed empty, but the air was thick with sadness.

He closed the door gently. "Mother?"

Silence.

He moved carefully in the shadows, in case something had been added to her room: a chair or a side table not yet on his mental map.

He halted by the nearest window.

"Mother, I'm going to open the curtains."

He pulled at the heavy brocade fabric, and light blinded him for a moment. Then Ashdown Park unfolded before him in all the tender green shades of early summer.

Bedsheets rustled softly behind him. "Marcus?"

His mouth quirked ruefully.

He turned.

She lay on her side, a small heap in the vast bed, one hand tucked beneath her cheek.

"No," he said. "Just Tristan."

Her eyes were tired. Her hair snaked over her shoulder in an untidy coil, more gray than brunette, he noted with unpleasant surprise.

She moved not a muscle as he approached, nor when he took a seat in the visitor's chair.

An acrid medicinal smell accosted his nose.

Her nightstand was cluttered with the numerous bottles of poison they fed her. There was a tray with a bowl of soup and a slice of bread, looking dried up and untouched.

"Good afternoon, Mother."

"My beautiful boy," she said softly, her eyes searching his face.

He reached for her hand. The feel of her bony fingers sent a shudder down his back.

She appeared not to notice. "Why have you not come to see me sooner?"

"I have not been back for long."

"Liar," she said without heat. "Carey told me you returned before Christmas."

"A faithful little spy, your lady's maid." It failed to draw a smile. When she was in this state, it was akin to talking into a void. Even her face changed in subtle ways. Her body was here; she was not. It would make the most jaded man believe in the human spirit, because its absence was plainly visible.

"Why are you not eating?" he said. "Should I have words with Cook?"

No reply.

His muscles were tense; his body demanded he walk away from

this fragility. Her lady's maid had kept it from him in her letters, how bad it was. Or perhaps he had refused to read between the lines.

He eyed the bottles on the nightstand more closely. Laudanum, naturally, and some other tinctures, likely snake oil. They used it on her when she had the morbs, and tried to use it on her when she became the overly bright, frantic version of herself who ordered thirty new dresses at once or tried to sail to Morocco on her own. When he was a boy, either version of her had unsettled him. Being around her and Rochester during those times had felt precarious, like shoveling water from a sinking barge with a spoon.

"Mother, did I tell you, in Delhi, I was a guest of General Foster," he said. "He keeps a pet elephant in his garden."

His mother's brows pulled together. "How curious—a whole elephant?"

"The whole thing. A small one, however, still a youngster. One day, he had figured out how to stick his trunk through the kitchen window and very prettily beg for food. You would like him."

How would she fare, in India, under General Foster's roof? She looked brittle, as though a mere carriage ride would shatter her. He wondered whether she was still a friend to Lucie's mother, for the women had sometimes spent some leisure time together in one of Wycliffe's smaller country homes. Friendly company might do her good. However, even if the women still shared a connection, Rochester would hardly allow his wife to convalesce away from Ashdown, since she was now his bargaining tool . . .

"An elephant," she said, still puzzled. "How does he keep it from trampling the roses?"

"The general has his eccentricities, but he makes for good conversation," he replied. "He fancies himself vastly knowledgeable on the gods of Hinduism and lectures for hours on the topic."

Her frown lines deepened. "Do you think it wise to mingle with aspiring heathens, dear, and the lecturing kind, too?"

"Right," he said lamely. "Well, I'm here now."

A glimpse of her shimmered at the bottom of her blue eyes. "Will you stay?" she whispered.

He wanted to run.

"Only if you eat," he said. He pulled the bell string over her nightstand and backed away, deciding to take his leave altogether. He had his information; she was obviously unfit for travel, and not particularly intrigued by Foster. He'd return some other time, when his plans had progressed. Any spoon-feeding of broth, the maid could do; he wasn't a bloody saint, after all. As it was, tonight he had a tête-à-tête with a man they called Beelzebub.

Night had fallen when he arrived in London, but this corner of the city was always steeped in darkness regardless of the time of the day. The address was most elegant, and presently well-lit by tall street-lights, but the polished white façades and pillared entrances hid back rooms and basements where powerful men assembled to revel in their vices. And where power was limitless, so was the vice.

Years ago, this had been his routine—letting a door knocker fall in a certain pattern, presenting passwords to hulking gatekeepers, descending narrow staircases. In the very heart of London, he had passed through Sodom and Gomorrah. Had it not been for the poets and their lines about all that was noble and true, the murkiness might well have taken permanent root in him. People recognized him even now, their eyes lighting on him from the shadows as he crossed the darkened antechamber of the town house.

He could smell that Blackstone was here before he entered the last card room. It was the distinct absence of fresh cigarette smoke, which normally masked the stink of old carpets that had been soaked in various fluids over the course of decades. No one was allowed to smoke in the investor's presence. Speculations abounded over the reasons, with half the people suspecting Blackstone had an unseemly concern for the condition of his teeth and lungs, and the other half insisting he just took pleasure in controlling the men around him. Tristan knew him long enough to be certain that both were the case.

Blackstone was sprawled in an armchair, facing the door with his back to the wall. His harsh features, made harsher by a once-broken nose, gave no indication he had taken notice of Tristan entering. He was not paying attention to anyone in particular, and his cards hung loosely from a careless pale hand. The other men in the circle who dared to gamble with him might as well not have been there at all. In looks and mien, Blackstone more resembled the underworld lords who ruled the docklands than his actual class of legitimate businessmen.

Tristan passed the group without slowing, but the small nod he gave indicated he wanted a word, and Blackstone's dark lashes lowered a fraction in acknowledgment. This was promising, for while they might still follow each other's moves privately, they had not purposefully crossed paths in a few years' time.

He sought out an empty side chamber and made himself comfortable in a creaking leather wing chair. Blackstone could take ten minutes, or hours. A patently tedious game, sitting and waiting and breathing the fetid air. In the past, it hadn't bothered him. He had been keen, then, eighteen years of age and greedy for the hunt. He had just become aware that not only women, but some men, too, were drawn to his face, and the entire demimonde had been enchanted by the newness and youth of him. They had pulled him into the dimly-lit, sweltering, and sleepless underworld of gambling and debauchery, and it had been quite easy, pulling them in in return, securing their trust when they were drunk on Scotch and pleasure or stupidly tight on ether. Incriminating secrets were easily extracted during those hours, and he had made others gamble deep, all while he was still stone sober beneath an exuberant veneer of intoxication. Soon he had had a ledger with a carefully calibrated mix of legitimately owed debts and favors as well as secrets he could occasionally turn into coin by way of extortion. His personal, portable bank account, his last trump card.

It was how he and Blackstone had met: attempting to pluck the same pigeon one glittering night. Their strengths had been too well matched to be pitted against each other effectively, and after some juvenile posturing, they had joined forces for their covert robberies. The brute and the snake. One had provided enforcement, the other access to exclusive circles. It had worked well for a few years. It had worked better for Blackstone, financially speaking—he was now one of the wealthiest businessmen in London. Then again, the man hadn't been yanked from his early moneymaking activities by an overbearing father. Blackstone, Tristan assumed, did not have a father to call his own.

A shadow fell across the floor. Speak of the devil: the financier's brawny build was darkening the door frame. Hard eyes the color of slate locked with his.

"I have business to discuss," Tristan said.

Blackstone contemplated, then nodded, turned, and left. They both knew the chambers here had strategically placed holes in the plaster to accommodate the ears and eyes of third parties. They knew from their days on the other side of the wall.

They were headed toward the east exit where the coaches waited. Blackstone motioned for Tristan to climb aboard his unmarked carriage. The vehicle jerked into motion a moment later, and unless discussed otherwise, it would take them a few streets down to Belgravia, which allowed for enough time to talk business if one was succinct; then Tristan would alight and Blackstone would vanish, presumably to one of his various properties whose locations he liked to keep undisclosed. He did have one well-known town house, in Chelsea, filled entirely with his collection of art and antiques, and Blackstone knew the price of each of these objects and the value of none. The investor was crass—commonplace in someone born on the wrong side of the blanket who had come into his fortune later in life, Tristan supposed.

"I need money," he said. "Tomorrow."

Across the footwell, Blackstone was watching the dark of night pass by the window, light and shadow playing over his blunt features. He apparently was still not much of a talker.

"How much," he finally asked, his gravelly voice dispassionate, his Scottish lilt a mere whisper these days.

Tristan named the sum, and Blackstone slowly turned his head to face him.

It was a rather speaking glance the man gave him. Well, yes. It was rather a lot of money.

"I'm almost curious what brought this on," Blackstone murmured.

"Women," Tristan replied. Lucie, his mother, and the unknown, unwanted fiancée, to be precise.

"Naturally." Blackstone was looking out the window again. "The money shall be in the account by noon," he said after a pause. "Meet my man to sign the papers at Claridge's tomorrow morning at eight."

There was no need for further discussion. Blackstone clawed his money back come what may, and Tristan knew the conditions. The last time he had asked for a large sum, he had been two-and-twenty and had just received his marching orders. It had been the second occasion where he had seriously contemplated becoming disowned and emigrating to America, and again, he had held back. He had, however, had the presence of mind to make an investment with an eye on the future before his regiment's ship sailed. In addition to an ambitious interest rate, his old friend had asked for a few debts to be transferred from Tristan's ledger into his own—Blackstone loved owning the debts of noblemen, only to call them in at the most inopportune times, inopportune for the indebted noblemen, that was. Ruined livelihoods lay scattered in his wake. Tristan smiled faintly. A viscount had to be mad to do business with Blackstone.

Chapter 8

L ucie's breakfast was disturbed by a disheveled runner boy ringing her doorbell. The note he delivered was from the Snug Oyster, and Lucie hastily dressed. When the Oxford brothel sent for her rather than have one of its occupants turn up at her doorstep in the black of night, something was afoot. She made her way toward Cowley Road in a hackney rather than on foot.

In the dim light of the brothel's vestibule, the sweet smell of Far Eastern herbs was already overwhelming. Incense, but employed with deliberate overabundance. As always, it blasphemously forced her mind back to early mornings in the Wycliffe chapel.

It was eight o'clock, and the Oyster was readying for sleep. The woman who had let her in looked tired, the kohl lining her dark eyes dissolved into gray smudges.

"Good morning, Lilian," said Lucie.

Lilian's curtsy was wobbly. "Milady. How good of you to come."

Lucie followed her along the corridor, then down the creaking stairs to the kitchen.

"It's young Amy," Lilian said over her shoulder. "She's had the baby, and now she's got nowhere to go."

The kitchen was cold, and dirty bowls piled up on the long table. Red Meg was dispassionately moving crumbs back and forth on the tabletop with a grimy rag. She glanced up when Lucie entered.

"Milady." She made a halfhearted effort to bow her head. Like most women at the Oyster, no, like most *women*, she was unsure where to place a lady who would set foot into a brothel.

Young Amy had to be the thin girl staring at her from across the room. An untidy blond braid tumbled over her right shoulder. She was clutching a bundle to her chest, which presumably contained the infant.

Lucie turned to Lilian. "When must she leave?"

"Now. The madam wants her gone."

"She should already be gone," said Red Meg, "but she's been begging to stay until you come, so we've let her. Lord knows why, Madam would have our heads."

It was the usual predicament. A man got a prostitute with child. The madam would give the girl two choices—leave with the baby into an unknown future, or give the baby away. Most stuck with the devil they knew. But every so often, a woman decided to keep her child. Young Amy seemed determined, judging by the death grip she kept on the bundle. She held herself very still when Lucie approached.

"Why did you call for me, Miss Amy?"

Amy's red-rimmed eyes darted nervously about the room. "Some of the girls said you help," she said. "You've helped girls in the Oyster before, and so I thought . . . I thought you might help us, milady."

Her voice was scratchy, making Lucie's own throat tighten uncomfortably. Screamed through the night while giving birth, no doubt. It was a miracle the girl was on her feet.

"And what is it you want?" she coaxed.

Amy hugged the bundle closer. "I heard you know of places where we could stay."

"You should've just been careful," came Red Meg's irritated voice.

Within seconds, the girl's nose turned pink and her eyes were brimming with tears. "I had planned to give her up. But when I held her . . . when I looked at her wee face . . ."

"Have you approached the father?"

Amy's chin quivered. "He wants nothing to do with us."

Red Meg let an armful of soup bowls clatter into the sink. "What did yer expect," she said. "He was comely and rich, and you were daft to think he'd have a care for a whore or a whore's babe."

Amy trembled, and the bundle in her arms gave a thin squawk of protest.

"Oh shut it, Megs," said Lilian. She went to Amy and put an arm around her slim shoulders.

"Milady," she said, "do you know who writes this? They could write about Amy." She pulled a paper from her skirt pocket and thrust it at Lucie.

The angry red header was at once familiar. It was a crinkled copy of *The Female Citizen*, the radical pamphlet whose editor was unknown, but which, for some reason, always found its way into the most unlikely hands.

"Write about Amy?" Red Meg snarled. "Why would anyone write about bleedin' Amy? No one reads about the likes of us."

"But it ain't right," Lilian said. "The father has money. He promised her things, and now she's got nowhere to go. And this paper prints stories about whores all the time, look—"

"It's horseshit," said Meg. "Printing stories about the Oyster? Making us all look bad, and ruining business? The madam would throw you out on your arse, too. As for Amy, it's her own fault. She's thick, not much up here." She tapped her finger against her gleaming forehead. "Nineteen years old, still believing in fairy tales."

Amy's eyes were overflowing with misery. "I can't give her away, milady. I hear they do terrible things to the babes . . . they sell them, or worse—"

"You do not have to give her up," Lucie said firmly. She pulled notebook and pencil from her skirt pocket, swiped debris off the table, and set pencil to paper. "Have you packed?"

Nodding and crying, Amy toed a battered brown bag at her feet.

"And have you any money?"

The girl shook her head. "I had saved some, but Madam took it when I couldn't work no longer."

"It's only fair, isn't it."

Lucie exhaled an audible huff. Red Meg's commentary was not going to cease, was it?

She tore the page from the notebook, tucked it into her pocket, and went to pick up the brown bag. It was dishearteningly light. "Come with me."

The stairs were a struggle. Amy was limping but wouldn't part with the baby to ease her burden. It took a long time to reach the side entrance. The fresh air outside was like a gulp of clean water after a drought. Back on the main street, it mercifully did not take long to hail a hackney.

Lucie tossed the driver a coin, then began counting more money into Amy's palm.

"This covers a Great Western Rail ticket. Take the train to Wokingham at a quarter to nine. Wait at Wokingham station—I shall send a cable now and have you picked up and brought to Mrs. Juliana's Academy for Single Females."

Amy blinked. "An academy? But I can't read all that good."

"It's simply a respectable name for a discreet halfway house. You may, however, learn how to read and write there, or other skills, if they appeal."

Amy's apprehension only grew. "Will there be nuns, milady?"

Lucie shook her head. "It is run by women trying to help." She handed Amy the note she had written earlier in the kitchen. "Give this to Mrs. Juliana, so she knows you are the one I sent."

The girl nodded. She was in a daze. She should not be traveling at all.

Lucie hesitated. She could feel the sovereign she had put into her coat pocket last night, heavy like a lump of lead. A sovereign earmarked for a ticket to Bond Street, London, and a set of new dresses.

Perhaps a powder blue one, in the style she had seen on the fashion magazine cover at the Randolph. It had grated to admit to it, but the truth was, she had felt drab like a crow at Blackwell's three days ago, when the shopgirls had spilled into the coffee room. In their colorful, snugly fitted cotton dresses trimmed with crisp white lace, they had brightened the room like a bouquet of fresh spring flowers. They had smelled like flowers, too. It was testimony to how overindulged Tristan was, how he had sat and signed his Ballentine cards with such languor; clearly, being accosted by eager young women was commonplace for him. God help the woman he would marry. His next mistress would simply fall into his lap whenever he took a seat somewhere.

The hackney horse snorted and pawed the cobblestones with an impatient hoof.

She thrust her hand into the pocket and fished out the coin.

Amy's eyes widened when she pressed the small fortune into her palm.

"Promise me you will use this to see a doctor and have them take a look at the babe as well," Lucie said. "And a few new clothes seem in order."

The girl stared at the coin in her hand with awe. "I promise," she whispered.

Lucie gave a nod. "Good day, then."

"Milady." Amy was offering her the bundle, starry eyed. "Would you hold her? To bring her good luck?"

Lucie took a step back. "You are making me sound like a fairy godmother, Miss Amy, which I assure you I am not."

The girl's face fell. "Of course not. I beg your pardon." She cradled the child close again, her cheeks flushing crimson.

"Oh, all right," Lucie said. "Let me hold her, then."

The baby was asleep. She didn't stir when Amy gingerly placed her into the crook of Lucie's arm.

Lucie stared, mesmerized, at an impossibly tiny face. A tiny button nose. A wispy black curl peeking out from under a tiny knitted hat. She counted three astonishingly sweeping lashes on each of the baby's eyelids.

"What will you name her?" she asked softly.

"Elizabeth," Amy said. "After me mum."

The infant's smell rose from the blanket, wondrously sweet like sugared milk and powder, edging out the incense odor that still clung to Lucie's coat. Something gave a painful pull inside her chest.

Carefully, she handed the little girl back to her mother.

"Elizabeth is a good name," she said, "the name of a queen. May you raise her to be a strong woman."

"I hope to raise her to be a bit like you, milady."

Her smile was crooked. "May the Lord help you both, then."

She offered a hand to help Amy up into the hackney, then stood and watched as they clattered off into the distance.

Nineteen years old, still believing in fairy tales.

Some women never stopped believing. Up and down the land, in brothels and manor houses alike, women sat waiting for a man to rescue them.

Were they aware that the cure they were hoping for could easily become their curse? Oh, they were. But ten years of glimpsing behind quiet, decorous façades had taught her that some never saw other options, and others never dared to seize them; and then there were women like Amy, who had never been presented with much in the way of options at all. And some days, she could not help but feel that no campaign in the world had the power to change this. She arrived back at her door in Norham Gardens feeling vaguely guilty about regretting the way her sovereign had gone. There was no doubt the coin had been put to its best possible use. But at the end of the day, it was a drop into a bottomless barrel. Even if she were to go in rags, there would always be more women and more babies needing money, needing shelter. The caravan of misery was endless. She could change a fate here and there immediately by going without, but what was truly needed were better circumstances for every woman, every child, independently of random acts of charity. And this was a matter of making just policies in Westminster. And tell herself as she might that frippery should not matter, with her fraying cuffs and slate gray skirts, she hardly looked the part for the corridors of Parliament these days, or any other part than that of a long-resigned spinster. She had been overly aware of it at Blackwell's. Perhaps even during her morning visit with Lady Salisbury, with the matron more than twice her age winking and mentioning lovers.

All pondering of fashion and policy ceased when she opened the mailbox. Mr. Barnes's nervous handwriting stood out amid the dozen letters with the effect of a beacon. She tore the envelope open while walking down her corridor, her heart racing. "Well well well," she murmured. "The power of a ducal connection never fails. Boudicca!" The cat gave an indignant growl at being seized and petted so vigorously. "Rejoice," Lucie demanded. "We are the new owners of London Print."

She took the sweeping marble staircase leading from the lobby of London Print to the office floor two steps at the time. Mr. Sykes, her solicitor, was hard on her heels, panting and with his glasses askew.

Mr. Barnes was awaiting her in his office with his own notary, a Mr. Marshall. Miss Barnes was seated demurely in her typist corner. And there, neatly assorted on the mahogany desk at the center of the room, lay the gleaming white papers of her contract.

"Your ladyship is aware that I shall have to read every sentence of this document to you?" Mr. Marshall asked.

She eyed the twenty tightly written pages. "I'm aware, but is it truly necessary?"

Both Mr. Sykes and Mr. Marshall exclaimed that yes, it was very necessary.

It took an hour and a half. Mr. Marshall read, Mr. Sykes interjected, both postured until Mr. Marshall annotated, and meanwhile, Miss Barnes was hacking away at her typewriter. Lucie's heart was beating unnaturally fast throughout, and her face felt fever-flushed. She urgently needed to see her signature dry on the dotted line.

Her throat was parched by the time Mr. Marshall placed the final contract page before her. "Please sign here, my lady."

The dotted line.

Someone offered her a gold-tipped fountain pen.

For a blink, she forgot how to confidently scrawl her own name.

And then it was done.

She lowered the pen on a shaky breath.

The penultimate step in their plan had been completed.

They rose and the men shook hands, then muttered perfunctory congratulations at her. They did not trust her. *They shouldn't.*

"If you are so inclined, you can meet the new co-owner right away," said Mr. Barnes as he stowed his fountain pen. "He took over his office today and should still be in the house."

She returned his expectant look with confusion. "A new co-owner?"

"Well, not exactly new, but he's taken over the other shares . . ." Barnes frowned. "You received my missive, have you not? I sent it the same day as my confirmation of offer."

A shiver of foreboding prickled up Lucie's nape.

"An oversight, perhaps," she said. Because she had rushed out of the house after seeing the takeover confirmed, instead of sorting the usual armful of mail first. "What has changed?" The shareholder structure had been ideal—no majority owner, hence no obstacles to her editorial choices.

"Lord Ballentine has returned from abroad and he has recently bought all other shares," Mr. Barnes said. "But perhaps your ladyship would like to discuss the details with your new partner directly . . ."

Chapter 9

The corridor drifted past without sound. Her face felt frozen. She all but shouldered past the receptionist announcing her into the office.

She was greeted by the soles of a pair of large shoes, propped up on a vast desk. A spread-open newspaper concealed the owner of said shoes.

Her heart plummeted.

Only one gentleman of her acquaintance would read the *Times* like a pantomime villain.

The paper lowered, and lion eyes met hers.

At once, the air between them burned. Her next breath scorched her lungs like hot steam.

"Lady Lucie." Tristan took his feet off the desk. "I've been expecting you."

Her throat was jammed with too many words.

He was dressed smartly, no crimson velvet in sight, just gray, immaculately tailored wool and muted silk. It made him look alien.

It made it all the more real.

He was watching her expectantly as he folded up the paper, and when she only stood and stared, her pulse thudding in her ears, he gave a shrug, rose, and meandered over to the sideboard.

Tristan Ballentine was walking around in the offices of London Print as if he owned them.

Because he did.

She swayed a little on her feet.

"May I offer you something to drink?" His long fingers played over bottle necks. "Brandy, Scotch, sherry?"

She crossed her arms over her chest, holding on tight. Her pulse was beating alarmingly fast. "Since when?" she demanded.

He uncorked a bottle and held it to his nose for a sniff. "Since when what?"

The innocent curve of his mouth sent lightning crackling over her nerves.

"Since when do you own shares in this company?"

"Ah. Well, I bought the first twenty-five percent around six years ago, before my first tour. The remaining shares I purchased yesterday. At a bargain price, too, once I informed the previous owner of a suffragist takeover. Are you sure you don't care for a brandy? You look a bit peaked."

Her heart thudded, threatening to pound a hole through her ribs. Her nemesis owned the other half of her publishing house.

Her gaze narrowed. "You," she said, "you were the one who alarmed the board and pressured Mr. Barnes."

"I did, yes." He did not look remotely contrite. "I had to buy some time, to secure the necessary capital and to confirm my suspicions that you were planning mischief before actually making an offer."

His suspicions—had this been the reason behind their meeting at Blackwell's? Of course.

She had known. She had known he had been trouble and she had gone to meet him anyway.

"Why?" she asked, hating the tremor in her voice. "Why London Print?"

He poured himself two finger widths of liquor as he strolled back toward his desk, taking the bottle with him. "Why would I not?" he said. "It's a publishing house with a vast readership, with still considerably under-explored potential. Anyone with an eye on publishing and a passive income stream would be interested."

The words hit like slaps. They were the same words she had given Mr. Barnes, when she had used economics to conceal her true intent of using the magazines to further the Cause. What was Tristan hiding? He should be living off his father's allowance like any aristocratic male heir, not pondering passive income streams.

"If it is money you want, pick another business," she said.

He cocked his head. "But why? Both my purchases preceded yours. One could say I was there first."

"You cad," she muttered, trembling.

It seemed to amuse him. "Throw a man a bone, Lucie. I'm back from the war. Perhaps I like the idea of having something to do. And London Print owns the rights to my literary works, so I suppose you could call me *emotionally invested* in my revenue."

"Literary works?"

He sent her a pitying look from beneath his long lashes. "Romantic poetry."

He might as well have talked Mandarin to her.

And then it dawned on her.

She shook her head, bemused. "Are you claiming *you* are the author of *A Pocketful of Poems*?"

"I am," Tristan said. He studied her over the rim of his whiskey glass, an expectant gleam in his eyes. "How do you like it?"

The poetry? The poetry was published by Anonymous. She had suspected a woman to be the author, as was so often the case with Anonymous. Apparently, the truth was more outrageous. Apparently, there was a reality where her business partner was a notorious rake and where Lord Ballentine, most shallow of men, was an acclaimed poet. She had quite possibly fallen through a rabbit hole.

"Do I like it," she repeated. "The poetry, I presume? Why, I never read any of it." She gave him a haughty look. "Pretty, empty things don't hold my attention."

The gleam in his eyes faded.

He tsked. "You surprise me—I had taken you for a thorough investigator and yet here you are, buying into a company without knowing the identity of fellow share-owners or the content of one of their best-selling products. You have been careless."

She seethed in silence, because he was not wrong. Her plans required no great knowledge of London Print at all, but she must not tell him that, and thus, she must keep quiet and let him think she was a fool.

"As it is," he continued, "we both profit from my intervention. My book is still selling six years after publication which is remarkable. However, figures have stagnated. Now, imagine I were revealed as the author." He looked smug, saying it. "We will need another edition, and we could—"

She held up a staying hand. "I am not doing business with you."

"Don't be obtuse," he said mildly. "You must."

"I must do no such thing."

He shrugged. "A pity, then. Your idea about my war diaries was good. They shall be published next."

Her stomach was a hard ball of dread. If only she had not gone to meet him at Blackwell's at all. Why had she? "Sell your shares to me," she whispered.

"Why—I have only just acquired them."

She drew closer. "If it is money you want, sell them to me." She would find the money, somehow, no matter how staggering the figures.

Tristan leaned back against the desk and swirled the whiskey in his glass, looking infuriatingly laconic and superior. "I have no interest in a lump sum, princess. I do, however, have a vested interest in London Print maintaining its profits long-term."

She glared at him, and his smile turned into a smirk. "Come

now," he said. "We both know you would never acquire wholesome women's magazines without ulterior motives. The pen is mightier than the sword and such. The *Home Counties Weekly*, in your hands? What is your plan—women's rights shenanigans instead of sponge cake recipes? No. I want control over the content."

Cold sweat broke over her brow.

He'd ruin . . . everything.

She swallowed, trying to force a surge of nausea back down.

"There are other ways of making money, if you must," she said. "Pick another way."

His expression hardened. "And idly stand by as you lose us readers? I cannot do that, I'm afraid."

Us.

She wanted to screech and snarl like a fox clamped in a trap. There could be no *us*. He had just sabotaged their every hope for this enterprise while casually swilling whiskey. Her blood roared in her ears. Anything she'd say now would be petty. She must not give him such satisfaction.

"This is not over," she said.

"Not in a long time, my sweet," she heard him say before she firmly closed the door.

The sky was already dark like smoke behind Oxford's chimneys and she was still pacing an angry circle on Hattie's Persian rug, round and round. The train ride from London had failed to calm her. The sight of Oxford's eternal walls had not soothed her.

"He tricked me," she fumed, "and I let him. How could I? He's not even sober half the time!"

Annabelle was watching her with overt concern from the settee. "You could hardly expect such a turn of events, no one could."

"It is all very curious, almost like a scene from a play," Hattie supplied from her armchair. "The odds for such a thing to come to pass, of both of you buying stakes in the same enterprise, are so low—it feels fateful."

Lucie whirled on her. "This is not a play, Hattie. This is a disaster."

Her friends fell silent, and she knew she had spoken too harshly. She took a deep breath. It did not help. She was still reeling.

"You know what this means," she said. "He will be able to veto anything. We cannot put our plan into practice—we cannot publish our report." She pressed her palms against her temples. "We have raised a fortune and purchased a publishing house—for nothing."

The silence became heavy and grave.

"Perhaps we find a solution while Parliament is in summer recess," Annabelle then said. "I shall ask Montgomery to reschedule the session for his amendment proposal when they reconvene in September."

"Thank you. But if it were easy to find another way, we would have found it by now."

"And if we just did it anyway?" Hattie said with a small voice. "What if we just went ahead?"

Lucie frowned. "The executive processes require two signatures at every turn now. There is no legal basis for us to proceed. I am vexed beyond words."

Catriona pulled her shawl more tightly around her shoulders. "And if we used the publishing house for some other purpose?"

Lucie blinked. "Which one?"

"It's still a growing enterprise, which is hardly a useless investment. And whatever we shall do with it, you have as much power as Lord Ballentine. You can both veto each other's ideas."

"Oh, grand. Spending our days bargaining and bickering with Ballentine instead of advancing our work? Blast, to even think I should have to endure his smirking countenance every week."

Annabelle looked intrigued. "I like it. We could use it to further the Cause in other ways. Why not employ as many women at London Print as we can? We could pay them the same wages as the men."

Hattie nodded. "Wouldn't that be much nicer than sending surplus women to Australia?"

Lucie paused. The idea was good; even as her stomach churned with emotions, she knew it merited close consideration. There was indeed the rapidly growing problem of middle-class women in need of office employment, chiefly because there were not enough men in Britain to marry and provide for them. War and emigration led too many prospective grooms abroad or to their demise, and the women left behind were deemed too proper to take up manual labor for a living. The government's current remedy of sending women to Australia with a one-way ticket so they could find husbands there was, as usual, a harebrained scheme. However . . . she shook her head. "A brilliant idea," she said. "But no."

"Whyever not?" Catriona looked genuinely confused.

"An office full of women workers?" Another shake. "It would be unwise, with Ballentine so close. He hardly needs the added acclaim of being a romantic poet—he could cause disruption just by flaunting himself around the office. And he will. Sensible women will turn against each other, competing for his attention. The one he lures will suffer a broken heart and do something deranged . . . you have all seen the headlines he causes. And I will have to dismiss her, because I cannot dismiss *him*."

Her friends were regarding her with a collective frown, as though she had quite lost her mind.

"Aren't you doing us an injustice?" Annabelle asked mildly. "I know he's a scoundrel, but it will take more than a handsome face and some flirtation to turn women into imbeciles."

"I agree," muttered Catriona. "Have some faith in our rational faculties."

Lucie blew out a breath. To an outsider, she would sound quite unhinged. "You have to understand something about Ballentine," she said. "He used to be a second son, and his hair was orange. There were rumors he wasn't even Rochester's. What does such an unfortunate boy do to survive? He becomes charming. And witty. He becomes a veritable Machiavelli of charm. He will eventually sense your desires and weaknesses from a mile away and will use them against you as it suits him. Now imagine that a boy with such a grudge and such skills grows into an extraordinarily handsome man, becomes the heir, and returns home with the Victoria Cross. Can you *imagine* what this makes him?"

For a long moment, only the crackling sound of the fire filled the room.

Annabelle's and Catriona's expressions had turned troubled.

"It makes him a dangerous man," Hattie finally said. "Forever out to gorge himself on the attention of admirers to soothe old wounds." Never mind that she looked half intrigued by the prospect.

"Bother," Annabelle said. "Can we not buy a different publisher? I shall speak to Montgomery; I'm certain he will not deny me more funding."

"If you find one on offer, with the same readership, certainly."

They all knew there was presently no such thing. While their plan to use London Print as a vehicle for the suffrage cause hadn't been perfect, it had been thought through within the constraints they were given. To think they could be executing the plan right now, rather than haphazardly collecting ideas of how to proceed!

"The more I think about it, the more I agree that Lord Ballentine shouldn't be in our offices," Hattie said pensively. "Just a few days ago, I was welcoming the ladies who have enrolled for the Oxford Summer School, and some of them were keen to admit they were taking the drawing course not because of Professor Ruskin's teaching, but because Lord Ballentine has set up home in Oxford. They are hoping to cross paths with him."

Lucie stared at her. "He has *what*?"

"Oh dear." Hattie ducked her head. "You didn't know?"

"No," Lucie bit out. "Where does he live, do you know?"

"In Logic Lane, I think—Lucie, what are you doing? It's not a respectable time to call on a gentleman. . . ."

Chapter 10

Tristan's manservant did not look at all surprised to find an enraged woman at his master's doorstep at an unrespectable time.

He did, however, bodily block her entry with his tall form. "His lordship is not at home," he said smoothly, his sleek black eyebrows exuding more arrogance than a full-fledged duke. He was not the valet she remembered from the days of Wycliffe Hall, either.

"You are new," she said. "What is your name?"

His dark eyes contemplated her down his nose. "Avi, milady," he finally said.

"Avi," she said. "Lord Ballentine and I have a business matter to discuss. Unless you think his lordship wants the entire street to partake in it, step aside. My voice carries, I have been told."

The brows swooped. "It does," Avi said. "Carry. You are not armed with anything sharp, milady?"

"Other than my tongue?"

The valet relented in the face of such belligerence, bowed his head, and stepped aside.

She brushed past him, her heart drumming an angry beat.

The stairway was narrow.

The landing was small.

Part of her wondered why the future Earl of Rochester would set up home in a commoner's house—

The door to the bedchamber was open, and the warm light of a fire and at least a dozen candles spilled onto the landing.

She rushed ahead and turned into the doorway.

She froze midstride.

At the back of the room, stretched out on his side and propped up on an elbow, the master of the house was lounging on a divan.

And he was naked.

She stared, for a breathless moment suspended in time.

He slowly raised his eyes from his book, looking . . . intrigued.

Her gaze jerked away like fingers touching something hot.

Too late. The sight was seared onto her mind and kept glowing behind closed eyes: the smooth, honeyed skin and chiseled muscle; wide, straight shoulders; a broad, broad chest . . . and a tattoo on his right pectoral.

Her mouth was dry. Her heart was pounding.

A trail of dark hair below his navel had dragged her gaze down and down. . . . He was not entirely naked. A pair of soft, low-slung trousers clung to his hips.

Still. Her face burned as if she'd stepped too close to a furnace. This was bad.

The divan creaked. She opened her eyes and, peering sideways, noted that his lordship had sat up. Her fingertips dug into her palms. *Let the circus commence.*

"Lucie." His voice was rough. "Should they become true at last, my dreams of you in my bedchamber?"

"Would you mind making yourself decent?" she said to the door frame, her tone unnaturally prim.

"I say," he drawled. "If nudity offends your sensibilities, I recommend you refrain from storming men's boudoirs after dark."

Some instinct told her not all nudity would make her nervous. It was this particular well-formed, golden nudity that had made her go a little weak in the knees.

In the periphery of her vision, she watched him rise and stretch with the grace of a large cat, his back muscles rippling beneath gleaming skin—could she blame herself for watching? It was as though a piece of art, a Roman marble, were coming to life.

Still, as he walked to the wardrobe, she was tempted to skip down the stairs again, past insolent Avi, and leave with whatever decorum she had left. Sometimes she had to wonder about her choices. She *had* just burst into a man's bedroom, utterly unacceptable behavior even for a confirmed spinster, scandalous even by her standards. Years and years of shared antagonism must have given her a false sense of familiarity where Tristan was concerned.

"Voilà," he purred.

She turned back.

He was standing next to the fireplace, not decent at all. He had slipped on a dressing gown of sorts: red silk, exotic floral trimmings. It fell open in the front and revealed a flat abdomen with well-defined slabs of more muscle. In the glow of the fire, his bare skin looked smooth like satin to the touch, and her lips responded with an excited tingle.

She steeled herself. This was as presentable as he would make himself. She strolled into the room with a nonchalance she did not feel, because hovering at the door like a ninny would be worse.

She noted a four-poster bed taking up near half the chamber to her right, and colorful wall tapestries and a wood cabinet to her left. The air smelled of him, and being cocooned in his scent was as unsettling as being confronted with him being in a state of dishabille.

"Did the cat get your tongue?" he asked, his voice soft.

He was watching her with a glint in his eyes. If he were a lion indeed, his tail would now have the telltale flick of a predator ready to pounce.

Except that he had already gone for the kill.

The resentment over why she was here in the first place surged anew; her body went rigid with it.

She propped a hand on her hip.

"Is it true?" she demanded. "You have set up residence in Oxford?"

He took his time contemplating her belligerent stance before granting her a reply. "For now, yes."

"Why?"

He gave a lazy shrug. "It is such a pretty little town."

She shook her head. "You would never voluntarily settle in such a provincial hovel," she said, the sweep of her hand encompassing the room. "First you buy half of my publisher, then you set up house in my city—what are you scheming, Ballentine?"

He raised a brow, rather superciliously. "*Your* city? A bit grandiose, don't you think?"

Her hands curled into fists. "We cannot both be in the same room, or the same town, for a minute without quarreling," she said. "Working together is impossible, you must know this. Sell me your shares. I shall put it in writing that your books will be well cared for."

He cocked his head. "Perhaps I enjoy our quarreling," he said. "It adds a certain piquancy to my day."

Of course, he would draw it out and try and make her beg.

She'd sooner give her first vote to the Tories.

"See reason," she tried. "We cannot both own exactly half."

Again his brow went up. "Because it means I can—and will—veto anything endangering our sales, such as, say, radical women's politics?"

"Yes," she hissed.

She realized then that she was closer to begging than she'd ever been. Her plans, for two years in the making, dashed. By *him*, of all people. To her horror, tears of frustration were burning in her nose, when she couldn't remember the last time she had cried.

Tristan's brow furrowed. "Come now," he said. "Potentially ruining your own business cannot be in your interest, either. And I know I played pranks on you during those summers at Wycliffe Hall, and some were not in good taste. But we are both adults now, so can you not forgive and forget and let us begin anew? I shall apologize for my youthful transgressions if that settles it."

Bells of hell. She saw red. A lecture on grace by a man, who, if rumors could be trusted, had recently jumped from a balcony into a rosebush to escape an enraged husband. But he'd toss her an apology, if doing so made her biddable?

Any sense of defeat went up in angry flames. "You think I dislike you for your childish pranks?"

His eyes narrowed. "What else could it possibly be?"

"Your ignorance is astonishing."

"Enlighten me," he said darkly. "Just what crimes have I ever committed against you to merit such a degree of dislike?"

"Dislike?" she said. "Very well, this is why I *dislike* you: you are a libertine. You seduce people for the sake of it, for sport. You will use and discard a woman just to pass an afternoon . . . you value trivial things and mock serious matters, and you talk a lot but say very little, which leads me to conclude your mind is lazy or foolish, or both . . . you misuse your superior station with your hedonistic ways, when most people cling to their positions by the skin of their teeth, and, worst of all, you have been assigned a seat in the House of Lords and yet you have not used it once—not once!—when millions go without a voice in this country. Truly, I can think of few men more useless than you, and I don't dislike you, my lord, I detest you."

A dam in her, long cracked, had broken; the toxic words were pouring out of her like a waterfall.

The ensuing silence was deafening. There was only the sound of her breathing, shaky and erratic.

Tristan stood as still as if shot.

Eerily still.

There was no mistaking the angry color slowly tinging his cheekbones.

An uneasy sensation stirred in her stomach. A line had been crossed she hadn't known they had heeded until now.

He took a deep breath. "*Useless,*" he said. The word dripped from his lips in cold contempt.

She crossed her arms over her chest. "Well, yes," she muttered. "And I cannot share a business with you."

"I see." His tone was controlled, but in the depths of his eyes simmered something sinister. The deliberate slowness of his gaze traveling over her, from her face down to her toes, raised all the fine hairs on her body. She had terribly provoked him.

He turned to the fireplace and stared into the glowing embers on the grate. In his flowing robe, with one hand on the mantelpiece and his profile hard and brooding, he looked like a vengeful young god contemplating the firelight.

"Tell me, Lucie." His voice was silky-smooth. "How badly do you want it?"

The question slipped like a satin rope around her neck. She could feel her throat tightening.

This was a trap.

She raised her chin. "Name a price. And I shall see whether I can pay it."

"Oh, but you can."

The fingers of his left hand had begun an idle exploration of the objects on the mantelpiece, trailing over the smooth curve of the ceramic clock, an oblong box, the heavy candlestick turned from oak wood. They lingered on the candlestick, slid around it, tested its girth.

Heat poured over her like liquid fire.

"You can," he repeated, and turned to look at her. His eyes were fathomless pools in the flickering shadows. "The question is whether you are willing."

His hand circling the candleholder languidly slid up over polished wood, then down again, a lewd gesture if she'd ever seen one. Terribly mesmerizing, too, because the firelight was playing over his bare chest and he had well-formed fingers that knew every shameless caress under the sun.

That he should dare it left her breathless.

"Your price," she whispered. "Name it."

A glint of canine teeth. "You're an intelligent woman," he said. "Take a guess."

"You are leering at me whilst fondling a phallic object," she said. "It does not take great intelligence to assume you are propositioning me."

"Mmh," he hummed. "Assume that I am."

"Lecherous, shameless creature."

"Are you speaking of me, or yourself?"

She could only stare and loathe him.

He took his hand off the candlestick. "Darling, you forget who I am. I know lust from twenty paces, and despite your outburst of virtuous severity earlier, you are roiling with it. It's in the shine of your eyes and the charming flush of your cheeks. If I were to lay my fingers against your throat now, I would feel your pulse beat unnaturally fast and hard."

Her body was suddenly too heavy for her legs. The heated cheeks, the quickened pulse, were all true.

"You are ridiculous," she said, and it came out husky.

His smile was pure vindication. "And yet neither one of us is laughing," he said. "One night. One night in your bed for one percent of company shares. *And* you shall give it to me in writing that you look after my books. That is the price."

She was breathing too fast, she was dizzy from it. "So you lied," she said. "You said you never force your attentions."

His brows rose. "I don't. I doubt anyone else in my position would even contemplate the potential ruin of their business by making any kind of offer. Decline it, and things shall rightfully remain as they are. Take it, and London Print shall be yours." His attention moved past her, to the bed. "We could begin now. You would wake up tomorrow morning well-pleasured and the owner of a publishing house. I'm a fool to offer you such a bargain."

The bed was close, a step or two to the right. His tone, for all its derisiveness, was matter-of-fact. Her hands clenched; for a fleeting second, she had almost felt the softness of the counterpane beneath her palms, had seen his bare throat and shoulders move over her. His seduction was already at work, naturally—he must have honed it by years of practice. . . .

The perverted entrancement he had spun around her with his silken voice and sliding hand shattered.

"If you think I'd trade a company share for the pox, you are deluded," she said coolly.

He made a face. "There are ways of preventing such things."

She doubted he used any of them.

She turned on her heels.

"I shall make it a standing offer, until the end of summer," she heard him say, and there was a smirk in his voice.

She spun back round to face him. "You sound rather desperate for me to take your offer."

His smile left his eyes stone cold. "I'm always desperate, princess. Take your time to consider it—as it is, I'm not all that *useless* in the bedchamber."

She knew. Women talked.

"Go to Hades," she said, and stomped out of his room.

The window's bull's-eye pane grotesquely distorted Lucie's cloaked shape as she disappeared into the shadows of Logic Lane. Tristan continued to stare down into the dusky emptiness of the street. The heat wave engulfing him minutes ago was abating only slowly. He realized he was fingering his cheekbone, quite as though he were twelve again and felt the sting of her slap.

He dropped his hand and gave a puzzled laugh.

Useless. Of all the insults she could have chosen, the little witch. She might as well have flown at him brandishing a scimitar. In fact, he would have preferred a knife attack, as he would have dealt with it rather more smoothly.

He turned to the room and sprawled back down onto the divan, and the piece of furniture shrieked in protest. To hell with it. Nothing in this *provincial hovel* was built for his size. Except the bed. The bed was built for two.

His gaze lingered on the silken counterpane as he reached for his brandy flask. What a sobering chain of events. He had not expected her to hold him in such contempt, nor that it would grate on him so to learn that she did. Apparently, his youthful preoccupation with her ran deeper than he'd known; so deep, it had become invisible beneath the years piling up upon it. But there it was, a furrow carved across a forgotten part of his soul, and it had filled up with want like a wadi in a flash flood when he had seen her stand next to the bed. He must have still thought of her as a fairy, had held an idea of her frozen in time. In truth, she was a red-blooded woman and he did not know her much at all. And she desired his body, which changed everything. Pleasure spread through him as he imagined her under him, on top of him, wanting, needing . . .

By the time the brandy had burned down his throat, he had decided to seduce her. And he would have to seduce her until she would consider it worth it regardless of the company shares, because he'd have to lose his mind before he ever let those go.

Chapter 11

⎯⎯⎯⎯⎯⎯⎯❧⎯⎯⎯⎯⎯⎯⎯

She had crossed the Oxford town center and walked the length of Parks Road at a brisk pace, but when she arrived at her house on Norham Gardens she was still shaking with emotions.

She nearly stumbled over a bag of mail Mrs. Heath had deposited in the dark corridor. On her way to the kitchen, she snatched an unsuspecting Boudicca up into her arms and the bemused cat sank five claws into her left palm. She dropped the animal with a hiss. At least the stinging pain diluted the urge to go back to Logic Lane to shoot Tristan in the knee.

There was a pot of cold stew in the kitchen, and she ate two spoonsful before her stomach became tied up in knots and she admitted defeat. There were days when one had to just retire to bed early and wait for a new morning.

Her room was overwarm, here under the roof in midsummer, and the standing collar of her dress jacket was constricting like a noose. She unhooked the skirt and let it fall to the floor, then discarded the jacket with equal carelessness, followed by her underskirt, her corset, and the chemise. A chill touched her bare torso.

The ceramic basin in her wash corner had been filled with fresh water. She grabbed the clump of soap and rigorously lathered up the flannel. She scrubbed the scratches Boudicca had inflicted and it stung, however, there was no need to end a tedious day with an infection. She rubbed the flannel over her face, her neck, her arms, as though Tristan's lewd proposition could be washed clean off.

Unfortunately, the matter went beyond skin-deep. Images kept flashing: rippling back muscles beneath fire-tinged skin. The up-and-down motion of a well-formed hand.

She dropped the flannel into the basin and started at her reflection in the mirror.

Tonight, he had treated her with utmost disrespect.

You were not exactly kind to him, either. . . .

She leaned in, blinking away the soap in her eyes. A tension around her mouth and between her brows had her looking a hundred years old.

Her pupils narrowed to small black dots as she studied herself.

Her face, presumably, was still a fine enough face.

She pulled back until the tops of her breasts were visible in the mirror.

Her body was useful, never sickly and reliably carrying her everywhere.

But as an object of a man's desire?

She had overheard comments about her person, uttered just loudly enough for her to hear. *There's more meat on a butcher dog's bone . . . bedding her would be like pulling a splinter . . . would she rattle, you think?* It was enlightening, the words coming out of purported gentlemen's mouths when they did not consider a woman a lady. Naturally, a woman's appearance was an easy target; even the most dull-witted could hit with great effect. She knew this. The words still returned to her now as she was trying to see herself through the eyes of a man.

She laid a finger against her collarbone. It felt hard and pronounced, beneath skin that was never touched, not by sunbeams, not by glances. Never by another's hand.

She traced a vein from the hollow of her throat, down across her chest. A tingling sensation followed in the wake of her fingertip, raising the fine hairs on her arms. The shallow curve of her left breast was petal soft and cool against the back of her knuckles. But she was hardly a fashionable size. *No bubbies on this one.*

She slid her arms around herself and squeezed. How would it feel, if someone were to embrace her?

Possibly equally disappointing as kissing. A young man from the Law Society had had the honors of her first kiss. She had thought him shy and guileless, but soon after the event, rumors had reached her through the society that he had won fifty pounds at White's for daring to kiss the Tedbury Termagant. Fortunately, the whole affair had not been as exciting as she had hoped; it had been oddly detached and their teeth had collided—hardly a loss.

But Tristan's lips looked soft and sensual, and he would certainly know how to kiss . . .

Angry heat sizzled through her. If it were not for his charming looks, his *offer* would not merit a second's worth of consideration, which told her exactly how bad of an affront it was. Besides, he had not propositioned her because he desired her—he had done it to provoke her. And he probably liked the idea to have her surrender to him in the most primitive way possible.

Her gaze made a slow journey around the Valentine Vinegar cards flanking the mirror, the hatchet-faced suffragists and the withering rhymes about women who dared. They had been sent to her to intimidate her in her own home. She had taken them into the sanctity of her bedchamber and made them hers, until familiarity had blunted the cutting words and mellowed the ugliness. This was how she dealt with adversaries: she met them on the field. She would deal no differently with Tristan. When she locked eyes again with her reflection, her face was determined. If his lordship wanted war, he'd better batten down the hatches.

Chapter 12

The clock had just struck ten, too early in the day for a nobleman to be in the process of getting dressed, but recent events compelled Tristan to summon fast-fading military habits and rise at the hours of the working people. The desk back in his bedchamber bore evidence of his matutinal productivity: a stack of formal letters to London and India, already sealed. Now he was observing his valet as the young man did whatever he deemed necessary to his jacket sleeves with a clothing brush.

"Avi," he said. "You are from Calcutta."

"I am," confirmed Avi.

"Now, knowing what you know of my person, and of Calcutta, and of the British as a whole—do you think a British lady and myself would find life more pleasant in Calcutta or in Delhi?"

For a beat, the brush continued its work as smoothly as though he hadn't spoken at all, and then Avi's dark lashes lifted. "The lady would certainly find life more pleasant in Calcutta. His lordship, neither. He would be best suited for Hyderabad."

"Right. Hyderabad," Tristan said, his tone bemused. "Write me a list of all the womanly things an English countess would require for her comforts in Calcutta, and another list of the families she should call on there. Then I require the same for Delhi. I need the lists by next Tuesday."

"Of course." Avi put the brush back onto the tray and picked up a cuff and the emerald cuff links.

"Not these," Tristan said. "The plain, chained ones today."

"Certainly. Milord, are you planning to take us back to India?"

Avi stoically ignored the rule of staff not speaking until spoken to, which made for entertaining, less lonely mornings.

"If I were, what would you say?" he said. "Be frank. Should you miss England terribly?"

This time, there was no pause. "No, milord."

"No?" He found himself intrigued. "Whyever not?"

Avi looked him in the eye while his slim fingers expertly secured his left cuff. "Because the climate is cold, and the food is bland," he said. "And I find that many of the ayahs of my acquaintance here are poorly paid by their English masters. I shall not miss England much at all."

This surprised an amused huff from him. "Cold, bland, and exploitative," he said. "There is an obvious line between frankness and insolence, Avi, and I'm impressed by how boldly you cross it."

"Thank you, milord. May I ask you to raise your chin, please?"

While Avi fixed his cravat with a silver pin, Tristan said to the ceiling: *Many* of the ayahs of your acquaintance, hm? Am I paying you enough to entertain multiple women?"

Avi stepped back and assessed his handiwork. "I'm an economical man."

"I see. Remind me again why you agreed to follow me to this cold, bland island?"

Avi's smile revealed perfectly straight teeth. "I wanted to study at Oxford."

"Oxford—but I was taking you to London."

A shrug. "Oxford, London, all the same, when you are from Calcutta."

He supposed it would feel like that—the distances in India made the length of Britain look puny. "It is not easy to gain admission to Oxford," he said instead.

"I hear Rabindranath Tagore studied in London, and Brighton," Avi said. "Great poet."

"Well, damn. To think you crossed an ocean in the hope to enroll, while I just squandered my time here."

Avi shook his head. "There were other reasons, too. Trouble with a girl's family in Calcutta. More importantly"—he picked up the other cuff—"it is a pleasure to dress you."

Tristan arched a brow. "It is, is it."

"Yes. You are perfectly proportioned."

"I see."

"Your build does justice to fine clothes. A dreadful thing, a beautiful, exquisite waistcoat which is wasted on its wearer. No garment is wasted on you."

"Well," Tristan drawled. "Fortunately, then, these charming proportions are attached to my person regardless of where we set up house."

"Yes, milord. When will we leave?"

As soon as I have seduced the Lady Shrew.

What an absurd thing to first spring to mind.

He brushed it off with a shrug; after all, on the list of things presently requiring his attention, from protecting his accounts and business from Rochester to surviving travel with a melancholic woman, bedding Lucie was the only task that appealed.

"We leave no later than six weeks from today, possibly sooner," he told Avi. It would see them leave England well before exhausting Rochester's three-month ultimatum. Admittedly, it was ambitious timing for seducing a woman like Lucie. She would resist out of spite alone, and unless she was in the London offices often, there were few occasions to woo her.

"One way or another, she will surrender," he murmured.

"Milord?"

"Never mind, Avi."

Friday noon bathed Oxford in sunshine and birdsong. Stained-glass windows sparkled, swallows flitted. The breeze carried the scent of the wisteria cascading down the façade of Somerville Hall. Lucie was marching down Woodstock Road, tight-lipped, her skirts snapping around her ankles.

The night had been short, fraught with pondering how to proceed with London Print and unwelcome erotic dreams of Ballentine's tattooed chest. By the time dawn had winked through her curtains, two things were clear: one, Ballentine had the power to make her life hellish. As much as society pretended to be shocked—shocked!—by him, he was a war hero, a peer of the realm, and next in line for a wealthy earldom. In Darwin's words, he presided over the food chain, which had led to the second realization: she now needed every social and political ally she could muster. Her position in society had long been tenuous at best, but over the years, she had achieved a status which had allowed her to advance the Cause despite her outspokenness. Now the moment she had secretly dreaded had come—she had to try to . . . be nice. She had to pick up the weapons of a good woman: Demureness. Gracefulness. A benevolent management of contrarian males. Very well, it was too late to be credibly demure and graceful, but a more benevolent approach to males was still within reach. She had sent a missive to Annabelle, requesting an urgent meeting at the Randolph this afternoon. Now she was about to fulfill the second point on her battle plan: order a whole new set of dresses.

The shop window of Mrs. Winston, the most recommended dressmaker on Oxford's High Street, displayed three mannequins which she supposed were fashionably dressed. The interior beyond was small but neatly organized, with tightly spaced rolls of fabric affixed to the walls and a gleaming cherrywood counter at the center of the room.

She entered, and a deafening clanking sound nearly made her jump out of her walking boots.

"Good gracious!"

She glared up, her hands covering her ears. A large . . . cowbell was swaying menacingly right above her face. It was most definitely a cowbell because it looked exactly like the ones she had seen on cows in Switzerland when visiting there as a girl.

"Good morning, missus. How may I help you today?" From the corridor leading to the depths of the shop's back room emerged a tall, thin woman with a measuring tape coiled around her neck. A pair of glasses was hanging on to the tip of her nose. Already her brown eyes were moving over Lucie from head to toe, taking mental notes— height, notably short; waist, notably small; bosom, largely absent.

Lucie placed her card on the countertop. "I require seven dresses after the latest fashion."

Mrs. Winston frowned at her, confounded by an accent announcing a lady while the card introduced a plain *Miss Morray*. Well, she could never be certain where she ran the risk of being recognized, and whether she would be served. Today, she had no time to waste.

Mrs. Winston picked up a pen and a wooden board with a sheet of paper attached to it.

"One morning dress," Lucie said. "A carriage dress, three walking dresses, and two evening gowns, complete with matching gloves. These are my measurements." She slid a note toward the scribbling Mrs. Winston.

Mrs. Winston side-eyed the note. "I prefer to have my assistants take the measurements."

"I'm rather pressed for time. The figures are accurate."

The seamstress put down her pen, her expression grave. "With all due respect, it is my experience that measurements tend to fluctuate greatly between a customer's measuring tape and the tapes we employ here."

Fluctuated greatly between reality and desirous thinking, rather.

"I suffer no illusions in regard to my size," Lucie said. Her skin itched at the thought of being stripped and measured and turned to and fro. The sooner she could go to the Randolph to plan her next moves, the better.

"Very well." Mrs. Winston's eyes flitted between the figures on the paper and Lucie's torso. "These measurements do not seem to account for a proper corset."

"They do, but it laces down the front and I prefer it to be quite loose."

Mrs. Winston's brows nearly reached her hairline. "I suspected this was the case."

"I expect it shall pose no problem for a seamstress as acclaimed as you?"

"None at all," Mrs. Winston said coolly. "We are proud to deliver outstanding elegance no matter the challenge. Have you any preferences regarding the fabrics and colors?"

She eyed the fabric bales on the walls. Pale hues of pink and blue and sunshine. Gatherings of ladies everywhere resembled baskets full of Easter eggs this season.

"Cotton in lemon yellow for the morning dress," she said. "Tafetta silk for the walking dresses in light blue, powder blue, and mauve. Cerise silk for the evening gowns. Finest new wool in dove gray for the carriage dress."

Mrs. Winston nodded along with revived enthusiasm; as usual, Hattie's color choices pleased the experts in the field.

"No trains on the carriage dress or the walking dresses," Lucie said.

Mrs. Winston stilled. "No trains?"

"Not one inch."

"Very well," Mrs. Winston said after a poignant pause. "I do recommend adding some strategic applications to create an illusion of buxomness."

"You mean ruffles? No ruffles, please."

"Very well. May I suggest velvet details for the walking dresses? I had some exquisite navy-blue velvet delivered yesterday; it would make an excellent contrast with both light blue and powder blue."

"Approved," Lucie said. "I also need three pockets in each skirt."

Mrs. Winston nearly dropped the pen. "Three pockets?"

"Yes."

"There is one pocket at the most in the skirts we order in or fashion ourselves, and in the walking dresses only."

"Well, I need three in each skirt, in convenient reach and quite large."

Mrs. Winston had a hostile look about her. "It is common to have one pocket, a small one, in the skirts of a walking dress. But three is quite unheard of."

"I have a lot of items on me," Lucie explained. "I'm quite discerning, you see."

"With all due respect, you required dresses after the latest fashion. The latest fashion can be described in one word, *snug*, but in any case, bulging pockets destroy the lines of any kind of skirt and thus the look of a lady." Mrs. Winston's voice had steadily risen and she was quite agitated on the last word.

Lucie reached into her reticule and placed coins onto the counter. "This lady pays extra for them."

Mrs. Winston picked up her pen again with pointy fingers. "It can be paid for, certainly," she muttered. "It does not, however, make it any less of a crime against a perfectly innocent skirt. Say, are you part of this new Rational Dress Society?"

"I am not," Lucie said, but *drat* it reminded her of the pile of correspondence back at home. Somewhere in the stack lurked her unfinished reply to Viscountess Harberton, newly minted founder of the Rational Dress Society. Should said society dare to postulate a recommendation on women's unmentionables (*no woman shall wear under-garments exceeding seven pounds in combined weight*), Lady Harberton had asked. And: would Lucie support a campaign in favor of women riding bicycles? The answer to both questions was yes, and she'd prepare a bicycle petition, but so far, she had not found the time. No thanks to the added work on London Print. Damn Tristan Ballentine, obstructor of women's progress on every front.

The cowbell exploded behind her as the shop door opened again.

"Good gracious," came a woman's aristocratic voice, "have we entered Switzerland?"

Lucie froze.

No.

No, this was not possible.

Mrs. Winston was looking past her at the new customer, her lips moving with a greeting.

She couldn't hear over the heavy silence filling her head. It had been ten years since she'd last heard that voice.

She glanced back over her shoulder with some hesitation.

An angel had entered the shop. Glossy curls in hazel shades. Large crystalline blue eyes. A mouth poets would have likened to a rosebud. She had never beheld this paragon of womanhood before. But next to the young lady, with her thin brows raised in consternation, stood—her mother.

So she hadn't imagined it. It was Lady Wycliffe, clad in high-necked pale silk and lace.

She had used to wonder how it would be to see her mother again. Her stomach had plunged at the thought. And now she felt—nothing. Just her heart beating away with eerie calm.

The countess looked thinner; she was stretched tight over her fine bones. Or perhaps it was the shock—first the cowbell, now her daughter.

A footman had accompanied the women; he stood back against the wall, bedecked in bags of varying sizes.

"Lucinda." Her mother was still staring at her. *A lady does not stare.*

"Mother."

Her eyes on Lucie, the countess gripped the angel's upper arm. "You remember your cousin Cecily?"

For a moment, she remembered nothing.

The young woman, Lady Cecily, tilted her head. "Cousin Lucie."

At the sound of the sweet voice, she knew. Memories returned, of a six-year-old girl who easily cried. Cecily's parents—her father one of Wycliffe's first cousins—had perished in a train accident, so she had come to live at Wycliffe Hall. At now one-and-twenty, she was a beauty, no doubt a toast of polite society.

"May I offer the ladies some refreshment?" Mrs. Winston's voice was unnaturally bright.

"Cecily excels at watercoloring," her mother said. "She was immediately accepted by Professor Ruskin for a place in Oxford's Summer School program."

"How delightful," Lucie said.

The air in the shop was suddenly thick as London fog. Had her mother just announced that she and Cecily were in Oxford for the summer?

"Are you often in this part of town?" her mother asked.

"It is a small town, Mother."

They were bound to cross paths. It was hard to tell who of them resented this more. The countess had finally released Cousin Cecily's arm, but a displeased flush reddened her cheeks.

"Cecily, we are taking another turn outside. This is a small shop, it cloys easily."

"Yes, Aunt," Cecily said softly.

"I was about to take my leave," Lucie said quickly. There was no need to cost Mrs. Winston an order, as reticent as the woman was on the matter of pockets.

Her mother gave a contemptuous sniff.

Lucie turned back to the seamstress. "Have you any crimson silk?"

Mrs. Winston looked at her sharply over the rim of her glasses. "I do. In the back room. Do you wish to take a look?" She said it reluctantly, no doubt worried the ladies would leave after all.

"Crimson is crimson, I suppose. I need a ball gown fashioned from it by next week. Feel free to embellish it, but no ruffles."

Mrs. Winston blinked. "By next week?"

"I shall pay double."

"Well, it's certainly possible," Mrs. Winston said, her pen flying over her paper.

"Excellent," Lucie said, and a little louder: "And do make the waist a few inches smaller, because for this one, I shall tighten the laces."

She could not remember the route she had taken to the Randolph and was vaguely surprised to find herself standing in the doorway to Annabelle's study.

Annabelle was seated behind her desk, surrounded by open books, translating something, for her lips were moving silently. The heavy mass of her hair had been pinned haphazardly on top of her head.

She glanced up. "Lucie." She cast a confused look at the clock on the mantelpiece while rising. "Forgive me, I had not yet expected you—I'm covered in ink."

"I just ordered a crimson ball gown."

Annabelle chuckled as she wiped her fingers. "Oh dear. Hattie has finally worn you down, has she not? Do not feel bad, we all succumb in the end."

"No. It was my mother."

Annabelle's brows lowered. "Your mother?"

"The very same. She did not look much changed."

Annabelle was by her side. "What happened?"

She must have looked rattled, as Annabelle spoke to her in a soft, concerned tone.

"I must apologize—I'm calling on you too early."

"Nonsense. Come."

She followed Annabelle into the drawing room, onto the green divan.

"She just walked into the tailor shop on High Street," she said. "With my cousin Cecily. I understand they are staying in Oxford for the summer so Cecily can improve her excellent watercoloring techniques at Ruskin's school."

Watercoloring—one of few pursuits a lady was encouraged to study in depth. Many young women had enjoyed a trip to Europe, even, to perfect painting techniques. Her mother had used to exclaim in despair over Lucie's lack of finesse with a paintbrush; no tour across Europe would have improved her.

Annabelle had paused the process of ringing for some tea. "Oh Lord," she said. "They will be in town for the whole summer?"

"It appears so. I reckon they will stay here, in the Randolph—it is the best hotel in town, after all." Today's awkward encounter might well repeat itself. And here she had thought the matter of Tristan owning half her business was troubling enough.

"I was petty," she said. "I ordered a red dress and ensured that they heard about how I wear my unmentionables."

"It was a shock," Annabelle said, quick to excuse her pettiness, as a good friend would.

A shock? She refused to admit to anything of such magnitude.

"It could have been worse—she could have given me the cut direct." Her brows pulled together. "She and Cecily seemed close."

"Were you close to your cousin?"

Lucie shook her head. "She was still a child when I left home. We never had much in common." By the time she was eleven and Lucie was leaving, Ceci had had one face and voice for men, and another for the women, and it wasn't quite clear which was the real one, something Lucie had found disconcerting. "Cecily is lovely, I suppose," she said. "And she liked Lord Ballentine. She followed him around every summer as if he had her on a string, like one of those wooden ducks on wheels." And Tristan had indulged her, with comments on her dolls and her ribbons. Sometimes he had made coins dance between his fingers, or toffees had appeared from midair. Even Lucie had been impressed by these tricks.

"If you are ordering ball gowns, may we assume you are coming to our house party?" Annabelle said with a smile.

"You may," she said, her own smile a little forced. "All four of us will be together. Hooray."

We assume . . . our house party. It grated a little, how husband and wife ceased to exist as *I* and became *us.* Annabelle had been changing accordingly since her wedding; her country accent was making way for the steeper vowels of the upper classes, and her hand-altered dresses had been replaced by the constraining gowns befitting a duchess. It was reassuring to still see ink stains marking her fingers, even though her study was now located in a plush hotel rather than her little student room at Lady Margaret Hall. Still, as she sat here in Annabelle's rooms and enjoyed the comforts of their close friendship, she was painfully reminded that some day soon, Annabelle would be lost to their circle of friends and the Cause, because at the end of the day, she was a married woman. And while Montgomery granted her time away from Claremont, he was an excessively dutiful man, and he would soon require his duchess to have his heir. . . .

"Oh." Annabelle made a face. "I'm scatterbrained these days. The going back and forth between Claremont and Oxford, and learning duchess duties . . . Lucie, I think your mother and your brother are on the guest list. As I believe is one of your father's cousins, the Marquess of Doncaster."

Her stomach gave an unpleasant twist. "Don't you worry," she said lightly. "I shall be on my best behavior—and avoiding relations during such gatherings is impossible; we are all, more or less, related."

"I never doubted your behavior."

"I just ordered a *crimson* ball gown. Clearly my comportment cannot be accounted for in their presence."

"Families are complicated," Annabelle murmured. She knew this from personal experience, judging from the few glimpses Lucie had caught of her friend's past.

She leaned back into the soft upholstery of the divan, the tensions slowly draining from her limbs. "I never told you why my father banished me, have I?"

"No," Annabelle said carefully. "I always suspected it was because of the incident with the fork and the Spanish ambassador."

"Ah. But no. It was because of the Contagious Diseases Act."

Annabelle's green eyes widened. "The same act we are still trying to have repealed?"

Lucie nodded. "I was seventeen years old and restless to *do* something other than just read about the adventures of Florence Nightingale and annotate Wollstonecraft essays. Whenever my family was in London during the season, I had access to newspapers other than the *Times*—and by chance, I came across Josephine Butler's manifesto against the act in the *Manchester Guardian*."

Annabelle bit her lip. "I imagine it was eye-opening?"

"Spectacularly so. Mrs. Butler had just founded the Ladies National Association to repeal the act and she was touring the country to gain support. Around this time, a factory girl had nearly drowned at the London docks, because she had jumped into the Thames to evade the police. It made headlines; the patrolling officers had thought she looked like a prostitute and wanted to apprehend her. At the time, word had already spread among working women that they would be subject to a forcible examination if caught—sometimes in view of male workers. Oh, I feel angry just thinking of it. Anyways, the girl flew into a panic and jumped to spare herself the humiliation, and Annabelle, I was enraged. Forcing examinations for venereal diseases on *any* woman struck me as abominable."

Annabelle visibly shuddered. "And all to protect men who use prostitutes from catching the pox."

"Indeed. So naturally, I stole away to attend one of Mrs. Butler's rallies in Islington."

And there, she had found something remarkable: a woman who had spoken in a loud, clear voice about ugly things. A woman who used words as weapons on behalf of girls who saw no choice but to jump. While the ladies in her mother's salon drifted over the agony of choosing the correct wallpaper in hushed tones, Mrs. Butler talked about forcibly apprehended women, and injustice, and double standards, and she had hung on every word. A diffuse anger coursing round and round beneath her skin for years had finally found a direction.

"I felt a great sense of relief," she told Annabelle. "Half my life I had felt strangely asphyxiated in the presence of my mother and her friends. But there, I was at ease. As though I were finally wearing clothes that fit rather than chafed."

Because these women had mobilized. *Fight*, she had wanted to tell her mother after the fateful morning in the library. *Fight!* when Wycliffe's indiscretions and belittling comments, relentlessly sprinkled over their daily lives, continued. But her mother never fought. She had pressed her lips together, and become thinner, and paler, and haughtier, until she had haunted Wycliffe Hall like a wronged wraith, and the more martyred and quieter she had become, the louder Lucie had wanted to yell. Years later, as her work with the Cause progressed, she had understood that she should have directed all her youthful anger against her father. She had not yet truly comprehended power then, and how treacherously easy it was to side with it, and to ask that the downtrodden ones change before one demanded the tyrant change.

Annabelle was looking at her with a small smile. "And this was how Lady Lucinda Tedbury as *we* know her was born."

Lucie gave a nod. "Mrs. Butler introduced me to Lydia Becker that night who had just founded the first suffrage chapter in Manchester. I should lose my birth family not long after."

Annabelle's brow furrowed. "But I understand quite a lot of ladies joined the movement against the diseases acts—and I imagine not all of them were banished?"

"They were not," she confirmed. "However, I worked with Mrs. Butler and Mrs. Becker in secret. My father found out during a rather unfortunate encounter two years later. I had gone to Westminster with a group of suffragists to confront Secretary Henry Bruce—he had not delivered on any of his promises, much like Gladstone today, hence, a reminder was necessary. Unfortunately, Bruce was with my father and another peer. And I chose not to abort the confrontation."

"Oh, Lucie. It must have been dreadful."

She shrugged. "It was that, or try and hide at the last moment, which would have been prudent, I suppose, but it felt as though it would betray the women whom I had worked with for two years. It felt as though I would betray myself. So I made a choice."

"So you did," Annabelle said softly.

"He did wait until we were home to let me have it." And her mother hadn't intervened. She had hovered at the back of the study, looking pallid and appalled, and had not said good-bye when the earl had sent Lucie from the house with just a trunk full of her possessions. Aunt Honoria had saved her from beyond her grave, having set up a small trust for her in wise foresight, and Wycliffe had not objected to Lucie claiming it before reaching the age of majority. He had considered this a grand concession, she supposed. Granted, he had never publicly denounced her—all the public knew was that she had relocated to Oxford to indulge her bluestocking tendencies.

It was the reason she was not shunned by society, and found allies for her work, but she had no doubt that Wycliffe had done so only to spare the family name a scandal.

She shook her head. "Old stories are not why I called on you today."

"What is it?" Annabelle asked. "Your missive was rather, erm, brief."

"I meant to ask you to tutor me in feminine wiles."

A baffled silence followed her announcement. "I don't quite understand," Annabelle then said.

Lucie sighed. "If I am to steer us through the current situation with Ballentine and London Print, I need every ally. Ballentine will try and paint me as a harridan who should best be ignored. . . ."

Annabelle leaned forward. "Have you really called on him last night?"

She must not blush now, she must not. "I have," she said, smoothly, too.

"Do tell?"

He is built like a Greek god and his mind is pure filth, and I dreamt of him all night.

She cleared her throat. "I need hardly tell you that it led nowhere. Under the circumstances, we need to concentrate on garnering sympathies for our report elsewhere—which means I must try and inspire some sympathy in men, at least until Parliament reconvenes in September."

"This sounds wise, and I would gladly assist you," Annabelle said wryly. "However, I am the Scandalous Duchess, remember? Before that, I was a scandalous bluestocking. I'm hardly in a position to give advice."

"And yet *you* brought the most calculating duke in the kingdom to heel—clearly your strategy works."

"Hmm. But the truth is, I had no strategy. I didn't make Montgomery do anything he did not wish to do."

Lucie's brow flicked up. "I doubt he longed to become embroiled in scandal."

Annabelle looked amused. "Let me say this: I was the most stubborn, reticent creature the duke had ever encountered—I just said no to everything he offered." She gave an apologetic shrug. "I suppose when a man truly wants something, he will do what is required. It is quite simple."

It might be simple, but it also sounded dishearteningly uncontrollable.

Her stomach snarled into the silence, and Annabelle gave her a pointed look. "How do you feel about taking luncheon together?"

"I suppose some lunch would be lovely," Lucie admitted.

Annabelle was on her feet and headed to the assortment of bell strings dangling from the wall. "An Indian restaurant has recently opened on High Street," she said as she rang for a footman. "I'm of a mind to try it."

"It sounds intriguing."

"We could then return here and read books together for as long as we want."

"Splendid idea," Lucie said. "Though I would prefer to work on my correspondence here instead. And I have to go to the reading room at the Bodleian later, they have the legal works."

Annabelle smiled. "Whatever puts you best at ease."

She had an inkling she would not really feel at ease for some time to come.

Chapter 13

Later in the day

Oxford had scored a victory over Cambridge during the annual cricket match this evening, hence the Turf Tavern was hot and crammed with obnoxiously exuberant patrons. Tristan used his size to plow a path through the crowd toward the bar, already of a mind to leave. The Turf was damp and reeked of centuries of spilled beer and piss on a regular night. Then again, this was every tavern in Oxford.

His Lagavulin arrived in a sticky tumbler. Braying laughter shook the rafters. There must have been a time when he had enjoyed himself immersed in the noise and excitement of revelers, but tonight, it was simply loud and felt hollow. As though they were all a little lost and tried to cast an anchor in the fray by way of their own booming voice.

Somewhere in the shadows at the back of the room, Lord Arthur Seymour, second son to the Marquess of Doncaster, was lurking and watching him in a sulk, all while pretending to have a jolly good time with his friends. He had noticed the boy's mop of curly blond hair on his way in. Ah well. Unrequited lust compelled people to do all sorts of ridiculous things.

He would know.

His whiskey glass came down hard on the counter.

Lucie was lying low, the little coward. She had not been in the London offices today, nor had she sought him out this evening, if only to berate him some more. *Lust* must have compelled his mind to circle around her today . . .

"By God, you are beautiful."

A young man his age had been crowded against his left shoulder. Tall, but not as tall as him. Well-drawn lips. Overlong dark hair curled around his collar. His blue gaze was intent on Tristan's face, tracing his features with the singular concentration of an artist.

Tristan leaned in close to keep his voice low. "And a good evening to you, sir."

"Such a face should be eternalized in oil and marble, so that future generations may behold it and weep over the glory of the bygone days," said the man.

Tristan gave his near-empty glass a little spin. "There's weeping already, I hear, though it is caused by my lack of character rather than my face."

The chap threw back his head and laughed. "Don't be modest. Your beauty causes the tears—the carelessness of a plain fellow is rather forgettable." He offered his hand. "My name is Oscar Wilde."

"I know who you are, Mr. Wilde. You won the Newdigate Prize for your 'Ravenna' poem two years ago."

The playwright inclined his head. "Why, I'm flattered. You enjoy poetry?"

"On occasion."

"You write yourself? Lord Ballentine, is it?"

"Yes, and yes."

Oscar Wilde was delighted. "A fellow scribe! I shall pay for your next drink. Brandy." He shouted for the barkeeper and fished for coin on the inside of his coat—a remarkably sharply tailored, midnight blue coat, with velvet lapels and silver buttons depicting peacocks. Tristan would quite like to have it for himself.

He slid his hand over the velvet, over Oscar's hand beneath the fabric, halting the futile scrabble for money with a light press of his fingers.

Wilde's gaze jerked toward him, surprise flashing in his blue eyes. Tristan watched it heat to intrigue at a startling speed. He had already dropped his hand again. *Playwrights.* The one species with even less regard for convention than he.

"Allow me." He procured a shilling from his own pocket and flipped it at the bartender. "Brandy for my friend, more of the same for me."

Wilde was still contemplating him with a half-lidded gaze. "Just what are you doing in this student-infested pub when you could have the best of London at your feet?" he murmured. "Or better yet, Italy."

The corner of his mouth twitched.

And he realized what he was doing—*seducing people for the sake of it*, as Lucie had called it. *Shouted* it. Damn, but he was doing exactly that.

The smile faded from his lips.

"London gets old. Variety's the very spice of life that gives it all its flavor," he cited, because using someone else's words could convey a lot without saying much at all.

A second or two ticked past until Wilde gave a wry little nod. "You like Cowper, then?" he asked in a neutral tone, and slid the freshly filled tumbler across the counter toward Tristan.

His nape prickled with awareness as he closed his fingers around the glass.

He looked up and met Lord Arthur's wounded stare from the other side of the bar. Arthur's expression was as glum as though someone had just shot his puppy. Well. He would not invite impressionable young things along to an orgy again if this was the result. What a nuisance.

"Oh dear," Wilde said, his gaze discreetly lingering on the lordling before he peered back up at Tristan. "What an unhappy fellow. A matter of romance?" He chuckled. "But of course not. It's a matter of sex, isn't it."

Tristan clinked his glass to his. "It's always about sex."

"Everything in the world is about sex," Wilde agreed. "Except sex."

"Then what is the sex about?"

The playwright smiled. "Power. But you know that already, don't you, my lord."

When he left the Turf three, maybe five, drinks later, he was not exactly staggering, but his head felt heavy. At least Oscar Wilde was in worse shape; by the end of his last brandy, he had made slurred promises to write Tristan into his first novel, one about the perils of eternal beauty; and the story would be gothic and dark.

How about the twisted tale of an earl intent on sending his own wife to an asylum, Mr. Playwright, gothic and dark enough?

The weather had turned; a fine spray of summer rain dampened the air and smudged rainbows around the gaslights lining Holywell Street. There was a halo fanning out from the pale blond crown of a woman hasting past.

A petite, very much unchaperoned woman.

He halted and squinted.

A rush of cold spread through his chest. Lucie. He would recognize her determined stride anywhere. And only she would be flitting about the town alone at night. She was weaving her way around a flock of students, already shrinking into the distance.

His body was in motion before his head had decided to follow her.

She was out alone when the night was crawling with drunken men, each one of them feeling masterful after a sports event. Foolish, reckless woman. When he got his hands on her—someone grabbed his arm, breaking his stride.

"Ballentine. A word."

He reacted on instinct, twisted sideways, gripped the attacker, and yanked him close.

Grand. Lord Arthur Seymour was staring back at him, wide-eyed, his hands clutching at the hand that had locked around his throat.

"Never approach me from a dead angle, you fool." He released his lordship with a shove. His pulse was thrumming fast, the blur of liquor gone. The night had edges again, wet black streets, glaring gaslights.

Lucie, he noted, had just reached the road junction at the end of the row of sandstone buildings. There was a silvery flash of hair as she turned off the main street into Mansfield Road. . . . Incredibly, Lord Arthur lurched back into his path. "Hear me out," he slurred, unleashing a wave of offending whiskey fumes. Where were his friends to save him from himself?

"You're drunk," Tristan said. "Go home."

At her brisk pace, Lucie would soon reach the eastern edge of the park. Was she contemplating crossing the park?

Arthur latched onto his arm. "Let us meet, just once."

Tristan's muscles tensed. Holywell Road was always lively even when it was not a sports night, as the narrow street connected two large pubs and was home to a number of small concert houses. Revelers were passing them on the pavement, and there was a steady supply of patrons tumbling from the closing taverns on the other side of the road.

"I saw you with Mr. Wilde." Arthur was loud and belligerent. "You drink with him, but not with me—"

He hooked his arm through Arthur's, pulled him hard into the side of his body and half dragged him along. Now they were just two fellows in their cups, propping each other up.

"Have a care," he said, his voice low. "Do not approach others in this way, it might get you into proper trouble."

Arthur's free hand clutched Tristan's coat lapel. "I am already in trouble. My every thought revolves around you."

Christ.

"We have spent no more than three times in each other's company; we drank, we gambled, as gentlemen do, and once, you were in the same room as I while I fucked. That is where our acquaintance ends."

Arthur twisted in his grip, hot with rage. "Don't deceive me. You knew what I was and yet you took me along . . . and your eyes were on me that night, while you were—"

He yelped when Tristan's arm tightened like a vise.

"Seymour. I may not consistently limit my preferences. It does not mean I have any particular interest in you." And while he might have been looking at Arthur, it would have had nothing to do with the young lord, and everything with the dark mood to watch or be watched, which sometimes struck at random. Ironically, the abundant stimulations of great debauchery could send his mind sprawling as hopelessly as reading a dull treatise in old Latin. There was, of course, no point in explaining any of that to an infatuated whelp.

He pulled Arthur with him when he rounded the corner onto the road to University Park.

People were drifting past them, exuberant and chattering. Lucie's small form was nowhere in sight.

"This is where we must part," he said, and abruptly let the young lord go.

The wet cobblestones, or his stubborn efforts to hold on, made Arthur lose his balance, and down he went.

This was bad, Arthur on his knees before him, in the middle of Mansfield Road.

He stepped round him, and an arm lashed around his calf.

"Gad—why are you so keen to see us arrested?"

"You are a monster," Arthur cried, still attached, "you have no care."

A group of students moving past hollered and jeered.

"Your pardon," Tristan said and gripped the white, clinging hands to bend back Arthur's thumbs. A squawk of outrage, and he was free, his long strides eating up the dark street.

The gate to University Park was locked after nine o'clock, but there was a well-trodden path to a gap in the fence a few yards to the left, large enough to admit children or slight adults.

Lucie breathed easier the moment she had slipped through the iron bars. She had long resolved to walk alone wherever she went; it was most practical, and furthermore, the idea of a spinster guarding another spinster struck her as ridiculous. However, a woman who walked through Oxford alone should know the university's schedule for sporting events. She had forgotten it was the day of the annual University Match, an understandable but still negligent lapse in attention after the bizarre encounter in the dress shop. Bands of student athletes and drinking societies roamed tonight, eager for brawls with townsfolk and each other. Shouting and fragments of lewd songs echoed from the street across the dark meadows of the park. The footpath to home, however, stretched before her blissfully empty and well-lit by a row of tall gaslights.

She walked rapidly. The misty rain had turned into a drizzle; cold rivulets ran from her cheeks down into her collar, and her skin rippled with goose bumps. She'd drink a hot cup of tea at home and go to bed; for once, her work would have to wait. Her *mother* was in Oxford. She'd add some brandy to her tea tonight.

She heard them first, raucous singing that made her ears prick with caution.

She slowed.

A group of men appeared on the footpath ahead.

Her shoulders tensed. It was five of them, some in pairs, arm-in-arm, weaving toward her. They must have set up camp in the park, drinking until night had fallen. Or perhaps, they had avoided the gates via the Cherwell, and their abandoned punt was now drifting downstream.

Wet steel glinted as they passed beneath a streetlamp. Foils. Her stomach gave a nervous lurch. Members of the fencing club? They frequently practiced in the park. They were also known to cause trouble around town.

Their bawdy singing ceased, and she knew they had spotted her. *Bother.* They had not stopped out of politeness. A woman alone in a park near midnight was not a lady, and the awareness crackled in the dark air between them. Their faces came into focus: leering mouths, eyes keen. Three sheets to the wind, each of them, and wealthy, judging by their top hats. The entitled ones were the worst.

Her heart was beating unpleasantly fast. In a moment, she'd have to walk right through them. There was no evading to the right—risky and humiliating, to leave the lit footpath and stagger over the lumpy grass of the meadow. The copse of trees to her left was a menacing black mass.

She squared her shoulders. They were young, just students.

As if on a silent command, the men fell in line next to each other, shoulder to shoulder, a wall of smirks and lewd anticipation.

Fear ran down her neck, cold like ice water. They were not going to let her pass.

Her right hand slid into her skirt pocket.

Too late, she noticed the man who had come up from behind.

Her body recognized him before she did, from the familiar warm scent of tobacco and spice, and it quelled the rush of alarm.

"There you are," Tristan said lightly. "For someone so short, you are bloody fast."

His hand slid around her waist and pulled her flush against his side. She let him sweep her along, dumbfounded, wrapped in the strength of his arm.

The rigid front the men had formed across the path dithered.

Tristan moved toward them as if they were not there at all. And then he slowed. Intent coursed through his body in a dark current, and for a breath, panic flared. Was he not aware there were only two of them and five of the others? No, he became slower still, his heels grinding to a halt on gravel.

"Bloody hell," someone said. "It's Ballentine."

Tristan stopped in front of the tallest one of the group, an inch too close as was polite. The stench of liquor breath and male sweat assaulted her senses. Her right hand was in her pocket, clutching cold metal, but she turned her face into Tristan's coat and held her breath.

"Gentlemen," he said. His voice was amicable. His voice lied. She was held snug against him, and through the layers of wool and cotton, she sensed something sinister crawling beneath his skin, something primal and keen. The feel of it raised all the fine hairs on her body.

The athletes had sensed it, too. They stood straighter, a little more sober.

"A fine evening for a stroll, isn't it," Tristan said, still friendly.

"Indeed," drawled the young man with whom he was toe-to-toe. "Very fine."

"Lovely and mild," said Tristan.

"We should continue with it," the ringleader remarked, "the strolling."

"An excellent idea."

Top hats dipped as nods were exchanged.

Still Tristan did not move. They had to walk around him, and therefore Lucie.

"Let me challenge him, and you grab the female," someone slurred, a few paces on.

"He will make mincemeat out of you, idiot," said another.

"I have a sword, he has a shtick."

"There is a blade in the stick, fool."

Their voices faded as the distance between them grew.

Her back was still tense, as hard as rock, half expecting an angrily hurled foil to hit between her shoulder blades. After a few paces, she glanced back.

The athletes swaggered onward in a disorderly heap, slapping each other's backs. Someone laughed.

A shudder ran through her. They would have tried to make casual sport of her and moved on, looking like exuberant but respectable gentlemen. No one on the other side of the park gates who saw them walking down the street would have been any wiser.

Tristan's arm around her tightened, and her cheek was pressed against the smooth fabric of his coat. The smell of damp wool mixed with his scent. Her shoulder easily fit under his, like a chick under a wing, protected from the elements and predatory eyes.

She felt anything but safe. The way he moved, on the cusp of a crouch, called to mind a predator's prowl, and his silence was entirely too preoccupied. Just like there was apparently a blade hidden in his silly cane, there was a mean, well-honed cutting edge to him, concealed by his glibness and his crimson waistcoat.

She peered up at his face.

He was focused on the path ahead, a faint smile on his lips. A shudder ran down her arms. A Nero would smile this way, while turning down his thumb. He was a thousand shades of angry.

She strained against his hold, and he released her easily. The night was immediately colder without the shelter of his arm. She'd have welcomed any one of his annoying remarks now, but he remained silent as they walked side by side. He wordlessly stood back as she wriggled through another gap in the park fence and watched as he, somehow, vaulted the fence without becoming stuck on the wrought-iron spikes. He followed her like a formidable shadow down Norham Gardens, and she knew better than to try and send him away.

She would have to thank him.

Her lips were still trying to form the words when they arrived at the gate to her front garden. Still trying when she climbed the two steps to her door.

She slid the key into the lock and glanced back over her shoulder.

Tristan had remained standing at the bottom of the stairs. It put her slightly above him, an unfamiliar vantage point.

The rim of his hat cast most of his face in shadows, revealing only his mouth and the clean curve of his jaw. The usually alluring, soft lines of his lips were tense.

She turned to him fully and took a deep breath. It was just three simple words, was it not? *Thank you, Ballentine.*

Instead, she said, "Go on then, say it."

His lips gave a humorless twitch. "Say what?"

"Are you not eager to lecture me on the perils of walking around alone at night?"

His head tilted speculatively to the side. "Would lecturing you keep you from doing it again?"

She blinked. "No," she conceded.

He gave a shrug. "Then I would be wasting my time. There are more pleasant things upon which to waste time."

He was still seething; she could tell from the silky coolness of his voice and the stiffness of his usually languid posture.

"It might make you feel less displeased," she suggested.

He gave her a dark smile. "Oh, it would not be nearly enough for that."

"I don't make my excursions unarmed."

He processed this with an unreadable expression. "A pocket pistol?"

She nodded.

His chin tipped up in appreciation, and then he held out his hand. "May I see it?"

She reached into her skirt pocket and pulled out the double derringer. It was dainty and ornate, made for a woman's hand, but it was cold and impersonal to the touch.

Tristan turned it over in his palm with deliberate care, checking the lock and running his thumb over the shimmering pearl handle.

"Lovely," he said, and handed it back. "But are you prepared to use it?"

The line of leering faces in the park flashed before her eyes. A primal aggression had swirled around the men, and the mere memory tightened her throat.

"I am," she said.

Tristan was quiet.

"You disapprove," she said, and wondered why this would give her second thoughts.

He shrugged. "It is a funny thing, shooting at a fellow man," he said. "You go about it as the situation requires, but few people, if any, will tell you that a while later, you may turn morose at the oddest of times, and your nights may become haunted by peculiar dreams."

"Haunted," she echoed.

"Just try and avoid putting bullets through people unless you must."

Rain dripped off the rim of his hat. He could not stand here indefinitely—he'd catch an ague; besides, he must not be seen at her door, as it would cause talk.

Why *was* he still standing there?

Because she had not thanked him yet, and of course he would want to hear her say the words. This was the man holding her suffrage coup hostage and blackmailing her in a most appalling fashion, after all.

"It's a good thing then that you have no need for a pistol," she said. "You can walk around on your own quite undisturbed. Your mere presence was enough to let us go on our way even though they vastly outnumbered you. Remarkable, isn't it?"

"Vastly outnumbered?" He sounded surprised. "Hardly. And approaching a woman who is already claimed by another man goes against instinct; I expected no trouble."

She leaned against the door frame. "I had no desire to be claimed," she said quietly. "I was merely walking home on a public footpath."

She felt him study her sodden form. She was too fatigued to pull herself together; her strength was rapidly draining from her legs into the damp bricks beneath her feet.

"You know," he said casually. "I could still go and shoot them. On your behalf."

A chill spread over her skin, which was not caused by the cold nor the rain. It was the dark thing she had sensed coursing through him in the park, simmering just beneath his attractive surface again.

"You just told me to aim wide," she said.

"Oh, you should," he said. "However, I have long missed the boat."

He would have, she thought; he had been in the army for years.

Did he feel morose? Were his nights haunted?

Her knees were shaky. Her collar was drenched inside and out. She wanted to crawl beneath downy covers, already warmed by a bed heater, and demand a sugary drink, like the spoiled girl she had once been: an earl's daughter with a vast bed at her disposal and kindly servants who brought hot chocolate at the ring of a bell.

The last thing she needed now was to let Ballentine see her unravel. He would take it and forge it into one more weapon for his armory, to be used against her on a better day, because this truce was an illusion. Midnight was near; he'd soon turn back into a scoundrel and she into a woman with a target on her back.

"Thank you, my lord," she said. "For escorting me home."

She turned and unlocked the door.

Boudicca's accusing cat face greeted her. She had sat right behind the door like a furry little sphinx, overhearing every word and not liking it. She was wary of men.

Lucie removed her damp glove and bent to run her hand over Boudicca's soft black back.

To her surprise, the cat strode past her, her green eyes fixating on Ballentine.

He hadn't moved from where she'd left him, a sentinel in a top hat at her doorstep.

"Good evening," he said politely, surprisingly, to the cat.

Incredibly, Boudicca slunk down two rainy steps to investigate. If there was anything her cat disliked more than men, it was getting her delicate black paws wet.

She watched with narrowed eyes as Boudicca made a figure of eight around Tristan's legs. He bent and scratched beneath Boudicca's chin with two fingers, just the way she liked it. "That's a dear girl," he crooned.

"How do you know she is a she?" Lucie asked indignantly.

He looked up. "Because she took one glance at me and was enamored?"

There was the Tristan she knew, smug and alive behind his eyes.

What he said was true, as well. Boudicca was rubbing her head on his trouser leg, shamelessly demanding another stroke.

Traitress.

She whistled. "Come inside, Boudicca."

Tristan straightened.

It still took two more progressively insistent whistles until her feline ladyship obliged and came back up the stairs.

Tristan stood waiting until she closed the door in his face.

Her arm full of damp cat, she peered out the reception room window from behind the curtain and caught a glimpse of Tristan vanishing into the night. For the first time since the encounter, she wondered what had brought him to the park at that hour of the night.

She had not slowed down. The thought kept circling with the grim persistence of a vulture as Tristan strode through the rain. Round and round the image went, of Lucie's narrow shoulders pulling back as she marched toward five men.

His feet took the turn onto Broad Street on their own volition, driven by a cold emotion which had to be rage. Was she unaware how easily she could be harmed? Was she suffering illusions about her size and strength? *She does know.* She carried a pistol in her skirts. He was the fool, having for inexplicable reasons deemed her unbreakable.

His pulse was still high by the time he strolled into the ivy-covered porter's lodge of Trinity College and infused his gait with an inebriated sway.

A porter manned the desk, looking as uncircumventable as his position demanded: stout, and with a decidedly resolute face beneath the hat of his uniform.

Tristan placed his signet ring onto the counter.

"This must be delivered to Mr. Wyndham posthaste," he announced. "Room number twelve, in the west wing."

The porter squinted at him, then the ring, and back at him, his watery eyes assessing.

It was past the curfew, and thus the gates to the Oxford colleges were locked and blocked by porters who had become quite inured to lordly behavior after years of managing student antics, and as such were a rather formidable match for a would-be intruder. Any students returning at this hour required a special permission to enter; any visitors would find themselves out in the cold unless they, too, had a written permission. Or, unless they remembered from their own student days where to climb the wall surrounding Trinity gardens from the Parks Road side.

"I would place it in his pigeonhole," Tristan said, leaning in close and speaking too loudly. "But as you may have guessed, since you have the look of a clever chap about you, this"—he gestured a vague circle around the ring—"has some sentimental value attached to it."

The porter's expression became very stolid. "Indeed, my lord."

"Excellent," said Tristan, his eyebrow arching expectantly.

"If his lordship returned tomorrow, during the daytime, Mr. Wyndham would be available, here in the lodge, for a safe delivery of the valuable."

He shook his head. "This is a matter between gentlemen which must be brought to conclusion tonight." His voice had lowered to a dramatic murmur. "So if you were so kind as to deliver it to room number twelve, in the west wing, right now, I should be much obliged."

"The hour is late, my lord."

"Much obliged," Tristan repeated.

The porter clearly wished to boot him out of the lodge posthaste, but much as Tristan had expected, he decided to bow to rank on a matter as inconsequential as a room delivery rather than rile an already troublesome and intoxicated nobleman.

"Very well," the man said. "Is the ring destined for room number twelve in the west wing, then, or for Mr. Wyndham?"

"Good man, you speak in riddles. I'm not in the mood for riddles."

"No riddles—Mr. Wyndham is not in room number twelve in the west wing."

Tristan tilted his head. "You are jesting, then."

"I don't jest, my lord."

"Oh good, for I'm not in the mood for jests, either."

He really was not, in fact. He wanted to get his hands on Mr. Wyndham.

The porter's lips set in a line. "You have either the room correct, or the recipient—which one shall it be?"

"Who delivers things to rooms?" Tristan wondered. "What would a room do with my ring? Of course it must go to Mr. Wyndham."

"Very well," said the porter, at this point, quite possibly, thinking the French had had the right idea to cull the titled classes. "I shall deliver the ring to Mr. Wyndham."

"To room number twelve," Tristan said brightly.

"No, because he does not reside there."

"And yet I have it on good account that he does," Tristan said. "It saddens me to say so, but I am losing faith in a safe delivery at your hands." His eyes narrowed. "Is it a trick, perhaps? Assuring me the ring will be brought to Mr. Wyndham, but because of an unfortunate confusion over the room number, it never arrives at all? Ends up in the wrong hands altogether, perhaps?"

The insinuation that the man was presently planning to steal his signet ring had the porter draw himself up to his full height and straighten his hat. "Tricks!" he snarled. He turned to pick up the sacred leather-bound ledger from the porter's desk, to which it was attached with a chain, placed it onto the counter, rapidly flicked through the pages, then spun the ledger round and thrust it toward Tristan, his blunt fingertip tapping on a line.

Mr. Thomas Wyndham resided in room number nine in the east wing.

"I see," he said softly. "A misunderstanding, then. No, no." He placed his hand over the ring before the porter could pick it up. "Perhaps the matter is not quite as pressing. I shall take my leave."

The climb over the slippery garden wall to reenter the Trinity grounds was satisfyingly compensated by the look of horror on Wyndham's long face when he found himself facing Tristan on the doorstep to room number nine. He was in his shirtsleeves, probably in the process of readying himself for bed.

"What is this?" he said sharply, when Tristan used the moment of surprise to push past him into the room. Without the company of his fellow fencers, he did not quite display the measure of bravado as earlier in the park, when Tristan and he had stood toe-to-toe the first time.

"Wyndham," Tristan said, and closed the door. "I have a proposition for you."

"The hell," said the man whose name was Wyndham. "We have never been introduced!"

"Indeed, we have not," Tristan said. "But your scarf is rather chatty." He nodded at it, the scarf, dangling from the clothing rack next to the wardrobe, having fulfilled its function for today's sporting event. And when the young man looked from him to the scarf with a painful lack of comprehension, he added, almost gently: "Your college colors. And it happens to have the Wyndham coat of arms stitched onto it rather prominently, too."

Wyndham's dark eyes narrowed, but his throat moved nervously. "What—what do you want? We parted ways in the park; no offenses were taken."

Lucie's tired face flashed before his eyes. He had never seen the little shrew in such a sorry state as when she had leaned against her entrance door, damp and somewhat crumpled. Something about the idea of her being laid low by a band of cowardly dimwits grated on the aesthete in him, and it made him irrationally bloodthirsty.

"I was wondering, old boy," he said to Wyndham, "how highly you prize your sword hand."

Chapter 14

Monday morning, three days after escorting Lucie home, Tristan was summoned to Ashdown at short notice, and he was fairly certain why Rochester demanded his presence.

His suspicion was confirmed the moment he strolled into the crypt. Rochester was hovering next to his desk, dark with fury like an angel of wrath.

A newspaper was spread wide open on the tabletop.

The gossip rag the *Pall Mall Gazette*.

"Explain. This." Rochester's index finger repeatedly came down hard on the page.

No need to take a closer look. The paper was yesterday's news. He knew the page showed a caricature of an overly tall, well-dressed gentleman with a lusty grin (himself) leading a keen-looking puppy down a cobblestoned street. With some imagination, the tag on the dog collar bore resemblance to the crest of Doncaster. *A gentleman's evening stroll*, read the caption. Fairly tame. The audacity had left the cartoonist on the last yard.

"What do you have to say for yourself?" barked Rochester.

He clasped his hands behind his back. "It was Oscar Wilde's fault."

"My pardon?"

"It's a silly cartoon."

Rochester looked about to breathe fire. "It nearly cost me your engagement."

His muscles hardened to stone. His engagement. It could have been amusing, had it not been for Mother languishing upstairs in the west wing, a chokehold around his neck.

"Lord Arthur was drunk," he said. "Other drunk students saw him acting like a fool. Someone thought it would be amusing to draw a cartoon."

And this was really all he *could* say.

Rochester took a step and stood rather close. A black emotion broiled in the depths of his eyes. "You were hard to stomach as my second son," he said softly. "As my heir, you make me sick."

Well. That managed to twist his gut. Rochester's disregard for him was hardly a secret, but right now, the depths of his contempt felt bottomless.

Rochester moved back to the desk. "This needs to be fixed," he said. "Here is how." He picked up a piece of paper. A list. The man had written him a list. Because Mother was *still* languishing in the west wing, he took it and gave it a perfunctory glance.

A bemused frown crinkled his brow. "I'm to attend the house party of a scandalous duke and court an old acquaintance? That is your plan to clear my name?"

"Montgomery is a fool to have married his strumpet," Rochester said, "but at the end of the day, the man cannot be ignored when he sends an invitation and the prince is his guest. One of us must attend. Under the circumstances, it shall be you." He said it with an expression of disdain. It had to grate on Rochester's soul like a rusty knife that someone had rebelled against the holy trinity of Queen, Tradition, and Society and was still standing when the dust had settled. It was quite impossible to truly bring down a duke; once a man like Montgomery broke the chains hampering his mind, he was free to pursue his carnal desires instead of strategy. A loathsome thing, an unchained mind, so very uncontrollable.

"The Prince of Wales is particularly supportive of the campaign in Afghanistan," Rochester continued. "Act normal when he approaches you."

"Yes, yes." He tucked the list into his breast pocket. "And I have already taken steps to *bolster* my reputation."

Rochester's gaze turned suspicious. "What are you planning, Tristan?"

"It shall be in the *Pall Mall Gazette* tomorrow evening. Or in any other newspaper in Britain."

After the scene with Arthur Seymour, he had no choice but to do something distracting. And society loved few things more than a grand reveal.

In the west wing, his mother was asleep. She didn't wake when he pulled back the curtains and daylight slanted across the room, right into her face.

Another untouched tray had gone cold on her nightstand.

"Mother," he said loudly. "You have a visitor."

She didn't stir.

He drew closer to the bed. Her cheeks looked sunken. A pale blue silk ribbon kept her braid together, a ludicrous scrap the color of the sky.

When he sat down on the mattress, the bed dipped under his weight. No reaction. She was as cooperative as a sack of flour. Would she even care where she languished? Perhaps she'd be the last person to notice the difference between General Foster's guest room and a bed in an asylum.

His hands clenched and unclenched by his side. Perhaps he was playing along in Rochester's ridiculous marriage game and laying himself bare in newspapers and entangling himself with one of the most ruthless businessmen in Britain—for nothing.

"Is it worth it?" he asked the room. His voice sounded harsh to his own ears.

He looked back down at the stubbornly sleeping countess.

"Are you doing this to be closer to Marcus?"

Perhaps they were meeting in the twilight into which she had descended. Perhaps she *liked* being there. He certainly saw more of Marcus in his nightmares than he had during his lifetime. They ended with Marcus staring at him with blood pouring from his eyes, when he had in fact cleanly broken his neck and would have experienced neither bleeding nor suffering. Neat and efficient, Marcus, in death as he had been in life. But he, Tristan, woke covered in sweat from these encounters with a crushing weight upon his chest. Why? He sometimes wondered. As a child, he had devotedly trotted after Marcus whenever he had been released from heir duties for some play. As adolescents, their relationship had been courteous, for their roles had been clear: Marcus was the heir, Tristan the misfit—but he had never envied his brother his position. After his marriage, Marcus had distanced himself thoroughly, his wife fearing Tristan's bad influence, presumably. But there had been a continent between them by then. So why the dreams? Perhaps because the good die first, as Wordsworth said, *and they whose hearts are dry as summer dust burn to the socket.* The weight on his chest might well be guilt because the good brother was gone.

He picked up the spoon from the tray and held it under his mother's delicate nose. As the metal turned misty from invisible breaths, a tension drained from his muscles.

He gave the spoon a little spin.

"Did you know Rochester hates me?" he asked. "I've known it a long time, since when he had Jarvis drown Kitten—do you remember her? You had given her to me for my thirteenth birthday."

Mother slept. Not a flutter of an eyelash.

"She was a beautiful little thing, ginger and white, and soft as down. She came hopping when I whistled, as a puppy would. And I remember thinking the only reason one could possibly stick such a charming creature into a bag and toss it into the pond was hatred."

It had been an autumn day, crisp blue skies, the smell of dry leaves in the air. The splendid weather must have distracted him from his Latin translations. Or he had bolted one time too many to go and run around the park instead of doing tabulations. He could not quite recall. He remembered very clearly Jarvis's glee as he hurled the bag containing the kitten out over the pond. After the splash, the bag had floated on the dark surface of the water. Rochester's hand had been heavy on his shoulder. *Do you see this, Tristan? This is what happens when you are careless and unfocused. This is what happens when you do not do your duty. You will fail, and things in your care will perish.*

The bag had bopped erratically; a tiny cat inside had struggled and cried for her master to save her. Her master never came. He'd been pinned to the banks of the pond by an iron grip, his throat aching from the screams he was holding back. Kitten and bag had been swallowed by the waters, leaving barely a ripple.

Afterward, he still had not mastered himself enough to sit still for the length of a day, to concentrate on tasks he found dull. He had rejected the fluffy puppy his mother had tried to gift him for his next birthday.

He rubbed a hand over his neck. There was a certain irony in that he could keep comrades safe under fire but not the women in his coddled life at Ashdown, not even the felines. *Useless.* Within these walls, he was that.

He put the spoon back onto the tray, and something on the night-stand caught his attention. A wooden figurine. It had not been there during his previous visit. A Christmas angel, and the clumsy carvings and mop of gilded wires miming hair looked familiar. He picked it up and turned it over in his hand.

"I made this for you," he murmured. "It was the first thing I carved with the pocketknife you gave me."

Somehow, the misshapen thing had survived over two decades.

He carefully put the figurine back among the medicine bottles.

He pulled the blanket up over his mother's shoulders. "I don't know if you still read the papers," he said. "If you do, don't be surprised to read about me sometime this week. I published some poetry a while ago and circumstances are compelling me to own it."

There were other things he contemplated telling her. *I offered to shoot five men for Lucie Tedbury, and I am not certain what it means.*

"I'm attending a house party at Claremont this weekend," he said instead. "I shall come back and bring you all of the gossip."

Monday afternoons were Lucie's least favorite part of the week, for they were dedicated to the administrative matters pertaining to the Cause: sharing the latest news, processing membership applications, settling the accounts for the Oxford chapter, compiling the schedule with meetings and events for the upcoming week. And because Annabelle had to be with her duke in Wiltshire four days a week, their ranks had been diminished. She had drafted Mabel, Lady Henley, to replace her, as the widow had long been a member of the chapter and she lived next door. However, since the foiled interlude with a certain lord in their front yard shrubbery, Lady Henley had become too busy on Monday afternoons to help. No good deed went unpunished.

Then again, pitting herself against an avalanche of tasks and duties diverted her mind sufficiently from recent events. The night in the park. Tristan, looking stern and masterful, at her doorstep.

"Thank you for coming," she told Catriona and Hattie, who had faithfully gathered round the table in the drawing room, their notebooks and pens prepared. Hattie was also munching on one of the dainties she had brought from the bakery in Little Clarendon Street, liberally scattering crumbs.

"To begin, here is a copy of Millicent Fawcett's latest lecture at the London School of Economics; it is quite a riveting read on the education of girls," Lucie said, and slid the transcript to the middle of the table.

Hattie peered at them. " 'These considerations force upon us the conclusion that the popular view of the duties of wives and mothers is a very low and incorrect one,'" she read, "'one which assigns almost supreme importance to the animal rather than to the intellectual and moral functions of womanhood . . ." She looked up. "It's quite odd, isn't it—Millicent is allowed to give clever lectures in London, and yet here at Oxford the female students are not permitted to matriculate and graduate in the same fashion as the male students?"

"Oxford was created for monks, and has since been administered by living fossils," Lucie said. "Time moves differently here. But also, don't forget Millicent's husband has a position at the LSE. Now, as for the first point on our agenda: have we found a solution for our Property Act report? I have not. I wrote to the *Manchester Guardian* again to request a meeting and have not even been graced with a rejection."

Catriona shook her head with a regretful shrug.

"I asked my father what he would do if he wished to publish a piece no one wanted to publish," Hattie said.

"And?"

"He said he would just create his own publishing house," Hattie said apologetically.

"Hear, hear," Catriona muttered, irony drenching the words.

Lucie rolled her eyes. "Very well. On to the second point: the current state of the Property Act letter count?"

Catriona, in charge of everything pertaining to numbers, glanced at her notebook. "The current state is at fourteen thousand, nine hundred and some. However, we are still missing the count from the Scottish chapters—I suspect a delay in mail delivery."

"Right. The mail shall be the demise of the Cause one day."

"What do you mean?"

"The delays—or think of the mail lost altogether," Lucie said. "For example, take the letter Millicent sent along with her lecture transcript. It contained outdated information—I had informed Lydia

Becker about a notably conservative shift in the Primrose chapter at least two weeks ago, and she should have passed it on to Millicent. It keeps happening, and it is getting worse—Millicent sends us commentary, or is in need of aligning a plan, and we comment, send it back, she sends it to Lydia Becker, who comments, and sends it to Rosalind Howard, and so on."

"Well, the more recipients we add to our mail chains, the more confusing it will become."

"Surely there must be a better way to organize ourselves."

"But how?" Hattie asked. "You can hardly travel to London solely for suffrage meetings every day—neither can the other suffrage chapter leaders."

"We can't," Lucie said darkly.

"Besides, we already have the Central Committee in London," Catriona pointed out.

"I'm aware," Lucie said. "It just is neither as efficient nor as effective as it should be. I imagine it will get worse—there are dozens of local suffrage chapters now, and a few societies, and unless we all talk to each other regularly, fat good will it do us."

"Imagine a world where mail does not travel for days," Hattie said. "Or where we could all be reading the same letter at the same time."

Catriona smiled faintly. "We'd have a woman's army rising within weeks in such a magical world."

"As it is, we should have at least one monthly meeting where we all try and align ourselves."

"Like a clan gathering," Catriona said.

"Clan MacSuffrage?" Hattie suggested.

Lucie gave a snort, but Catriona was chuckling into her plaid.

"Right—third point on our agenda: Catriona is checking the accounts. Hattie is in charge of membership applications. I shall make notes on necessary campaign work arising from my correspondence."

Atop her letter pile was a gentle reminder from Lady Harberton about the campaign for women on bicycles. She groaned. How could she keep forgetting about the bicycles? No, she was not forgetting them, she just could not seem to find the time. . . .

"How strange." The puzzled note in Catriona's voice made Lucie look up. Catriona was rarely puzzled.

Her friend was frowning down at the list of donations before her.

"What is it?"

"There's a donation from the Oxford University Fencing Club."

Lucie sat very still. "Are you . . . certain?"

"It says so clearly. But it must be a mistake."

It could be that.

Or it was something far more complicated.

"How much?" she asked, and heard her voice squeak.

Catriona glanced up. Her blue eyes were wide behind her glasses. "A hundred pounds."

"Good Lord." It was everyone else's monthly donation to the Oxford chapter put together.

"How curious," said Hattie, her eyes round. "Why would they have an interest in women's rights all of a sudden?"

Catriona made a note on the ledger's margin. "I shall confirm this with their treasurer."

"Please do," Lucie said, but her mind continued to race. The donation was not a mistake, she knew it in her bones. She could see the menacing glint of wet steel as clearly now as if the young men were squaring up to her again. Even if they'd known who she was, they would not have felt compelled to pay such a penance come morning— unless something, or rather, *someone* had, in fact, compelled them to do so.

Tristan. Who else.

But why? A two-pronged attack, perhaps, a tactic of carrot and stick to confuse her?

He had succeeded at confusing her.

She was tempted to ignore it. Unfortunately, she would have to address the matter—did not bear contemplating how Tristan had extracted the money, and the suffrage chapter could not afford to make personal enemies out of the upper-class males at Oxford. She made a note in her diary to resolve the situation after the house party.

Chapter 15

L ucie had been twelve the last time her family had paid a visit to
  Montgomery, so the landscape now slipping past the carriage
window was unfamiliar. She had memories of Claremont, a sprawling gray limestone palace dominating the view of the green hills of
Wiltshire. The entrance hall had been three stories high beneath a
domed glass ceiling.

"It should not be difficult," she said out loud. "I present myself in
fashionable clothes. I shan't mention a word about women's suffrage,
diseases, or politics. I shall make conversation with the most staid of
society matrons we can lure into being seen with me. I will dance a
waltz."

On the bench opposite, Hattie sat up straighter. "A waltz? That is
a new addition to the list."

It was. It had just popped out of her mouth. Perhaps because she
was preternaturally aware of a crimson ball gown taking up half of
her luggage trousseau.

Hattie surveyed her—again—and made a happy noise. "You shall
have no problems at all with the first point on your list—you look
most elegant. I know, I must stop saying it." Every time she did say
it, she pressed her hands over her heart and her brown eyes grew
dewy. Hattie really took pleasure in other people looking their best—
especially when they had followed her fashion advice.

Lucie smoothed her hand over the dove gray skirt of the carriage dress. The scent of fine new wool wafted around her when she moved. The new gowns *were* very flattering, modern, and sleek. Also quite constraining, as the sleekness was achieved by making them a snugly fitted one-piece. All her old dresses were three-pieces. By the time she had to present herself to the baying crowds, she would hopefully be used to the limited movement of her arms. Then again, none of her fashion choices would adequately counter Tristan's most recent move.

The news that he was the author of *A Pocketful of Poems* had hit the papers on Tuesday. Wednesday morning, she had received a shrill cable from Lady Athena, who was standing in as secretary at London Print: what was to be done with all the mail? The office was being flooded with letters, half of them heavily scented. Ballentine cards were pouring in, demanding to be signed and returned. Lucie had traveled to London and had had to give her fiercest scowl to escape a gang of journalists lurking by the side entrance of the publisher. By Thursday afternoon, it had been clear that they needed to issue a new edition of Tristan's poetry as fast as possible. And Tristan? He'd shone with his absence. After sending runners to the four winds to find him, she had discovered a note on his office desk: *Editing the war diaries—you can thank me for the increase in sales later.*

A small growl escaped her throat, and, at Hattie's alarmed expression, she added: "Him."

Hattie bit her bottom lip. "Ah," she said. "Him."

And Hattie didn't know half of it. She'd never bother her friends by repeating his lewd proposal.

"I maintain that the publicity for London Print is a good thing." Catriona had been silent throughout the ride, sitting next to Lucie and reading. She was still looking down at the tome on her lap.

"Is it really?" Lucie asked. "Have the company value and number of book orders soared overnight? Yes. Has Lord Ballentine just become more powerful? Again, yes."

Silence filled the carriage, leaving each of them to brood.

Hattie was never able to brood for long. "Have you read it yet?"

"His poetry? No."

Hattie was studying her with the intent expression she wore when she stood in front of a painting, mentally dissecting the composition. "May I ask why?"

Lucie gave a shrug. "It's romantic poetry."

"But . . . why?"

"Most gentlemen write poetry to their sweethearts, I believe?"

"I certainly hope they would."

"And how many gentlemen take a mistress soon after the honeymoon?"

Hattie's tawny brows pulled together in a frown. "A few, I suppose."

"More than a few. And I imagine I should feel doubly fooled as a wife when he is out frolicking with another while I am at home with a pile of paper declaring his undying adoration. It's all lies."

Hattie's sweet face fell. "I feel this may be a little cynical."

"I like to call it realistic."

Hattie's jaw set mulishly. "Even if romantic sentiments cool over time, the poems could well have been true in the moment."

Lucie shrugged. "I suppose I don't rate truths that last only for a moment. Truth should be more durable. If you must put something in writing and make it rhyme, let it be timeless. In fact, consigning fleeting emotional outbursts to the bin instead of using them to lure an unsuspecting lady would be the true mark of chivalry."

Hattie blinked as if she had splashed water at her face. "Heavens. It's just poetry."

Catriona slowly raised her gaze off her page and stared. "*Just* poetry?"

Hattie threw up her hands and raised her gaze to the carriage roof. "Shall we make a wager? This house party is going to be scandalous—again—because it happens whenever we make an appearance together."

A pang of alarm made Lucie point a warning finger. "Harriet Greenfield, do not jinx this house party."

"Yes, don't," Catriona said. "Annabelle would be exceedingly cross."

"I can hardly control my intuition, can I?"

"Please try, will you?" Lucie said.

When their carriage pulled into the vast quadrangle of Claremont Palace, Lucie was amazed. A building last seen in childhood normally appeared smaller upon a revisit. Not so with Claremont. It was still a palace the size of a small city, its long row of pillars fronting the main house looming like sentinels.

A queue of elegant carriages snaked around the quad, most of them carrying people she hadn't dined with in a decade. Most of these people considered her a traitor.

Her stomach tightened uncomfortably. As adept as she had become at balancing on the edges of respectability and genteel rules day in and day out, the thought of having to dust off this particular rule book made her bristle with apprehension.

The duke was personally receiving his guests by the main entrance, the stillness of his lean figure rivaling that of his gray pillars. He was a cold man and he looked it—pale skin, wintry eyes, Nordic blond hair. A stern mouth. His scandal had not humbled him. The mere sight of so much stuffiness would have tempted the old Lucie to ruffle a feather or two.

The feeling was clearly mutual. The duke was vaguely emotive when welcoming Catriona and Hattie—was that the hint of a smile hovering over his lips as he greeted them? But when it was her turn, a glacier would have been more expressive than Montgomery's face.

"Lady Lucinda. Welcome to Claremont." His voice was glacial, too, cool and smooth, without inflection.

She curtsied. "I thank you kindly for the invitation, Your Grace."

Granted, the man had an impressive way of looking straight into people with his cold gaze, inducing guilty urges to confess to something, anything. She attempted a docile expression. It failed to fool him, for he inclined his blond head and said: "I understand the duchess is very fond of you."

This could be taken as a compliment. Or a warning, that a friendship was at stake if she mis-stepped. She would go with the warning. Not long ago, the duke had been one of her most powerful opponents on the political parquet, and compliments would not be on offer for a while.

"Lucie!" Annabelle appeared by Montgomery's side, her face brightened by a wide smile. "How wonderful to have you. I shall have to steal her," she said, peering up at the duke as she reached for Lucie's hands.

Montgomery's austere features transformed into a startlingly warm and handsome countenance as he looked at his beaming wife. "Steal away," he murmured, his voice dipping low. The intimacy in the glance they shared was so palpable, Lucie felt a blush blooming just witnessing it.

Annabelle looped an arm through hers and pulled her into the domed Great Hall, where Catriona and Hattie were already waiting, relieved of their traveling coats and bonnets by attentive maids.

"I'm glad you came," Annabelle said and took Catriona's hand without letting go of Lucie. "Lucie, I adore your dress. I trust your journey was comfortable? Truly, an adorable dress."

Lucie slowed. "Are you all right?"

Her friend looked impeccable in an emerald gown with gossamer sleeves, her mahogany hair a gleaming coil over her left shoulder. But her cheeks had high color and her back was too rigid, even for a duchess.

"I am just glad you are here." Annabelle's smile remained fixed on her face as her green gaze flitted between the various guests coming toward them. "I can feel them waiting with bated breath for me to commit a major faux pas."

Lucie had never seen Annabelle quite so nervous before, and they had shared various adventures.

She gave her arm a reassuring squeeze. "You are doing very well. And no one in attendance wants to get on the wrong side of your husband."

"Well, we already had the first incident—Lady Hampshire's cat has escaped. If you spot a ginger Maine Coon the size of a small tiger, please report it immediately."

"Oh no," said Hattie, "what happened?"

"Apparently, a footman put down the cat crate too hard and the door sprang open. The cat made a dash for it. Her ladyship is beside herself and demands the footman's head, and half the staff is presently chasing the animal instead of helping to accommodate guests."

Lucie made a face. The marchioness was a vocal opponent of the suffragist cause and women in general. Society humored her, and so she continued to successfully bully newspapers and journals into publishing unpardonable falsehoods on the inferiority of female brains and disposition. Frankly, Lucie would leg it, too, if she were a Maine Coon in Lady Hampshire's possession.

They were shown their rooms and given some time to change out of their travel gowns, then Annabelle returned to take them to a vast, richly decorated reception room. It was already populated with guests who were standing in small circles, sipping drinks and chatting in low voices. A string quartet played a subtle tune in the far corner.

The shift in attention toward them when they entered, the slight pause in conversation, was not subtle.

"I must leave you and tend to the other guests," Annabelle murmured as she steered them toward Hattie's parents and her brother, who had already arrived from London and were assembled near an imposing Greek marble. "Please make yourselves at home. I shall see you before dinner."

Lucie stood back as Hattie was absorbed by her family's warm welcome. Mrs. Greenfield had the same wine red hair as Hattie. Her father, the mighty Julien Greenfield, looked like everyone's jolly uncle who told the scandalous jokes at dinner: short, rotund, his cheeks ruddy from a lifetime of enjoying wine and food. A mustache resembling walrus tusks framed his mouth and chin. Word had it that he was utterly ruthless.

He squinted at Lucie over Hattie's head, not unfriendly.

He doesn't belong here, either, Lucie thought. He came from banking stock, his family's fortune and influence based on a century of unapologetic grafting. Nothing about him recommended him to the class of people currently surrounding them but his ability to give them substantial financial credit.

An unpleasant sensation tickled the back of her neck. Someone was watching her. She tilted her head and glanced surreptitiously back over her shoulder.

Cecily. Barely two yards behind her stood her cousin, observing her with innocent eyes. Her gown was white and blue like the summer sky; she was an angel on her cloud.

Lucie turned to face her, and Cecily's gaze promptly darted away. She was escorted by a young man who all but hovered over her. He was handsome, and . . . familiar. Light blond hair, gray eyes not unlike her own.

Her heart gave a little leap.

"Tommy," she blurted.

Her brother was a far cry from the fifteen-year-old youth she remembered. He had grown quite tall, and precisely sculpted sideburns framed his long face. He was staring as if she were an apparition.

He cleared his throat. "It is Thomas now," he said.

"Oh. Of course. Thomas."

He did not offer his hand, nor a bow. He also could not give her the cut direct in a room where both of them were guests.

He grabbed Cecily by the upper arm. "Do you remember your cousin Cecily?"

Cecily's eyes widened in pained surprise. Tommy—Thomas—had to have quite a grip on her. She recovered quickly. "Cousin Lucie," she said demurely.

"Cousin Cecily. A pleasure to see you again so soon. I trust your journey here was uneventful?"

"Quite," Tommy said. He had gathered his wits; his face had shuttered. A disapproving flush reddened his cheeks. He looked a lot like Mother this way.

Speaking of Mother, she was not far behind. Her stiff back was visible behind her brother's shoulder, and she appeared to be in deep conversation with Lady Hampshire.

She obviously knew Lucie was here. She had always had eyes in the back of her head, catching Lucie in the act, and even facing the other way, awareness rippled between them. Everyone else in the room was probably aware of it, too. Their estrangement was a secret, but then again, it was not. Intrigue already swirled like toxic fog, and her skin prickled as covert glances raked over her. Normally, this would have sparked belligerence in her, the kind that was required to take on opponents larger, stronger, and meaner than herself. But here in this opulent reception room, faced with strategically turned backs of people who once must have loved her, and she them, her throat became worryingly tight.

She plastered on a smile. "Splendid," she said to Tommy. "I hope you have a splendid stay. I think you can safely release Cecily now."

His gaze flitted to his right hand, which was still clamped around Cecily's arm.

His hasty apology faded into the chatter of the crowd behind her as Lucie started toward the ornate wing doors.

She was unsurprised to find herself in front of Montgomery's stables. She had noted the arched entrance to the stable court with longing when they had sat waiting in the carriage, admiring the fine horses that had been paraded past the vehicle's window.

She entered through a side door. A high, airy ceiling and white-washed walls greeted her, and she breathed deep, savoring the sweet smell of hay and well-tended horses. A smile stole over her face. She had spent a few wonderful, carefree summers in the stables as a girl.

At the sound of her footsteps down the aisle, half a dozen curious horses stuck their heads over their doors and watched her, all ears standing to attention.

Her own ears pricked.

Somewhere, a man was cursing away.

"Bloody creature. I'll give you to Cook when I catch you. He'll make a dozen pies out of yer furry arse."

Well, that was unpleasant.

"And I'll have yer bleedin' tail made into a duster, you 'ear me?"

She turned into the next aisle on quiet feet. To her right, a low wall separated a large alcove filled with tack from the aisle, and in the alcove stood a young man, hands on his hips, and he was threatening the rafter above.

Or rather, the large ginger cat hunching on the wooden beam.

Lady Hampshire's Maine Coon.

A ladder was already in place.

"Yer posh-faced, flea-riddled—"

"Why don't you go up and retrieve her?" Lucie said coolly. "She'll hardly descend the ladder on her own."

Not with him standing there, bellowing to have the poor thing skinned and cooked.

The man's head jerked toward her.

A young groom-gardener, she assumed. His cap was bunched in

his left fist, and his red hair stuck up as if he had pulled it in exasperation.

"Milady." A fierce blush turned his face the same color as his locks. "My apologies. The . . . cat . . ."

"Yes?"

She entered the alcove, and the groom eyed her approach warily. "I tried, milady." He held up his right hand. Four ruby-red streaks furrowed across the back. "It doesn't want to be retrieved."

High above their heads, the cat gave a drawn-out yowl.

"She does," Lucie said. "Can't you hear how she's crying? She is scared."

"Bit me, too." He held out his other hand. Two angry-looking puncture marks marred the fleshy bit between his thumb and index finger.

She gave him a stern look. "Are you telling me a big lad like you can't retrieve a small kitten?"

His gaze began flitting between her dark face and the vocal cat.

Clearly he found his options equally dreadful, so he stood frozen and mute on the spot.

She sighed. "Why don't you go and fetch some help."

He moved immediately. "At once, milady."

Off he went in his big boots. She imagined them stomping after the cat, giving her a proper scare.

She tilted back her head. "They will save you in a moment," she told the cat.

It gave her a baleful stare.

"You really should not have climbed to heights you can't come down from again on your own. Believe me, I know."

It occurred to her then that saving the cat could, potentially, kill two birds with one stone: returning it wouldn't make Lady Hampshire like her, but the marchioness would have to restrain her attempts to undermine her, lest she wanted to risk looking ungrateful.

She eyed the ladder. It looked fairly sturdy. She had certainly scaled worse as a girl. Against her better judgment, she began to climb.

She had not worn fashionable skirts as a girl. She had to climb sideways, and her progress was slow and awkward. Halfway up, a step creaked loudly under her right foot.

She paused and glanced back down, and her hands instinctively gripped the ladder more tightly. She was up quite high now. But still not near the cat. In fact, the Maine Coon began edging backward. By the time Lucie's head was level with the rafter, the animal was at least three feet out of reach.

"Come now," Lucie coaxed, stretching out her arm, or trying to. The snug silk detained her like a lovely-looking straightjacket. Her next effort produced the suspiciously crunching sound of straining seams. "Blast. It."

She tried flattery instead. "Goodness, you are huge, aren't you," she cooed. "Fifteen pounds, I reckon?"

The animal didn't budge. Its tail, thick as a fox's, batted softly, angrily, against the beam as she fixed Lucie with distrustful yellow eyes.

Silly creature didn't know what was good for her.

"Come now," she wiggled her fingers. "Come now, what a pretty kitty."

"I say," drawled a dreadfully familiar male voice from below. "Montgomery's stable boasts some lovely, unexpected views."

She froze, her arm awkwardly extended.

Tristan.

She peered back over her shoulder. He was on the other side of the low wall and made to enter the alcove. Of course he would be at the house party—his snob of a father would have never made a show himself. And now he was standing right beneath her, pretending to look up her skirts. No. Not pretending. His gaze was brushing over her ankles, noticeable on her skin like a physical touch.

She closed her eyes and silently counted to five.

It was the moment the cat decided to accept her person as the bridge to freedom and make a dash for it. Lucie opened her eyes to fifteen pounds of determined-looking cat hurtling toward her face, ears flat, tail crooked. Ginger fur muffled her shriek; claws dug into her neck sharp like needles. Her hands closed over thin air, and, with a hissing cat wrapped around her head, she fell backward into a void.

Chapter 16

I t would hurt. Her body curled and prepared for hurt.

The pain never came.

She crashed into something solid, but it gave; she went down yet again, and it was over.

For a moment, she lay prone and motionless, the hammering beat of her heart in her ears.

One by one, she accounted for her limbs. They all felt intact. A negligible ache in her ribs. White stars still flashed behind her closed eyelids. Her eyes snapped open when realization dawned that she was lying atop a man. Her nose was pressed into the V of starched shirt above his waistcoat, breathing in the warm scent of his skin.

Grand. She was draped over Tristan's supine form, no part of her touching the ground. He had caught her and the cat, and his body had taken the full brunt of the flagstone floor.

He would mock her ruthlessly about it, forever.

It was tempting to close her eyes again and feign unconsciousness.

But he just lay still, suspiciously so. Not a breath moved his broad torso.

She raised herself up on his chest and peered down at him.

His eyes were closed, his lashes sooty crescents against his cheeks.

His hair was spread around his head on the stable floor. He had lost his hat. It lay on its side, a good five feet away.

Lord. His head must have taken a hit on the stones.

"Ballentine."

No reaction.

Her chest turned cold inside out. She gave his cheek a firm pat. "This is not funny."

No reaction.

Had she killed him? No one would believe that it was an accident. *Nonsense.* There was no blood—none she could see.

She peeled off her gloves and tossed them aside. Leaning over him, she sank her fingers into his hair. It slid through her fingers, slippery and cool, as she swiftly searched his temples, then the sides and back of his skull with urgent fingertips. No lumps, no blood.

"Don't be dead," she murmured, "or permanently damaged." He was a rogue, a scoundrel, but . . .

A sound rumbled in his chest.

Her hands stilled. It had sounded . . . like a laugh.

His eyes opened, bright pools of mischief looking up at her.

The blast of mixed emotions stunned her. She glared down at his indolent face, panting, unable to move.

He slowly shook his head. "I cannot believe you fell for that."

Her fingers tightened reflexively in his hair. "I *hate* pranks," she whispered.

His smile widened. "I know," he whispered back.

She felt his hands on her hips.

Everything slowed. Tristan went still beneath her, the amusement fading from his eyes. Heat bloomed on her skin, aware that she was laying on him, hip against hip, her skirt on his legs like an exotic wing. . . . She tried not to move, not press more closely against him, but she felt him so well: his chest, hard and solid as flagstone beneath her. The sensuous sleekness of his hair between her fingers. The dull beat of a needy pulse between her legs. Tristan's breathing turned ragged, and his gaze was hot, molten gold, as if he felt what feeling him did to her. Her hands began to tremble, and he felt that, too. His mouth softened, and she gazed at it, entranced. He lightly slid the tip of his tongue over his bottom lip, leaving it damp, and a tiny noise escaped her. She wanted to feel his mouth against hers, and in this slow, warm haze, it made sense. Her head dipped.

A subtle movement brought his thigh up between hers, right where it ached. She gasped. Too much. The harsh, earthly smells and sounds of a stable flooded back.

She was, in fact, on a stable floor, in a most compromising position.

She arched up. "Release me."

"Lucie." His voice was unsteady.

"Now."

What a disaster. They were embracing on a stable floor, barely shielded by half a wall.

His grip on her hips eased, and he slowly raised his arms over his head and lay under her in a pose of mock-surrender. It still took her a moment to move, to roll off him and struggle to her feet. The tension in her limbs did not ease; she was fair aching with it.

Tristan unhurriedly drew himself up in a sitting position and braced an arm on his bent knee. Straw stuck from his hair. He looked indecent, and his mouth was edged with a knowing arrogance. She had very nearly kissed this mouth. Her lips were burning, angrily, because she hadn't.

She turned and strode from the stable, her head held high, not knowing whether she was more put out with him or with herself.

Tristan watched her go, breathing hard and aware that he was slipping. He could not recall ever losing control to the point of grinding himself against a lady on a stable floor. Appalling, and yet his blood still rushed with ecstasy. Ecstasy from a near kiss.

He had seen Lucie cross the courtyard, because he had arrived late at Claremont, and he had made the spontaneous decision to follow her. When a terrified groom had all but rushed toward him from the stables, yammering about a formidable lady and a cat, he had sent the lad to the other end of the courtyard. A good foresight. His hands had not obeyed him at first when he had willed them to let go of her skirts. He had been fighting the urge to roll with her in his arms, to pull her body beneath his. It would have taken another second or two to drag up her skirts. *On a stable floor.* He had, until today, fancied himself a somewhat sophisticated hedonist. Apparently, it wasn't so.

He closed his eyes, waiting for the heat to fade from his limbs. The look in her eyes, such a clash of want and fury. When they would finally come together, it would shake foundations, or, at the very least, break the bed.

He felt a watchful gaze on him, and a quick glance around located the source: the large orange menace Lucie had tried to save earlier. It had crammed itself backward into a nook in the wall opposite. Cats. The smaller the box, the more attractive they found it. He came to his feet and winced and adjusted the front of his trousers.

The daft animal purred when he approached. It didn't resist as he carefully extracted it from the nook and lifted it into his arms.

He couldn't have bolstered his reputation among the respectable matrons any better than by strolling into the reception room holding a grousing cat. The Marchioness of Hampshire sailed at him through the crowd with the force of a schooner, exclaiming incoherently while taking the animal off him and pressing it to her bosom. A growing ring of spectators circled them, murmuring praise.

"The stable, you say?" the marchioness cried. "She could have been trampled. Why, *you* could have been trampled, Lord Ballentine."

"It was a risk, but I persevered," he said modestly, eliciting a soft chorus of appreciative sighs.

Lady Hampshire sniffed. "I daresay, mayhem was to be expected over the course of this party, given the nature of our hostess," she muttered under her breath, shooting an indignant glance in the direction of the new duchess, who had kept a tactful distance during the reunion. "But the loss of a pet is going decidedly too far," her ladyship continued. "This is a highly delicate animal! Anything could have happened."

The moment Lady Hampshire took herself and her growling pet to her rooms to recuperate, the Duchess of Montgomery started toward him. He dipped his head to acknowledge her superior station with a wry smile. During their last encounter, she had been Annabelle Archer, a country bumpkin from Kent, and he had approached her, out of sheer ennui. She was also a remarkably beautiful woman: tall and radiant with a latent sensuality that was vigorously bred out of the ladies in his own class. . . .

An icy glare positively skewered him. When he looked up, his eyes locked with those of Montgomery, who stood at the very opposite end of the room. *Bother her and I shall kill you*, said that look, and so he dipped his head at His overly protective Grace, too.

The duchess assessed him with cautious appreciation. "Thank you for bringing the cat back, my lord."

"I did what anyone would do."

"She has reportedly mauled several footmen and a groom, but it appears you are uninjured?"

"Of course. I have a vested interest in keeping my looks as they are."

"Of course," she murmured. If she weren't a duchess now, she would have rolled her eyes.

Welcome to the world of petty constraints, Your Grace. Her stakes in this house party running smoothly had to be exceedingly high—and society matrons like Lady Hampshire could make or break a woman's standing.

"My lord," she said. "I shall have to impose on you once more, I'm afraid."

He obligingly inclined his head. "Impose on me, duchess."

Her gaze strayed to the group of ladies nearby, watching them from behind erratically fluttering fans. "Due to popular demand, I must ask whether you would read us one of your poems in the drawing room this evening."

A flicker of resistance licked through him. His days of writing pieces that held meaning, fueled by the now irretrievably lost Sturm und Drang of his youth, had cumulated in *A Pocketful of Poems* years ago. Selling the works was one matter, reciting them quite another—it reminded him of the florid fellows who held forth about their three-decade-old adventures in Crimea because they had not done anything worth mentioning since. But soirees and recitals had been inevitable the moment he had revealed himself as an author.

"If it pleases the hostess, I'm keen to oblige," he said.

This gained him a grateful nod. "The request is specifically for 'The Ballad of the Shieldmaiden.'"

"Naturally."

Just then, the duchess's gaze slid past him, and he sensed someone approaching.

"Lord Ballentine." The sweet voice made him go still.

He stood with his eyes fixed on the duchess.

The last time he had spoken to the young woman now hovering by his arm, she had been nothing but an acquaintance. She was considered a diamond of the first water, and he had to be the only man in the kingdom who'd rather not make conversation with her. But the moment had been inevitable. He plastered on a smile and lowered his gaze to meet the sky-blue eyes of his would-be fiancée.

Chapter 17

⁂

"Lady Cecily."

She was gazing up at him, long enough that he couldn't miss the admiration in her eyes, and then she shyly looked away. Then she peeped back at him from beneath lowered lashes.

She had grown into a lovely thing since he had last seen her, with a healthy glow on her cheeks and charming curves that would fill his big hands nicely. Her nose was sprinkled with pale golden freckles, which she had not taken the pain to bleach as was the custom. If she weren't a lamblike, gently bred virgin, and his intended at that, he could probably muster some interest. A lot of *ifs*, that.

"Lord Ballentine," came a reserved voice. Lucie's mother was flanking Cecily like a thin, cool counterpoint to her niece's golden sweetness.

"Lady Wycliffe. A pleasure to see you."

Her gaze snagged meaningfully on his cravat pin—a large lapis lazuli from Kabul. Rochester's list hadn't specified anything about cravat pins.

"You are the hero of the hour again, it appears," she said without inflection.

"I was in the right place at the right time."

"A useful habit every man should acquire," she remarked.

Impossible to tell from her expression whether she approved of her husband's ward being betrothed to him of all people. She had once been his mother's closest friend, but her fine-boned attractiveness was permanently marred by a vague, deep-seated antagonism she must have cultivated for decades. Not unlike her daughter, except that Lucie's antagonism was lovingly honed like an arrow and had a clear target.

"I'm so glad you saved the poor creature," Cecily said softly, "all the ladies here are."

He suspected she knew about their arrangement—there was something in her eyes that struck him as . . . conspiring. Grand. She shouldn't be in favor of a match that was never going to be. Had she not been a parentless ward but Wycliffe's daughter, he doubted the man would have offered her up as his bride. Wards, as a rule, were more easily passed on to a reprobate than an earl's direct blood.

"Come, Cecily," said Lady Wycliffe. "We are going to take another turn around the room. Lord Ballentine, you will surely be so kind to regale Cecily with the heroic tale at dinner. She is your table partner."

"Splendid," he said reflexively, his gaze shifting to the duchess, who quietly stood by. She was in charge of the seating order. Had she been informed about the whole betrothal business?

Did Lucie know? was the next logical question.

His body tightened with an acute sense of alarm.

Lucie must not know. She would never come near his bed if she thought he was going to marry her cousin.

As he searched the crowd for her icy-blond head, he spotted Lord Arthur's sulky visage near the Rembrandt on the east wall. Slouching next to the Marquess of Doncaster himself.

He felt Cecily's intrigue, though she was not really looking at him, and he excused himself to go and have Avi brush the cat hair off his jacket.

Two hours later, he found himself boxed in between Lady Wycliffe and Cecily, and Lucie was three tables away, neatly out of sight in the sea of heads between them.

Every one of those heads was slightly tilted to the head of the main table, where His Royal Highness Albert Edward, Prince of Wales and future king of England, was seated next to the duke as the guest of honor. The air of the vast dining room was quietly vibrating with hushed excitement as every interaction between Bertie and Montgomery was noted with Argus eyes.

Only Cecily was wholly uninterested in the prince. "It was such a surprise to read that you were behind *A Pocketful of Poems,*" she said, her big eyes seeking his.

"I imagine."

She looked like a polished doubloon in a white and gold evening gown, occasionally making a dainty pick at the piece of venison on her plate. Her aunt was unnaturally distracted by her own table partner. Giving the love birds some time to engage in conversation, wasn't she?

"I don't remember ever seeing you write anything during those summers at Wycliffe Hall," Cecily prodded gently.

Had she noticed him at all, then? She had still been a girl during the last holiday he had spent at Wycliffe's, no older than twelve, all gangly legs and braids.

"Writers often work at night," he said absently.

He had gleaned that Lucie was seated between the Greenfield heir, Zachary, and Lord Melvin, an outsider in the House of Lords thanks to his overt support of women's suffrage. Melvin was Lucie's age and still unattached. They were probably going to flirt outrageously under the pretense of a policy debate or some such. A twinge in his right hand drew his attention to the fact that he was gripping his fork as though he meant to strangle it.

Vaguely appalled by his unnatural preoccupation, he relaxed his grip and forced his gaze back onto Cecily.

"And what do you enjoy doing for a pastime nowadays, Ceci?"

She blushed at being addressed with her old pet name. She sipped her wine and cast him a coy glance over the rim of her glass. "I'm afraid you shall think me forward if I tell you."

Darling, there is nothing you could do in your lifetime that I would consider forward, he wanted to say. He gave her a smile that came out wolfish. "Try me."

She leaned a little closer. "I do like to try my hand at poetry, too."

He tutted with mock horror. "I declare I am shocked."

She giggled, very prettily.

"Will you present some of it tonight during the recital?" he asked.

Her eyes widened. "Oh, oh no. Perhaps one day. I'd choose the piece I thought of when you entered the reception room with Lady Hampshire's cat in your arms."

"You don't say."

"Yes. It is about a cat, you see—a kitten, to be precise." She had leaned in closer still, wrapping him in the warm scent of her rose perfume. There was no way around it. She very much wanted to recite her poem to him.

"A kitten," he said. "Would you do me the honor and recite it to me?"

"Oh, I couldn't," she protested duly.

"You don't know it by heart?"

"I do, it is not long."

"A short poem—that is rare. I'm afraid I must hear it now."

"But I could not, not here at the table."

He shook his head. "You are not half as forward as you led me to believe, are you? How disappointing."

She bit her bottom lip. "I suppose I must, since you insist," she said, the color in her cheeks high. She lowered her soft voice to a murmur and began:

"Hark! Who hears the kitten's cry,
So sweet, so soft, so yearning?
She's lonely in the black of night,
And those shadows, so concerning!

Her siblings gone, the bed so cold
Where is master, to whom she's sold?
Oh, it's such a cruel fate,
To mew and shiver, fear and wait.

But! Here comes young master, after her demand,
His caress doth fear destroy,
Cupped gently in her master's hand,
The kitty purrs again with joy."

His gaze was riveted on her upturned face. Her expression was perfectly guileless. Mildly expectant.

His eyes narrowed slightly. "Is this a figurative or a literal poem?"

Cecily gave a slow blink. "I'm afraid I don't follow?"

"It is about an actual cat, then, whiskers and all."

"Well, of course. I adore kittens. I shall happily leave the crafting of metaphorical meanings to the gentlemen. Although I do remember you being fond of my aunt's cats at Wycliffe Hall, so perhaps you don't consider them entirely unworthy of a stanza or two."

"They are worthy." One wily feline in particular, he thought darkly.

Ceci's eyes brightened; she was taking his agreement as a compliment. Etiquette, and the proverbial noose around his neck, demanded he give her a real compliment on her accidentally salacious monstrosity of a poem. A non-cynical, non-rakish one. Briefly, he was at a loss.

"It has a good rhythm, your poem," he finally said.

She looked cautiously delighted. "And is the rhythm important?"

"Some would say the rhythm is everything."

She tilted her head. "And what would you say?"

That you play a good game of seduce-the-male for a purportedly shy and lovely lamb. Men made of less depraved stuff than him would be feeling tall and wide like Hercules by now, under her ever admiring, maidenly blue gaze.

He looked into her eyes and leaned closer. "I have always supported the idea that it hardly matters what you say, but it matters very much how you say it. So yes, much is to be said for a good, steady rhythm to provide a satisfying experience."

"Ooh," she breathed. A hectic flush spread over her face.

He decided she sensed that he was being lewd but failed to understand the specifics.

He picked up his glass, and, drinking, he studied her angelic features and imagined a life where she was his wife. She'd expect regular husbandly things from him: pretty children, being kept in the fashion to which she was accustomed, compliments. She wasn't delicate, but she looked malleable as butter and was trained to please her husband. She would be more complex than that, secretly, but he'd never really know her thoughts if he did not care to hear them—she would accept it if he pursued his own endeavors elsewhere. It would be conventional, life with Cecily. He would become horrifically bored after a week and make her unhappy. It wasn't her fault. He was not suited to care for helpless creatures, or even the self-sustaining ones. Even had she been his perfect foil, the fact that Rochester had chosen her made her the last person he'd consider for the position of his wife.

Cecily squirmed in her seat, and he realized he had been staring at her intently.

He emptied his wineglass. The time for Scotch could not come soon enough.

The ducal banquet was surprisingly good. Claremont's kitchen served a unique blend of French and rustic cuisine and Lucie hadn't indulged in such fine food in years: perfectly round, golden pies; choice pieces of tender game and fish; well-seasoned sauces; and a bouquet of colorful vegetables. It was enough of a delight to distract her from what had almost transpired on Montgomery's stable floor a few hours ago . . . No. No, she would not think of the stable floor—again. Or of the feel of soft hair between her bare fingers or the solid male body against her own.

She stabbed her fork into the pie on her plate. The crust broke with a crunch and a warm, savory fragrance wafted up. Her eyes drifted shut, and the chatter around her faded. When had she forgotten how much she loved to eat?

She took a big, impolite bite. Heaven. Her housekeeper was a marvel, but she wasn't a cook; but then, she ate mindlessly half the time anyway, her thoughts circling the desk in the drawing room like eager vultures while her body was sitting at the kitchen table.

"The cooks have outdone themselves," she said to Lord Melvin when she realized that she had been enjoying her pie in greedy silence, leaving her table partner in a lurch.

Melvin had to gulp down his food. "It's certainly lengths better than the new refreshment service at Westminster," he said, dabbing at his lips with the napkin. "I wish they would reopen Bellamy's; the veal was ghastly the other day."

Lucie gave him a sardonic smile. "I would not know."

Bellamy's, the canteen of Westminster, hadn't admitted women activists while in operation, and she was not entitled to join the male politicians for the in-house refreshments.

Melvin gave an amused shake. "Well, you do seem to be everywhere; it is hard to imagine there are still places in Westminster Palace where Lady Lucinda should not unexpectedly pop up."

Her brows rose. "Why, it almost sounds as though I were haunting the place, Lord Melvin."

"Enough people would say so," he said with equanimity.

This was not going according to plan—her notoriety should not be part of any conversation here at Claremont.

Melvin's dark intelligent eyes turned speculative. With his beakish nose, it made him look like a magpie contemplating a heist. "Would you do it," he asked, "take up a seat in Parliament and endure the luncheon food?"

"Of course," she said without hesitation. "And I will. One day."

Melvin nodded. "You must work harder on Gladstone, then."

She frowned at the unsubtle prod. During his recent election campaign, Prime Minister Gladstone had paid enough lip service to the women's rights movement to raise even her hopes. The suffragist chapters across Britain had thrown whatever support they could muster behind him, had marched and petitioned for him and submitted their policy demands to him in good faith, but during his now three months in office, he hadn't said a word on the Cause. Business in Westminster coasted along as usual, on the back of empty promises. Soon they would have to harass him, and he would tell them to be patient and wait, as every administration had done before him.

She put down her fork and picked up her wineglass. The Sauvignon was lovely and crisp. It still left a sour aftertaste in her mouth.

"Until I have found a way to actually be everywhere at once, I'm presently not in a position to increase my activities on the Gladstone front," she said.

"Consider delegating tasks rather than thinking of yourself as irreplaceable," Melvin said. "Delegating is an art form."

"Such brilliant advice," she said blandly. "It had not occurred to me."

He nodded, politely or obliviously. "You see, the curious thing about causes is that they usually continue well without you. The question is whether you can continue well without the cause. Now, have you read Montgomery's amendment proposal yet?" He chuckled. "But of course you have. What is your opinion?"

Montgomery was currently saying something that had the Prince of Wales nodding and chuckling.

"There were no objections to either wording or content from Millicent Fawcett, nor our legal advisors," Lucie said. "I do have a few objections."

"Naturally."

She shrugged. "But if they were addressed, the amendment would not get past our usual suspects in the House of Lords. The current proposal stands a chance. We could build on it in a next round of amendments."

"Montgomery knows how to draft his policies," Melvin said. "He makes them as slick as an oiled eel and before you know it, they have slipped through your grip and passed."

"Indeed." She eyed her plate. The vegetables were wilting. And the image of an oiled eel pressing on her mind rather tempered her appetite.

Melvin's eyes were still on the head of the main table, ever a politician, drawn to power like a moth to the flame. "It's the influence of the duchess," he said, his voice low, "Montgomery's new policies."

For a moment, they both sat and watched discreetly how Annabelle was making an interested face at some tale the Prince of Wales was telling. The heir to the throne became animated, his right hand threatening to knock over his wineglass as he gestured without taking his eyes off the duchess. And everyone else in the vast hall was seeing it, too. Lucie felt a swell of satisfaction. Cat incident or not, no one could dismiss the approval of the prince, and he was presently stamping it all over Annabelle.

"Astonishing, isn't it. I can see why my fellow men would object to giving the fair sex more power," murmured Lord Melvin.

Lucie slowly turned in her chair to face him. "Whatever do you mean, my lord?"

He kept his eyes on the prince. "Her Grace used to be a country woman, wasn't she?"

Her defenses were rising on Annabelle's behalf. "She was, yes."

He nodded. "And yet here she is, influencing a duke and charming the future king. Most men only obtain such a position through birthright, then tireless politicking. Naturally, people wonder why women should need political powers when they already hold so much power simply by being women."

Her smile was bemused. "I assume you are playing devil's advocate, Lord Melvin."

"Assume that I am—how would you declaw someone who argued this?"

"I'd suggest he study the definition of *liberty* under *L* in the *Oxford Dictionary*."

Melvin raised his brows, as though she were an ill-mannered pupil.

"Truly," she said. "How many of your hypothetical fellow's female acquaintances equal the duchess in all her beauty, youth, and wit?"

His brows came down. "A gentleman has nothing but compliments for the appearance and accomplishments of any lady of his acquaintance."

"Of course," Lucie said evenly. "And niceties aside, Her Grace possesses a rare combination of attributes that would drive most men to distraction. But is a gentleman's influence and dignity contingent upon something as fleeting as his natural charms? Must he be outstanding to count? No. He officially has a voice simply because he is a man."

The corner of Lord Melvin's mouth tipped up. "Unless he has no property. Then his voice counts for little."

She had a feeling that he quite liked the devil's advocate position. "A man's lack of voice is connected to his lack of property," she murmured. "A woman's lack of voice is forever connected to the fact that she is a woman."

"Indeed." Approval glinted in Melvin's eyes, and he raised his glass to her. "I'm well pleased with tonight's seating order. Always a pleasure to converse with someone who hasn't yet lost their passion. Too many treat politics as a self-referencing play these days."

She could see herself in his dark iris, the complicated coronet of blond hair and silk flowers atop her head an unfamiliar sight. Belatedly, she gave a nod.

Lord Melvin was intelligent. He was on her side. Parliament heralded him as the next John Stuart Mill, and she respected and admired him for his work, when she rarely admired much of anything.

Could joy be had from him? Would he make her feel molten and mindless, as she had today when staring into the mocking eyes of a man who had very little to recommend him?

She looked away and looked back at him again. Faint lines bracketed his mouth. She suspected that while he was passionate in his speeches, in private he would display the stiff upper lip of any self-respecting aristocratic male. Likely, he was *starchy*.

Lord Melvin's expression turned bemused under her inspection.

She reached for her wineglass.

A lady should never be seen indulging in food and wine, and it would be best if she did not take enjoyment from it at all—pace your bites, Lucinda; you are a lady, not a horse.

The past was nipping at her heels, here in the ducal dining room amid glinting crystal and silver terrines. Another version of herself could be attending this very same event tonight, could be sitting in the same seat: a respected lady, a mother of children, married to someone like Lord Melvin. Not necessarily content; if it was not the state of women's rights in Britain one took issue with, one could be discontent about the curtains, or a lousy season, or a tyrannical husband. All that separated her from that woman had been a few books and pamphlets, read at the right time . . . or had the diversion begun sooner? Had there always been something in her disposition that had gradually edged her off the beaten path?

She brushed the musings aside. However she had reached this point, the only way now was forward.

Lord Melvin made himself her escort to the green drawing room, but his attention was on other members of the House of Lords drifting alongside them through the Great Hall.

Ahead of her in the throng was Tristan. And on his arm was Cecily. Her face was in profile, her eyes riveted on her escort as though he had just hung the moon and the stars for her. A memory flashed, of Cecily the girl running after a lankier version of Tristan, her blond braids and the strings of her white pinafore flying behind her. Now her cousin was gliding along on Tristan's arm with the poise of a swan on a pond, the train of her snowy dress languidly trailing behind, and the sight grated. Why was her mother nowhere in sight to keep an eye on Cecily's reputation? At least there was Tommy—Thomas—a few steps behind the pair, his back stiff with displeasure.

"Lady Lucinda?" Melvin was looking down at her quizzically.

"I beg your pardon?"

"Are you looking forward to the evening program?" he repeated patiently.

"Certainly."

"I heard Lord Ballentine will gift us with a poem."

"Riveting," she said dryly.

"You do not sound charmed," Melvin observed.

"Oh, I am charmed," she said quickly. "Excessively charmed."

The evening would be a terrible bore.

Thankfully, Hattie and Catriona were waiting for her at the entrance to the menagerie. The cavernous green-walled room had been rearranged to accommodate a semicircle of four hundred gilded chairs with thick red velvet upholstery. At the center of the circle gleamed a black lacquered Steinway.

She followed Hattie down one of the two aisles that allowed guests access to their seats. Close on her heels was Lord Melvin, when there was really no good reason for him to keep escorting her.

The crown prince sat next to Montgomery in the first row opposite, in a special chair that blocked the view of anyone unfortunate enough to be seated behind him.

Hattie was craning her neck around the room the moment she had arranged her skirts on the chair. "Have you heard?" she murmured. "Lord Ballentine is going to recite a poem."

"I heard."

"I hope it is going to be 'The Ballad of the Shieldmaiden,'" Hattie said, her eyes still searching.

"He is seated right opposite, second row to the left."

"I wasn't looking for him," Hattie lied.

There would be no escape. This would be the sole topic of conversation among the ladies once the men had retreated to the smoking rooms: Ballentine and his poems.

And all the while, his prank in the stables continued to smart, like the prolonged sting of a burn. To add insult to injury, he had apparently become society's darling the moment he had returned the bloody cat, which she had, quite literally, dropped into his lap.

"That is your cousin, next to him, isn't it?" Hattie murmured, watching Cecily.

"The very same."

"Very pretty," Hattie said, "a Botticelli. The angel kind, not the Venus."

"I suppose," Lucie said. She didn't have an artistic bone in her body. She did, however, notice the look of rapture on her brother's face while he was watching Cecily, while she was making conversation with Tristan. Interesting.

The program opened with the rapid tune of Mozart's *Alla turca*; a young lady had taken her place at the Steinway and let her fingers fly over the keys.

Inevitably, her mind wandered back to the incident in the stable. She would feel less preoccupied had Tristan just been his usual self during the past week. But he had helped her in the park, and she had received a mysterious donation from the fencing club. It must have raised her expectations of him despite herself. At the very least, it had made her *wonder* about him, and now she knew how good his hair felt, and she would not be able to unfeel it.

The piano piece ended in a sound round of applause. The crown prince gave a start; he looked around, blinking, and belatedly joined the clapping crowd. Three further, forgettable piano performances followed.

And then Tristan strolled to the center of the room to a chorus of aaahs and ooohs.

Next to her, Hattie released a suspiciously yearning sigh.

Lucie's head turned to her a little too sharply.

Hattie shrank away, embarrassed color flooding her cheeks. "I know, I know," she whispered, "and I'm awfully sorry. I can't help it. He's so . . ."

". . . obnoxious?" Her voice was a hiss.

"Beautiful," Hattie said, and gave a helpless shrug. "He's beautiful. His jawline, just look at it."

She looked at it as he assumed his stance next to the piano and gave a bow.

". . . Yes?"

"It has a perfect right angle. Do you know how rare that is? The whole composition of him—I *must* have him sit for my series of archangels."

Lucie pursed her lips. "Can't you just draw it on?"

Hattie looked puzzled. "What do you mean?"

"The jawline. Can you not just draw one with a right angle?"

Hattie was genuinely aghast. "That is not how it works, Lucie."

"Hush," someone said.

Faces turned toward them, none of them friendly. She could feel Lord Melvin's probing gaze on her.

"Your Royal Highness, ladies, my noble friends," Tristan began when silence was restored. "Allow me to take you along on the journey of . . ." He paused, and the room held its breath. ". . . the Shield-maiden."

The room swooned.

"This is a good one," Hattie breathed. "So much like Tennyson."

Lucie folded her arms over her chest, and Tristan stepped forward.

> *On either side the forest lie*
> *Cold blue lakes which hold the sky;*
> *Where she goes to see the eagle fly;*
> *The shield-maid of a time gone by*
> *A princess with no people . . .*

How vexing. Five lines was all it took and there was no doubt: he could write. And recite.

And she had to sit still and witness how his baritone changed effortlessly from velvet to silk, from light to dark, until the meaning of his words was of no consequence and the poem became a melody. Eyes glazed over, breaths were held; four hundred people, entranced.

Apparently, he too knew that words could be used as weapons, and he wielded them with formidable effect.

When he eventually fell silent, there was a pause before everyone stirred as if released from a spell.

The Prince of Wales came to his feet, clapping. "Bravo," he cried. "Bravo."

The rest of the audience scrambled to follow His Royal Highness, sending chairs scraping across the floor as they rose and rattled the chandeliers with the thunder of their applause.

Amid the commotion, Lucie slipped away.

Tristan bowed again, using the brief moment to assume a neutral expression. Very well. A standing ovation from the prince annulled a multitude of sins on the spot.

His performance must have concluded the first half of the evening program, because groups of women began encroaching upon him, enveloping him in clouds of ambergris and excited titters. Cecily hovered among them, regarding him with an ardent expression that would have struck him as rather possessive, had he not become distracted.

"Lord Ballentine."

The prince approached, his right-hand man Lord Manchester at his heels, parting the flood of admirers like the Red Sea before him.

Tristan clicked his heels together, just sharply enough to transform a mock salute into a real one.

"At ease, Ballentine, at ease," Bertie said jovially. "Once a lieutenant, always a lieutenant, eh? Good man. And such a way with words. Why are you not at court more often?"

Because your mama would not be amused. In fact, he was the last person Queen Victoria would want near her heir, whom she considered to be a lothario and crushing moral disappointment in his own right.

"I'm afraid I'm occupied with editing my diaries from my latest tour in Afghanistan, Your Highness," he offered. "I hope to publish them in a few months' time."

"War diaries—from this man's pen. What do you say to that, Manchester," said the prince, prompting Manchester to declare that it was a splendid idea, that it would undoubtedly make for a splendid read.

The prince nodded, his eyes still on Tristan. "Splendid, splendid. Dedicate these diaries to me, won't you?"

"It would be an honor, Your Highness."

The prince's voice had been loud enough to reach any bystanders in a ten-foot radius. By tomorrow, everyone of importance would know that the heir to the throne was the patron of his latest work, and they could triple the figure currently planned for the print edition.

His official mission of bolstering his reputation was done.

As for his unofficial mission . . .

A glass door led from the green drawing room onto the spacious terrace. Lucie had slipped away through it, largely unnoticed during the mayhem of four hundred guests coming to their feet.

He bowed to the prince.

He strode toward the door, past a narrow-eyed Lord Arthur Seymour, whom he ignored as if he didn't exist, away from Cecily, away from the armada of longingly batting fans and lashes.

Chapter 18

After descending the terrace stairs down to the French Garden, she had, on impulse, taken a left on the gravel path. Against the weathered terrace wall, next to a granite lion, stood a granite bench.

She sank down on the hard surface and took a deep breath. She probingly rubbed her bare upper arms. The evening air was still tepid enough for her not to catch a cold; besides, three glasses of wine were warming her from the inside out.

Beyond the symmetrical rectangle of the French Garden stretching before her, hills rolled into the distance. On one such hill stood a folly, strategically placed to please the eye from the terrace, and behind the folly, the clouds were afire with the last of the sun's rays. The wistful song of a blackbird floated from one of the neatly trimmed hedges. The simple tune gradually edged out the echo of the Shieldmaiden.

She was not left in peace for long.

Footfalls approached, of a man with a long, leisurely stride, and sure enough, a tall, familiar figure appeared on the path.

Her palms turned damp. "Stop following me, Ballentine."

"Don't flatter yourself. I came outside for a smoke."

He made himself comfortable next to her on the bench, sprawling uninvited, and pulled a silver cigarette case from the inside of his jacket. "Do you care for one?"

The case appeared under her nose, presenting a row of cigarettes lying neatly side by side like peas in a pod.

Trust him to offer a lady a smoke. Or to smoke in the presence of a lady. Clearly, he did not consider her a lady.

She turned away. "You were in the park. You were in the stables. I don't believe in such coincidences—you are following me."

He closed the cigarette case with a snap. "If you truly prefer to grapple with five men at once or to fall off a ladder the whole way down, I shall desist."

She ground her teeth, and they sat in silence, him smoking, her struggling with why she was not taking her leave.

Because it was not simple anymore. Equal and opposing forces, or perhaps the wine, were holding her in place, right in the spot between the granite lion and him.

"What did you think?" he asked, his eyes on the horizon.

"Of the poem?"

He nodded.

That, too, was complicated.

"It was good," she said grudgingly.

Even if her expectations had not been low, she would have been amazed. She had tried to escape these tumultuous emotions by taking some fresh air.

"You do hold poetry in an atrociously low regard," he said, a hint of amusement in his voice. "Or is it just *my* poetry?"

"Don't flatter yourself," she said without heat. "I do not loathe it."

"But?"

She sighed. "I don't appreciate the elevated station it enjoys, considering it is largely hot air."

"Is it?" He was watching her rather intently from the corner of his eye.

"Of course. The great Romantics were dreadful husbands and lovers."

To her surprise, he turned to her, his expression intrigued. "I am all ears," he said.

"I'm certain you know all about it."

"It would please me to hear it from you."

Why, she wondered, and why should she do something to please him?

"Very well," she said. "Take Shelley—there were rumors his first wife drowned herself in the Serpentine while expecting, because he had abandoned her yet again to be with his mistress."

He winced. "That is true."

"As for Coleridge, he made no secret of the fact that he detested his wife, and he gave himself up to opium. Byron is the most loathsome of them all—his lover never saw her daughter again after he snatched the girl and put her into a convent." Her hand gave a small flick of contempt. "'She walks in beauty like the night,' he says, but he takes her child, then abandons the girl, and the child dies soon after. His grand words do not exude much charm when one knows such things."

Tristan's expression was unreadable, and he was silent.

She put up her chin, inviting his rebuttal.

He just nodded and resumed watching the sun set again, exhaling smoke.

She shifted on the bench. "Well?"

"Well," he drawled. "It poses an interesting problem."

"Oh," she said, and then: "Which problem?"

He glanced at her, then, a cynical edge to his lips. "By your logic, only a flawless paragon of a man is entitled to create things of beauty," he said. He smiled widely enough to show teeth. "There goes poetry, then. How about music? The composers were by and large insufferable."

And, when she was silent, he continued: "We would also have considerably fewer paintings. The adorable Pre-Raphaelites, with all the titian hair and knights and maidens? Millais stole Ruskin's wife from right under his nose to make her his own—rude, I admit, but will you not look at his Ophelia again?"

"Your feathers are ruffled," she said, astonished.

He stilled. "Ruffled feathers," he repeated, his eyes narrowing. "God. You will tell me not to worry my silly little head next, won't you."

"Would it help?"

His head tipped back on a surprised bark of laughter. "Not at all."

She gave a shrug. "Naturally. It never helps us to hear it, either."

"Duly noted," he said, grinning still.

Strange. She had never seen him laugh before. He'd mastered every variant of a seductive smile, but he never laughed. A good thing, perhaps, because his cheeks dimpled very charmingly when he did, and he had enviably attractive teeth.

Behind the folly, the last pink-hued clouds were usurped by midnight blue.

It wasn't wise to sit with him alone in the dusk, warmed by wine, drawing the cigarette smoke leaving his lungs into her own. They were on their way to a civil, if not intimate, conversation, and she should truncate it now.

"I do not demand a paragon, nor perfection," she said instead. "I just want the truth."

She felt him sober then, and when she glanced at him, she saw that the mirth was fading from his eyes.

"Just," he repeated. "Just the truth."

"Honesty, truth. Authenticity. However you wish to call it."

"That is, in fact, a lot to ask."

She gave a shrug. "But is anything worth having without it?"

"Little puritan," he muttered. "You truly are a fervent idealist."

Her brows rose in surprise. "I don't think I have ever been called such."

"An idealist?"

"Yes. They usually call me a terrible cynic."

Why she would tell him this, she did not know. She knew his words about the paragons had made her think, and she was intrigued that he would have this effect on her.

"It's quite the same," Tristan said. "Idealism, cynicism. Two sides of the same coin."

"And the coin, what would it be?"

He waved his hand with the cigarette. "A yearning to control our fickle destinies." His tone was faintly dramatic. "The cynic is but an idealist who preempts the shock of disappointment by deriding everything himself. Both have expectations that are rather too lofty. And you should consider reading Tennyson, if you haven't already. I have a feeling both the subject matter of his poems and his moral character would pass your scrutiny."

Her stomach fluttered with unease. Recommending books to her now, was he, as a friend would.

The air warmed around her, or perhaps it was the heat of his body, because the distance between them had melted. She could smell him, the note of his shaving soap more prominent tonight.

She slid back an inch or two. He refrained from following, he was too clever for that. But a knowing smile played over his lips, and it made her bristle.

"You made the fencing club donate a handsome sum to the suffrage cause," she said.

He looked unsurprised but took his time to blow a smoke ring before saying: "I did?"

"Yes," she said, impatience creeping into her tone. "How?"

His smile was vague. "I'd rather not disclose it. You would condemn me bitterly, little puritan."

"At least tell me why?"

He raised his brows. "Who knows. Perhaps I am trying to get into your good graces, so you will give in to your attraction at last and come to me."

His resonant voice had gone deeper and scratchy on the edges when he said *come to me*, and it sent a hot jolt of emotions from her middle down into her toes. For a beat, she was back in the stables, on top of him, possessed by the dark need to feel his mouth on hers.

She shifted uneasily. She had let things go too far tonight, here on this bench. She could not trust him; worse, she could not trust herself around him. Tristan would never reliably act the gentleman and save her from her own audacity. He would go along as far as her curiosity, no, her *weakness*, would take them, and provoke her to go further still.

She came to her feet. Her legs were stiff. The cold of the granite had seeped through her thin skirts into her skin unnoticed.

"For a reputed gambler, you show your hand rather carelessly," she said coolly.

He laughed softly. "Hiding in plain sight can be quite effective in certain cases. Why don't you try it yourself, sometime."

She looked down her nose at him. "Hiding in plain sight?"

"No. Seduction."

She scoffed. "From what I observe, being female and breathing is enough to provoke interest in most men."

"Not men," he said derisively. "A low standard by anyone's imagination. No, try society. That ignorant, fickle, illiberal monolith."

She found his eyes unfathomable and wondered how much he knew of her current attempts to become more likable. Wondered whether all this was part of his seduction of her, too.

He gave her a placating smile, as if sensing the turn her mind had taken. "Society is dumber but stronger than you," he murmured. "Be devious. Be subtle. If you can."

She left him as quickly as her narrow skirts allowed, feeling the weight of his gaze between her bare shoulder blades. Her pulse was running high. She had long assumed Tristan was careless and grew bored easily because his mind was lazy. She had been wrong. He grew bored easily because his mind was working entirely too fast.

She found she was not inclined to mingle with guests and chatter about inconsequential things when she reentered the green salon, and so she took to her room.

Give in to your attraction and come to me.

His words were pure provocation, but his baritone kept resonating, kept heating her from the inside out. Words mattered. She knew this. The manner with which they were said mattered, too. This, she might have underestimated.

She pulled a handful of copies of the *Discerning Ladies' Magazine* from her carpet bag and spread them out on the small cherrywood desk, next to a stack of copies of *The Female Citizen*, which she had not yet had time to read.

She soon transferred the periodicals onto the rug in the middle of the room, each issue open at the beginning of a different section.

The structure of the content was the same in each issue: first the reports on major society events—balls, weddings, exhibitions—then the prints of fashion plates and advice on good manners, then the recipes. Miscellaneous household management advice filled the largest section. The final page featured a piece of sugary fiction. In between, elaborate advertisements for corsets, potions, dressmakers.

A story of sorts on each page, each in their own way trying to appeal. All of them trying to regulate, stating rules on how to do things right. Bewildering. If it was truly in woman's nature to be an ever demure and pleasant sunbeam in the gloom, why then, it took an awful lot of ink and instructions to keep reminding woman of this nature of hers. . . .

Be devious. Be subtle.

She was in no mood to go and search for Hattie and Catriona in this cavernous house, and Annabelle would be occupied past midnight with hosting duties. With the help of obliging footmen, she had a note delivered to each of her friends' rooms, requesting a meeting in her chambers before breakfast come morning. Upon second thoughts, she wrote a fourth note and sent it to Lady Salisbury.

Chapter 19

⸺◈⸺

I may have an idea how to use the magazines," she said when everyone had gathered round the rug on her chamber floor.

Her friends looked up from the chaos she had created last night, eyeing her with varying degrees of intrigue.

"I'm all ears," Lady Salisbury said. She was comfortably settled in the wing chair in a pool of morning sun, her cane leaning against the armrest.

"It is not a coup anymore," Lucie conceded. "But rather, a gradual undermining." She picked up a copy of the *Discerning Ladies' Magazine*. "These periodicals tell women everywhere, every week, how best to dress, cook, act, and what happens in society. These could be powerful vehicles, Trojan horses, if you will, as long as we ensure that every section relegates a suffragist message—but in a subtle manner."

Blatant astonishment filled the room. Possibly because she had used the word *subtle*.

"See here," she said impatiently. "It is hardly a new idea to use periodicals to inform women readers about politics. There was the *English Woman's Journal*, and the *Female's Friend*, for a start. However, these magazines all perished after just a couple of years in circulation. The readership was too small; even if all women miraculously agreed with the Cause, budgets are still tight, and much as it pains me, few can afford to choose critical essays over advice on how to run an efficient household. I therefore suggest we make it convenient and feasible for women to have both: household and fashion advice, and gentle reminders that we are, in effect, chattel. In one periodical."

Her suggestion was met with silence.

"You look like Lucie," Hattie said, her eyes suspicious slits. "But you do not sound like her."

Lucie gave her a speaking glance. "I'm not incapable of changing tactics."

"I do like the sound of it," Annabelle said. "But what precisely is the plan? We cannot just abandon our report."

"No," she said quickly, resentment hollowing her stomach at the very thought. "No. We will publish our report. Each of us must try and look for a solution, preferably before the vote on the amendment in autumn. In the meantime, we must put these periodicals to a good use. For example, I should like to add a new section. We print the less harrowing letters, altered and shortened, from the pool of letters we have collected, and we shall have them answered on the page by a lady of good standing." Her gaze landed on Lady Salisbury. "It would resemble a dialogue rather than a lecture or provocation. It would still bring delicate matters into respectable drawing rooms."

Catriona was nodding along, which was a good sign because she was usually the first to see a problem. "I like it," she said. "This format already exists in science journals: readers send in questions and the answers are printed for everyone to see." She hesitated. "It's on matters of science only, of course, not of a private nature."

"But women's matters are of a private nature," Annabelle said. "It is why we feel alone with them."

"I like the idea, too," Hattie said. "It reminds me of the question-and-answer section in my subscription periodical for girls, which is very popular."

"What questions do they print?"

"Oh, nothing political. Queries regarding recommendations on novels; experiences with dieting pills; how to pronounce certain words and the meaning of foreign-language terms. . . ."

"Dieting pills," Lucie said. "Rather sinister, if you ask me."

Lady Salisbury cleared her throat. "Have I understood you correctly—you suggest I counsel women in a magazine column with camouflaged suffrage messages?"

"Not just a column—at least two pages. And we can write the answers if you don't wish to ponder them—but we do require a well-respected name on those pages."

Hattie rubbed her hands. "It's cunning."

"The idea has merit," Lady Salisbury agreed. "I shall give it due consideration."

"We could undermine the fashion section, too," Hattie suggested, her cheeks flushing with excitement. "There's the new Rational Dress Society and I think quite a few ladies would be open to new, more accommodating designs."

Lucie gave her an appreciative nod. "That is exactly the sort of thing I had in mind."

"How about the story on the last page," Catriona said. "We could feature only heroines who aspire to be free and equal."

"Or the ones who are terribly wronged by society," Hattie said, "so the reader wants to begin a revolution on her behalf!"

A smile tugged at Lucie's mouth. For the first time since Tristan had invaded London Print, she was excited at the prospect of having a publishing house at her disposal, half of it anyway.

"Presently, we just have to all agree on the new direction," she said. "Pandemonium by stealth."

"It is an excellent direction," Annabelle said.

"Hear, hear," said Lady Salisbury.

"But how shall we get these reformed periodicals past Lord Ballentine?" Catriona asked. "Nothing would stop him from vetoing these changes, either."

"I'm quite put out," Lady Salisbury said indignantly. "Lord Ballentine is a resplendent specimen of a man, but how very rude of him to ruin our plans at the very last minute."

"Indeed," Lucie said darkly. "Leave him to me. If he hinders us purely out of spite, when our changes might well prove popular with readers, I shall just have to spite him back."

"That sounds awfully juvenile," Lady Salisbury remarked.

"Oh, it is," Lucie said. Then she groaned and buried her face in her hands. "It will take years before our manipulations show any effect—how am I going to stand the wait?"

"By keeping your eyes on our victory," came Annabelle's voice.

"A long queue of women on Parliament Square, ready to cast their first vote," Catriona added.

"Lady Lucinda, first female member of the House of Lords," Hattie said. "I'm demanding the exclusive right to paint your portrait for Westminster."

Lucie looked up. "I'll try not to be insufferable until we launch the revised issue."

"We shall hold you accountable," Hattie assured her. "You are doing very well so far." Turning to Lady Salisbury, she added: "Lady Lucinda is in the process of improving her reputation."

Lady Salisbury's brows rose high. "Ah. I have noted that you look very fashionable." She appraised Lucie's mauve walking dress with a sweeping glance.

"It is not just my wardrobe," Lucie said. "Reacquainting myself with certain factions of society is next on our list." She glanced at the ornate clock on the mantelpiece. "I should not miss the main breakfast time."

Lady Salisbury tutted. "Why did you not tell me that you were ready for such a thing?" She reached for her cane and heaved herself to her feet. "Come. I shall make introductions for you."

Lady Salisbury's idea of making introductions was to herd them out onto the sunlit lawn of Claremont's English Garden after breakfast. Gauzy white canopies and wicker chair arrangements invited meandering guests to gather and chat and have a cup of tea al fresco. A croquet game had been set up in the middle distance near a copse of trees, and the players' squeals of amusement reached their small group with the breeze.

Lady Salisbury walked ahead with Catriona, who was a lady herself, while banker's daughter Hattie and black sheep Lucie were to inconspicuously trail behind at a small distance. And then the countess surprised Lucie by approaching Lady Wycliffe of all people, who, with Cecily in tow, was making conversation with two elderly matrons. Lucie and Hattie were half past the small group when Lady Salisbury's head whipped round.

"Ah, Lady Lucinda," she exclaimed, as if surprised to see her. "Why, what a lovely dress, what an unusual color. Come closer, let my old eyes see."

Right. Lady Salisbury was taking a great gamble, sticking her nose into the politics of an estranged family. Of course, it would work very much in her favor if she *were* to be seen conversing with her mother. . . . The countess closely admired perfectly regular shades of mauve. "Isn't it lovely?" she asked with such enthusiasm that Lady Wycliffe was compelled to feign a double take at the dress and admit that yes, it was lovely indeed.

A polite exchange on fashion ensued among the older women, when from the corner of her eye, Lucie saw Lady Hampshire approach, gesticulating and in deep conversation with a white-haired, bearded gentleman.

The marchioness's eyes promptly lit on Lucie's mother. "Lady Wycliffe," she exclaimed. "I have been looking for you—we were just discussing Professor Marlow's latest research on hysteria."

"I say," her mother said faintly. "How intriguing."

"Very much so," Lady Hampshire said. "Professor Marlow shall head the Royal Society in no time, mark me." The ladies shuffled backward as she determinedly maneuvered the man into their circle. "The duke extended an invitation to the professor upon my personal request, and I declare there is something greatly philosophical about a man who places knowledge above etiquette when required. Now, do you recall the article I am drafting on the unruly wombs of spinsters—"

Professor Marlow cleared his throat, his expression grave. "Considering the presence of innocent ears, may I suggest we close this delicate subject for the time being?"

Lady Hampshire stiffened, then assessed Cecily and Hattie with a dour glance.

"We were just sharing stories about cats," Lady Salisbury said cheerfully, when there had been no such sharing. But Lady Hampshire's imperious visage brightened at once. "Well, you would," she said. "Like myself, Lady Wycliffe is an expert on the subject and one of the few with foresight on the matter of housecats. When the rest of society still considered these elegant creatures lowly mousers, we remembered how the ancient Egyptians revered them as gods, did we not?"

"Indeed we did," Lucie's mother said.

Lucie vaguely remembered her mother's cats: pampered, ill-tempered beasts that had roamed freely in her chambers and that had been transported to obscure cat fairs in plush crates. She had always suspected her mother had done it to annoy Wycliffe, who had never ceased to comment on the inanity of keeping kitchen animals upstairs.

"The Egyptians mummified them," Lady Hampshire said. "I have had the fortune of obtaining one such cat mummy from Dr. Carson—I presume you have heard of him?"

"I'm afraid not," Lady Wycliffe said, looking repulsed.

It was the moment when something possessed Hattie to say: "Lady Lucie has a cat."

"Oh?" Lady Hampshire said. And nothing more. Her beady eyes, however, were sweeping over Lucie from head to toe, as though she had only just noticed her.

Her mother leaned toward her, ever so slightly. "What breed?" she asked.

"I wouldn't know," Lucie said slowly, a little alarmed at having her mother leaning in on her. "She's black. She's a foundling."

"Faith," Professor Marlow said. "A barn cat—in the house?"

"A misplaced cat, rather," Lucie said. "Her attitude is far too entitled for a cat of humble beginnings."

The professor frowned, but her mother nodded, as though she found it a perfectly valid argument, and so Cecily began nodding along, too.

"Her name is Boudicca," Lucie said, feeling Lady Salisbury's prodding stare.

"After a belligerent pagan queen," Professor Marlow said. "How droll."

Lady Hampshire was still quietly assessing her.

"You are very trim, Lady Lucinda," she now said, scrutinizing Lucie's narrow waist. "Have you employed a tapeworm, by any chance?"

Her mind blanked. Was this a trick question? An insult? A jest?

"Excessive slimness in a female is usually a sign of a highly nervous disposition," Professor Marlow remarked. "I recommend long, regular lie-downs."

She was of a mind to do the man bodily harm with Lady Salisbury's cane, but both Hattie and Catriona suddenly remembered they were urgently required at the croquet game, and whether they could be excused, and their arms looped through Lucie's, left and right, and steered her away.

"Now," Hattie said brightly as they headed toward the copse, "this went well."

"Well?" Lucie said. "They loathed me. Tapeworms?"

"She was just trying to make conversation, Lucie."

"She insinuated I have a parasite."

"Some ladies ingest them to stay slender," Hattie said earnestly. "A lot of ladies bond over dieting advice."

"And yet I cannot see her asking my mother such a question."

"No. She'd rather discuss hysterical wombs with her in front of a crowd," Hattie said.

An unexpected giggle bubbled up in her throat. "Oh, Mother was not impressed."

She glanced back over her shoulder. Her mother was still making conversation with Lady Salisbury. But she caught Lucie from the corner of her eye. Lucie held her gaze. So did the countess. The subtle connection lingered until Cecily leaned in close and drew Lady Wycliffe's attention to herself.

"I think it was a success," Catriona said. "You were seen having a conversation with influential people and, most importantly, your mother . . ."

"Look," Hattie said. "Lord Peregrin is playing—he will let us join."

Montgomery's younger brother had already spotted their trio. He delayed his swing with the croquet mallet and raised a hand to where his hat would have been in a more formal setting. He was casual today in one of Oxford's colorfully striped boater jackets, and his blond hair, lightened by the sun, was ruffled by the breeze.

Catriona suddenly became heavy on Lucie's arm. A nervous flush had spread over her cheeks. "Perhaps I'd rather go and have some punch," she muttered.

"You can't," Hattie muttered back. "He has already seen you."

"My ladies, Miss Greenfield," Lord Peregrin hollered, and as if to leave no doubt that he had seen them indeed, he gave a wave with the mallet, missing Lord Palmer's curly head by a margin.

"Drat," Catriona whispered.

It was a little bewildering, seeing her normally unflappable friend so flustered, but Lucie recalled that a few months ago, Catriona had taken Peregrin's side during a tiff with the mighty Montgomery himself. She slowed, baffled. "Do you . . . like him?"

"Shhh," hissed Catriona.

"He can't hear us yet," Hattie murmured; evidently, she was well-informed on the matter.

"It does not matter, anyway," Catriona said, sounding glum. "He called me a good chap."

Hattie came to an abrupt halt, her mouth an O of outrage. "He has done what?"

Catriona adjusted her glasses. "After the episode in the wine cellar, when he thanked me, he said I was a *really good chap*. Clearly, he does not class me as a female of the species."

"The cad!"

Catriona sighed. "He's hardly the first to do so. Onward."

Pay him no mind, Lucie wanted to say. At nineteen, Lord Peregrin was wet behind the ears compared to Catriona's three-and-twenty, and in any case, he was underservant of her brilliance. However, there was apparently, sadly, no logic to emotions pertaining to men. As they had approached the group of gentlemen, she had caught herself looking for a tall libertine with copper hair among them, despite his crimes being far more insulting than calling her *chap*.

She took Catriona's hand and nodded at the players. "Will we have to feign ineptitude and miss all the goals?"

"Of course," Hattie said cheerfully. "At least if you wish for one of these gentlemen to ask you to dance tonight. A waltz, wasn't it? I recommend Lord Palmer, he has light feet and a secure grip."

"I despise having to hit a croquet ball at just the wrong angle."

Catriona clasped her hand more tightly. "I shall win it for us," she said softly. "I never dance."

Tristan couldn't recall a ball duller than this, and it had not even begun. Cecily hung on his arm, smelling and looking like a rose in a pink gown with rows of tassles and pleats. He was shadowed by Lucie's taciturn mother and Tommy Tedbury, who held a grudge against

him, and the constant presence of the trio felt more constricting than
the knot of his bow tie, which was choking him unpleasantly ever
since he had picked up Cecily and the countess from their suite.

As they crossed the Great Hall, a few chaps of the old Eton posse
loitered in his path, tumblers in hand. Weston, Calthorpe, Addington, and MacGregor, from what he could tell at a glance, and they
promptly cried his name with brandy-inspired enthusiasm.

He turned. "Tommy. May I entrust you with Ceci for the remain-
der of the way?"

He was already planting her gloved hand on his former playmate's
arm.

Thomas Tedbury gave him a sullen stare. "It's hardly seemly to
pass a lady off like a parcel, Ballentine."

"I'd never consider her less than precious cargo," Tristan said, and
sauntered off toward the cluster of Etonians.

Their demeanor had hardly evolved since boarding school days; it
was the same banter, the guffaws, the shoulder-slapping. The changes
were on the surface; hairlines were receding, floridness advancing.
Still the better company right now, all things considered.

"I would rib you about your pretty poetry," Addington said, tipping
his glass toward him, "but I'm not hankering after a knife in my back
when I least expect it." His grin didn't touch his eyes. Addington had
earned a proverbial knife or two in his back at Eton, because a younger
boy's only option to defend his place in a boarding school hierarchy
was to become creative. And what Tristan had lacked in discipline,
he had always more than adequately compensated with creativity.

He signaled for the footman carrying a tray with refreshments
and chose a brandy for himself. "How's estate business, Weston?"

Weston's country exploits were known to bore Addington, and he
reliably launched into a lengthy oration about his bovines. Until his
voice faltered. His eyes widened, and he whistled softly through his
teeth. He must have spotted a woman.

"I'll be damned. That's the Tedbury Termagant."

It took some effort to not just turn around but to do so with a measure of visible disinterest.

He caught her descending the last few steps of the main stairs.

And the Great Hall fell away. For a beat, there was only the dainty woman in red. Not red; crimson. Like his favorite coat. Like the ruby on his ring. Like the color of blood on its way to the heart.

His mouth went dry despite the brandy.

With her light hair, she was fire and ice. An evil genius had attached a gauzy, crimson cape to the back of her sleeves, the fabric so fine it gently lifted up around Lucie at every step, giving the impression that she was floating down the stairs on a breeze like a creature with wings.

She was a phantom of delight,
When first she gleam'd upon my sight
A dancing shape, an image gay,
To haunt, to startle, and waylay . . .

The voice was all but blaring inside his head. It was Wordsworth.

He raised the tumbler to his lips, gulping down the contents. Wordsworth meant he had it bad. His stomach churned with an emotion he found difficult to endure while standing still.

"I say. She scrubs up nicely." Weston sounded impressed.

"Don't be fooled. She would still freeze your bollocks off," Calthorpe said.

"Withering them, with a glance," MacGregor added, sounding worried.

"I'd show her bollocks," muttered Addington.

Calthorpe chuckled. "You wouldn't dare."

"Don't be wet, old boy. Women like her are rebellious because men are too timid with them. They desperately crave a firm hand and a firm prick to keep them in their place, so the more you kowtow to them, the more hysterical they become."

"Ho ho," Weston exclaimed.

MacGregor gave a lackluster laugh and shuffled his feet.

"Careful, Addington," Tristan said, pleasantly enough. "She's still Tedbury's sister."

A sober man would have heard the threat thrumming in his tone.

Addington smirked. "Tedbury. Is he here?" He shaded his eyes with his hand and cast an exaggerated glance around the hall.

"I'm taking offense on his behalf." Lucie had halted at the bottom of the stairs, hesitating. An escort was nowhere in sight. She would enter a ballroom filled with people who regarded her as a freak, alone. In a bollocks contest with the men presently surrounding him, this woman would leave them all in the dust.

A warm tide of pride rose in his chest, briefly filling all the empty hollows.

He would contemplate the significance of this later.

"Twenty pounds that MacGregor shan't dare to ask the harpy for a dance," Calthorpe said.

MacGregor's tawny brows flew up. "I prize my bollocks higher than a paltry twenty pounds, thank you."

"Thirty," Calthorpe said quickly, "and double that if you can make her dance the first dance with you."

"MacGregor? Waltzing with *her*?" Weston laughed. "Here, I double the stakes."

"You fiends," Addington said. "As if MacGregor could turn down a hundred quid—his old man is tight-fisted as a clam."

MacGregor groaned like a man defeated.

"What say you, Ballentine," Addington said softly near his ear, "are you not partial to the boyish ones?"

Someone was intoxicated beyond caution.

He turned. "Hold this, would you?" He pushed his empty tumbler into Addington's free hand, and the man's fingers clamped around it in surprise.

Lucie stood near an overspilling flower arrangement, last in the slowly moving queue to the ballroom.

The coil of white-blond hair between her pretty shoulders looked too heavy for her slender neck. He had known she was slight, but she was tiny. He could probably lift her up with one arm and tuck her into his chest pocket and knowing this made him feel restless and hot.

She did not grant him a glance when he halted next to her, in the spot where her escort should have been.

"We have discussed the matter of you following me," she said stiffly, keeping her eyes fixed on the back of the gentleman queuing in front of her.

"Good evening, stranger."

She shifted a little, as if she had something pointy in one of her shoes, bothering her.

"Do you wish to make a statement and enter alone," he continued, "or would you consider taking me as your escort?"

Now she looked up at him. He blinked. A curl had been pulled down her forehead, and red flowers were tucked into her coiffure. It was the current fashion, he knew, but at first glance, it made her look like a stranger in truth.

"Entering with you is a statement, too," she said.

He inclined his head in acknowledgment.

"I was forced to lose at lawn croquet today," she added cryptically.

"That's . . . dreadful?"

"It quite makes me want to make an entrance," she murmured, and eyed his arm.

His heart beat faster. "I reckon it also makes you want to dance the first dance with me."

She was staring at the back of the fellow in front of them again. When she spoke, a smirk was in her voice. "Why don't you try and find out, my lord."

Why don't you try and find out, my lord.

Apparently, a farcical game of croquet made her want to do something reckless. Or perhaps it had been the two glasses of champagne, drunk in haste in the dressing room. She was contemplating entering the ballroom on his arm, as if her in a crimson ball gown with a surprise cape was not enough to raise eyebrows. She was contemplating whether to waltz with her nemesis or not to waltz at all.

Despite her defeat on the croquet lawn, no gentleman had asked her to dance. It would have made a statement to the rest of the ballroom that they were apparently unwilling to make. Tristan, of course, was quixotic enough to find gossip about him and the Nefarious Nag amusing.

She scrutinized him from the corner of her eye. Naturally, he looked dashing, wearing the formal black-and-white evening attire with an alluring casual ease. She should reject his dance request, preferably in full view of everyone. But they entered the ballroom the moment the soft sway of a French horn announced the "Blue Danube" waltz, and an electric burst of excitement shot through her legs and curled her toes. She had not danced in years.

Tristan faced her, with one arm held very formally behind his back.

Her breathing quickened. "You are going to ask, aren't you."

"Of course." He performed an old-fashioned bow. "Will you honor me with this waltz, Lady Lucinda?"

The ballroom was watching; the attention coming their way was palpable like a cold draft in the air.

She looked past the hand he offered to his face. His eyes held an emotion far more complex than mockery. This was another truce. The languid song of the violin celli changed into a perky three-quarter time, and as if on command, dozens of couples began to twirl past them.

She placed her right hand into Tristan's left.

Something sparked where their palms connected. She watched him raise their clasped hands into position, feeling unsteady. The warm pressure of his hand on her waist was already sinking through layers of silk and corset right into her bare skin. *Keep your enemies close, but this close?* A bad, bad idea.

Too late. He stepped backward into the fray, pulling her with him. And she was flying, literally, as the momentum briefly lifted her off her toes. Her little shriek was swallowed by the swelling music and the rhythmic shuffle of heels on parquet, but Tristan had caught it; his hold on her tightened, and a memory flashed, of the feel of his hands on her hips as she had lain on top of him in the stables.

She fixated on the knot of his white bow tie, which was still above the level of her eyes.

She tipped back her head. "You are very tall." Her voice was decidedly too high.

He tilted his face down. "You have great observation skills for a woman. I imagine you occasionally frighten the gentlemen with your pluck?"

Pluck?

He smiled, and she glanced away again, to a less dazzling place. His throat. Too intimate. His left shoulder. She had seen it naked, bronzed and smooth. A hot flush spread up her neck. No part of him was neutral tonight.

"Where did you come from all of a sudden?" he teased. "I have not seen you before." His gaze grazed over the edge of her low, square neckline.

"I believe this counts as flirtation, my lord."

"The shameless kind," he confirmed, and pulled her closer. Well. *He* had never been afraid of her pluck. Warmth still tingled on the path his eyes had casually drawn across her chest. The combination of champagne and tight lacing was perilous; it was making her light-headed and overly forgiving. Round and round they went, the skirts and fans and garlanded pillars surrounding them melting into a color-fully streaked blur.

"It is now your turn to deliver a witty reply," Tristan remarked.

"Well then," she said. "Where is your earring?"

His brows rose in surprise. "Not what I expected."

She had, now and again, wondered about this since their meeting at Blackwell's.

He was quiet for a turn. "The earring went the same way as your skirt-trousers," he then said.

"My skirt-trousers?"

"They looked as though you had fashioned them from an old skirt with wide, billowing trouser legs," he said. "You tried sneaking to the stables while wearing them and you almost did not get caught—it was the summer when you were fifteen, I believe."

She remembered. It had been the summer she had become too old to steal Tommy's breeches for riding Thunder. But she couldn't ride astride in skirts; hence, she had fashioned a pair of trousers. That Tristan should remember it was astonishing, but then again, there had been a memorable commotion when they had caught her.

"I loathed riding sidesaddle," she said. "Tommy snitched on me, the lout. They locked me in my room for three days to make sure I knew it was wrong."

He claimed his earring had gone the same way. Someone had told him to remove it—but who, she wondered, had the power to dictate a nobleman's fashion choices?

They flew past Lord Melvin and his dance partner, and she returned his nod with a smile.

"Lord Melvin," Tristan said, when she looked back up at him. "Is he your beau?"

She would have tripped, had he not been leading. "You are not entitled to ask such things."

"You looked very familiar during the recital."

They had not; more significantly, had he been watching her? If he were any other man, she would think he was displaying signs of jealousy. But Tristan would never be so gauche as to be jealous, even if he had a claim.

"Remarkable you should have noticed," she said, "considering you were preoccupied with Lady Cecily. What was my mother thinking, partnering the poor lamb with you?"

She had hit a mark, inadvertently, for his expression shuttered.

"You have not heard her cat poem," he finally said, sounding ominous. "You would reconsider who the poor lamb was in our partnering."

"A cat poem? Very well—I do like cats. Was it a good poem?"

"Atrocious. But very naughty. Although that was an accident, I believe."

She laughed despite herself, and his eyes lit on her with intrigue. Round and round they went. She tried not to lie to herself. And the truth was, she felt drawn to Tristan in all his wicked glory. It was why her skin prickled as if she were floating in champagne when he put his hand on her waist, it was why sometimes she felt hot when thinking of all the ways she disliked him. It was a sick desire outside the bounds of reason, which was perhaps why it appealed. A good woman was not even supposed to have words for the parts of her body that ached when he looked at her like this, his gaze reaching deep as though he wanted her secrets. But she had long been deemed a shameless woman. She could safely enjoy herself for the duration of a dance with no reputation to lose.

From the shelter of a ballroom pillar, two pairs of eyes were watching the unlikely couple dance more closely than the others.

"You are admirably calm, considering this should have been your dance," Arthur said.

Cecily did not look at him. Her eyes were on the dance floor, where Tristan whirled with a woman in a crimson dress to a waltz that, by an unspoken understanding, should have been hers indeed, and she was not nearly as calm as she appeared. The stinging sensation in her nose said her tears of dismay had risen precariously close to the surface.

"It is clear that she accosted him," she said softly. "She was probably worried no one would ask her for a turn. He was too much of a gentleman to reject a lady of his acquaintance. Not even a lady like her."

Arthur nodded, for this was the regular reaction to Ballentine's callous behavior: making excuses for him. He'd heard it all before. He had done it himself. But then, he had probably been in love with the man for as long as his cousin. It had been the summer when he had turned eleven, when his parents had sent him to spend his first summer at Wycliffe Hall with distant relations rather than take him along on a tour to India over the holidays. He had sulked for days, for Tommy had found him dull from the lofty height of his fifteen years, and Cecily, his own age, had struck Arthur as dull. And then, he had arrived. He remembered it clearly, the carriage halting, the door swinging back, and the beautiful youth jumping out onto the gravel, his hat under his arm. His hair had glowed like a flame in the summer sun. His movements had been graceful as a dancer's. He remembered how his mouth had turned dry and how his stomach had felt hollow. Much, much later, he had understood that it had been his first taste of infatuation. Tristan had strolled past the line of greeters and had carelessly ruffled Arthur's hair, saying, *Who have we here?* Ten years later, their paths had crossed again in a den of iniquity, and Tristan had not remembered him, not at all—it was as though he had never been at Wycliffe Hall, never been running after him for a month with boyish ardor or dreaming of him for much longer.

Now Ballentine was twirling the scandalous Lady Lucie as though he were above everyone's judgment, and while Arthur was quite drunk already, he was not nearly intoxicated enough to watch

it without chagrin; in fact, he was just drunk enough to feel uninhib-
ited frustration. He had nothing against his cousin Lucie, personally;
their paths had barely crossed during his stay at her home. She had
been older than Tristan and had preferred to seclude herself in the
park or her room. But right now, seeing her in Tristan's arms, he did
not like her much.

He turned to Cecily, and contempt and pity colored his voice
when he said: "He won't marry you, Cecily."

She turned her head toward him, blinking slowly. "Why would
you say such a thing?"

"He is not the marrying kind."

"But . . . he must. The contracts are all but drawn up."

When Arthur was quiet, she said: "The only reason it hasn't been
made official is because my uncle demanded Lord Ballentine right
his reputation first, so it wouldn't tarnish our family in any way.
Which is unfair—he's been terribly misunderstood."

Arthur scoffed. "Look at him. Look at him, my dear."

She turned back to the dance floor. She was looking. She hadn't
taken her eyes off him in two days. There wasn't a more attractive
man in England, which meant there wasn't a more attractive man in
the world. His amber eyes, smoldering, his beautiful mouth, smiling,
making her feel . . . feverish. Her skin warmed the moment he looked
at her. Every woman in the room wanted him.

She had known he was hers the first time she had clapped eyes on
him as a girl. Well, perhaps not the very first time, but even when he
had not yet been spectacular to behold, he had always paid attention
to her. He would marry her. Arthur was just being morose, a regrettable streak in his disposition.

"I see a man gracious enough to dance with my unfortunate
cousin," she said, a little too gracious of him, in her personal opinion.
"And the Prince of Wales likes him."

Arthur's lips twisted with impatience. "This man cares nought for contracts. Or honor. He has nothing but contempt for people who admire him, and I wager he even laughs at the Victoria Cross. Marriage is the last thing on his mind, mark my words. There are only two things Lord Ballentine cares about and those are himself and his pleasure."

Cecily frowned. "You say ghastly things with great certainty."

"Because I know him."

"I know him, too."

"I know him in ways that you don't."

Cecily felt moved to stomp her delicate foot. She knew gentlemen tended to have bonds that eluded the women in their lives. She didn't like it.

"Be that as it may, I shall marry no one but him," she said tightly.

Arthur gave her a long look, blinking as though she were out of focus. "Cripes," he then said, slurring faintly. "You really do want him."

She dropped her gaze, her cheeks unnaturally hot.

"And what about the woman who seems to have inspired him to write a whole book of romantic poetry?" Arthur said, for it was clearly a woman at the center of Ballentine's poems.

"It is perfectly natural for artistic men to depend upon a muse," Cecily said. "Or perhaps she is a figment of his imagination entirely." And she, Cecily, was much preferable over an imaginary woman. Over many existing ones, too, if she was being honest.

Just then, Tristan tipped back his head and laughed, his white teeth flashing. When he looked back down at Lucie, he pulled her indecently close in the next turn of the waltz. And there was something in his gaze . . .

A stabbing sensation pierced Cecily's chest. Her gloved hands reflexively balled into fists.

Of course, this meant nothing. It was only Lucie, after all. No one liked her.

But to witness him look like this at another woman? What if he danced with an eligible woman next? She swallowed. Could it be true? Her engagement was not as certain as they said it was?

Black dots began dancing before her eyes. Her hand scrabbled for the support of the column.

Arthur's gaze filled with pity. "Ceci—"

She raised her other hand. "I do not enjoy this conversation. And I do not enjoy that he is dancing with Lucinda."

He paused. Studied her flushed cheeks and glittering eyes. "All right," he soothed. "All right. If someone must have him, I would want it to be you."

The tears still threatened to spill. "But if he refuses? You seem so certain that he will."

"You know." His fingers wrapped around her small hand. "I could tell you something that might help you if he refuses to do right by you. You would have to be courageous, however."

She blinked, a flicker of hope in the watery depths of her blue eyes. "I can be courageous."

He felt a little ill. He was much more sozzled than he had thought. "He does not deserve you, this you must know."

Cecily gave a shaky sigh. "You have always been a favorite cousin of mine, Arthur."

He returned the feeble press of her fingers. He wished he could say that playing the knight in shining armor for his pretty cousin was what had just compelled him to make his offer. Alas, it was much less noble than that. It was, admittedly, a petty desire to see Ballentine needing to bend or down on his knees, his arrogance and appetites at least in part curtailed by wedlock. Perhaps that would give the man a taste of how it felt to never quite get what one wanted.

Chapter 20

⁂

The disaster happened the next morning, on an empty stomach. Lucie was running late for breakfast, because she had indulged in a lie-in, lingering on last night's waltz in the twilight hour between dreams and conscious thought. Then she had asked the lady's maid for another complicated coiffure and had taken frivolously long to select the best silk flower as a crowning glory.

The moment she entered the breakfast room, three hundred or more heads turned toward her, each movement subtle, but together, it created a veritable disturbance in the air.

She slowed.

The hall was quiet as a tomb. And just as frosty.

Reflexively, her hand rose to her hair. The flowers were still firmly in place. It couldn't possibly be her gown. . . .

Annabelle was watching her from her seat at the head of the table, wearing a pleasant little smile. Formally pleasant.

Her stomach sank. Something had happened, between the early-morning hours and now, and whatever it was, it wasn't pleasant at all.

The crowd found its bearing, people moved, and chatter swelled again.

Her thoughts racing, Lucie turned to the breakfast buffet, reached blindly for a plate, and began selecting fruits from the tiered platters. Whatever it was, she wasn't guilty of it.

The scent of lavender wrapped around her. Lady Salisbury had appeared by her side and pretended an interest in the oranges in the large silver bowl.

"Some of us found something strewn along the corridors this morning," she murmured without preamble.

"Found what?" Lucie said quietly.

Now Lady Salisbury looked at her. Her usually watery blue eyes were piercing. "Pamphlets."

A shiver of alarm ran down her back.

Pamphlets of any kind had no place in a ducal corridor. Certainly not when the Prince of Wales was in attendance. Not when Montgomery was trying to restore his reputation. . . .

"It was *The Female Citizen*," Lady Salisbury said tightly. "The prince found one, too."

Her palms turned damp. Apples and oranges began to blur.

She could see the pamphlets on the cherrywood surface of the vanity table before her mind's eye, placed there carelessly when she had spread out the *Discerning Ladies' Magazine*s, because who would come to her room and see them, and take offense?

Lady Salisbury had probably seen them there yesterday morning. Did she believe Lucie had done it? Of course. Everyone here believed she had done it.

She turned to the crowd, her plate forgotten.

No one was facing her directly now; they were looking past her, through her. She might as well not exist at all. Wrong—one man was staring right into her. The Duke of Montgomery. His pale eyes were assessing her from his place at the head of the long table, his face as still and cold as if carved in ice. The prince sat next to him, champagne flute in hand, looking deceptively bored.

Her gaze began darting around the room. Every face in her field of vision closed up like a fist.

She did catch Lord Melvin's eyes.

He glanced away.

"Excuse me," she said to Lady Salisbury, and made for the exit.

She kept her pace measured in the Great Hall; still, the clicks of her heels were echoing like gunshots off the walls. She overtook a group of chattering guests and they fell silent. Their stares bore into her back until she reached the bottom of the grand staircase. The narrow new skirts forced her to take the stairs one dainty step at a time, *step step step*. She turned right on the landing, toward the corridor to the east wing.

Two women were ahead of her.

Hazel ringlets, and her mother's unmistakable slim frame. Lady Wycliffe crept down the hallway like an old woman, slightly lopsided and leaning on Cecily's arm. Oddly, the sight stung, right into the depths of her chest.

When they vanished into an antechamber, she quickened her stride to follow them and entered without knocking.

"Mother?"

They stood with their backs to her, facing the tall windows. Her cousin glanced over her shoulder and gasped, her eyes widening with—fear?

Lady Wycliffe kept her back turned, her thin frame stiff like a frozen reed. "Leave now, Lucinda."

The cold contempt in her mother's voice stopped her hesitant advance like a wall.

Cecily's gaze had dropped to the tips of her shoes.

"Now."

Lucie nodded. "As you wish."

She was at the door when the cold voice came again. "You just had to do this, didn't you? You simply could not help yourself."

She stood facing the winter blue of the doorjamb, uncertain what to say.

"You always had a desire to spurn me. So disobedient, so difficult, since you were a girl. I really should not find myself surprised today. But that you would go to such extremes as to humiliate the duke and his wife in front of the Prince of Wales to indulge your politics . . ."

A roar starting up in her ears, she turned back. "It wasn't me."

The countess wheeled round to face her, the glitter in her eyes as sharp as broken glass.

"You are selfish," she said. "You always were."

Cecily was hiding behind her hands like a child.

She should leave. It appeared her mother could still work herself into a passionate outburst after all, and they had had enough scandal for a day.

"Good day, Mother."

"Of course. You have no scruples to just walk away from the chaos you create." The blend of imperiousness and disappointment, so unique to her mother, erased years between them and made Lucie feel like an awkward girl in a woman's body. Her hand had all but frozen on the door handle.

Her mother's expression turned oddly triumphant. "There are other ladies who dabble in political activism," she said. "Have you never wondered why they have not lost their family? Why they are still well-received?"

Beyond her shoulder, Cecily was still covering her face with her palms. Well, when one was not used to them, confrontations could be frightening. And presently, the Countess of Wycliffe very much wanted to confront. Her wrath was an old wrath, pulled from the very depths of her. She would not be appeased.

"If you must know," she continued, "Wycliffe might have forgiven you, had you not embarrassed him in front of his peers. But you do not care whether you cross a line, do you, as long as it serves your immediate gratification. Indeed, I used to think how similar you and your father were in your selfishness. The difference is, of course, that Wycliffe is a man—he can't help himself."

Her gaze traveled over Lucie from the tips of her new slippers to the silk flower in her coiffure. "It was all a ploy, wasn't it, the lovely gowns and polite conversation?"

Lucie's skin crawled under her inspection. "Whatever do you mean?"

Her mother sneered. "Please. Do you truly believe that adorning your hair with flowers will disguise what you are?"

The snide words made her feel numb. She opened the door and escaped into the corridor.

"That is what you fail to understand." Her mother was following her. "Your peculiarities are not skin-deep. They are at the very core of you—how could I possibly have corrected them? I tried. Oh, I tried." She was right behind Lucie, close, breathing down her neck. "Know that any normal man and woman can sense your masculine nature from afar. Know that nothing will hide what you are, Lucinda—you cannot outrun the truth."

She stopped abruptly and turned back.

"The truth?" Her tone was metallic, impersonal, the kind she used on heckling strangers. "The truth is that while you speak with great authority, your authority is a mirage, Mother. Wycliffe can take it away with a snap of his fingers, like this. You hold no rights, not even over your own body, because you are a married woman. Your pedestal stands on quicksand, and if you are satisfied with this fate, for yourself, for half the human race, we shall never agree. So forgive me if I would rather *run* than stay and let you berate me."

Lady Wycliffe drew herself up to her full height. "There is dignity in quietly bearing a woman's cross," she said icily. "There is no dignity in your stubborn refusal to do so—only humiliation. Your shrieking, your marches, your pamphlets: humiliation."

Lucie's lip curled. *Remember the morning in the library at Wycliffe Hall, Mother? There had been a world of humiliation in your shrieking and pleading for a scrap of your husband's love while he flaunted his mistresses for all to see. Could there be a humiliation greater than begging for love?*

"Do you think these activists you have chosen over your family have a care for you beyond what you can do for them?" Again her mother was rushing after her with quick, angry steps, hissing words under her breath. "They have not. Mark my words, you will be a bitter old spinster with not one child, not one friend to give you comfort in your twilight years."

"I promise I shall not bother you if that comes to pass."

"What if your trust fund runs out? You won't be proud in the workhouse."

Her foot nearly caught in her hem as the words slithered into her heart, beneath the doors she kept firmly shut between her and a secret world of dread. She could not afford fear. The only way for her was forward, always forward.

As the corridor split to a left and a right, she turned right the moment her mother tried to turn left, and they stood facing each other.

They were both breathing hard.

When she tried to step around her mother, her hand shot out and clasped her arm. "Lucinda." Her voice was low. "No one can abide a selfish woman. You must know that."

"Oh, I do. I do know."

A damp sheen blurred the countess's blue eyes. "You . . . you could have had everything. Everything." Her little shrug was almost helpless. "And yet here you stand, wasting your life—and for what? For what?"

For something you will never understand.

For something she, Lucie, could never go without again.

She looked her mother in the eye. "For freedom."

This time, no one followed her.

The copies of *The Female Citizen* were gone from her vanity table. Someone had positioned a few of the *Discerning Ladies' Magazine*s in

their place. Well. Whoever had tried to sabotage her, they had succeeded.

Her carpetbag and the travel trunk were stowed in the dressing
chamber. Mechanically, she began pulling gowns and petticoats into
her arms, carried them to the bed, and dumped them on the counterpane. Her senses were still overheightened, her blood still racing.

Years ago, when she had been new to activism, she *had* wondered
how the other ladies who were taking up the Cause retained their
positions and people's good graces. Their families usually displayed
unusual degrees of tolerance. But most ladies also stayed clear of the
truly ugly matters and left them to the activists from the middle
classes. And usually, they were more patient than her, and contented
themselves with gradually carving out space for a project here or
there. Another foundling home, another school for girls, an academy
for fallen women. A position as policy advisor on health matters
thanks to personal connections, as Florence Nightingale had done.
All valuable work, none of it enough. And she, Lucie, was greedy.
She found the endless waiting difficult. She wanted to see women
advisors in the Ministry of Economics. She wanted fewer academies
for fallen women, and more changes to the circumstances that made
women fall. Her mother was right—she *was* selfish. She was indulging her impatience and wanted too much, too fast.

She pulled the flowers from her hair and tossed them onto the
disorderly heap of clothing. *Masculine nature.* How many of them had
been laughing behind her back at her attempts to look nice?

She began stuffing the dresses into the trunk, crushing velvet and
silk.

A soft but determined knock sounded on her door.

"Enter," she said without interrupting the packing.

Annabelle appeared on the doorstep. At a glance, she took in the
pile of clothes on the bed and the open trunk.

She closed the door behind her. "Surely you are not thinking
about leaving?"

"I think it would be best, considering the circumstances."

Annabelle drew closer. "What makes you think so?"

"Please. Everyone thinks it was me. Including you." Forgivable in her mother, who had never known her much at all. So hurtful in a friend, she couldn't breathe, thinking about it.

"I do not think you did it."

She glanced up. Annabelle was staring at her with hurt in her eyes.

Lucie swiped a dislodged lock of hair behind her ear. "I saw how you looked at me when I came into the breakfast room."

Annabelle shook her head. "It would be stupid, and disloyal, and you are neither."

It didn't soothe the jagged emotion stabbing away in her chest.

"I'm glad. But I would have appreciated a warning before I walked into Antarctica."

Annabelle blew out a breath. "I could hardly leave Montgomery's side—we were busy pretending that everything was fine." She hesitated. "But it is true that I *had* seen the pamphlets on your vanity table yesterday morning. And . . ."

"Yes?"

"And I know that you are not fond of Montgomery."

Lucie gave a nod. "It is true. I'm not fond of him."

"He is not hindering our cause now," Annabelle said calmly. "In fact, he is fighting in our corner."

"Is it still *our* corner?"

A look of surprise passed over Annabelle's face. "Of course—why would you even say such a thing?"

Because you have everything a woman supposedly should have, and it shall be a matter of time before it keeps you from pursuing masculine *activities.*

Lucie shrugged. "I suppose I do not like how the duke is changing you."

"Changing me? Whatever do you mean?"

It would be unwise to keep talking. So naturally, she did keep talking. "You are not really part of the student body anymore, and are only present at Oxford two, at best three days a week, when studying the classics used to be your dream."

Annabelle gave a baffled shake. "I'm a married woman now. I cannot live apart from my husband seven days a week—I do not wish to, either."

"Precisely. It just strikes me as a lost opportunity, considering how few women have access to anything resembling a higher education."

"Lucie, Oxford does not even allow women to fully matriculate."

"Oh, I'm aware of that—I am writing a letter a week and speak to more bigots than I care for to change that. It means we have to fight harder, not withdraw."

"But I'm not withdrawing—I'm compromising. Just because I am married does not mean I shall ever give up the fight."

"It usually means exactly that."

Annabelle regarded her warily, as though uncertain what had got into her friend. "Presently, Oxford does not allow us to take the same final exams as men, and they teach us in the upstairs room of a bakery. We are not deemed fit to enter the same lecture halls as the men. You can hardly expect me to strain my relationship with Montgomery for their disregard and a third-class diploma, especially not when I am perfectly capable of fulfilling much of my coursework from afar."

She was right, of course. "Still," something possessed Lucie to say, "you do not walk with us as much anymore because your gowns are too constraining. And your speech is changing—is he making you take elocution lessons?"

And she had gone too far, she knew even before she heard her friend's sharp intake of breath.

"I should not have said that," she murmured, a sinking feeling in her chest.

"No," Annabelle said quietly. Her beautiful face was white. "You should not have."

"I'm a beastly friend."

"You are not being fair." Annabelle crossed her arms, the air around her crackling with the sparks of her own temper. "Has my life changed? Why, yes, it has. I have changed the constraints of poverty to the constraints of protocol—guess which I prefer? I enjoy being safe and well fed. I prefer constraining gowns over having to mend my old ones, over and over, worrying how I would replace them before they turned into rags. I *like* having strength and resources at my disposal for matters beyond my immediate survival. I am of much more use to the Cause as I am now than I was before. But none of that signifies—what signifies is that Montgomery gave up near everything he once considered important to be with me. And I would have shared my life in a hovel with him. Because there is no one who sees me better, and no one I trust more."

Lucie was cringing. "I apologize."

"How could he possibly give me any more? He could lay down his life for me, but I daresay he would do so without blinking if required." Annabelle's eyes were blazing like emeralds on fire. She had worked herself into a right mood, and Lucie could hardly blame her.

"I apologize," she repeated, feeling dreadful. "Truly, I spoke out of turn."

Annabelle's arms remained firmly crossed.

Lucie sank onto the bed next to the tangle of remaining gowns.

This was worse than what had just transpired in the breakfast room. Worse than the confrontation with Lady Wycliffe. She was unraveling in some fashion, had been so for days, with resentment sprawling destructively around her like the arms of a kraken. Could she blame her friends for having doubts?

She raised solemn eyes to Annabelle. "It does not excuse my tirade, but for what it's worth, I felt hurt." It made her feel queasy to say this out loud, as if she were revealing a soft, pale flank to a marksman. "I was ghastly to you because I felt hurt when I thought you thought it was me. I would never try and embarrass you, in your own home no less."

Annabelle's face fell. She rushed to settle next to her and clasped Lucie's hand in hers.

"I'm sorry, too." The green of her eyes was muted again, all temper gone out of her. "Please believe me." She gave Lucie's hand a squeeze. "I never meant to give you this feeling."

Lucie shrugged. "It's all these years of me being known as a troublemaker. It's bound to confuse people."

Annabelle's eyes looked suspiciously shiny. "I'm not people, I'm your friend. My emotions are running high—will you accept my apology?"

Lucie sighed. How could she not?

"There is nothing to forgive," she said, and gave Annabelle's hand a squeeze in turn. "And I'm happy for you. I am."

Even when contrite, with her regal posture and proud cheekbones, Annabelle looked as though she had always been destined to be someone. Poise and pride were in her marrow. It was just a bitter pill to swallow that it had taken the money and the protection of a man to help her achieve her destiny. But that was how it was. And perhaps, she, Lucie, was turning into a bitter old crone before her time.

Annabelle toyed with a tassel on the belt of her dress. "If you must know," she said, "I don't relish constraints of any kind, be they gowns, protection officers, or protocol. But Lucie." She raised her eyes, and the depths of emotion in them stunned Lucie for a moment. "Lucie, I have never been so *happy*. Perhaps I am greedy, but I wish to believe I can do both: be a wife to the man I love, and work for women's liberty."

Lucie had to yet see such a thing.

But if anyone could hope to do both, it had to be Annabelle, hadn't it. "It's your prerogative to wish for however much you want," she said.

Besides, even to her bitter crone eyes, it was obvious that the duke was besotted with Annabelle. He wasn't an expressive man but inevitably, his attention shifted and settled on his wife, wherever she happened to be in the room. In terms of affection, their union appeared balanced. It was hardly degrading to fawn over a man who was fawning right back.

"What are you going to do now, about the pamphlets?" she asked. "Is the prince terribly annoyed?"

Annabelle scoffed. "Between the two of us, I think he's dying from ennui, so he is grateful for diversion of any kind. That said, he doesn't suffer provocations against his person gladly."

"I imagine—what will you do?"

Annabelle smiled without humor. "Montgomery already convinced him that the pamphlets were the idea of some inebriated ladies in the wee hours after the ball; a wager between foolish women."

"Ingenious. The most expedient way to take the gravity out of any situation."

"Of course. No red-blooded male would concern himself with such a frivolous matter."

"The women, however, are another kettle of fish," muttered Lucie, remembering the turned backs, Lady Salisbury's piercing eyes . . . her mother's seething embarrassment. "They think I tried to make a fool of a duke. Or tried to draw attention. The question is, who did it? And why? Are there any clues?"

Annabelle's face darkened. "Nothing yet. Montgomery has plenty of detractors among his guests who would like to make him look less than in control."

"As do I," Lucie murmured.

Annabelle's eyes widened. "You think this was directed against you?"

"That was my first thought, although why someone would go to such lengths—oh." A thought struck her, and it sent her stomach plummeting straight to the floor. She knew one person who might have a rather acute interest in sabotaging her credibility. Someone who had ample experience with playing cruel pranks on her. Tristan.

Her palms turned damp, and she noted that her heart was pounding.

"We will find out whoever it was," Annabelle said, confidence in her voice. "In the meantime, the whole affair is only a provocation if we make it so. As long as we make light of it, the people who continue to take offense will look terribly gauche. No one here wants to look gauche."

This was true. She still reached for her bag. Mollified prince or not, the thought of spending another day under covert scrutiny made her skin crawl. The magic of last night, the warmth of Tristan's hands, the easy laughter and champagne, it had gone in a blink, leaving her chest feeling hollow. Her body was reacting far too strongly to a potential betrayal by Tristan Ballentine.

Annabelle folded her hands in her lap. "Lucie, I don't want to pry, but . . ."

"Go on?"

"Is there something that is troubling you? If I may say so, you do seem a little angry lately."

She chortled. "I'm always angry."

Annabelle shook her head. "This is different. If you wish to speak about something in confidence, I am here."

Half an hour ago, she would have appreciated the offer. But if Tristan had scattered the *Citizen* around Claremont, she was back to despising him, a simple emotion that required no further analysis.

A flurry of knocks hit the door, and Hattie and Catriona tumbled into the room a moment later.

"I told you so," Hattie said as she flung herself onto the bed. "Did I not tell you so?" And, when everyone looked at her blankly, she raised her hands toward the ceiling. "Whenever the four of us attend an event, there's a scandal." She shot Lucie a speaking glance. "And this had absolutely nothing to do with me not controlling my intuition."

Annabelle looked from Hattie to Lucie to Catriona. "Has she taken leave of her senses?"

"Never mind," said Catriona, and claimed the last available space on the mattress. "Do we have a suspect? Do we know whether Lucie or Montgomery was the target?"

Hattie nodded. "And we need a plan how we will catch the culprit and keep the awkwardness contained at a reasonable level until our departure."

Lucie's heartbeat slowed. The hollowness in her chest filled with warmth, and she surveyed her friends with a lump in her throat. "No culprit yet," she said. "But we will pretend to be unbothered."

"We *are* unbothered," Annabelle said firmly.

Then she rang the bell to order up a tray with a full breakfast for Lucie and more tea and pastries for everyone.

Tristan arrived in the breakfast room bleary-eyed and in need of coffee, black as tar, please. The ball had petered out shortly after midnight, which was when he had convinced a handful of gentlemen including the duke's younger brother, Lord Peregrin, that it was necessary to play vingt-et-un in Claremont's blue smoking room. They had dealt cards and poured drinks until everyone was red-eyed and badly disheveled. He had emerged victorious from a drawn-out battle of card games, but because he had still been clearheaded enough to think obsessive thoughts about a certain woman in red, he had coaxed young Lord Peregrin into raiding Montgomery's port cabinet. The lad, easily inspired because he was only nineteen, had selected an impressively ancient bottle that was now giving him an equally impressive headache.

It was always the last bottle that did it, he surmised as he surveyed the empty breakfast buffet with a vise clamping down on his skull. He beckoned one of the footmen lining the brocade-papered walls, because it appeared that Montgomery's spartanic household really did clear the breakfast tables before one o'clock. He asked that the footman bring up a breakfast tray and to come find him outside at the back of the house.

Light glared through the tall glass doors leading to the terrace, right into his pounding brain. He squinted. He should have taken a back exit, away from the crowds. The whole regiment of house party guests was promenading out here and in the French Garden below in their Sunday finery.

He was about to retreat when she found him.

"My lord!"

Cecily was bright-eyed and rosy-cheeked, because she hadn't been drinking and gambling until past the darkest hour. She was of a mind to take a turn around the French Garden, she told him, the hope that he accompany her written plainly in her eyes, while Lucie's ever-present mother raked him with a cool glare. Unlike innocent Ceci, Lady Wycliffe was not fooled by his meticulously assembled attire and too-tight cravat knot but saw the brandy and port still sloshing in his innards.

He wanted to tell everyone to bugger off.

What he did was offer Cecily his arm, and her small hand latched on with a surprising grip.

She chattered about something as he descended the steps leading to the French Garden—the weather, presumably.

His attention was consumed by the group of women coming toward them at a leisurely pace, their arms entwined, their merry voices drifting toward him. Lucie and her lady friends.

Lady Catriona, the Greenfield daughter, and the duchess returned his greeting when they passed each other.

Lucie gave him a dark, assessing stare, and he just knew she considered him guilty of something. He nearly stopped right then, to demand what had ruffled her feathers, but an ice wall rose around Lady Wycliffe when the quartet passed them by, and short of abandoning the woman on his arm in full sight of the ton and run after another, there was nothing he could do but move along.

"The duchess is very generous," Cecily murmured as he led her deeper into the garden. "Though some people say it reveals her own radical inclinations to be so forgiving of such a prank."

He squinted, evidently still too drunk to follow. "A prank?"

"Haven't you heard?" Cecily said, her voice hushed. "Apparently, Lady Lucie left some radical suffrage pamphlets around Claremont so that the Prince of Wales could find them."

His expression didn't change, but she now had his full attention. "Did she say it was her?"

Cecily gave him a puzzled look. "No. At least I did not hear her confess," she added quickly.

"Ah well. Then it wasn't her."

"How certain you are," Cecily said, her blue eyes amazed.

"It's a pointless provocation, which is stupid, and considering the duchess is her friend, it would also be disloyal. Your cousin is neither stupid nor disloyal."

Cecily's smile was sugary enough to make a man's teeth ache. "You know my cousin well."

"You don't have to know her well to know this about her."

"How quick you are to judge a person's character," Cecily marveled. "Do you think it is your observant writer's eye?"

Mother of God, help, he thought as he smiled at Cecily so brilliantly, she tripped over her own feet.

Lucie ambushed him on his way back to the breakfast room. She looked as warm as black ice, and he knew he should have had a coffee first before engaging with that.

"Did you do it?" she demanded.

He was unprepared for the bodily reaction to her accusation. His muscles turned rigid. A warmth that had lingered in his chest since last night dissipated.

"Did I scatter a few pamphlets around a ducal palace?" he said. "To discredit you? When no one with an ounce of brain matter would contemplate such a thing?"

Her gaze was sharp like the point of a dagger, trying to make forays into his very soul. "It is no secret that you are trying to outmaneuver me."

She did not think he had much of a brain, he remembered. Lazy or a fool, she had called him, or maybe both, and it seemed she had returned to regarding him such.

"I suppose you think our dance last night was also part of a ploy," he said.

"I don't know what to think about you anymore." She stepped closer, bringing with her the clean scent of lemons. Her upturned face was tense with rancor. "Sometimes, I think you do not know whether you would rather seduce or sabotage me."

He shrugged. "It would amount to the same thing, would it not?"

Her chin jutted out. "I admit, I briefly thought there was more to you."

He could have handled it like the adult man he was. Instead, he allowed the carrot-haired boy to take the reins. "Why not take my offer and be certain, how much there is to me?" he murmured. "It stands for the summer, remember?"

He didn't bother to watch her walk away. Her back would be rigid, her skirts snapping, and all things considered, it was better that way. He needed a brief respite from her. He might have set out to seduce her, but dancing with her, flirting with her, revealing pieces of himself to lure her in had evidently begun to affect him, too, laying parts of him he had not realized he still possessed bare to her attacks, and he needed to regroup.

Chapter 21

"I favor this one." Lucie slid the magazine toward Hattie across the office desk, her index finger on the open page.

Hattie briefly peered at the fabric sample beneath the black-and-white lithography, then shook her head with such vigor, the pearls on her earrings clicked together. "You need them to be heavier, and they most certainly should not be purple. Purple, Lucie?"

"Why not?"

"Because it is purple."

"A color that has gravity, but is not gray, which is drab, as you informed me. And I prefer a lighter fabric over a thick one—airy rooms lift the human spirit. It says so in the piece on page twenty-seven in this magazine."

Hattie's lips remained firmly pressed into a line.

"All right," Lucie said evenly. "No purple."

She should have never become involved in selecting curtains—there were only twenty-four hours in the day and there was presently little progress on more pressing tasks on her list. But since last week at Claremont they had decided on a gentle reform rather than a coup, it stood to reason that London Print would continue to exist, if not expand, and therefore it required a look reflecting their new direction and a space accommodating of female employees. To her surprise, Tristan had simply nodded and signed off her budget proposal when she had presented the measures required for the refurbishment. Ever since, new furniture arrived, worn carpets were discarded, and a partition was being torn down. The process stirred up a lot of dust, and the heavy thud of workmen's boots echoed up and down the hallways of the office floor. The staff grumbled as they continued to work amid the chaos. They could not just take a week's leave, thanks to an explosion in orders for Tristan's works—word that the Prince of Wales had endorsed the diaries had quickly spread far and wide. The production manager was already in an uproar. "We can manage one of the books on time, but not both of them, certainly not if you also wish to redesign the periodicals," he had cried at their last meeting, red in the face with exasperation.

A faint ticking began in Lucie's temples as she recalled the meeting. Her life, so carefully calibrated over the years to accommodate all her different duties, was perilously close to staggering around like a drunk. *Consider delegating more . . . delegating is an art form.* Easy for Melvin to say. She could of course put Hattie fully in charge of the décor, but just yesterday her friend had proposed wall tapestries depicting kittens for the women's office, and much as she loved cats, this was not her vision for London Print. If she tasked someone other than Hattie, her friend's sensibilities would be hurt, which would result in a drawn-out sulk. Lord help whoever got between Hattie and her quest for her next project.

"What do you think of midnight blue?" Hattie said. "Blue is calming—"

The largest of the bells on the wall behind them rang; whoever was currently staffing the desk in the antechamber was asking for permission to enter.

"Excuse me." She gave her own bellpull a tug, and a moment later, Lady Athena, niece of the Countess of Salisbury, stuck her strawberry-blond head into the room. "Apologies for disturbing you, but the overseer of the workmen is asking where to place the crates with the new stationery."

Lucie gestured at Hattie. "Lady Athena, allow me to introduce Miss Greenfield. Hattie, Lady Athena is currently standing in as staff for, well, every vacant position, and she shall be in charge of curating the content for the *Discerning Ladies' Magazine.*" She glanced back at the young woman at the door. "Please tell the man to place the crates in the storage room, as we discussed this morning."

"I did," Lady Athena said tightly. "He insisted I confirm it with the gentleman in charge."

"Naturally. Do you feel comfortable telling him that you are tasked with giving the instructions and if he wishes to get paid, he refrain from disturbing the gentleman in charge?"

"Exceedingly comfortable," Athena said, determination hardening her intelligent face as she closed the door.

Hattie gave her a questioning look. "She seems very competent."

"So far, she is."

"Is she a suffragist?"

"At heart, I think she is; officially, not yet."

"You shall recruit her eventually," Hattie said with confidence. "Whatever happened to the old receptionist?"

"He handed in his notice on the day Mr. Barnes left."

"Oh."

Lucie shrugged. "It left an additional vacancy for a woman in need of employment. I scheduled a first round of interviews to staff the positions for tomorrow."

"Now, that's exciting." Hattie's eyes were sparkling, because as someone who would never have to apply for a position unless she insisted she wanted one, she found breadwinning, applications, and interviews exotic and intriguing to witness.

"The advert was in all major newspapers yesterday," Lucie said. "We are also looking for a new typist, as well as an additional copy editor."

Hattie's brows rose. "I understand it's not entirely uncommon for a woman to train as a typist these days, but I haven't heard of any female copy editors."

"There are—there must be. Emily Faithfull ran Victoria Press in the sixties, and her office was staffed entirely by women. I made some inquiries last week, and I understand the press is in a man's hands now, but I am planning to pay him a visit, to take a closer look at the press and to speak to any remaining female employees."

"That sounds clever," Hattie confirmed.

"Still," Lucie said, "what I really need is a woman capable of running the entire operation."

"Which operation?"

"This." Her sweeping gesture included the desk, the half-emptied, sagging shelves, and the chandelier with its dusty crystal drops. "I cannot run a publishing house in addition to the suffrage movement. I was in a position to bring enough women investors together to purchase it, and I must help ensure the right future direction, but running the day-to-day business—how?"

"No, of course you cannot," Hattie said. "Do you have anyone in mind?"

If only. She rubbed her temples. The pulsing headache was a frequent companion lately. It would vanish if she took a few days in the country and rested her eyes, but she would not have time to do so for a while.

"I reckon Lady Athena shall rise to the occasion, but the transition period is a challenge," she said, wondering not for the first time about the all-around haphazard planning. "And now there's also the added difficulty of her needing to handle Lord Ballentine."

Hattie made to say something, which she swallowed back down, her white throat moving, and she settled for a polite "Hmm."

"Hmm?"

Hattie closed the magazine, then opened it again. "Perhaps it will be less challenging than you think," she said, "finding a woman who will be able to handle Lord Ballentine. Just make sure she's older and acting very stalwartly, like a headmistress, perhaps."

"But I *am* older and acting stalwartly."

"Of course," Hattie said quickly. "But wouldn't you agree that there is a rather, erm, special antagonism between the two of you?"

Lucie's brows came down. "No. I feel our antagonism is perfectly normal."

Though she couldn't deny that it had taken a turn for the worse. After mildly intoxicated discussions on garden benches and a dreamy waltz, the return to reality had been jarring. It was still unclear who was responsible for the pamphlet incident, but she had not apologized for suspecting Tristan, for he hadn't denied it, and now he was more villainous than before. Since their return, he had scheduled several meetings pertaining to his books with staff and suppliers and she had not received an invitation. Every time they were both in the office, she saw him strutting around and sticking his nose into the different departments, asking questions, requesting ledgers, and yesterday, he had drawn up a plan outlining changes he deemed necessary for the distribution process of the book division—again without consulting her. But while he was certainly trying to provoke her, it was more worrying that he appeared to take a genuine interest in the workings and improvement of the enterprise. And unlike her, he had a lot of time on his hands to be in the office from morning till night and to delve into the details. Worse, though their truce appeared to be over, her erotic dreams of him were not. Ludicrous scenarios slipped into her sleep at will at night, and no matter how heated the chase, he always dissolved with his lips still an inch away from touching hers. It left her with a perpetual irritability throughout the day.

The bell on the wall jingled again, the sound shrill and grating against her thinly stretched nerves, and before her hand could reach her bellpull, the door swung open and Tristan's broad shoulders filled the frame.

Her stomach dipped, as if she were falling. Speak of the devil.

He looked angelic. Burgundy waistcoat; immaculately fitted jacket; a healthy glow about his face and hair.

"Lady Lucinda. Miss Greenfield."

"Lord Ballentine," Hattie said breathily.

The nonchalance with which he now strolled into her office, his gaze wandering around the half-renovated room with a guileless expression on his face, had her nape prickling with foreboding.

She leveled a stare at him. "How may I help you?"

There was a black binder in his left hand. She did not like the look of it.

He halted before her desk.

When their eyes locked, her heart leapt against her ribs. Something shimmered in the air between them, and for a fleeting moment she could feel the warm pressure of his hand on her waist when he had pulled her into the dance. She shifted in her seat, the surface of her skin sensitive against the cotton of her undergarments.

As though he had guessed this effect on her, he dropped the binder on her desk and leaned against it with easy familiarity. "I just wanted to inform you about the new production schedule," he said.

She stilled. She hadn't discussed a new schedule with production, or anyone else.

"As you know," he continued, "our capacities are overburdened thanks to about a thousand preorders of my war diaries and the second edition of the poetry—"

"You discussed a new schedule, with production? Without me?"

He looked mildly irritated at the interruption. "I have."

"You must not rearrange the schedule without consulting me."

"Don't worry," he said in a benevolent tone. "I organized everything with the company's best interest in mind."

Her nails bit into her palms. "If the magazines are affected—even if not—I need to take part in these discussions."

"But we already know that the books must take priority. Potential profits based on preorders after a mere week are higher in absolute terms than profits in the previous three months put together. Take a look." He opened the binder and tapped his attractive finger at one of the figure columns.

Her gaze bore into his as she rose from her chair. "I wish to be present during meetings that affect us both."

"I am sure you do, dear, but it's hardly necessary." He had leaned in, too, was close enough for her to smell him, and smiled. "The men will listen to me over you anyway."

She wanted to smack the smirk off his soft mouth. She wanted to do all sorts of things to his mouth. How feebleminded, to want a man she disliked.

Her face was hot, her voice cold. "Your games do not change the fact that my party owns half of this company."

"Ah. That." He dismissed it with a shrug. "Fact is also that men reflexively turn deaf to the shrieking voice of an agitated female. Even more so when a rational, male voice is available instead."

She nearly did shriek then.

"Tell me who loaned you the money for your shares, for I should quite like to have him poisoned," she said instead.

He gave a surprised laugh. "I'd like to see you try," he said, "but even you would struggle to take down Blackstone. I reckon he gargles with strychnine as part of his morning routine."

The name told her nothing, but Hattie gasped in surprise, reminding her that she was still in the room. Her friend was regarding Tristan with wide eyes. "How?" she asked.

He tilted his head at her. "How what, Miss Greenfield?"

Embarrassed heat reddened Hattie's cheeks, but she pressed on: "I presume you are speaking of Mr. Blackstone, the investor?"

"The very same."

"Well, he is incredibly elusive, so I'm wondering how you possibly secured a deal with him," Hattie said. "My father speaks of little else at dinner lately; he is awfully keen to win Blackstone for an investment project in Saragossa, but I understand he never responds to invitations."

"And naturally, your father would be delighted that you are sharing classified information with us, yes?"

"It isn't classified, not at all," Hattie said hastily, but her blush was deepening. "Still, it would probably be best you did not mention it to anyone? Except, perhaps, to Mr. Blackstone," she added, her brown eyes beseeching.

Tristan shook his head. "No, dear. I am not going to broker deals between the mighty Julien Greenfield and his business archrival."

"No, no, of course not . . . but perhaps you could tell me which club he visits? Which places of leisure?"

There was a pause.

"Right," he said. "Well, he does frequent places of leisure."

The faint undertone in *leisure* made Hattie fall into a confused silence, and in Lucie's mind, it conjured up images of Tristan wearing his slippery red silk gown as he stood surrounded by bodies in various states of undress, the prince of debauchery in his realm.

She cleared her throat. "We have work to do here," she said, and his attention shifted back to her. "I shall see you later on the matter of the production schedule."

To her surprise, he simply nodded and picked up the binder. "Of course. I look forward to it."

He sauntered from the room, looking complacent even from behind.

She slowly blew out a breath. Her thoughts were whirling. She needed to speak to production. She needed to get rid of Tristan. She needed to help Lady Harberton with her campaign for women on bicycles. She required her days to be forty hours long.

"I gather he has not made Mr. Blackstone's acquaintance in a reputable establishment," Hattie said, still staring at the door where Tristan had vanished.

"You can be certain of that," Lucie said dryly. "May I ask the purpose of this vigorous little interrogation?"

"It was hardly an interrogation," Hattie murmured.

"You wouldn't let him leave the room."

Hattie's shoulders sagged. "All right," she said. "As you know, I contribute little to the Greenfield family fortune, with my overriding interest in the arts and my poor numeracy skills." She worried her bottom lip with her teeth. "Zachary is the heir, my sisters make reasonable investments, and Benjamin is the apple of Mama's eye. I'm none of these things. I might as well not be present at all during dinner. If I could have helped secure a meeting between my father and the notorious Mr. Blackstone . . ."

"What is so notorious about him?"

"Well. For one, he is very wealthy, and very cunning." Hattie's voice had lowered back to a murmur. "Don't mistake me, he is recognized as an investor and man of business, and the merchant class does want his money. Lord Ballentine was right to call him a Greenfield rival because his investments are good. But very few people have actually met him in person. No one knows where he comes from. And he has driven several peers into financial ruin for seemingly no good reason at all. And he ignores my father's requests for a meeting—only a greatly impudent man could afford to do so." She shuddered. "Some people refer to him as Beelzebub."

Beelzebub?

"Grand," Lucie said coolly. "Whether he is officially a man of business or not, it appears that de facto, he is more of an underworld lord, and presently, he owns part of our publishing house."

Hattie sucked in a breath. "Oh dear. If you put it that way—"

"I must get rid of him."

Hattie's tawny brows flew up. "Of whom?"

The tinny sound of the bell interrupted—again. She made a mental note to uninstall it.

The tension in her shoulders eased when it was Lady Athena, not

Tristan, who made a return. The lady looked a little flushed. "Apologies for disturbing you again," she said. "Several large boxes of Ballentine cards have just arrived and we haven't discussed where to put those."

Lucie blinked. "*Boxes* full of them?"

Lady Athena gave an apologetic shrug. "Apparently, a trader in Shoreditch has taken up the proper production. It appears Lord Ballentine ordered them here."

Lucie's eyes narrowed. "I see. Why don't you have them deposited right in front of Lord Ballentine's office door."

Athena hesitated. "Right in front?"

"Yes."

"Of his door?"

"Yes. Stack them high, if you please."

"As you wish," Athena said slowly, a frown on her freckled forehead as she vanished.

Hattie was smirking at her from the corner of her eye, looking like a red-haired imp. "Perfectly normal antagonism, is it?"

"You just witnessed him—he's a nuisance."

Hattie's smile faded. "To be frank, if he sees eye to eye with men like Mr. Blackstone, I worry he goes beyond being a mere nuisance."

Lucie wouldn't admit to it out loud, but she had reached the same conclusion, and it worried her, too.

After her arrival in Oxford in the evening, she stopped and hovered in front of the Randolph on her way home, because there was light behind the curtains of Annabelle's rooms on the first floor. She must have returned from Claremont after the house party to resume her classes. Presumably, she was alone. Montgomery never spent any time at the hotel; she understood the duke was in London when Annabelle was here.

She navigated the stairs and hallways of the hotel as quickly as the heavy satchel on her hip allowed, keen to avoid any unexpected encounters with her mother or Cecily, who had indeed set up home here for the summer.

Annabelle looked pleased to see her despite the spontaneous nature of the call. She ushered Lucie into the drawing room, and into the most comfortable armchair next to the fireplace, and fussed when she heard her stomach growl—would she be interested in some of the hotel kitchen food, chicken breast in lemon sauce with a side of roasted potatoes?

"A brandy sounds even more interesting," Lucie said, uncertain whether the spirit would ease or compound her headache.

"I have sherry," Annabelle offered. She started toward the elegantly curved liquor cabinet below an equally elegant landscape painting. She hummed softly while selecting a bottle and pouring a glass, looking serene in the muted light filtering through the rose-colored curtains. Lucie's fingers absently drummed on the chair's armrest while something inside her grated against the room's rosy, tidy surfaces and plush upholsteries and the lingering fragrances of jasmine perfume and linen starch. Easy contentment floated up from every corner, underlined by the sedate ticks of the clock, and she vaguely felt like an intruder.

Annabelle handed her the sherry glass. "How was your day in London?"

Frustrating.

"It's a flurry of activities," she said instead. "There's the refurbishment, and I have scheduled interviews for tomorrow. The production manager is on the brink of an apoplexy—we have well over a thousand preorders for new Ballentine books, and the reprints for the old ones." She raised the glass to her nose and sniffed. "I think we shall have to purchase some printing capacity elsewhere, if we wish to deliver on time."

Annabelle settled in the armchair opposite. "I would have thought that a high number of orders was a reason to rejoice?"

The sherry ran down her throat stinging and sweet. "It is." It also gave Tristan more power. She had seen the figure columns today; depending on production costs, he was well on his way to making their enterprise substantial profits.

She lowered her lashes as another tide of pain hit the back of her eyes.

"Are you quite well?" she heard Annabelle say.

She nodded. "I am, however, worried that we won't find another way to publish our report," she said. "It would have been of great use to us to publish it before Montgomery puts the amendment before the House of Lords."

"Indeed."

"Currently, we are not only *not* finding a solution; I am preoccupied with an entirely new, unplanned undertaking that demands time and resources away from my actual work."

They fell into a drowsy silence. The sherry was taking effect; Lucie's core was warming, and her head spun in lazy circles, not unpleasantly. She studied Annabelle, looking cozy and benevolent in her armchair, and the grating sensation returned.

I'm jealous, she realized. *I'm jealous of a dear friend.*

She did not envy Annabelle her besotted duke, though she supposed it had its charms to be the wife of a man who was keen to lavish his enormous wealth and affection upon her.

No, she envied Annabelle her contentment and her grace and softness, wrapped around a core of steel, and that she was able to receive and bend a little if required, and thus she would not break even when a formidable force like Montgomery was bearing down on her. She was like a blade of grass, could be near flat one day, upright again the next.

She suspected it was quite the other way around with her—her exterior was steely, useful for plowing paths where there were none, but beneath the rigid shell, outside the facts and figures and goals to be achieved, matters were quite nebulous. Her emotions were rarely graceful, and they had been an unrefined riot ever since she had watched a naked Tristan take a candleholder in hand. Hard shell, malleable core. She was not a blade of grass. She was more in the way of an exoskeletal insect. An overwrought one, as of late.

She swallowed the remaining sherry in one gulp and put down the glass, feeling dizzy. "Annabelle. If I were to take a lover, what would be the consequences, do you think?"

Annabelle went very still.

She was shocked, Lucie supposed. And she would have never put this question to any other woman, but she suspected that Annabelle and Montgomery had not just left it at exchanging longing glances before deciding to jilt convention and get married. Surely, her friend could not be *too* shocked on the matter of taking lovers.

"Well," Annabelle finally said. Her gaze was uncompromisingly direct. "I believe you know the effects an intimate association with a man can have on a woman better than most, given your occupation."

Lucie inclined her head. "Possibly."

"Your now asking me to lay it out for you leads me to believe you desire confirmation that it would be a poor decision," Annabelle continued. "Which in turn leads me to believe you are already rather too fond for your own liking of making that poor decision."

"I have always admired your deductive skills."

Annabelle huffed. "I suppose," she said, "I suppose it depends." Her mouth curved into a hesitant smile. "Have you met a gentleman you like, then? Though I suppose if he were truly a gentleman, he would not just offer you a dalliance."

"Goodness, no—I don't like him much at all."

Annabelle's face fell. "Then I'm afraid I don't understand."

Neither do I.

There were Tristan's sinful good looks and his reputation, of course, which could lead a woman to think it would be worth it despite his ungallant character. But it was more complicated than that.

She might think about him precisely because he was a scoundrel. The thought of an intimate affair with an upright, mild-mannered gentleman bewildered her—as Annabelle said, such a man would offer marriage, which was not an option for her, and entanglement of any sort with such a man would be destined to end in disappointment. But a rakehell like Tristan? She would never owe him her courtesy. She would never have to struggle to maintain a sweet disposition or prove herself to be someone she was not around him—he'd care nothing for her manners anyway.

"It would still be risky," she muttered.

"Indeed," Annabelle said evenly.

"If anyone found out, my reputation would be ruined." Plenty of married women and widows discreetly took lovers with little consequence, but never-married ones? She'd had a taste of how it would look like back in Claremont's breakfast room: stares and turned backs, as though she were contagious. Her daily experience magnified tenfold. Except that the people who mattered to her would be compelled to ignore her, too—the women and activists she'd come to admire and rely on over their shared efforts.

"There's certainly the danger of rumors and a soiled reputation," Annabelle said. "But there's always the risk of more severe consequences."

"A child."

Annabelle gave a small nod.

"There are ways of preventing that." She was familiar with them all. She was also aware that none were guaranteed to work.

"And diseases, since we are already shockingly frank," Annabelle said. "And then, of course, all the other ways in which a man like him can ruin a woman."

Lucie froze. *A man like him?*

"Don't worry," Annabelle said pointedly. "I don't know who he is. But if you contemplate a clandestine affair with a man you do not care about, I certainly know his sort. He must have captured your attention thanks to base attraction alone; he strikes you as an outstanding lover. He probably is, and Lucie, these men all have one thing in common: a mere affair with them hurts a woman's soul."

Lucie made a face. "But I told you I have no care for him."

"Very well." Annabelle leaned closer. "What I know is that a good lover can addle your brain. He can make you feel things you neither expected nor wish to feel. And what if the passion you share with him is second to none, and ruins you for all others?"

Lucie waved a dismissive hand. "But if one takes a lover, there's hardly a point in selecting a mediocre one? I do, however, worry about jeopardizing my reputation—it would hand the opposition to our cause splendid ammunition."

Annabelle's features softened. "What about yourself?"

"Me?"

"Yes, you. If you did wish for a happy-ever-after with a man, you could have it."

She gave a little huff of surprise. "I confess I find a fairy-tale ending involving a man difficult to envision, given the circumstances."

She used to think that she was lucky to have been born now, rather than a century or two ago. "Spirited" girls with ambitions could respectably get by as spinsters these days, or eventually settle down with staid old professors called Bhaer.

Annabelle sighed. "Well, whichever path you choose, doing something in your mind is different from doing it. Reality has unpredictable consequences. You could accidentally cross the Rubicon."

The following morning, she took an early train to London in her powder blue dress, her hair locked into the most sensible bun she had managed, because that was precisely what was required of her now: being sensible. It hadn't come naturally, lately.

Bemusement set in when she approached the imposing granite façade of London Print.

An orderly queue of smartly dressed women lined the pavement up the front steps to the publisher's lobby.

The queue continued across the foyer.

Covert glances and nervous smiles greeted her as she strode past, and still it did not dawn on her until she had reached her office floor, where the queue had derailed into a small crowd around a flailing Lady Athena, that these were her applicants for the positions she had advertised.

"Good morning," she said, baffled and to no one in particular.

A chorus of *good morning*s rang back, reminiscent of a class full of well-trained pupils in a village school.

A small smile spread over her face as she made her way into her office. What an unexpected, wonderful development this turnout was.

The first applicant was a Miss Granger, five-and-twenty years of age, from Islington. Hectic red splotches bloomed on the woman's neck above her high collar as she pushed the binder containing her references across the desk.

Lucie gave her an encouraging smile and picked up her pen. "Miss Granger, why don't you tell me a little more about why you are interested in working for London Print?"

"Well, milady, there just aren't enough gentlemen to go around for marriage these days, are there?"

". . . Right."

"I considered applying for one of the government grants that help single women find husbands in Australia, but after due consideration I decided I'd prefer to stay in England and find employment instead. Either way, we must be prepared to make our own bread these days."

"Indeed," Lucie said, "but why should you like to work here rather than say, a government office?"

The blue of the woman's eyes lit up. "Oh. I do enjoy the magazines. My mother has a subscription to the *Home Counties Weekly* and I read every issue."

Lucie nodded as her pen scribbled away in her interview diary. This was the enthusiasm she needed to see. Working life in London held challenges for a woman; some motivation besides a wage would help sustain anyone who joined the office.

"I also adore *A Pocketful of Poems*," said Miss Granger, a slight pitch in her voice.

Lucie slowly raised her eyes from the page. "You do?"

The nervous flush claimed Miss Granger's cheeks and nose. "Yes," she said. "I was so surprised to hear Lord Ballentine was the author."

"Weren't we all," Lucie drawled, not liking the heated gleam in Miss Granger's gaze.

"He has such a scandalous reputation, but his poems made me believe it is based on rumors," Miss Granger enthused. "Surely a true rogue wouldn't be capable of such emotional depths?"

"What an interesting thought."

"Is he here at London Print often? Lord Ballentine?"

"I'm afraid not, no."

It had come out decidedly too dark, for Miss Granger's face assumed a vaguely embarrassed expression, as if she'd been caught in the act of doing something naughty.

Lucie took a deep breath. To no avail. The headache returned with pounding force.

The next applicant was a Mary Doyle, heavily freckled, and twenty years of age. She had traveled all the way from Birmingham and the purple smudges beneath her eyes said she had risen at an ungodly hour to reach London on time.

"Miss Doyle—you are applying for the typist position, but from your papers it is not quite clear for how long you took typewriting lessons or where you worked before," Lucie said, rifling through the woman's application with a small frown.

Miss Doyle was studying the wood grain on the desk. "I have not yet fully trained as a typist, milady."

Lucie arched a brow. "I see?"

A demure glance. "I was hoping I could acquire all the necessary skills here, at London Print."

Lucie shook her head. "I commend you for your aspirations, but this position requires a fully trained typist," she said, and when disappointment turned Miss Doyle's mouth downward, she added: "It is, however, a good idea to establish a course here to teach women these skills."

Such a good idea, in fact, that she was making a note of it in her diary.

"Would working here also involve tending to Lord Ballentine's administrative needs?" came Miss Doyle's voice.

For a blink, the swirls of her own handwriting blurred before her eyes.

She looked up, half-surprised that the girl didn't turn into stone as their gazes locked.

"No position here," she said, "involves tending to Lord Ballentine's *needs*."

Mary Doyle's shoulders fell. "I heard he owns London Print."

"Half. He owns half."

The little time waster from Birmingham perked up. "Are you in need of someone serving refreshments, then? I have some experience with handling a tea cart."

By the time the next candidate walked in, a woman in sunshine yellow muslin with a suspiciously enthusiastic spring in her step, the pulse in her temples radiated heat with every beat.

She cleared her throat. "Good morning, Miss . . . ?"

"Potter, milady," the girl said, then blushed, curtsied, and pulled back the applicant's chair.

"Miss Potter. What made you apply to London Print, apart from the possibility of catching a glimpse of Lord Ballentine in the flesh?"

The girl quite froze in the act of lowering her bottom onto the seat, her mouth opening and closing without producing a response at first. "Nah," she said. "I must make my own bread, my lady. I'm in need of employment, here in London, to care for my mum." She bit her lip and gave an apologetic shrug. "But I'm afraid it's well known that his lordship looks like an angel."

"I see," said Lucie. "Do excuse me for a moment."

In the antechamber, dozens of faces turned toward her, pale ovals beneath hat rims and artfully arranged front locks. How many of them had done their hair this morning with special care, with only one thought on their mind? By the time Tristan's office door came into view, her heart was thrumming harder than her headache.

He sat behind his desk in only his waistcoat and shirtsleeves, head tilted, writing something. A lock of his overlong hair had slid loose and fell into his eyes.

She pulled the door firmly shut behind her.

He glanced up and looked bored to see her, though his eyes lit with faint intrigue on the interview diary in her hand. That was how she noticed she was still holding it. It would be satisfying to hurl it at his stupid, handsome head.

"I'll take it," she said.

A puzzled expression passed over his face. "Well, that's lovely. And what would *it* be?"

She flung the diary onto the nearest chair.

"Your offer." She raised her chin. "A night in your bed for a percent of shares. I'm taking it."

The bemusement was wiped clean off his face. His expression was an utter blank.

Her chest rose and fell violently, her head filled with the bright roar of a storm hitting a forest.

"Are you now," came his voice, a low murmur.

She gave a nod, her throat feeling too tight for words.

His eyes bore into her, and she stared back into the golden depths, face hot, hands clenched. Let him try to call her bluff.

She watched his gaze fill with an unholy light.

He leaned back in his chair, toying with the fountain pen between his fingers for a beat or two.

"Then I suggest you lock the door."

Chapter 22

She had gone and done it. There was no stopping it now; her words were on the loose like hounds on a hare, like a tumbling rock already setting off the avalanche.

She blindly searched the door behind her back for the lock.

The metallic click of the key raised the fine hairs on her nape.

Tristan was not moving a muscle there behind his desk; he appeared transfixed.

She crossed her arms. "Did the cat get your tongue, my lord?"

His lids lowered, making slits of his eyes. "Come here."

Her heart was trying to flee her chest, the erratic thumps almost painful. She dropped her arms to her sides and approached as commanded, but she slowed when she rounded the corner of his desk.

She halted an inch outside his reach.

The chair scraped across the floor when he pushed away from the desk to face her. His knees spread, head cocked, he was contemplating her, and she endured his inspection with a defensive little sneer fixed on her face, endured it as the silence between them stretched and hummed—

He gestured at her head, a lazy flick from his wrist. "Take down your hair." His voice was husky.

Her knees turned shaky. He was going far to try and call her bluff. Or perhaps he was not calling her bluff at all. Perhaps he was serious. Perhaps he wanted to begin *it* right here—he would be depraved enough to try.

She raised a hand to her hairpin.

The audible hitch in his breathing made her pause.

His eyes were fixated on her fingers as they hovered over the pin, looking . . . hungry.

Interesting.

He might sprawl and issue commands, but unaffected, he was not. It made her give the pin a tug. Another twist, and her hair slid free. The scent of citrus soap wafted up as the long strands unfurled and cascaded down around her to her waist.

Tristan shifted in his chair, color tinging his high cheekbones. Tiny flames of vindication licked amid her loathing, and she brushed her hair back over her shoulder, the flick of her wrist mimicking his, mocking him.

His gaze was on her face as he patted his left thigh. "Take a seat," he said, his voice very soft.

She froze, all sense of triumph dissipating. "That is not necessary."

His smile was a little cruel. "You would sit on vastly more intimate parts of me very soon if you took the offer."

If? Took?

"Fine."

She stepped between his legs, stiffly turned her back to him, and sat.

His left arm immediately slipped around her waist, his hold light, but the gesture alone was deeply possessive.

She stared ahead at the wall, dimly aware of a wooden cabinet, busily patterned wallpaper, outdated sconces.

The alien, muscled power of a male thigh beneath hers registered even through layers of fabric. It made her body so weak, she could not have struggled had she tried.

Tristan leaned closer, bringing his chest against her back.

"Why are you here, Lucie?"

His breath touched the sensitive side of her neck. His chest was warm and hard like a sun-soaked brick wall against her shoulder blades. Goose bumps prickled down her arms. *You would sit on vastly more intimate parts of me very soon.*

"I am taking the deal," she managed. "You said it was a standing offer."

He made a noise, half scoff, half growl. "Do you want me, then?"

The gruff question was disorienting. The wall, the cabinets, the sconces, were swaying before her eyes.

"I want you far away from London Print."

His free hand delved into her hair at the back of her head. She tensed, but his touch was careful. Confusingly careful. He let a lock slide through his fingers, and then another, slowly, as though he were studying each pale strand before releasing it again, and a different tension entered her. She clamped her knees together to quell the urge to move. Her scalp was warming from the minute tugs of his fingers intimately combing through her hair, and the heat filtered down her nape, sank heavily into her breasts, low into her belly, down to her toes.

She gasped when his thumb grazed her bared nape.

His lips moved softly against the shell of her ear. "My dear, it is a simple question: do you want me in your bed, or not?"

She gritted her teeth. "Anything to get rid of you."

"I see."

He slid his fingers from her neck, down her arm to her wrist. The warm pressure of his hand flattened her palm against the inside of his right thigh, and he guided her up. And up.

Sparks flashed across her vision, knowing where he was going.

She made a tiny noise in her throat.

His pause was infinitesimal. Then he moved her hand over him.

Heat poured through her. Her breathing was the loudest sound in the room. She was touching a man's part, an astoundingly hard, hot, and heavy part that briefly made her wonder: how? How would it . . . work?

She tried to pull away. "Let go."

He did, but it was too late. Now she knew. This was the stark reality of the deal, leaving no illusion, nowhere to hide. She would never be able to undo this, once it was done.

"Are you so vain as to want to be wanted for yourself?" she bit out. "But of course you are."

"The bravest woman I know, so evasive." His tone had turned conversational, as though he had not just splayed her fingers over his rampant arousal. "Why can you not answer me?"

Her palm was still burning with the feel of him. She made a fist. "The answer is simple: you leave me no choice."

"Is that what you must tell yourself to get your fill?" he murmured. "The permission you need to lie with a man like me—that you had no choice? Very well." He pulled her flush against him and buried his face in the crook of her neck. "Lucie, Lucie. I shall include you in every meeting at London Print whether it pertains to your interests or not. I shall sign off whatever you wish unless it will damage our revenue. No more games in the offices, on my honor. What say you now?"

Her heart was battering against her ribs, against his constraining forearm. He was reading her with his body, nosing her skin and breathing her in, like an animal taking scent, and it scattered her wits to the four winds.

She turned her head to face him. The emotion in the depths of his eyes was glowing hot like embers.

"Honor, you?" she said. "No. I think you are trying to dissuade me. You are trying to repel me because you wish to keep control of the company after all, and you'd rather not rescind your offer like a fickle coward."

His smile was dark. "Think of me what you must. But understand that I'd rather be damned than shag you unless you want it for acceptable reasons—and the only acceptable reason is lust. Pure, plain lust."

She felt molten and hot, and the realization that it could be *lust* made her spring to her feet. She nearly took a tumble because Tristan had released her with no resistance at all.

She spun back round to him and found his expression had cooled. "I was rattled when I made the offer," he said. "You had provoked me, with your righteous raving about my uselessness, all while you were making lustful eyes at my chest."

She blanched. "You are a wretch."

He raised a shoulder in a shrug. "Well, yes. I gather it is part of my appeal."

She stared at him, how unruffled he appeared now, how he was not even attempting to cover the prominent bulge at the front of his trousers, and the mad thought flashed how very badly she wanted to see him on his knees.

But first . . . oh, it took effort to look him in the eye.

"Assume I want you," she said. "Assume I want you. I still want my shares, as offered."

Tristan stilled.

He slid an indecipherable glance over her, a number of emotions chasing behind his eyes.

"Go," he said, and abruptly came to his feet. "Go home. Now."

A peculiar outrage crashed through her. "Why?" she demanded.

"So you can cool your hot head, and think again."

He was looming over her, and she glared up in his face, not moving an inch. "You started this, my lord. Do not change the terms now. I am expecting you at my house, tonight. Eleven o'clock would suit me."

He hesitated. "Very well," he then said tightly. "But leave now."

He moved, forcing her to take a step back, and another, lest she wanted to be snug against him. He had paled a shade beneath his tan, she now saw. There was an unfamiliar tension around his mouth, and the tendons in his neck stood out. He was, she realized in a part of her mind separate from the bizarre situation, in an agony of sorts which he only contained with difficulty.

He was also bodily herding her toward the door.

She turned to take her leave but glanced back over her shoulder. "You must be discreet at all costs—take the small alleyway between my house and the house to its left. Then step over the wall enclosing my backyard. I shall let you in through the kitchen door."

He muttered a curse under his breath. "When you change your mind, do not come to the door. Do not open that door. And I shall take my leave."

"I shan't—"

"Go," he said hoarsely. "Unless you wish for me to sample the goods right here on my desk."

"You are very crude." Her hand on the key, she turned back once more. "We need an agreement that you will give the shares to me."

"Of course." He shot her a sardonic glance. "A contract, perhaps? Do you wish for me to summon my lawyer now, to record you as my mistress—to be paid in company shares for services rendered?"

"I need certainty that you will keep your word."

He was silent for a moment.

"May the powers that be strike me down if I don't," he then said roughly, and, perhaps foolishly, it made her nod and leave his office, her knees still trembling as though they had carried her through battle when this had only been the beginning of it.

Long hours later, when the narrow sickle of a moon had risen over Oxford and the cries of little owls drifted across University Park, Tristan reflected that he did not appreciate the irony of the situation. And there was fine irony indeed in being on his way to the house of a woman he had long dreamt of seducing, only to tell her no. To tell *himself* no. Once the immediate temptation had stormed from his office this morning, the sense of triumph over her surrender had not come; he had been too aroused from the feel of her in his lap, and once that had abated, it had been clear that he could not have her as long as she wanted her shares.

He slowed at the corner to Norham Gardens. The night was innocent, the air still and mild, smelling faintly of wood smoke and flowers. The bright haze of the Milky Way arched across the sky. If he were to go through with his offer, he would take the encounter to a secluded spot outside. But he would not.

There were options to keep control over an income without equal co-ownership of London Print, but those options were tedious and risky, given that he would be abroad and unable to keep an eye on matters. He could, of course, bed her, and keep his shares anyway. It was a safe guess she would then try her utmost to ruin the success of his books, and she would succeed, at the latest during his absence. She would probably do the same if he failed to show in person tonight to tell her no. She might want him, but she quite loathed that she did; thus, rejecting her now would elicit emotions he would have to take to his face. Therefore, there was a very rational explanation indeed why he now stood in front of her address in the deep of night.

The house was steeped in silence, its black windows staring broodingly into the night.

He entered the small, dark alleyway she had mentioned, and when he emerged again, the low wall surrounding her backyard was to his right.

The kitchen door was easily found, too. He knocked against it with his cane, and the stained-glass panes rattled in their rotting frames.

Interesting. He'd thought someone like her would be meticulous in the upkeep of things.

His body tightened with anticipation when her face appeared behind the window, a pale heart shape in the dark and without a sound to announce her, as though she had floated across the kitchen.

He unclenched his hands. She would have opened the door.

The key turned in the lock with a squeak.

"Hush," she said, craning her neck past him and hastily looking left and right.

She grabbed his sleeve. "Quick."

The kitchen was a blur, traces of light glinting faintly off the wall tiles. Her scent surrounded him, fresher, more pungent than usual, as though she had just taken a bath. Utterly distracting.

Now he noticed she was clutching a robe in front of her chest: of undecipherable color in the dark and overlong, the flowing, shiny material pooling on the floor around her. He could have been intrigued. He *was* intrigued.

"All right," he said reluctantly. "I shall be quick about this—"

"Yes, I would prefer that. Come."

She turned and vanished into the shadows as quietly as if carried on wings—was she barefoot?

He cursed under his breath but followed the trail of lemon fragrance into a pitch-black corridor. A few strides ahead, orange flickers danced on the wall, cast through an open door on the left through which Lucie must have disappeared.

When he turned the corner, he abruptly came to a halt.

At the back of the room shone an isle of light, created by a semicircle of gas lamps and candelabras. At its center, before the fire roaring on the grate, she had spread out a thick layer of blankets.

She had built them a love nest.

He was not lost for words often, but he was now. This . . . complicated matters.

Lucie straightened from lighting a last candle and turned to him, a reddish glow outlining her slim form. Her hair slid freely over the sleek fabric of her robe, and he felt himself heat and stir at the memory of the smooth strands against his palms, of her weight on his thigh, the press of her soft hand on his swelling cock. . . .

Sweat dampened his brow. He hooked a finger into his collar, loosening it. "Lucie. We must talk."

Her chin tipped up. "We have talked quite a lot, don't you think?" Her hands rose to the knotted belt, gave a tug, and the robe parted down her front.

A flash of white, white skin.

She was naked.

He made a sound, primitive and uncontrolled.

She yanked the robe shut again, but he'd seen enough. Enough to know things he would never shake again. She was infinitely sweeter than his depraved mind had allowed him to imagine. And she was blond—everywhere.

"Now that," he said, hoarsely, "is not fair."

She tossed her head. "Well. They say all is fair in love and war."

Right.

"Then war it is," he murmured. From a distance came the clatter of his cane hitting the floor. His coat, his hat, his jacket thudded behind him as he stalked toward her; by the time he towered over her, she looked alarmed and he was on the last button on his waistcoat. Her gaze followed the deft movements of his fingers, then flew to his face when the garment had landed on the blankets with a swish.

"What," he said, pulling the braces off his shoulders, "surrendering already, Tedbury?"

"I—"

"You will," he promised, sank his fingers into her hair and kissed her. She gasped, and he plunged his tongue between her lips.

Finally.

For a beat, he floated, absorbed in velvety, intimate heat. He knew her taste at last, *at last.*

He licked deeper into her mouth, already enchanted. A last, sane remote of his mind expected her to bite. There was a scrape of teeth, clumsy rather than angry. He'd let her draw blood if it pleased her.

He gathered her in his arms and pulled her up, mouth on mouth, chest to chest. Her mewl of surprise reached him through a haze. A riptide of sensation was dragging him under at the feel of her: sweet lips, soft tongue, her lithe strength in his arms. The need to be closer was ferocious, a drowning man's urge to come up for air.

He broke the kiss and set her down only to drag his shirtsleeves over his head.

Her gaze was on him, moving from his chest to the breadth of his shoulders, then down to the ridges of muscle on his stomach. An assessment every woman made when deciding: would it be worth it?

He hadn't wondered whether he passed muster in years. He was wondering now.

Their eyes locked.

She looked glazed and drunk.

Good.

Because any finesse had left him, and instinct made him artless and fast. His hands were on her shoulders and pushed rather than eased down the robe. Heat swept his body at the sight of her— breasts. A gentle flare of hips. Remarkably shapely thighs.

He was on his knees.

She squeaked when he grabbed her hips and buried his face against her belly.

"Tristan—"

He kissed below her navel, then licked, and she fell silent. She bucked when he did it again, and his grip tightened, because he was drunk, too; on her nudity and her fragrance, a heady blend of citrus soap and silky skin and more intimate notes of arousal. He kissed a downward path, following these notes, the feminine scent that turned a man more animal when it was right. When his mouth brushed over the spot where all her pleasure centered, he paused.

Heat pulsed against his lips, the beat of hidden places filling with desire. Oh God. It was very, very right.

He pressed the flat of his tongue against her. *Yes.*

He'd gladly spend the rest of his life right here, with his head between her thighs, murmuring filth and praise between his kisses . . .

A sharp tug on his scalp pulled him rudely from his bliss.

Above him, her face was flustered and flushed.

"Does it not please you?" His voice was rough.

Her eyes glittered with a million emotions. "I think yes," she said. "I think it does." She did not release the fistfuls of his hair. He was too hasty, he realized, shredding his reputation as a skillful lover in the wake of his greed. Greed? Or perhaps, a less flattering, more whimsical emotion—that she would dissolve in his embrace like a fae and he would never hold her again.

"May I?" His hands slid from her hips to her waist—a tug, and she tumbled down into his arms. She stared up at him wide-eyed, disoriented as though she had landed in a foreign country. A confused Lucie, naked, in his arms. A picture he knew so well from his daydreams, he could have sketched her with his eyes closed: the parted lips. The huge pupils. Her delicate throat moving in nervous anticipation.

Daydream Tristan proceeded to do dark and wicked things to her.

Daydream Tristan hadn't expected the ache. Holding her like this *ached*, deep within his chest, and the sensation spread outward, squeezing his throat and locking his muscles.

He quickly laid her down and stretched himself out beside her, trapping her with a still-clothed leg over her bare thighs.

Shadows and flickers of fire danced over fine female skin.

She looked small next to him. Hurting her would be easy. Too easy.

He rested his hand lightly on the sweet curve of her belly. The beat of her heart was noticeable even there, a hectic echo against his palm.

He splayed his fingers wide. "How do you like it best?"

Her gaze met his, uncertain. Did her lovers never ask?

"The usual way," she said, her eyes opaque.

"I am intrigued by *your* usual," he said, amused.

She gave a small shrug. "Why do you not try and find out?"

She wanted him to learn her by trial and error? "My pleasure."

He heard a mew when he put his mouth back on her again. He smiled darkly against her. She had made *that* sound despite herself. He lost all sense for time as he was pleasing them both by eliciting more soft noises of pleasure with his fingers and his tongue, until his back was covered in sweat and the urge to be inside her pounded in his blood like a battering ram.

She squirmed, slippery and panting. "I'd quite like for us to do it now."

So would he. But she was still tight enough around his one finger to make him cross-eyed. Not even Daydream Tristan would have proceeded with this.

He shook his head. "We are not ready."

Her feet drew restlessly over the blankets. "Please."

He pushed a second finger in, perhaps too impatiently, but just then she thrust up into his hand. Her eyes squeezed shut and she gave a sharp hiss of discomfort.

He stilled.

This was not a reaction he knew. Certainly not one he liked. Not one bit.

Her face relaxed only gradually. In renewed bliss? Or to conceal her emotions altogether?

A heavy feeling stirred in his gut.

His lust diffused, the room came back into focus—the crackle of the fire. The roughness of the wool blanket against his side. Details floated to the surface of his mind: the clumsy kiss, the little gasps of surprise, the way she was clamping too tightly, too anxiously, around him . . . surely not. Hell. Surely not.

He withdrew from her gently, not daring to look.

"Lucie."

Her eyes snapped open, wary and alert.

The brazenness of her greeting him in the nude. A worldly woman might do such a thing. Or a woman whose instinct was to fight rather than flee when presented with a challenge. Whatever the challenge. He felt a little sick.

"You . . ." He tried again. "You do have experience. With men. Don't you?"

Chapter 23

You do have experience. With men. Don't you?

The turbulence at the back of his eyes made her want to lie. But she never lied.

"Does it signify?" She sounded rather recalcitrant.

Tristan was regarding her as if she were a stranger. "Does it signify?" he repeated. "It does. Because I don't bed virgins."

"You don't?"

"Not ever," he bit out, and sat up.

She sat up, too, grabbing the edge of a tartan blanket to cover her chest. "Why?"

"Because they are virgins." He sounded prim, rather incongruous with his bare, tattooed chest.

"Goodness," she said, amazed. "The rogue has a conscience."

He blanched. "I do not. I just don't care for dramatics. A woman fumbling and crying in my bed—not my taste." He snatched his shirt off the blankets. "And they require training, which would be tedious."

A pang of panic hit her stomach when he came to his feet. He was leaving. The bite of pain he had caused was only just fading. He'd leave her with the pain and none of the pleasure.

"So it is a matter of convenience," she ventured.

"Absolutely." He struggled into his shirt, attempting it the wrong way first, and, when his head appeared again, he said, "No shag is worth major inconvenience. Therefore, no bedding of virgins, or sisters, daughters, or mothers of close friends—dealing with lawyers: major inconvenience." He stooped and picked up his waistcoat.

"Mothers?" she said, aghast. "Daughters?"

He was buttoning himself up with military precision.

He would leave.

She fought a surge of nervous anxiety. "I won't be inconvenient," she said. "I never cry. And I read widely on the matter, all sorts of accounts, lascivious ones—I know enough."

His eyes were cold. "You know nothing."

She came to her feet, her own temper rising. "You never asked whether I take lovers. And I never claimed I did."

"You talk about women acknowledging their desires," he said under his breath as he strode toward the heap that was his jacket. "A while ago, I noticed your coat smelled like my men's when they returned from a brothel—then again, you would walk through neck-deep debauchery just to take notes for an essay or such, of course you would."

She drew herself up to her full height. "It was hardly my intention to break your virtuous rules," she said to his back. "But it is too late. I'm afraid they have been broken; the virtue, and the rules."

He stilled. The hand that had caressed her so intimately clenched and unclenched by his side.

The speed at which they had gone from ecstasy to awkwardness was astounding. She was reeling from it. He was right, she knew very little. Still.

"Since my virtue has been disposed of, perhaps consider staying."

He turned around, disbelief plain on his face. "Disposed of," he echoed.

She gave an apologetic shrug. "I confess I never relished the idea of dying an old maid."

Of going to her grave never having been touched. Never having been kissed.

She had used to wonder how it would be, kissing Tristan, and her imagination had been lacking. It was a glorious and terrifying thing, the moment all-consuming, akin to hurtling toward the glittering surface of water after jumping from a great height. Of course, she had been punished for hurling herself off the rock back then.

It felt as though she was being punished now, too.

He was staring at her with anger in his eyes.

It dawned on her that his exaggerated reaction might be of a pragmatic rather than a moral nature. He had mentioned lawyers. He was a nobleman. And at the end of the day, she was still the daughter of an earl, unattached, and young enough to bear children. Men like Tristan could not ruin women like her with impunity; marriage was usually the only way to atone for such a transgression, and rakehell or not, the most sacred tenets of polite society would still run deep.

She sighed with relief, and his brows lowered censoriously.

"Tristan, you must know that the virtue of a woman my age is not a prize," she said. "It has low bartering value. Don't frown so—I don't understand precisely how it works myself. But one moment, a lady's virtue is her sole worth, the one attribute that determines who, if anyone, will marry her; the next moment, it's something to pity and snicker about because the lady failed to give it away fast enough. In my position, it is, frankly, quite useless."

Tristan slowly shook his head. "Do not use politics to try and command me to bed you."

He walked out, not taking his hat.

She stood staring at the empty doorway, a sinking feeling threatening to pull her to the floor. The most indiscriminate seducer of England was leaving without a backward glance, after merely sampling a taste.

"You have already *ruined* me—at least do it properly," she tossed into the room.

The answering silence could not have been more pointed.

She sank back down onto the blankets. "Please."

A numbing cold spread through her from a place inside her chest. She closed her eyes and forced a calming breath. It was unacceptable to feel unsettled over a man. Especially over such an indecisive one.

When her eyes opened, he loomed in the doorway, cutting her a look she would not be able to read in a hundred years.

She bit her lip. Had he come to collect his hat?

He walked straight past it, back into the circle of light, making the flames of the candelabra flatten and sway.

He went down on his knees before her, his expression a commingling of apprehension and want.

"Hell," he said softly. "I cannot deny you when you say please."

He curved his hand around the back of her head, and his mouth was on hers. Her hands fluttered up, startled, then settled on his shoulders. Worrying, how fast her lips softened beneath his again, how she already clung to him again . . .

Tristan raised his head, his breathing ragged. "Have you locked the cat away?"

She blinked slowly. "Why?"

He gave her a speaking glance. "The only claws I'm of a mind to enjoy on my back tonight are yours."

"Oh. I put her outside before you came."

He gave a nod. "We shall begin your tutorial, then. Lesson number one: never tell a man you won't be inconvenient."

She made to reply, and he shook his head. "Never," he said. "You would both be sorely disappointed. Now. Undress me."

He sat back on his heels, a challenging look in his eyes.

Her gaze traveled over his torso, assessing. There was a purpose to this, and she was not certain which.

"Very well." She raised her hands to push the topcoat off his shoulders, and her blanket slipped and pooled around her hips. Her cheeks heated. He was fully dressed, and she was naked, save the curtain of her hair.

He kept his eyes on her face. "Go on."

"Patience, my lord."

She divested him of the topcoat, then set to work on his jacket. He was not assisting her, and it was a near embrace as she wrestled his arms out of the tailored sleeves. The tips of her breasts brushed the silk of his waistcoat, and the delicate contact shot an electrifying current all the way to her toes. At her soft gasp, he shifted. She glanced up and found his face tense, his eyes black mirrors for the erratic play of the firelight.

"Courage," he murmured. "It won't bite." He nodded at his chest, at his waistcoat.

She hesitated. There was something rather deliberate about undoing buttons. A shyness came over her she had not felt when he had been on his knees before her earlier, doing scandalous things with his mouth. It would be easier, she reflected, if he were to just overwhelm her again now.

The waistcoat's buttons were mother-of-pearl, smooth against her fingertips. By the fourth, she was proficient at it.

"This is you still trying to change my mind, is it not," she said as her hands worked.

His smile held no humor. "If this part gives you doubts, you should refrain from what comes next."

He was not just giving her more time to reconsider, she realized. As cotton and silk slid through her fingers, she was learning his body, too: the strength and size and textures of him, the hardness of his shoulders when she pulled off his braces; the warmth and smoothness of his skin when she dragged her palms down the planes of his abdomen, and farther down, to the fall of his trousers. A haziness entered her and left her breathless at the first button there. By the time she had undone the last, she was burning. She touched him without looking, but the way Tristan's lips parted so helplessly when her fingers brushed over hot velvet made her head swim.

He snatched her hand off him and rid himself of his remaining clothes with remarkable speed. She was nudged flat onto her back, and he was on top of her, large and naked and radiating heat.

"Wait."

She had come prepared; she reached behind her and nudged the small wooden box containing the sheaths toward him.

The dark intent in his gaze never wavered, he just nodded and handled himself adroitly and with ease. But when he gathered her close again, the inevitability of what was to come made her weak in his arms. He rolled over her, keeping his legs well between her thighs, and his body on top of hers was heavy and overwhelming. A look into his lust-glazed eyes, and she knew she would never succeed at disengaging from his embrace unless he let her.

He must have sensed it, because his urgency eased.

"Lucie."

Her breath was coming in gusts.

"Lucie." He was holding her face.

"Yes?"

"Do you wish to stop?"

She eyed his broad shoulders, dwarfing her. She felt his desire humming in his muscles, barely leashed. "Will you be able to stop?"

Surprise sparked in his eyes. "Of course. Always."

Her hands, locked behind his neck, loosened again and flattened against his nape.

He lightly stroked her cheekbones with his thumbs. "I am not asking you to trust me. But trust me tonight. If you wish for me to stop, a word suffices."

Her longing returned as an aching, yearning pull.

She tugged his head back down. "I do not want you to stop."

He kissed her hard. But he came to her gently. He was careful with her, she felt it in the slowness of his advance, as though they were moving through honey. It was in the tenderness of his lips against her cheeks, her nose, her brow, as he sought to soothe the pressure of his possession. He was careful as though she were breakable in his hands. An entrancing sensation, to be fragile and to be handled with care. Entrancing also to see his face above her, wholly unguarded. He was a stranger and he was moving inside her, and she gave over to the steady, sliding rhythm, to his warm scent and his gasps of pleasure. She was floating, watching them from above sur- rounded by a ring of fire, his broad back over her, her slim white legs wrapping around his hips. She watched until Tristan arched and threw his head back on a broken yell.

She lay across his chest, and he had his arms locked around her as though he did not wish to be separated from her again just yet. She lay stiff in his embrace, feeling his heart beat hard and fast be- neath her ear, her own pulse still hammering from what had trans- pired. But as her mind rallied, trying to assert whether being held so intimately afterwards was a regular thing, her body was already soft- ening against his. As though it was quite familiar now with his phys- icality and considered him a safe place for resting.

As his breathing slowed, her head grew heavy on his shoulder. "You never stole my pamphlets at Claremont, did you?" she asked softly.

"Of course not, silly." He sounded drowsy. She lay and listened as he fell asleep.

Some time between the darkest hour of the night and dawn, he reached for her again, or she for him. She found herself back under him, caressing warm, firm muscle and kissing silk soft lips, until the growing urgency pulled her from her dreams enough to say yes, she would have him once more. He was one with the dark, but his hands raised her knees, and heat bloomed wherever he touched, and this time, his passion and patient persistence consumed her. When a white heat blazed behind her eyes, she bit down hard on her lip to stifle her cries.

Chapter 24

───❦───

*M*ost men are by nature rather perverted, and if given half the chance, would engage in the most revolting practices—including performing the act in abnormal positions; mouthing the female body, and offering their own vile bodies to be mouthed in return.

She was curled up on her side, the floorboards hard against her hip, and watched the morning sun draw gentle patterns onto walls and curtains. The room looked different, viewed from a blanket nest by the fireplace. A tranquil tableau of age-worn furniture and fading oriental rugs, all the lines softened by the fuzzy gold of dawn.

There was a dull ache between her legs that was new. She had expected this. The surprise was that the feeling wasn't entirely unpleasant. She smiled at the room. An old maid no more.

Some young women actually anticipate the wedding night ordeal with curiosity and pleasure—beware such an attitude!

She had read any variety of immoral publications to understand the relations between men and women, and yet it was prim Ruth Smythers's advice for new brides that kept intruding. The Smytherses of the world would have the vapors seeing her now, naked and glowing with warmth from her fingertips down into her toes. There wasn't an inch of her body where Tristan hadn't put his mouth. Not one part he hadn't licked or kissed by the time the morning chorus had filtered through the windows. She squeezed her eyes shut, her face flaming. The things she had let him do . . . A soft puff of breath behind her back had her freeze.

He had stayed the night.

What did one say, the morning after?

His even breathing said he was still asleep.

Gingerly, she rolled onto her back and paused. When he didn't stir, she slowly, slowly, turned over to her side.

He slept on his back, the powerful shoulders exposed, his face turned toward her. His forearm was flung carelessly above his head.

He had not been as cavalier last night. He had fallen asleep with his arms locked around her from behind, and whenever she had tried to creep to a cooler, less disturbingly intimate spot, he had dragged her back into the curve of his body without waking. Perhaps this was why some of his affairs ended in headlines of women threatening to jump into rivers—how easily he gave his lovers the feeling of being the only woman in the world, and that even asleep, he knew he must keep her close. Admittedly, it was a heady feeling.

The sun's rays streaming in made him golden, too. He was hardly in need of gilding. His scheming mind at rest, the structure of his face was uncorrupted by dissolution, cynicism, calculation. Here was the clean, gloriously symmetrical countenance of the angel Hattie and every Old Master aspired to eternalize on canvas. *The slumbering Gabriel in repose.*

Odd. She preferred him awake. Not one artistic bone in her body, and even she could tell that his wicked mind turned his face from perfection to alluring.

Her right hand slipped from beneath the blanket. Her fingers traced the air above his brow. The noble bridge of his nose. The ridge of his left cheekbone. She had once seen it bloom red with her handprint. How angry she had been at the ways of the world that day in Wycliffe Park. How helpless.

Her hand drifted lower, to his throat.

A sudden motion, a rustle, and her wrist was trapped in an un-compromising grip.

Tristan's eyes were on her, half-lidded but alert.

He must have been awake awhile.

She gave a tug.

He held fast, but his grip relaxed. The lingering look he gave her held all the hours of the night. A shameless replay of every low moan and kiss and eventual surrender. Two surrenders, truth be told. Sure enough, a smug gleam entered his gaze and she felt her face warm with a blush.

"How did you know my hand was there?" she murmured.

The corners of his eyes crinkled. "I smelled you." He raised her hand to his face and nosed the spot where she had dabbed perfume last evening. His voice was unfamiliar, deeper and scratchy with sleep. Arousing. She was corrupted already, for shame.

She propped herself up on her elbow. "You have a good nose."

His hazy gaze met hers over her wrist. "An extraordinarily good nose," he corrected.

"The animal is prominent in you."

"I did not hear you complain about that last night." He brushed his lips against the beat of her pulse, and the soft contact made her restless. Tristan's lashes lifted, a knowing smolder in his eyes that would have grated only yesterday. Now it roused anticipation. But his expression sobered. His hand slid up her arm and cupped her face, and he touched his thumb to her bottom lip, where she had bit down in ecstasy. It felt sore. "In fact," he said, "I did not hear you much at all last night."

She drew back. "It's hardly a requirement."

He nodded. "It isn't. But there is no shame in being vocal about your pleasure."

She glanced away. There were some last defenses a woman had to keep when she was being foolish, and for reasons she could not name, *being vocal* would feel like abandoning a last bastion. She did not want to abandon it.

Tristan sat up and cast a glance about the room, his gaze briefly snagging on Mary Wollstonecraft's call for women's equality above the mantelpiece. "We fell asleep here," he said. "Together."

"We did."

He gave a slight shake, as if to rid himself of a private confusion. "Why here? And on the floor?"

"My bed is too narrow," she said absently.

A bare-chested Tristan was impressive to behold when tempered by shadows and firelight. In the morning sun, with the blanket slipped down to his hips, it was intimidating to look at him but also impossible not to.

In the light, the inking covering his right pectoral stood out in vivid detail. An intricately patterned circle the size of a saucer in different shades of blue, and at its center, a long-haired female dancer, waving . . . multiple arms? Studying it gave her some time to think, what to say, what to feel, as they sat closely together, smelling warmly of lovemaking and sleep.

The tattoo was remarkable: the dancer's expression was serene, her body caught mid-motion in a graceful turn. She was naked, but to Lucie's surprise, strands of her hair fully covered her modesty.

"It's charming, I suppose," she said.

"Charming? It's Pierre Charmaine's finest handiwork."

She raised her eyes to his. "Who is he?"

"Monsieur Pierre was a former officer of the French Foreign Legion. For reasons he never disclosed, he found himself in London a few years ago and now charges outrageous prices in a secret tattoo parlor in Mulberry Walk. I suspect a woman was behind his fall from grace."

"Aren't we always," she said dryly. "Why does the woman have four arms?"

"Because she is inspired by Lord Shiva."

"Right. And who would he be?"

The arms quivered when Tristan chuckled. "Shiva is one of the three principle deities of Hinduism, also called Mahadeva. He is the Lord of Divine Energy, creator of the universe, the god of transformation and destruction. He holds more roles and names, depending on which sect of Hinduism you study. It is complex. He is often depicted with blue skin, four arms, and a snake around his neck."

"A god of destruction." She was bewildered. "But naturally, you then go and ink a woman onto your skin."

He gave her a grave look. "I'll have you know that when I stayed in General Foster's house, I had conversations with the Pujari, the temple priest, after which I considered it wise not to tattoo all powerful deities onto my thoroughly debauched English body."

More rules and principles. And his debauched body had now thoroughly debauched hers. If she continued to blush so fiercely, her face would soon stay permanently pink.

"Mulberry Walk?" she said. "I was expecting a tale involving a sailor, a drunken wager, and a back street in Kabul."

He shook his head. "When I left Asia, my scars were still healing."

It took a moment before different pieces of information, collected and stored over recent months, linked together. He had been shot when saving his captain.

She peered more closely at the inking. The small podium beneath the dancer's pointy-toed right foot was not as smoothly executed. The texture of the skin was puckered, and the purple tinge wasn't ink. It was the color of scar tissue.

"How . . . awfully whimsical," she blurted.

"Isn't it just," he crooned.

She didn't think. She leaned in and pressed her lips to it.

It startled him as much as it startled her. When she glanced up, his features were oddly frozen.

He recovered quickly enough. "I suppose congratulations are in order," he said lightly, and, when she was silent with confusion, he dipped his head. "To the majority ownership of London Print."

She blinked. "Of course. Yes."

She pulled the blanket more tightly around her shoulders. From the corner of her eye, she spotted her robe, stretched out limply at the foot end of their makeshift bed. Next to it was the small wooden box.

She looked away. "I have to speak to the Investment Consortium before I can transfer the sum in full," she said. "It may take a few days."

"There is no hurry."

Discussing the transaction was the first thing since their coupling to make her feel like a trollop. He must have known it would have this effect. A rather distancing effect.

Hoofbeats sounded outside her window, and the fine hairs on her arms rose with a sudden bout of nerves. "My housekeeper will return soon," she said. "I gave her leave for the night, but she could be back any moment now."

Tristan was already sliding his shirtsleeves over his head, and she turned her head to give him privacy when he rose to reach his trousers.

She did steal a glance when his back was turned. The shirt was long enough to cover his backside. After touching it last night, she would have quite liked to know what it looked like.

"I shall pay the price you paid for the shares, rather than what they are worth now," she said.

He paused in the process of adjusting his braces. The look he gave her back over his shoulder was unreadable. "You drive a hard bargain, my lady. More fool me for not insisting on a contract beforehand."

She crossed her arms, and he turned to her fully.

"I jest," he said. "Considering that you have been shortchanged, it's perfectly acceptable."

"Shortchanged?"

He shrugged into his waistcoat. "You experienced the agony of bliss just once, didn't you."

The agony of bliss. The white heat wave that had overtaken her during their second joining.

"It was all new to me," she said.

His eyes softened. "It was not a reproach. Not in the slightest."

Her smile was a little evil. "But it would make for a most unflattering rumor, wouldn't it. Ballentine, infamous seducer, fails to satisfy."

His gaze narrowed. "Possibly."

He tipped up his chin and tied his cravat with the careless fluidity that came only with years of practice, a purely masculine gesture; surprising, too, since he had a valet, and it made her pulse flutter a little faster. He must have sensed it, for he slid a wholly indecent gaze over her rumpled appearance and said: "You could, of course, allow me to redeem myself."

Her heart gave an appallingly eager little pounce. Another night with him?

There was pause as reason grappled with older, baser instincts.

"I suppose I could," she finally said, not quite meeting his eyes. "I give my housekeeper leave every Friday night."

Another pause.

"Friday is tomorrow," he said, sounding casual.

"Correct."

"How convenient."

A sinking feeling took hold as she watched him pick up his cane and his topcoat. He would leave now, and she'd be here, alone with the enormity of what she had done. And with what she was about to do again.

He put on his hat and was fully transformed back into nobleman, albeit a rumpled one. The look he gave her went straight through the blanket she was still clutching like a damsel.

"The same time, the same place?" he asked.

She could only nod.

A wink, a bow, and he was gone. A moment later, she heard the kitchen door fall shut, the old windows rattling in their pane.

Normally when sexual stupor faded, a sense of well-honed detachment returned. Today, it didn't. He was waiting, but the feeling did not come, and by the time he had walked twenty minutes and reached Banbury Road, he was shaken. He had finally bedded the woman he had had an eye on half his life and walked away from it feeling *shaken*. His head swam, from the summery air or a daze wholly unrelated to the weather, and it took several attempts to hail a hackney.

In the dark heat of the cab, the night returned with full force. Lucie naked. Lucie flushed. Lucie flat on her back, gazing up at him with nervous anticipation. Every image seared onto his mind in brilliant colors, as though they had been his first taste of an erotic education.

His head dropped back against the battered upholstery, sweat sliding down his back. He never stayed until morning. He'd learned early that it created expectations, which created complications. He had not only stayed, no, he had asked her for an encore and he had to laugh at his foolishness. He had expected to bed exactly one virgin in his life—his wife, a faceless woman in a nebulous future. The carriage walls were decidedly too close.

Lucie's hands on him, with the feral curiosity of a kitten. He could see now that she had very much chosen him to *dispose of her virtue*, to use her ungallant turn of phrase, and he was at a loss as to how he had earned such trust. The urge to fling the precious, breakable thing away rolled through his body in waves. A deeper, darker part of him wanted to stash it at the very back of a cave and guard it possessively until kingdom come.

Another issue forced itself to the surface of his mind: if he wished to be a man of his word, he had a problem. Because she would insist on her bloody shares, and then she would go and do something hare-brained and progressive with the periodicals, and, in consequence, hurt London Print and thus, his bank balance.

He was calmer by the time he arrived at the front door of his lodgings on Logic Lane. Naturally, it would require a second encounter to satisfy more than a dozen years of endured slights and boyhood fancies. And of course he would find a way of keeping his source of income intact.

"Good morning, Avi."

"Milord." His valet unconvincingly pretended not to see him wearing yesterday's hopelessly crinkled attire.

"I'm in need of a bath. A hot one, if you please."

"Certainly, milord." Avi was following him up the stairs. "I placed the train tickets and the bouquet for her ladyship onto your desk, as milord requested."

He had no idea what his valet was talking about, until he remembered that he had promised his mother the gossip from the house party. He was traveling to Ashdown. Today. The real reason for a visit being, of course, that he had to assess her suitability for a sea voyage and decide how to best abduct her from the house.

"Bloody hell," he muttered, and then: "Stop making disapproving faces behind my back, Avi—you knew when you accepted this position that I was going to spend my days philandering and cursing."

"Yes, milord."

"It won't change, mark me, it won't."

"Of course not, milord."

A letter was on his desk next to the train tickets, without an address of the sender, but he recognized Blackstone's painstakingly even handwriting at a glance. The man could destroy people and apparently find out his address on a whim, but still wrote like a child practicing his ABCs. . . . The rest of the note was much in the way of Blackstone, too, congratulating him on paying off the first rate of the loan, and confirming that publishing was a solid investment these days. It read friendly enough, but it was above all a reminder that Blackstone kept an eye on his whereabouts.

Tristan dropped the letter in the bin. He should have handed his former partner his ledger of debts and secrets in full as payment and let it be done with. Let the investor deal with the tedium that came with collecting gambling debts and the delicate maneuvers required for extortion. He had not used it in years. But the mere thought of giving the ledger away made his gut twist in protest. And his instincts never betrayed him.

Half an hour later, he folded himself into the steaming copper tub, wondering whether his instincts had betrayed him for the first time last evening when they had urged him to spend the night between Lucie Tedbury's pale thighs. Muscles he hadn't known he possessed were aching, because he had slept on a hardwood floor. And he had woken up one company share poorer.

He sluiced soapy water over his chest. Pressed a testing finger onto his bullet scar, and it responded with the same dull ache as always, as though she hadn't kissed it better.

He closed his eyes and tried to relax into the pine-scented warmth swirling around him. The tension remained tightly coiled in his limbs, because although one might as well lay claim to the wind, a feeling returned and returned: *she is yours now. She is yours.*

Chapter 25

Rochester must have been lying in wait after learning of his arrival, for he came sailing at him with great purpose the moment he entered the Great Hall.

"Tristan—a word, if you please."

He faced his father with a polite mask in place. If Rochester had but a sniff of his private turmoil, he'd root for the cause like a hound for blood, and nothing good would come from it.

The earl fell into step beside him, staring ahead, his hands clasped behind his back. The eyes of a dozen long-dead ancestors followed their silent track along the portrait gallery until Rochester said: "I want to commend you."

Now, that put him on edge impressively fast.

"I heard you made a full success of Montgomery's house party," Rochester continued. "The prince, the matrons, everyone was pleased."

Considering all these were good things in Rochester's world, his eyes were oddly flat when he finally looked at him. "Wycliffe has signed the marriage contract as a result."

Everything inside him went quiet. Lucie was looking back at him, her usually pointy face trusting and soft. His knuckles cracked into the silence.

"Congratulations," he said, sounding bored.

Rochester halted. "It has also come to my attention that you are financing a business with Blackstone money."

And there was the reason for his father's mood.

"In part, yes," he said.

Rochester's pupils narrowed. "The man is dangerous."

"Is he," Tristan said mildly. "It must have escaped my notice."

There was a pause, where Rochester was deliberating. "Blackstone was one of the reasons I had you enlist in Her Majesty's army," he then said, and, when Tristan's face must have shown his surprise, he nodded. "I don't know what crimes you were involved in precisely, but it was only a matter of time before something would have besmirched the reputation of our house or seen you dead. And he may count as a reputed businessman now, but Blackstone has deliberately ruined the lives of peers before—mark me, he is ruthless."

"He is utterly ruthless," Tristan said, "and dangerous, and intractable—and quite beyond your reach, I presume." Precisely the reason why he had borrowed from Blackstone.

Rochester took a sudden, small step toward him. "I do not know yet what your game is," he said softly. "But I know that you are playing. And I am watching you."

Tristan tilted his head in acquiescence. "I would expect no less."

It was why he hoped he'd find that his mother was improving as he climbed the stairs to the west wing, because he couldn't shake the feeling that they were running out of time sooner than expected.

His hopes were answered when the lady's maid admitted him to a sun-flooded bedchamber. Mother was sitting up in bed, supported by several large pillows, her braid tidy and her eyes promisingly lucid. Her gaze lit on the bouquet he had forgotten he carried, pink hothouse peonies with big fluffy heads.

The maid scurried to take the flowers and to procure a vase as he approached the bed.

His mother raised a white hand toward him, and he bent over it.

"My dear boy, I'm cross with you," she said in a mildly chiding tone.

A hint of alarm sizzled up his spine. No, she could not possibly know about what he had done with Lucie.

He pulled a chair closer and sat. "What have I done, Mother?"

"You should have told me." She nodded at a letter on her cluttered bedside table, several pages crammed with erect and narrow penmanship. "Lady Wycliffe tells me you and Lady Cecily are engaged."

"No," he said, and, when her brow crinkled at his abruptness, he added, more gently: "I haven't signed any papers yet. Nothing has been announced."

"I see," his mother said, her frown easing, and then the corners of her mouth lifted. "No announcement is required. I can tell the change in you—there is a dazzling brightness about you." Her fingers made a fluttering motion toward his head, and he could not blame this on any of her tinctures, because it was the kind of thing she would say even when she was well.

"Still," she continued, "I should have liked to hear it from you, rather than have Rochester confirm it. How terribly unorthodox in any case, to leave the matchmaking to the lord of the manor instead of the mistress. But I suppose I'm not much of a mistress these days."

"Do not worry about it," he said quickly.

"Oh, I do—but I am so pleased for you, Tristan."

He blanched. "You are?"

Her lashes lifted, and the warm glow in her eyes nearly took his breath away.

"Of course," she said. "I badly wish for you to be happy. And a wife might settle you."

"Ah," he said, amused. "But I'm hardly unsettled."

"All officers are lost after the war, my dear. Like fish on the dry. Now. Tell me everything. Because while the girl was obviously besotted with you since she wore braids, I confess I never noticed any particular affection on your part."

She was looking at him expectantly while he processed the revelation of Cecily's enduring attachment to his person. Meanwhile, the maid was moving about with the vase, her head bent, her cheeks flushed, more mouselike than usual. She was all ears, wasn't she?

"Well," he said. "Rochester certainly recommended her wholeheartedly."

"Your father doesn't have a heart, darling."

"I cannot possibly comment on that," he said slowly.

There was something different about his mother today. Glimpses of her old gumption were shining through, possibly revived by the prospect of a wedding. Well, hell.

"Who would have thought such a demure girl would attract your attention?" she mused. "But then it's always the quiet ones who make for a good wife, I suppose."

"I suppose," he drawled.

"I'm so terribly happy." She sighed, and again her lips were making the effort to smile.

His throat constricted unpleasantly. "It pleases me to see you happy," he said.

She patted his hand. "You must take her out." She glanced back at the letter. "Lady Wycliffe says you reside a few streets away from each other—I understand they settled there to be close to you for the summer, to give you time to become more closely acquainted. And yet you haven't even had an outing in Oxford."

He was aghast. They had settled in Oxford because of him? "Lady Wycliffe is very involved," he said.

"Why, of course. We women are always worried about our charges. And a gently bred lady needs to be wooed, especially"—and now her tone turned a little stern—"when the groom has a past. You must leave no doubt in Lady Cecily's mind about your affection if you want your sweetheart to rest easy."

He shifted on his chair. "Right—"

"Why not take them on a picnic? No, I know—take them punting." She looked visibly invigorated by the thought.

A mental image of him, Cecily the Cat Poet, and the mother of the woman he had recently deflowered, in forced proximity on a wobbly punt, accosted him, and he'd rather enlist in another tour through the Hindu Kush.

"Oh, how delicious the sky looks from here," his mother said, her eyes now wistful on the slice of blue revealed by the tall windows. "Is it warm outside? I'm of a mind to take a trip."

"Grand," he said quickly. "What do you think of, say, India?"

She cast him an amused glance. "I was thinking of the folly."

The folly. Not even half a mile away from the house.

"Carey," she addressed the maid, "what do you think of an outing to the folly?"

Carey, who was hovering in the background like a listless ghost, solidified. "I don't know, milady." The worry in her voice was palpable. "Perhaps the fountain would do just fine for now?"

The fountain. Two hundred yards from the house.

A sea voyage with an invalid into an only rudimentarily organized future was looking less and less like a master plan. Had it ever been a master plan? Or just the illusory idea that he could do both: keep her safe and escape Rochester's marriage match?

What if he told her? *Mother, your husband is using you as bait and you are not safe in your own home.* She might expire on the spot. Already she was deflating before his eyes: too much talk and matchmaking excitement. She barely reacted when her lady's maid placed the vase next to her bed.

"Carey read me your poetry," she said when he had already taken his leave and was on his way to the door. "I am proud of you."

Her meaningful undertone made his nape tickle. He turned back and found that her gaze had blurred, and that she might not see him well at all.

"And Rochester does not hate you," she murmured. "He is afraid you could become like me."

Mad like me, were the unspoken words. He stood rooted to the floor.

"What a curious thing to say, Mother."

It had of course crossed his mind, many times, whether the moods ran in the family.

As though he had spoken out loud, she shook her head. "I have been a great disappointment to your father. To everyone, I daresay. His anger is part fear, Tristan. But you must never fear, my dear— you have all that was best of me, and none of the curse. At your age, I had long been afflicted. Unfortunately, Rochester is not one to recognize nuances; it is all the same to him."

He took a step toward the bed. "You are hardly cursed. What is the purpose of telling me this?"

She was already drifting into sleep, or pretended to be, and eventually, he left with his instincts for trouble high on alert.

Rochester's valet, Jarvis, stood lurking in the corridor, yards away from the chamber door. At least Rochester had not sent his spy right into the bedchamber with him.

"Milord." The hushed female voice made him turn back. Carey, the lady's maid, had slipped out the door after him. When she spotted Jarvis, she abruptly came to a halt, her dark eyes widening beneath her cap before she quickly dropped her gaze.

Instinctively, Tristan moved his body between the valet and the woman. "Yes, Carey?"

The tops of her ears were crimson. Any number of reasons could be the cause: addressing him without having been spoken to; looking at him; fearing the valet. She glanced up, her gaze not quite meeting his.

"Nothing, milord," she whispered, mortified. "Congratulations on your engagement." She hurried past him, her shoulders looking tense.

The time from Thursday morning to eleven o'clock Friday night had crawled by more slowly than the passing of a woman's rights amendment. Lucie had had ample opportunity to doubt and revoke her decision to invite a rogue back into her bed, and she had dithered. She had languished in the unfamiliar purgatory of suspense over a man, and she disliked it. Her stomach had somersaulted every time she thought of Tristan stretched out lazily on the blankets in the drawing room again. By the time he did duck through her kitchen door, looking unfazed and smelling deliciously of himself and hints of wood smoke, she had developed a bit of a temper.

He knew after taking one look at her face, for his mouth curved into a wicked smile, and before she could utter a word, his right hand cupped the back of her head and pulled her in close for a kiss.

Her mind was still spinning when he hung his coat and hat on the servants' rack next to the china cupboard.

"You are quiet," he remarked as he walked to the sink to turn up the tap. "A little tense, even?" There was a teasing note in his voice.

She was about to be skin to skin with him again. She was already shamelessly wearing her robe, and her feet were bare. Of course she was tense.

"Not at all," she said, her first lie in years.

"No? Well, good." He was looking at her with a soft heat in his eyes while tugging off his gloves, slowly, one finger at the time. By the time the gloves lay side by side on the kitchen counter, warmth tingled in her cheeks and lips. She was familiar now with what he could do with his fingers.

She watched him spread the creamy lather of soap over his hands, watched as a lock of his hair fell over his forehead, and how the gaslight cast his terrifyingly beautiful profile into stark relief, and the sudden force of her desire for him frightened her. *A good lover can addle your brain*, Annabelle had warned her. *He can make you feel things you neither expected nor wish to feel. . . .*

He was drying his hands when a growl sounded in the tense silence.

He raised an apologetic brow.

"Are you hungry?" she asked quickly. "Have you not eaten?"

He shook his head. "I came directly from the office in London. Come here."

She danced closer like a nervous colt. "You should eat," she told him.

The corner of his mouth tipped up in a small smile. "I shall," he said. "In a moment. Turn around." His index finger made a slow twirling motion.

She hesitated, but his smile became a challenge, and so she turned her back to him.

He brushed her hair forward over one shoulder.

"What—" She moaned in surprise when his thumbs expertly pressed into her shoulders.

His lips were warm against the bared side of her neck.

"Lovely," he whispered. "Do that again."

"You . . ." she murmured, and her voice faded, because he continued the delicate massage, skillfully manipulating his way to the sensitive hollow of her nape, then down again. He kneaded gently on either side of the pearls of her spine, until her head fell back against his chest. Her eyes were closed; she did not want him to see how much she wished for him to kiss her. How her body was already heavy with longing and needed his hands to slide forward over her breasts. . . .

His fingers fanned over her jaw and tilted her face up. She felt his lips against her own and then the heat of his mouth. She moaned, her thoughts dissolving. His other hand skimmed over her breasts, her belly, between her legs, where his fingertips pressed down. Darkness exploded behind her eyes; for a beat, all that held her upright were his hands. And they were bent on destroying her, one clever touch at the time.

His arousal was hard against her backside. At least the madness was affecting him, too. She arched, and he groaned, his grip on her tightening. She was turned in his arms and walked backward, kissing and grasping, and the edge of the kitchen table bumped against the back of her thighs.

He lifted her onto the surface and stepped between her legs.

Her gaze was heavy-lidded. "On the table?" she murmured.

He brushed his index finger over her damp bottom lip and dragged it down over her throat.

"I believe you told me to eat," he said, and sank to his knees.

A whimpering noise; it must have come from her. She was familiar with the things he could do with his mouth now, too. His hands slipped up her thighs, parting the robe wide, and his fingertips dug into her hips as he pulled her closer to the edge. Her eyes were shut again, but she felt him. He rubbed his face against the downy inside of her thigh, abrading her skin with the grain of his cheek, then the velvet of his lips, back and forth, rough and soft sliding into each other, until her shaking fingers tangled in his hair to try and pull his head to where she needed him.

A low laugh shook his shoulders. He looked up. "Tell me," he said, his eyes black with lust. "How much do you detest me now?"

She gasped. "This is not fair."

"Of course not," he said gently, "love and war, was it not?" He kissed her inches from where she ached. "Say it," he demanded, his mouth hot against her skin.

"I detest you," she whispered. "Very much."

But then he pulled her thigh over his shoulder, and she felt the liquid softness of his tongue, and the deluge of emotion flooding her was markedly far from the war side of things.

Chapter 26

When she woke the next morning in the drawing room, she thought of the kitchen table, and that she would never be able to look at it without blushing ever again. Could she have breakfast there now without her mind wandering back to last night? Leave it to Tristan to despoil a perfectly innocent piece of furniture.

He had again stayed, after he had carried her limp form from the kitchen to have his way with her before the fireplace.

He was awake now, up on his elbow, his chin in his hand, studying her with an expression of lazy satisfaction. His eyes were suspiciously free of guile.

Her own feelings were ambiguous. This was her last morning of waking up with a man. Last times had a touch of nostalgia to them even as they were still ongoing.

Tristan appeared oblivious; his free hand was playing with her hair, looping it between his fingers. "When I was here the first time," he said, "you said you had read *lascivious* accounts about lovemaking."

She blinked slowly. "Yes."

He tugged on the lock he had caught, and the gentle prick on her scalp sent goose bumps down her back.

"What was it that you read?" His voice was a low erotic rumble.

She gave a little shrug. "I suppose the most lascivious ones were in *The Pearl*."

He stilled. "*The Pearl*," he repeated. "By the Society of Vice?"

"Yes."

"Good Lord." He looked torn between shock and delight. "That is utter smut—the worst you could have chosen."

"So I gathered," she said, "vastly ridiculous, too."

"Ridiculous?"

"Yes. All these charming parlor maids and dear virginal cousins keen on sharing the unsuspecting male houseguest among them—it appeared to be a common theme in the stories."

He fell back and erupted in what appeared to be both laughter and a cough.

She sat up. "Are you well?"

He looked up at her, eyes liquid, and shook his head. "It is a recent publication," he said, his gaze turning calculating. "Either you started your education late, or you are diligently . . . maintaining it."

"What of it?" she muttered.

He touched her cheek. "Was there anything in those stories that you *did* like?"

There was a promise in that question. *Tell me your desires, your darkest ones.*

He would do whatever she asked of him, she understood. She looked down at him, glorious in his nudity, and briefly, she felt drunk on the possibilities that came with having a lover of few principles. It felt peculiarly close to freedom.

But this was their last morning. As it should be.

"You should leave."

He paused, then glanced at the clock on the mantelpiece.

"You are quite right." He let her hair slide free. "How rude of me."

He sat up and leaned in to kiss her forehead, his lips teasing and soft. He had to have a heart of stone, to indulge in such small intimacies and then go on his way without a backward glance.

She watched him as he turned and bent forward to reach his shirtsleeves, carelessly discarded on the floor next to their nest.

The morning light was bright on his back. It revealed a crisscross of faded white lines, from between his shoulders down to the small of his back, and it took her a moment to comprehend the nature of such scars. She laid a hand against his side.

"I thought the army had outlawed flogging decades ago," she said. "I was, in fact, under the impression that noblemen were not flogged at all."

Tristan had turned rigid under her palm. "It was not the army," he then said.

He came to his feet, and the disturbing pattern disappeared beneath a layer of fine cotton. She still felt unsettled. "Your headmaster, then?" she asked, because when she was unsettled, she investigated.

He turned to her, fastening his braces. "He must have dreamt of doing so on occasion, but no."

A cold sensation spread in her chest. "Rochester."

He nodded, and when her horror must have shown on her face, he gave a shrug. "Many fathers thrash their sons. Spare the rod, spoil the child."

"You were not thrashed," she said, her voice low. "This was cruelty. He must have had you beaten within an inch of your life."

"Oh, he did it all himself," Tristan said. "I give him that."

His expression was entirely untroubled, but she saw a lanky adolescent, who must have been bleeding and in pain, and a fierce emotion surged through her body and launched her to her feet.

Tristan paused in the process of buttoning his waistcoat, his eyes riveted on her, and she realized she stood before him in the nude.

She crossed her arms over her chest. "What Rochester did to you was wrong."

"What a lovely sight you are," he murmured. "Furious and debauched."

Unexpectedly, he reached for her and pulled her up against him.

The sudden feel of his clothed body against her naked length was a shock. She stood still as his one hand smoothed a slow, warm path down her back, then lingered suggestively on her bottom.

He knew what he was doing. He could make her feel things, he could change her moods with a well-placed touch. It was, upon closer inspection, horrifying.

And there was the sad truth of it: she did not want it to be the last morning.

Fleetingly, she wondered whether this was how it began for the wretched souls who ended their days in an opium den—with the thought: *only one more time.*

She peered up at him.

His lashes had lowered; he looked absorbed in the feel of her. But she sensed he would never ask her. *The male flaunts itself, the female chooses.*

It would not be sensible to ask him.

"I wish to see you again," she said.

His eyes opened, and her stomach dipped. She loathed it well enough—asking for things, and him of all people.

His hand flattened against her lower back.

"When?" he asked gruffly.

The tension in her shoulders eased a little. "Soon. But it cannot be here."

A pause ensued.

"I shall see to it," he said, and then his fingers came to her chin and tipped up her head, making her look him in the eye. "However," he said, "it means it is time for some rules."

Her brows swooped. "More rules?"

"Yes. Two nights can pass as an accident. Three nights are the result of deliberate forethought."

"And this is a matter of concern?" she asked, for there was an undercurrent of hesitation in his voice.

He shook his head. "No. Sometimes, it may take longer to slake a particular desire. But it requires that you tell me your expectations."

"What is the advantage, stating them?" She sounded skeptical.

"It may reduce regrettable misunderstandings."

He had done such things before, and she did not relish the reminder. She slipped from the circle of his arms to pick up her robe.

"Discretion," she said, turning back to him. "I expect you to be discreet." Her eyes bore into his in a warning. "My work and my reputation would be ruined if word got out."

"You are taking a high risk, my sweet."

She was aware, acutely so. "I am not above holding your books hostage," she said coolly.

"Charming," he muttered. "But clear. Anything else?"

She nodded. "Honesty."

"Honesty," he repeated, testing the word.

"Yes. Without honesty, there can be no trust."

"Ah, darling." His smile was lopsided. "My second rule is: do not trust me. Not in the deep, blind sort of way."

"Why?"

"Because even I do not trust myself such."

"Charming," she said wryly. "And your first rule?"

His tone was kind, but his eyes held a rare seriousness. "Don't fall in love with me."

Chapter 27

⸙

"How many letters have we presently?"

Lucie's inquiring gaze fell on Catriona. It wasn't Monday, but the additional workload caused by creating new magazine content and refurbishing a publishing house required additional meetings. She'd soon be able to span the length of her drawing room with her list of tasks.

"The count is at fifteen thousand, three hundred," said Catriona. "Give or take the reports delayed by poor mail service."

"Very well. On to our next point." Well, drat. She cleared her throat. "Are there any new ideas on how to publish our findings?"

As they were shaking their heads, her fingers tightened uneasily around her fountain pen. Now would be a good time to announce that she had, at least in theory, regained the majority ownership over London Print. Unfortunately, it felt quite impossible to tell the truth about how she had acquired it. Besides, she was, by now, rather fond of their new idea to gradually undermine the content of the periodicals. She should, however, have made a much more dedicated effort to finding a solution for the report.

It was her dalliance. Lingering preoccupation over their shared nights had begun to distract her during her days. Tristan had procured a room for them in Adelaide Street, half a mile from her home. The terrace house had a respectable façade and a well-concealed back entrance, and the housekeeper was never seen. She hadn't asked Tristan how he knew about such a place, which clearly only served one purpose: facilitating illicit encounters. For a week now, she had walked there near every night after dusk, had let herself in and left the door unlatched for him. Then she waited. For his footsteps. For the visceral clench of her belly when he appeared in the doorway. For the first bump of his lips against hers.

On all accounts, an affair with a scoundrel in a rented room was the pinnacle of tawdriness. Her detractors had classed her correctly all along, that she was not made right as a woman, that she was wicked. She knew because she *felt* right, lying sated on his chest, on a mattress that creaked, when she should have felt horrid. There was no honor in what they were doing, and yet she became alive in his arms in ways she had not expected to be possible; it was as though she were fully growing into her skin under his touch, stretching herself, in fact, when she had believed herself fully formed. She also never knew a word of judgment from his lips. His mouth only gave her pleasure. And since he was impossible to shock, she freely shared her thoughts, without any prior reflection on what would be an acceptable thing to say. In his arms, she breathed so deeply, she went dizzy from it.

"Lucie?"

She blinked at the three expectant faces looking back at her.

"Right," she said. "I am currently at a loss over other options for publishing our report."

This was not a lie; besides, the papers for the share transfer were still being drawn up by a rather confused solicitor Beedle—

"Lucie?"

Now they were looking at her with covert bewilderment.

"What is it?"

"We, erm, we are no longer discussing the report," Hattie said carefully. "We are currently discussing the St. Giles Fair."

"Apologies. Of course. The fair."

The annual fair on one of Oxford's main streets, attracting visitors from all of England.

"It is in three weeks' time, correct?"

"Correct," said Annabelle. "Will we have a booth? A banner? Shall we hand out leaflets?"

Lucie blew out a breath. "It's a gamble, politicking at a fair."

Granted, the St. Giles Fair was well visited, hence their chapter should be present. However, the circus music and overall exuberance constituting the atmosphere of a fair made suffragists and their pamphlets look particularly dour, as though they were bent on vanquishing the joy in people's lives, or so she had repeatedly been told on no uncertain terms when making a show at such events. And with its location at the heart of Oxford, there was a high risk of professors seeing women activists who were also students at the university, and the university frowned upon women's suffrage.

"We should do it," Catriona said. "I heard they will set up the wire with the flying trapeze again. Do you remember last year, when women and girls were allowed to use it for one day, and then the proprietor was asked to only admit men and boys? I imagine there will be plenty of women watching with resentment, remembering when they were allowed to partake."

Hattie nodded eagerly. "Low-hanging fruit," she said. "Who doesn't want to take a turn on a flying trapeze?"

Those were good points. She should have thought of them herself. It was unlike her, to overlook recruiting opportunities.

"Fine. Let us prepare some leaflets and tailor the message around the trapeze rather than something overtly political," she decided. "Annabelle, would you have time to help prepare this?"

Because she really didn't have time—she needed to be in the London offices tomorrow to interview the next batch of potential typists and secretaries, and the still-untouched bicycle campaign for Lady Harberton was hovering over her head like a Damocles sword.

"I shall draft you a leaflet," said Annabelle. "Which reminds me:

you have an alignment meeting with Lord Melvin on Montgomery's amendment proposal in Westminster in two weeks' time."

Lucie's pen made an unenthusiastic swirl into her diary. Another inch lengthening her task list. She could almost forgive her mind for straying ahead yet again to what the night might bring.

Would he come?

She had begun to wonder why he did, why he had not tired of it yet. Last night, she had wondered whether it was because possessing her body was not enough for a man of his appetite. She had wondered whether he was out for her very soul.

Tristan was stretched out on his back, still pleasantly sleepy, and relishing the feel of Lucie's hair flowing over his bare chest. *Winter rivers over sun-warmed rock.* The poet in him choked a little on the gauche image. She did inspire atrociously purple similes and sentiments, but beggars could not be choosers, and at least, at last, words were coming to him. She would of course balk at the idea of being a muse, passively inspiring a man just by the grace of her existence.

She slept, so he picked up a strand of her hair and let it slide through his fingers. He would never tire of doing so, would forever feel the temptation to wrap her locks around his wrist, his neck, his cock, until he was entangled in a sensual web that was all Lucie. But morning shone through the curtains at Adelaide Street, and from afar came the noises of an already busy street: buckets clanging, hooves clopping. Such was the peril of little rooms reserved for pleasure; one lost track of bothersome realities and time within their walls.

He carefully nudged Lucie onto her back and propped himself on his elbow to admire the view. She had not put her nightgown back on before falling asleep last night, allowing him to look his fill, so naturally, he did. He had fantasized about her breasts for years. Her stiff gray gowns had not revealed a thing, and so his mind had run rampant, envisioning everything from pretty nipples on a boyish chest to her binding an unexpectedly generous bosom. He liked them as they were, because they were hers, and he finally got to lick them. He did just that, lowering his head and putting his tongue to work on a soft rosy tip until it stood to attention.

Lucie stirred under his kisses. He raised his head and watched as her lashes gradually lifted.

Holding her in his gaze, he slid his hand down over her belly toward her thighs, and his caresses became intent. She shifted, her feet drawing restlessly over the sheets as his fingers danced over the softness between her legs until she gave him a tiny moan.

"Good morning," he murmured, and made to kiss her again.

She batted his exploring hand away with a cracking little slap.

He blinked. "Now I'm confused."

She closed her eyes again on a groan.

He leaned over her, frowning. "Are you quite well? Speak to me, Lucie."

She cut him an accusing look. "It must be bad for our health." Her voice was still drowsy with sleep. Perhaps she was dreaming still.

"Our—what is?" he asked.

"The frequency of us . . ." She huffed and drew the sheet up to cover herself. "You said it sometimes takes more than a night or two to slake a desire."

"I did."

"How many? How many nights?"

He drew back slightly. "A peculiar question, this."

She was staring up at the ceiling, her arms crossed over her chest with maidenly modesty. She had been far from maidenly last night; she had ridden him as though her life depended on it, and he felt heat pool in his cock just thinking about it.

"This . . . urge," she muttered. "It isn't going away. Do not say anything smug."

"It is early days," he said, and astoundingly, smugness was not on his mind. A mix of desire and alarm, perhaps, for she was right; the urge to couple with her was not abating. If anything, it grew stronger, and it was new for him, too. He had been trying to ignore it as best as he could.

"Twelve," she said. "It has been twelve days."

"Look who's counting." He entwined his fingers with hers and raised her hand to his lips.

She squeaked when he sucked her little finger into the heat of his mouth. Behind closed doors, she was full of little noises—dainty, fiery, noncynical ones, all of them intriguing. Never, however, when she came apart in his arms. Then she was silent. Even last night, when he had all but roared his pleasure. She was holding herself back, or something did despite herself, and it grated on him, though he was careful not to address it. There had to be reasons when the most outspoken woman he knew was silent.

He released her hand and said: "I was not honest with you."

Immediately, she tensed. "How?"

"Some urges cannot just be shagged back into obscurity."

"Oh."

"We may have a difficult case on our hands. Sometimes, it is a hunger that will only cease if you starve it. Indulging it makes it worse."

She contemplated this in silence, and eventually left him lounging in the bed to wash at the basin in the corner.

The room is wrong for her, he thought as he watched her carefully navigate the small space, and how she dried herself with a towel that was threadbare from too many washes. He wanted to bed her somewhere more befitting. A proper master bedroom in a country house, preferably one that he owned, with staff that brought her a breakfast tray in the mornings. She usually woke feeling ravenous.

Knowing her now, he reckoned that rather than being bedded on silk and down, she would prefer for him to tell her about his personal situation. Honesty was her second rule. Honesty probably meant him telling her about his father trying to marry him to her cousin, and him being India-bound with his mother to leave Rochester's tyranny behind once and for all. But where to begin with such a thing. Twelve days ago, even a week ago, it had been his personal affair, which had been none of her concern. He could not quite tell when they had crossed a line that made him suspect she would feel deceived and hate him if he told her now. He only knew, instinctively, that the line *had* been crossed. And that he did not wish for her to hate him just yet.

She had finished her ablutions, and restlessness took hold of him as he watched her pretty limbs disappear beneath layers of clothing.

"I won't see you tomorrow night," she said as she buttoned up her jacket.

The pang of disappointment he felt at the words was surprisingly strong. But he gave a nod—she did not owe him an explanation for not wanting to see him. Hell, he had just handed her all the reasons she needed with his little speech on how to starve desire.

He still sensed a hesitation in her, so he tilted his head in encouragement.

A rosy flush spread down her neck. "I expect I shall be indisposed," she murmured.

It took a moment for her meaning to filter through, as such a thing was hardly a topic of conversation among men and women. It was strangely touching that she would address such a private matter rather than leave him wondering in regards to her whereabouts.

He cleared his throat. "I presume you won't see me for a week, then."

She nodded and turned away to cast a final assessing glance into the small mirror. In a minute, she would walk out. And he would not see her. For a week.

"Forgive my asking," he said, "but are you indisposed during the daytime, too?"

She looked back at him, still pink-faced. "Why?"

"I should like to take you on an outing."

Her brows lowered in confusion. "An outing—just an outing?"

"There's no *just* about it," he said. "My outings are spectacular."

She was biting her cheeks not to laugh.

"Let me take you punting, the day after tomorrow," he said.

A flare of excitement lit her gray eyes to silver, but then she shook her head. "People would see us."

"Not if I take us upstream. There is nothing west of Lady Margaret Hall but rabbits and cows."

She liked the idea, and wasn't sure she wanted to like it; the struggle was written plain on her face.

"There would be a picnic," he said casually. "Strawberry tarts are in season."

She worried her bottom lip with her teeth, visibly torn, and he knew he had her. He didn't even try and hide his smirk. She was, in many ways, as much of a glutton as he.

Chapter 28

———⚜———

Strawberry tarts. Her mother used to be adamant that her sweet tooth would lead to her demise, but drifting along on the Cherwell beneath a clear blue summer sky was an unexpectedly enchanting path to doom. The sun was warm on her face. The air was still and filled with the scent of wild apple blossoms and the lazy ripple of waves as Tristan propelled them up the river.

She was watching him through slitted eyes. He was a dark silhouette against the glistening sun, his strong arms ceaselessly working the punting pole with languid, even strokes, and he was hers for the day. Taking her on an outing, as if he were her beau. She felt giddy and a little dazed. It was doom, all right.

Having forgone a straw hat, he shielded his eyes with his hand. "You may come up now."

She had climbed aboard upstream of Lady Margaret Hall's punt house to avoid being seen, and had thought it prudent to lie flat until they were out of sight of the footpath. The back of her light blue dress had been protected by a tartan blanket Tristan had brought.

She rose to a sitting position and placed the bonnet back on her head. "Oh, this is lovely."

Lush greens framed the riverbanks, and weeping willows dipped the tips of their branches into the glittering water. Her shoulders rose and fell on a deep breath. She hadn't been surrounded by such calm . . . in a while. She tugged the glove off her right hand and let her fingers trail in the cool softness of the Cherwell, and she felt Tristan smiling at her.

He eventually steered the punt onto a crescent-shaped patch of white sand where they could spread the tartan blanket.

"Let's see what my good man Avi deems essential for an outdoor luncheon," Tristan said as he went down on his knees to open the basket latches.

She slid her arms around his neck from behind and peered over his shoulder. "Intoxicating beverages, methinks."

Overwhelmingly, the basket space was taken up by a swaddled crystal pitcher, bottles of Pimm's, champagne, and lemonade, and a disappointingly small jar with strawberries. A longish object wrapped in brown paper turned out to be a peeled and sliced cucumber, to be added to the cocktail along with the strawberries.

Tristan scratched the back of his head. "I shall have to be clearer in my instructions next time."

"Don't be cross with the poor man," Lucie said pointedly. "He probably just packed what he normally packs for your outings with the scores of other women."

"My jealous one," he said, and shrugged out of his jacket to prepare the Pimm's in the pitcher.

His concoction turned out to be rather potent, and a few glasses and many champagne-logged strawberries later, Lucie's head was spinning. Tristan had stretched himself out long on the blanket and was using her lap as a pillow.

Looking up at her, his features were soft with languor. "I'll have you know that there aren't scores of other women," he said.

She laid her bare palm against his sun-warmed cheek. "The papers and scores of women say otherwise."

He leaned into her touch like a lazy cat. "Both lie," he said, his

eyes drifting shut. "Just think, I haven't been in the country much
since my deployment. My poor cock, it would be exhausting, bedding everyone who claims that I did."

She shook her head. "Why on earth would women lie about it?"

"I suppose once word gets out that you are good at bedsport,
enough people like to imagine that they took part in it. A lot of fellows are terrible at seduction in and outside the bedchamber, you see.
A lot of marital beds are cold."

Instinct told her there was truth to his words, and her stomach
gave a nervous lurch. She did not need reminding that the storm of
sensations she experienced in his arms was a rare thing, if not impossible to replicate. And a thought struck her that turned her insides
cold: how did one go on living well and fully present, knowing that
the brightest ecstasies lay already in the past?

She sat very still as the sparkling colors leached from the river-
bank. Surely, her greatest ecstasy would be casting her first vote in a
parliamentary election, the fruit of her life's labor. And that moment
most definitely lay ahead. Kept steadily moving out of reach like a
rainbow, in fact. . . .

She absently stroked Tristan's cheek. "So the affair with Lady
Worthington is not true?"

He chuckled. "I have never spoken to the woman."

"The incident with Mrs. Bradshaw in the linen closet?"

"Entirely made up by a mad editor at *Punch*."

"The jumping into the rosebush from Lady Rutherford's window?"

He opened an eye. "That one *is* true." He turned his head and
kissed her stroking fingers. "You are well informed about my movements."

"It's Hattie," Lucie murmured, distracted by the softness of his
lips against her thumb. "She reads and shares everything in the gossip columns. Why would you cultivate such a reputation if only half
of it is true?"

She felt the slickness of his tongue between her middle and ring finger and snatched back her hand.

"Very well," he said. "When I was young and juvenile, I noticed that it annoyed Rochester as well as made women I did desire take an interest in me. Such efficiency. So naturally, I fanned the flames. It soon developed a life of its own—the audience decides when to let a persona sink back into oblivion."

"True," she said wryly.

"You would know," he said, his eyes meeting hers. "Tedbury Termagant."

She smiled as an understanding passed between them, from one notorious figure to another.

He rose to a sitting position, only to wrap her in his arms and pull her back down onto the blanket with him, her back to his chest, his face buried in her hair.

It was astounding, how matter-of-course their bodies melded together these days. As though they had been made for it, despite their difference in height. Lying down, their fit was perfect.

The wool of the blanket was warm and rough against her cheek. A bee hummed and investigated, and she didn't lift as much as a finger to shoo it. A pleasant drowsiness enfolded her. She hadn't had a headache in weeks, she realized.

"You often sleep holding me like this," she murmured.

"I do." His voice was close to her ear. "It eases the night terrors."

"Terrors," she repeated. "Because of the war?" She remembered their conversation on her doorstep in the rain, after the trouble in the park. "Does it haunt your nights?"

"Occasionally."

She resisted the urge to press him for more and was surprised when he released her and rolled onto his back to say: "It was so ugly, you see."

She propped herself up on her elbow.

"Ugly," he said to the sky. "And senseless. The senselessness is the worst of it."

"Senseless—how?"

He still was not looking at her. "You want my opinion on the war?"

"I do." As it was, she wanted his opinions on many things.

"It is a crime, against them, and us," he said, and glanced at her. "Are you shocked?"

"Go on," she said slowly.

"I remember when I first knew it. I was pitching our tents on this barren plain, and all that surrounded me was foreign—the jaggedness of the mountains in the distance, the animals, the taste in the air. It could as well have been the moon, and was about just as far removed from Britain, as a month of travel lies between our shores. All of Afghanistan could have vanished from the earth, with no Englishman any wiser back in London, and vice versa. Instead, we take the trouble to voyage there, since they never came to us and never shall, and the natives starve and are butchered, and I had to bury good English men in foreign soil. All because of an expansionist Tory manifesto Disraeli drew up in a fit of personal ambition. Yes, there may well be economic interests via a long, convoluted chain of cause and effect, but the feeling of senselessness remains and it is the worst of it—one may well live and die for a worthy cause, but a senseless one?"

She sat up straight and looked down at him with a measure of alarm. "Is this what you wrote in your war diaries?"

He squinted up at her. "Possibly."

"You mean to ruin London Print with scandalous publications, but forbid me to do the same?"

Openly speaking against the expansionist wars had been tantamount to treason under the Tory government—the people who did so were considered radicals. As far as the current prime minister

Gladstone was concerned, at this point she had no faith he would be much different.

Tristan observed her with a glint of intrigue in his eyes. "Are you afraid for me? Do you worry they will put me in the dock?"

She shifted uneasily. She had not expected him to hold such radical opinions. She had also—naïvely, she now understood—underestimated the depths of the scars he had brought home from the war. And yes, she worried.

"I agree with your sentiments," she said truthfully. "I suppose I have grown overly fond of our publishing house."

"*Our*, is it," he said. "Do not worry. I have a way with words. They shall see whatever they wish to see in the diaries."

"You are good with words," she said, and not wishing to stir up his memories further: "What about poetry—will you write more poetry soon?"

Instead of this distracting him, his expression became darker still. "Who is to say."

"Whyever not?"

"As you made it known rather fiercely at Claremont, you want truth in your art."

She remembered it with a faint smile. "It ruffled your feathers."

"It did," he said. "For I agree with you. And the truth and I have a rather strained relationship."

Her frown lines appeared. "Go on."

He nodded, as if to himself. "My father tried his best to whip me into shape, as you know. He certainly enjoyed doing it more than he should have, but I think in part he did it in the hope it would make things simple for me, teach me very clearly right from wrong. I suppose he thought it would be easier for a man to be upright when things are very clear and simple in his mind. But despite his efforts, I find things are so rarely just one thing or another. And I find there is no end to the truth; reach for it, and it slips away. I only succeeded in holding on to it once, and I turned it into the poems in *Pocketful*. Then I went abroad, and I have not written anything meaningful since." He gave a shrug. "So who is to say."

She understood then that by truth he did not mean honesty, but something more essential: the same mystery perhaps that had Hattie looking vexed for days because her painting lacked "heart," or saw Annabelle working deep into the night to "capture the true spirit" of a long-dead script with her translation.

She brushed a fingertip over Tristan's brooding bottom lip. "For what it's worth," she murmured, "I believe your father beat you out of shape, not into one."

He went very still. A parade of thoughts and emotions rushed behind his eyes, there and gone when he next blinked.

He rolled over onto his side and rested his chin in his palm, his expression carefully blank. "And you," he said. "Have you any aspirations outside your work for the Cause?"

"No." She shook her head, amused by the ignorance of the question. "Never."

"Never is a long time," he said mildly.

"It is a necessity. Do you recall the quote over my mantelpiece?"

He thought a moment, then gave a nod. "'I do not wish women to have power over men, but over themselves.'"

"Yes. Mary Wollstonecraft wrote this line in 1792. 1792, Tristan. It has been nearly a hundred years, and yet here we are, still fighting."

His brows lowered with surprise. "That is a long time indeed."

"And take John Stuart Mill—he has tried to make us equals for the past fifteen years. Did you know that?"

"I did know, yes."

"He failed. Or take Gladstone—he promised us the moon as long as we supported his campaign. Now I learned he muzzled members of his cabinet when oppressive policies are tabled for a vote. He warned Millicent Fawcett's husband in person not to abstain; imagine, he is not even allowed to abstain from voting against us, against the interests of his own wife."

"It is a shame Gladstone would do that," Tristan said quietly.

"So you see, when I say never, I mean it. If they wanted to hear us, they would have by now. I try to believe otherwise—I must—but there is a likelihood I shall be cold in my grave before the women of Britain are free."

Tristan's hand enveloped hers with warm pressure. "And if that comes to pass?"

She gazed into his searching eyes. "Then I shall leave this world knowing I spent my life on a good cause, and not regret it."

He moved suddenly, and she was well pinned beneath him. Her surprised laugh faded fast, because he was looking down at her with an ardent glow in his eyes that left her a little weak in the legs.

"Ah, princess," he said, a rare tenderness in his voice. "How you humble me."

"As though anything could humble you." She turned her head to the side when he made to kiss her. "And why do you call me that? Princess?"

He sighed. "You still have not read any Tennyson, have you?"

"I have not."

"He wrote a poem called *The Princess*. It is about women like you."

Her smile was bemused, and a little flattered. "How so?"

"I'll cite a passage, and you shall see."

"If you insist."

He chuckled. "How could I deny such an ardent request?" The smile stayed in his voice as he continued:

"But while they talked, above their heads I saw
The feudal warrior lady-clad; . . .
That drove her foes with slaughter from her walls,
And much I praised her nobleness, and 'Where,'
Asked Walter . . . 'lives there such a woman now?'

Quick answered Lilia 'There are thousands now
Such women, but convention beats them down:
It is but bringing up; no more than that:
You men have done it: how I hate you all!
Ah, were I something great! I wish I were
Some might poetess, I would shame you then,
That love to keep us children! O I wish
That I were some great princess, I would build
Far off from men a college like a man's,
And I would teach them all that men are taught;
We are twice as quick!'"

Long before he had finished, a peculiar sensation had begun traveling up and down her spine. Thought fragments shifted, trying to find a way to fit together.

"I must admit," she said. "I do like this much better than Patmore's *Angel in the House.*"

"And yet you seem vaguely disturbed," he remarked; "why?"

She looked at him straight. "This poem expresses admiration for unconventional women, or is there a sinister conclusion at its end?"

His eyes crinkled at the corners. "No. It very much expresses admiration."

"And yet you have called me princess for years, when we have only recently begun to like each other."

His eyes turned opaque, like a well muddied by a sudden disturbance in its depths.

He was holding her face, and she felt his thumbs, very gently, touch her cheekbones.

"Perhaps I have always liked and admired you, Lucie."

Her mind blanked.

It was a statement as well as a question, and it left her breathless and fleetingly disoriented.

"And are you normally in the habit of dyeing a woman's hair blue when you admire her?" she said.

He did not smile. "I was a foolish boy when I inked your braids. And while I apologize for it, I cannot regret doing it—your hair was the silkiest thing I had ever touched and remained so for years."

He was touching it now, and she could feel the reverence. It had been the first thing he had asked her to do when they had crossed the line, that she take down her hair. How long had he dreamed of touching it again?

Her heart was beating far too fast. He was rearranging her past one careless sentence at a time.

"I'd rather you not say such things," she said softly.

His caresses ceased. "And why not?"

"Because I might believe them."

When he made to reply, she shook her head. Because above all, she was frightened—the racing heart, the shortness of breath, it was fear. It seemed logical and natural that when there was a tender past, and a magical now, there would be a future as well.

And there could be no future.

Nothing thrived, or even survived, unless it could continue to grow, and the attraction that had sprung between them had nowhere to go beyond these stolen, dazzling hours. Even if his words now were spoken in earnest and not part of some careless seduction, she did not wish to marry. He would have to marry. And in this moment, here by the river, drunk on Pimm's and the tender touch of his fingers in her hair, she wished all of it could somehow be different. And that frightened her most of all.

She glanced up at his handsome face, and her arms slid around his back. "Kiss me."

There was a hesitation in him, as if he were about to press for answers, but then a thought visibly crossed his mind that sobered him, and just before his lashes lowered, she wondered whether she had seen guilt in his eyes.

A few days later, she was at her desk, trying to comprehend a pesky legal text on divorce laws she had diligently avoided for days, when Annabelle called on her unannounced.

Annabelle's serious expression made it clear before greetings were exchanged that this was not simply an impromptu social visit. Lucie asked Mrs. Heath to please prepare some tea and serve it in the drawing room.

"We have a suspect in the pamphlet case," Annabelle said as she sat down at the untidy table.

It took Lucie by surprise how surprised she was—not about the potential suspect, but how much the dreadful day at Claremont had already faded from her memory. The past weeks had been a blur.

"I'm all ears."

Mrs. Heath bustled in and placed a tea tray onto the table, and Annabelle waited until she had left.

"We suspect it was your cousin Cecily."

This did have her sit up straight. "Are you certain?"

Annabelle nodded. "A lady whose description matches her very well indeed was seen entering your room the night of the ball and left again shortly after. We only obtained this information now because the footman who saw her—without thinking any ill of it—had gone on leave the next morning."

Lucie was quiet for a long moment. "This creates more questions than it answers," she finally said. "What could possibly be her motive?"

"I don't know but I asked Montgomery not to take any further steps without having consulted you first. It's your family, after all."

"I appreciate it," Lucie said, "though I'm uncertain what to do. Based on the evidence you have, I think my parents would be inclined to dismiss it, or worse, they will suspect I was trying to blame Cecily and use your influence over Montgomery to do it."

Annabelle nodded. "Which is exactly what I feared."

Cecily. Who would have thought such lovely blue eyes hid such deviance. *She has always been two-faced, remember?*

"I suggest we do nothing about it, for the time being," she said.

"I am sorry I had to be the bearer of such unsettling news."

"I'm very glad you told me."

She decided there and then that she, too, had something to tell. She rose and walked to her desk to pick up Annabelle's invitation she had written early this morning.

"It's an invitation for a celebratory lunch hosted by the Investment Consortium."

"Lovely." Annabelle turned the envelope over in her hand. "Any particular occasion?"

Lucie's pulse began to flutter. "Yes."

Annabelle glanced up warily.

"We are again the majority shareowners of London Print."

Solicitor Beedle had put it down on paper yesterday, and both she and Tristan had signed on the dotted line. Tristan had been quiet afterward, and she had not felt nearly the elation she thought she would.

Annabelle put the invitation on the table. "Somehow, I feel reluctant to ask how exactly you achieved this."

"I suppose I crossed the Rubicon."

Annabelle's eyes widened. "Oh Lord. It is Lord Ballentine, is it not?"

Lucie gave a tiny nod.

"Oh my."

For a terrible second, she wondered whether she had been wrong to strain their friendship with such a secret, whether she had been reckless and selfish to unburden herself.

But it was not just a guilty conscience that had just shoved the words out of her mouth. There was an urge to share with the world that Tristan was her lover; she had to frequently rein in the impulse of wanting to shout it from Oxford's spired rooftops.

Annabelle's hand moved toward hers. "Are you . . . all right?" Her green eyes were filled with deep concern.

"Oh. Oh yes. It was Lord Ballentine's idea. But entirely my choice." And she kept choosing him, night after night. As much as someone partial to opium chose to visit the den every day. . . .

Annabelle must have guessed as much, for her expression changed from worried to apprehensive. "Is he good to you?"

Was he good to her?

She knew she felt light, and dare she say it, happy in his arms. He made her laugh. After the disappointing dearth of strawberry tarts during their outing, he had brought her a whole basketful last night.

"I see," Annabelle said, and Lucie realized she had been sitting in her chair with a wide smile on her face.

"What have you told the consortium?" Annabelle asked. "How this, erm, change has come about?"

"Half a truth," she admitted. "I told them the daily close intercourse between Lord Ballentine and me at London Print convinced him of my competencies and goodwill, and that he would regain a more leisurely life, yet still reap all of the benefits if he sold us his shares."

"Daily close intercourse," Annabelle said wryly. "Very well. And Lucie."

"Yes?"

"When you wish to talk, do not hesitate to call on me."

When, not *if.* But of course, Annabelle was right.

"Now," she said brightly. "Have you any news on the pamphlets for the St. Giles Fair? I found out yesterday that we must give them to production before the end of the week."

She was lazing in the creaky bed in Adelaide Street a few days later, while Tristan was in the backyard to fetch fresh water from the pump, and she was studying her task list before her mind's eye.

She still owed Millicent Fawcett an answer on the latest amendment proposal for the Contagious Diseases Act.

She needed to prepare the July newsletter.

The first batch of new magazine content had to be readied for production.

She still had made no progress on Lady Harberton's blasted bicycle campaign.

And she had not yet sent Lord Melvin the summary on the last suffrage society activities.

Melvin. Melvin . . .

"Oh blast—"

The pre-amendment appointment on the Property Act with Melvin was today.

She had *forgotten* the appointment.

She leapt out of bed. Her gaze bounced around the room, locating scattered clothing.

She rushed to pick up a stocking.

There was a train at eleven o'clock, going straight to Paddington. She'd need to be very, very lucky though to hail a hackney right away. . . . She dressed with flying fingers, pantaloons, chemise, the right stocking, underskirt. Tapes and bows were slipping from her grasp; her adroitness had vanished together with her sense of duty.

It was how Tristan found her, spinning around her own axis and chasing the hidden clasps on the back of her skirt. A pitcher in hand, he eyed her frantic dance with growing bemusement. "I leave a sleepy vixen and come back to a whirling dervish," he said. "What happened?"

"I must go to London—I should be in London as we speak."

She also had to reconsider her priorities. She had been negligent. She had not been home in days.

Tristan put the pitcher down on the table. "London—whatever for?"

"A meeting. At noon. Help me, please."

He helped her into her walking dress. "At noon?" he said. "You will not make it."

"I must," she bit out and buttoned up the bodice.

"But—"

A button snagged and was unmoored, was left dangling by a thread. "Drat."

"Lucie."

She felt him touch the crown of her head, and her instinct was to jerk away.

But she could not blame him for this; this was of her own making. Granted, he had hardly insisted she go home and fulfill her duties, but why would he, if he could have her under him and flat on her back instead?

She took a deep breath and looked him in the eye. "We cannot continue, not like this."

He stood oddly frozen.

The corresponding twist in her chest nearly made her heart stop. One night. One night had turned into a juggernaut crashing through her life, making her forget her appointments.

Tristan still had not moved. "Are you ending the liaison?"

"I . . ." She shook her head. "It cannot continue like this."

His rigid stance softened by an increment. "It is the lady's prerogative to end a liaison. And normally, I would not ask for an explanation. However, given the astonishing speed at which you have turned from looking well-pleased to half-crazed, etiquette can go hang. What is it, Lucie?"

She spread her fingers with great annoyance. Where to begin with the list she had just tallied up in her head? "I have responsibilities," she said. "I have a lot of responsibilities."

"This has always been the case. It doesn't explain the hasty flight now."

He stood, gaze steely now, and waited. But if she were to decide to run from the room, back into her meaningful routine, he would not hinder her. Unfortunately, running from the room would not just restore her old life, would it.

"I missed an appointment with Lord Melvin," she said acerbically. "Because I was in bed with you."

His eyes flashed. "Melvin."

"I had not expected you to understand." She had, and was disappointed. "But I take my appointments seriously; they matter to me because the Cause matters to me, and I . . ." To her dismay, her throat tightened. "Where are my shoes?"

She spotted one, near the chair. Lying on its side, laces sprawling, like some creature that had been hit by a carriage and left on the road. She sat down hard on the chair and stuffed her foot into the boot.

Tristan went down on one knee, plucked her hands off the shoe, and laced his fingers through hers.

"Let me help."

"You," she said, looking down at him with surprise. "Help."

"I am trying not to take offense at your incredulity."

"I do not need help."

"Very well. Allow me the pleasure of making myself useful then, oh stubborn one."

She hesitated. "But you know nothing about my work."

His left brow arced. "You talk about your work constantly."

"I do?"

"Constantly," he drawled.

"And you . . . listened?"

He shrugged. "I listen. When I'm interested."

"Oh, and for how long have you been interested in women's suffrage?"

"I never opposed it. And I am interested in you—that suffices."

Very well. He looked serious enough.

Perhaps it was time they both found out whether the Cause could be interesting to him in its own right. The meeting with Lord Melvin had been soundly missed either way—she might as well try and proceed with work on other fronts, such as the mail at home.

Her breathing was still a little shaky. What an emotional outburst. She was learning she was that, emotional.

"I shall go ahead," she said. "I shall leave the kitchen door unlocked for you."

Chapter 29

When Tristan spotted the three bulging hemp bags at the center of her drawing room, he stopped dead in the doorway and whistled through his teeth. "When you said *bags* of mail, it was not an exaggeration."

He strolled toward the desk while shrugging out of his jacket, then briefly derailed her focus by rolling up his sleeves and exposing muscular forearms. He looked enticingly purposeful, doing so.

"What do I do?" He turned to her, his face expectant.

Kiss me.

She cleared her throat. "You pick a letter. You determine whether the writer is a married woman and whether her woes pertain to her marriage. Whenever that is the case, you sort the letter into a category."

She turned to unlock the doors to the cherrywood cabinet to take out the labeled boxes and the notebook for the tally.

"There are five main grievances married women experience," she said as she set the boxes down next to each other on the long table. "Emotional, physical, or financial maltreatment, melancholia due to a lack of purpose, or a combination of the four."

Tristan was silent, and when she glanced at him, he wore a frown.

"Right," he said, and waved. "Continue."

"You allocate each letter to a category and add up the numbers in this ledger. That is all there is to it."

"I see," Tristan said, his tone suspiciously neutral.

"Help yourself." She presented the opened bag with a little flourish.

"Lucie." The frown was back in place. "What, on God's earth, is the purpose of this . . . ghoulish exercise?"

"Ghoulish? This is research."

"Toward which end?"

"Do you know what the main argument of the opposition to a Property Act amendment is?"

He had the decency to look vaguely contrite. "I'm afraid not."

"They argue that we must keep the legal status quo because unless a woman's person is completely subsumed in that of her husband, it threatens the harmony in the home. They reason that only when a woman is completely dependent on her husband in all things will he feel obliged to care for her despite his selfish male interests. In the same vein, she will be deterred from nagging her provider and act like a good wife."

His lips quirked without humor. "There is a logic to it."

She shot him a dark look. "Logic matters not when its predictions are not grounded in reality. We have collected ample proof that coverture does not protect women from neglect or outright harm. We could in fact go as far as to claim that the opposite is the case. Which means the main case against amending the act is hollow, morally and also factually, and people who continue to insist upon it will have to do it in the face of overwhelming evidence to the contrary. This," she said, and made a gesture to include all the bags of mail, "is our case against the Property Act."

He gave her an unreadable look, but she could hear his mind working from here.

He shook his head and reached for the letter opener.

He took one of the envelopes from his bag and sliced it open with a smooth flick of his wrist.

"*My dear lady,*" he read out. "*It has been thirty years since Florence Nightingale sailed to the battlefields of Crimea, where she near single-handedly saved thousands of our wounded soldiers from certain death.*

"*Unfortunately, the existence of women such as myself has not changed despite Miss Nightingale demonstrating the tenacity and abilities of the female sex. And I call it an existence, rather than a life, because we much resemble a fancy bauble, decorative but ultimately useless, our place decided by others. I can't help but feel that our lives lack meaning, filled artificially by chores and rituals that are empty and do nothing to better our minds, or the cruel realities blighting this world—the poverty, the spread of diseases, the ill-use of children, to name only a few. There are days when I feel I cannot breathe, and my heart is racing, as I watch my life running through my fingers like sand through an hourglass . . . huh.*"

He dropped the letter onto the middle of the table and looked at her with raised brows. "I suppose this one is for the melancholy category?"

He selected the next envelope from the top of the pile.

"From a Mrs. Annie Brown. . . . *My dear lady . . . I am increasingly convinced that the struggle for a married woman's rights will be a longer and a harder fought battle than any other that the world has known. Men have been taught that they are absolute monarchs in their families, ever since the world began, and that to kill a wife by inches, is not murder—*"

He faltered. "Bloody hell," he said after a pause, and that was all he said for a while.

At first, she tried addressing him now and again, and he reacted with absentminded grunts, until she gave up. He did not touch the biscuits or the cup of tea she served him when the clock struck eleven. He waved away the brandy she offered, too. A focused Tristan, with furrows between his brows. She kept stealing glances at him in between letters. So many sides to a man she had once thought as shallow as a puddle.

Her bag had emptied and been replaced by the next as his looked still half-full, but then, she had developed a keen eye for the gist of the matter, and rarely needed to read to the end. He startled her by abruptly coming to his feet and staring into a nothingness.

She lowered her letter into her lap. "Would you like some tea?"

"No," he said absently, and then most ungentlemanly cracked his knuckles in his palms.

"If it is too tedious, you could also—"

"Oh no. This is interesting." The jeering note in his voice alarmed her. "Very interesting."

"In truth?"

His smile was positively sardonic. "Oh yes. It has been a veritable treasure trove of insights. So many gems. This one is my favorite." He picked up a letter he had set aside.

"My dear lady,

"I turn to you in confidence, in the hope that you could help me on a matter about which a woman should be silent as a grave, but I cannot be silent any longer.

"I know a man who tells his wife, 'I own you, I have got a deed to you and got it recorded, I have a right to do what I please to you,' and the law of a Christian land says she shall submit, to indecencies that would make a respectable devil blush for shame. Man, who is said to have been created in the image of God, is the lowest animal in the world, and the most cruel. It shatters my faith in the goodness of God, so much that it makes me tremble for my own reason."

Here, he stopped, and his gaze bore into hers over the rim of the page.

She inclined her head. "Yes?"

"You read such things every day, I presume." There was a disconcerting flicker in his eyes.

"I do, yes."

"Since when?"

She had to think about it. "They came pouring in around five years ago, when my name had become established. We have been collecting and categorizing them for nearly two years now."

"'We'?"

"The suffragist chapters across Britain. I consolidate the tally every fortnight."

"Ah."

He was pacing round the room, his hands clasped behind his back.

"How many?" he then asked curtly. "Letters, I mean."

"Presently, we have a count of fifteen thousand."

His laugh was harsh. "And those are just the ones who write to you."

"I expect there are many more who never speak," she acknowledged.

"Indeed." He was contemplating her with an alertness as though he had never really seen her before. "And it hasn't occurred to you yet to shoot the next man you meet on sight?"

Now he had her full attention. "What a curious thing to say."

"How about setting fire to Parliament?"

"You are angry," she said, amazed. "The letters shocked you."

"I knew my father was a dastardly husband." His gaze fell heavily upon the five boxes, now filled to the brim. "I had not realized all of them were."

"Not all of them," she said. "It is a rather filtered selection. Contented wives do not write to us. Though, of course, they would be no less trapped if their good fortune changed."

He gave her a hard look. "It is abominable. All of this."

A knot of tension she hadn't realized was there until now dissolved in her chest. The sudden sensation of lightness made her fingers curl into her skirts, as though it would keep her from floating up toward the ceiling.

Until now, she had not been sure how her lover would respond to realities most people refused to see. Until now, she had not been entirely certain whether he would fall victim to the peculiar, selective blindness which afflicted so many otherwise perfectly sensible people when confronted with something ugly; whether he would claw for explanations, no matter how ludicrous, or would try to belittle away what unnerved him rather than face inconvenient truths. She should have trusted him. His mind was fluid and fast, it resented the rigidness of conventions rather than find comfort in their constraints.

A smile broke over her face. Perhaps that was why she had not debated her work with him so closely until this morning. He gave her so much *joy*. A morning of lying in bed with him, entwined and content like a simple animal, had her feeling bright and warm all day. Her time of joy and warmth would have ended quick like a shot had he proven himself unwilling to see. She had not been ready to know. She had not been ready yet to give him up. And it appeared she could keep him awhile longer.

"They are all the same, aren't they?" His sweeping gesture included the three bags' worth of mail.

"I'm afraid so."

"And yet you sit there in your chair looking very calm."

She drew back. "I have not been calm in over ten years, Tristan."

His gaze narrowed. Several seconds ticked past in heavy silence.

"No," he finally said. "I suppose you were not. God." He speared his fingers into his hair, leaving it in disarray. "Lucie. You must publish the results."

She couldn't help a deeply cynical smile. "This certainly used to be the plan."

"Finding a newspaper to run it, however, should be a challenge—it's poisonous."

"It is near impossible," she confirmed. "We tried. But as you can imagine, people would rather not see it. Of course, society is well aware that women are in danger from their menfolk ever since *Oliver Twist*, you know, when Dickens had Bill Sikes kill poor Nancy. But Nancy was a drudge of the working classes, wasn't she? Surely you noticed that most of these letters here are written eloquently, sometimes on very costly stationery. These are middle-class and lady wives, Tristan. The maltreatment of married women is not a secret, but they want you to believe it is a problem of the poor. No, it is pervasive. It spares no one. We prove it. And that is the poison you speak of."

Tristan was pale. "You must take it to the House of Commons."

She sniffed. "And have these precious voices wedged between two agenda points on import tariffs? Only to be dismissed and forgotten, as is usually the case, or to hear again that we should wait some more? No. Men of influence have been fighting for women's suffrage on the floor of Parliament for twenty years. Don't think we have not considered all our options—we have been trying for twenty years, too."

He gave her a brooding stare. "You have tried the *Manchester Guardian*, I presume?"

"Of course. In the end, we decided to acquire our own means of distribution." She cut him a pointed look. "Unexpected circumstances ruined it."

A moment of confusion.

As the pennies dropped, one by one, his expression turned vaguely horrified before her eyes. "London Print."

She nodded.

"Oh grand," he said, and then, "This could have sunk the entire publishing house."

"Possibly." She gave an apologetic smile. "Of course, we very much hoped it would survive. Somehow."

He gave a shake as if waking from a dream. "You bought an entire publishing house for the purpose of a single publication."

"It is a very important publication. And it goes straight into the hands of tens of thousands of women of the kind who write to us. They would have known they are not alone. And there would have been headlines after all."

His mind was churning behind his eyes, rapidly like a flywheel. "The plan is rather convoluted," he finally said. "But bold, and strangely brilliant, given the circumstances. Ambushing women across the land from the pages of their divertive periodical. Brutal, too. I am, however, surprised you would gamble with the money of your investment consortium."

"Tristan." Her tone was gentle. "They know." And, when disbelief filled his eyes: "I would have never proceeded without the ladies' consent. No, they all knew they might never see their money again. For that reason, it was rather challenging to pull a consortium together. There are very few women in Britain who are both independently wealthy as well as so supportive of women's suffrage that they could be entrusted with the plans for our coup."

He wore the expression of a man who had just learned that the earth was not flat. "We have a circle of financially suicidal lady investors in Britain—little Lady Salisbury? In truth?"

She almost felt sorry for him then. "I'm not the only woman in Britain who is angry."

"No," he said slowly. "I suppose not."

His jaw set in a determined line, and he walked past her, straight out the door.

She came to her feet and rushed after him.

He was in the corridor, wearing his coat, taking his hat off the rack.

Her heart leapt in alarm. "You are leaving?"

He reached for his cane. "To London."

Will you come back?

One hand on the door handle, he glanced back over his shoulder, his eyes already focused on something that lay ahead. "If you want me tonight, wait for me in our room—though I cannot tell yet when I shall be back. Keep the back door locked, it is safer for you."

"But wait—how will you get in?"

He was already gone, and only later did it occur to her that he had skipped down her front steps in bright daylight. They were becoming careless in rather too many ways.

He returned when the night outside the curtains in Adelaide Street was as dark as a pit. She had long slipped into an unruly sleep and woke disoriented at the sound of careful footsteps. She blinked and found it made no difference whether her eyes were open or closed.

"Shh," came his voice from above. "It is me."

The bed sagged under his weight with a lazy creak.

She reached for him, and her hands met satiny skin and muscle. She had slept through his arrival, and him discarding his clothes.

"You came back." Her sleepy hand trailed over his back, down the indent of his spine, eliciting a purr.

He lifted the blanket and moved over her, one with the dark. He smelled good. The warmth of his naked body touched her skin, and anticipation began to simmer.

Her hand found the silk of his hair. "What did you do?"

"I met a few fellows." His lips teased her ear, then the side of her sleep-flushed neck. "And I have claimed my seat in the House of Lords."

Her eyes were wide open.

"One more sword for your troops, princess." His breath brushed against her chin. "I had meant to do it the day after you had told me about a hundred years since Wollstonecraft, but—"

She lifted her head and her mouth met his, and he made a soft noise of surprise. She touched her tongue to his and he grunted, and his weight settled heavily on her. Heat welled between her legs. She arched up, seeking the pressure of his chest against hers.

Not enough—she struggled, trapped in swathes of sheets and nightgown.

He broke the kiss, his laugh a dark rumble. "Such impatience."

Her nails bit into the balls of his shoulders, because it ached. She was aching for him. "I need you."

He made a soothing sound. "Then you will have me."

The bed groaned as he stretched himself out beside her and slid his warm hand beneath the hem, up her thigh, and up. The respite of being intimately touched was fleeting; a tension was tightening beneath her skin and it demanded all of him. She squeezed her thighs together, trying to trap his languidly circling hand.

"Poor darling." He shifted, and she heard the scrape of the small box that was ever present during their encounters.

Her fingers curled over his wrist.

He stilled.

"Leave them," she said softly, "if you wish. Be careful."

He rolled over her, and a haze took her, there was only liquid heat and the blunt pressure of him demanding to be let in. "Oh God," he said. She could not speak. The silky glide of his movements was unlike anything he had made her feel before. Noises climbed in her throat, uncontrollable, she was dissolving in sensations. Her one hand was on his shoulder, the other low on his back, she saw with her palms how he moved between her legs. From a distance came the rhythmic creaking of bedsprings. An echo of his voice, murmuring that she could enjoy him as long as she liked, as long as it took, the whole night, forever, if he lasted—she did not last, not at all. The tension curled her toes and broke in hot voluptuous spasms, and a starlit sky rushed at her as she screamed.

She was still panting when she came to, and a high-pitched noise rung in her ears.

Her fingers were mindlessly smoothing the damp hair on his nape.

Agony of bliss indeed.

When he stirred and raised his head, she could feel him looking at her.

"Of course." Soft irony tinged his voice. "I should have known that politics would please you best."

Her hands flattened on his sweat-sheened back. His muscles were tense, he was supporting his weight, careful not to crush her.

Her belly felt sticky. He had been careful.

"You please me very well," she whispered.

She strained to stay awake, to hear him tell her that she must not trust him, must not need him, but he remained silent until she was asleep.

He was lying on his side, his body protectively curved around the sleeping woman in his arms. His blood was still racing, his eyes and ears straining as though threats were hidden in the shadows, and he was ready for them. He would try and protect her from anything.

Of course, he was currently a threat himself. He felt her heart beating beneath his hand, his careless hand. Did she know she was in love with him?

He was painfully aware that he was. He had nearly lost himself in her when she had come undone. For a mad moment, he had wanted to do it.

He buried his face in her hair and breathed her in. Hubris came before the fall, they said. And he had fallen hard, and was falling still. It meant he could not stay in India. He had to make a new plan and it involved returning posthaste. And he had to do the dreadful thing and tell her everything. It was what a good man would do. He had not wanted to be good in half a lifetime, but now he did; he fair ached with it. Cecily, Rochester, India. He would tell her. His arms tightened around her of their own volition at the thought, as though to say they wanted to hold on to happiness just a while longer.

Chapter 30

The next afternoon when he arrived in his lodgings in Logic Lane, he had a letter from General Foster on his desk—it would be his pleasure to accommodate Tristan and his mother in Delhi until Tristan had set up a household of his own. The confirmation elicited no sense of relief, for at this point, he resented the idea of leaving Britain almost bodily. He still instructed Avi to purchase three tickets for a ship leaving Southampton in three weeks. It would give him enough time to settle his financial and administrative affairs and to oversee the production process at London Print. To lengthen his workdays as required, he decided to spend a few nights a week in the director's apartment on the publishing house's top floor. He resented that, too, for it would mean spending nights away from Lucie. He had, of course, not told her a thing this morning. Her eyes had been filled with an emotion that he, very selfishly, had not wanted to destroy. He would find a solution first; if he had to confess, he would not do so without being able to offer a solution along with the confession, whether she still wanted him or not.

Could he entice her to stay in the offices in London with him? Hardly. He wanted to bed her on silk, not another battered settee. Besides, she would balk at being taken away from her duties in Oxford. Only during their parting this morning, she had told him not to come see her tonight, as her work was weighing upon her.

He sorted through his remaining pile of mail. Another kindly threatening note by Blackstone, from the looks of it. He binned it unopened.

A cable from the editor of the *Manchester Guardian*. He set it aside on the *important* pile.

An envelope without a sender's address, the handwriting distinctly female, nearly followed Blackstone's letter. It wouldn't be the first time a woman had ferreted out his current address and sent an unsolicited love letter . . . and then he did a double take. Cold foreboding trickled down his nape. It was the hand of his mother's lady's maid. Familiar from occasional correspondence when his mother had been too listless to write herself. He ripped the envelope open.

Milord,

I write to inform you that my lady, the countess of Rochester, has disappeared from Ashdown last night, and there is no certainty of her whereabouts. There had been talk she might not be safe at Ashdown among some of the staff. I believe she would have wanted your lordship to be informed; your return had reawakened some of her strength. I hope this missive reaches you, as I have reason to believe that I am being watched. . . .

The letter was dated three days ago. It meant his mother had been missing for four.

"Avi," he said. His voice was ice. "Get ready. We are going to Ashdown."

Jarvis, his father's valet—spy—bodyguard stood in front of the door to Rochester's study, feet apart.

"You can stand aside now, or die," Tristan said pleasantly.

Jarvis leapt out of the way as though he had found himself barefoot on hot coals, and Tristan strode into the office unobstructed. "Where is she?"

Rochester was behind his desk, assessing his crouching stance with narrowed eyes. "Tristan. How timely. I was about to send for you."

"Strangely, a change in rules is not what I had expected from you."

Rochester was observing his approach warily. "I told you I was watching you. And what I saw was the usual lack of cooperation—"

Tristan had walked straight around the desk and gone toe-to-toe.

"You gave me three months," he said, thrusting his face close to Rochester's cold visage. "They are not up."

"There was no need since—"

"Where is the countess?"

"Sign this. And she shall be back."

Rochester never broke eye contact, but his fingers were tapping one of the documents laid out on his desk. Tristan glanced at them, barely deciphering the script through the red haze before his eyes, but it was enough to understand that it was a marriage contract. Already signed and sealed by the honorable Earl of Wycliffe.

He stepped back and pulled the blade from his cane so fast, a high-pitched ringing sound filled the air.

Rochester stood still as stone, his eyes flitting from the sharp steel vibrating near his cheek to Tristan's face. "You would not dare," he said, his lips barely moving.

"Dare what," Tristan said. "Slicing up Harry's old carpet? But I think I do." And the tip of the sword dug into Rochester's beloved royal tapestry, right into the heart of the tree.

"No!" Rochester made a grab for the blade, before thinking better of it and going for Tristan's throat.

Tristan was faster.

His father's fingers were digging into his arm, trying to dislodge the fist twisting his cravat.

"Where is she?" Tristan demanded.

"This is undignified," Rochester growled as he grappled.

Tristan gave a shake. "Where is she?"

"I don't know."

A flick of his right wrist, and century-old silk threads parted like butter.

"I don't know where she is," shouted Rochester, his handsome features distorted with fury.

Damnation.

Bright hot anger was pulsing through Tristan, but his intuition was rarely wrong—his father was speaking the truth. His mother was gone, but not the way Rochester had planned.

Which meant the bastard had just tried to get him to sign his life away by bluffing. Which meant he was worried that his leverage over Tristan had significantly dwindled.

He released his father's cravat. He did not lower the blade.

"What does her lady's maid say, or is she gone, too?"

Rochester touched the tip of his tongue to the corner of his mouth. The look in his eyes was murderous. Tristan had to look more murderous, for Rochester to stay put and compliant like this.

"The wench had run off," Rochester said. "We found her, but she claims she knows nothing, so we let her go."

"And put her under surveillance."

"Of course," Rochester snapped.

Tristan made a mental note to seek out the woman, to see whether she had been harmed, and whether she did know something. She had tried to speak to him during his last visit, after all. Bloody Jarvis has deterred her, and he had let it happen.

The earl peered at the foot-long gash that Tristan had inflicted on the tapestry. "I shall cut your allowance to nothing for this."

Tristan shook his head. "I have never seen you act as concerned toward a human being as you are acting toward this piece of cloth."

Rochester's upper lip curled with contempt. "People die," he said.

"Ideas and traditions and glory survive—long after your flesh has rotted into the ground."

Tristan nodded. Spoken like a tyrant, then. True to their ancestors eternalized on the tapestry, who had gained and defended their titles and estates by cleverly using their underlings as cannon fodder in this war or that. Considering the same blood rolled in his veins, he could probably be a lot worse than he was: an outright monster in addition to being a careless libertine. Except that . . . he was not.

He was not.

He stared at the family tree, the swirling names of all those who had come before him, and knew in his bones that he would save a beggar in rags before he worried about saving a material thing. There was a rightness to the realization, an instinctive quality like that of drawing breath. He gave a bemused shake. Here in this study, before the now maimed tapestry, Rochester had tried to beat this instinct out of him, year after year. Had killed a kitten or two in between, too. *He beat you out of shape, not into it.*

He sheathed the blade. He gave Rochester a pointed look. He strode from the room without a backward glance. Was his disposition twisted in places? Undoubtedly. But Rochester had not succeeded to upend his foundation. He had not succeeded at all. And the most remarkable thing was that it had taken him so long to see it.

As he climbed aboard the carriage awaiting his return at the back entrance, it occurred to him that his mother had perhaps planned her flight all along. In hindsight, her parting words during his last visit sounded suspiciously like parting words for good.

Now he just had to find her before Rochester did. Annoyingly, the one possible clue he had thus far required him to call on two ladies he would have gladly never called upon again. Back in Oxford, he stopped by at the Randolph Hotel and left a card addressed to Lady Wycliffe with an invitation to an outing.

He returned to Logic Lane to answer a few important letters and to write a couple of his own, then he made his way to Lucie's house against her orders, for he needed her tonight.

She didn't open the kitchen door. But she had to be home; he had seen the flicker of light behind the curtains of her drawing room from the garden. When she did not react to knocks on the drawing room window, he took the liberty of picking the kitchen door lock and let himself in.

"Lucie," he said softly into the silence. Her housekeeper was probably home, asleep upstairs. It was careless of him to be here. Lucie would be spitting mad. It would be worth it, he supposed.

He halted two steps into the drawing room.

She was curled up on her side before the fireplace, asleep on a pile of letters.

Behind her, the logs on the grate had collapsed into a softly crackling heap of embers, the glow delineating her curled-up form with a fiery edge.

His men would sleep like this, after battle, not caring where they lay.

Boudicca was sitting on her skirt, her yellow eyes fixing upon him in a quiet warning when he approached. The little black fury was guarding her mistress better than he could have hoped.

"Good girl," he murmured.

Her tail twitched, but she did not sink her claws into him when he lowered himself to his knees next to the slumbering Lucie.

She slept as she lived: entangled in her work. One hand lay palm up next to her cheek; the other was trapped beneath a still-open book, a big legalistic-looking tome that would send him snoring in minutes.

He felt a pang of tenderness, but also, guilt crawled uncomfortably down his neck. Pure exhaustion must have claimed her. He made demands on her most every night, and she never refused him, for her newly found ability to reach the highest heights with him made them both greedy. Then she worked relentlessly during the day.

Because she was afraid she would be cold in her grave before she and her fellow women were free.

He carefully lifted the book from her hand. Lucie didn't stir. Her forehead was smooth as a babe's in her sleep, her mouth relaxed into a rare softness.

His fingers lightly traced between her brows. He had to tell her about India. God, but he did, he should wake her and tell her now. He supposed he could ask her whether she wanted to travel with him. He certainly wanted her to, he realized, very much so. Embarking on a journey, any journey, with a woman like her by his side would make the difference between a chore and an adventure. He froze, there on his knees, mindless for a moment. Had he just acknowledged that there was joy to be had from shackling himself to a woman?

Not a woman.

Lucie.

The one who had dedicated her life to fighting the marriage laws of England.

"Well, then."

His arms slid beneath her knees and shoulders, and he lifted her up against his chest.

The stairs leading up to her bedchamber creaked under their combined weight.

The moon threw a rectangle of pale light across her chamber floor. Her bed was narrow, just wide enough to accommodate a lone woman.

She burrowed into him when he tried to deposit her under the coverlet.

"I told you not to come," she murmured, drunk with sleep.

He kneeled down next to the bed and leaned his forehead against hers. "I know. I did not listen. I shall leave."

Her hand searched and slipped beneath his coat, and he stilled.

"Stay," she said.

"Your housekeeper is in residence, my greedy one."

Her fingers became a fist in his shirt. "Stay," she slurred. "In here. Shall send . . . her away tomorrow."

"Right," he said. The floorboards were already uncomfortably hard against his knee.

He took her hand, now limp against his chest, and tucked it under the blanket.

He unlaced his shoes, took off his cravat, and stretched out on the rug before her bed.

Lucie rustled, making discomfited sounds.

"Tell me something," she murmured. "I like your voice."

He stared into the dark, fleetingly wondering whether there would be a way back to his life as an infamous seducer from this. But already, melodies were flooding his mind. . . .

"How do you feel about Yeats?"

"Hmm."

He took this as a yes.

When you are old and grey and full of sleep,
And nodding by the fire, take down this book,
And slowly read, and dream of the soft look
Your eyes had once, and of their shadows deep;
How many loved your moments of glad grace,
And loved your beauty with love false or true,
But one man loved the pilgrim soul in you . . .

A snoring sound came from the bed above.

He lay still. "Philistine," he then muttered. *Hell shall freeze over before there is a way back from any of this*, whispered a mocking voice in his head.

Spending the nights together in her home rather than Adelaide Street meant they could work together in the drawing room between breakfast and noon as long as she had sent Mrs. Heath away on a long errand in the next town. It was perfectly sensible to do so, since they would have to consult one another on major editorial decisions. And yet. Lucie kept stealing wary glances at Tristan. He lounged in her wing chair and made notes in the small notebook he always carried in his breast pocket while Boudicca irreverently climbed all over his person.

It was vaguely alarming, how lovely it was to work on her task list with him present in her space. She felt highly defensive of this room of her own, her sanctuary, and yet a comfortable domesticity had settled over them here, which felt entirely natural. Quite as though they had done this before and should be doing it again.

"I'm thinking about introducing a column where I explain how various unjust policies may affect the details of women's daily life," she said. "In simple words for the layperson, of course, and I have to find a way of making it sound pleasant, I suppose. What do you think?"

Tristan looked up, taking in the picture of her kneeling at the center of a circle of open *Discerning Ladies' Magazine* galleys with her yellow skirts carelessly bunched behind her.

He rose and meandered over, then kneeled next to her.

"A splendid idea at first glance," he said.

"I am also wondering whether I should remove a few of these advertisements."

She paused, half distracted by his fingers caressing the small of her back through the fine cotton of her morning dress. She had gone from a lifetime of never being touched by another to being kissed or petted in abundance when he was near, and the wondrousness of it was not wearing off.

She cleared her throat. "Look." She pointed at an open galley, where a written advertisement filled half a page. *"For reducing and shaping the waist to pleasing proportions—has your middle thickened beyond pleasing plumpness? Have tapeworm cures left you with an unbe-*

coming pallor? If you wish to please your husband, send a telegram to Dr. James Mountebank today to order your first sample of highly effective chemical Reduction Pills. I do not like the idea of women ingesting worms, but I do not like the sound of these pills, either."

"It is probably just snake oil," Tristan said. "Some herbs and flour and glue."

She leaned into his side, and he absently snuck his arm around her waist.

"What about this one." He nodded at another page showing the portrait of a smiling matron with a big bow tied beneath her chin. *"I am 50 today, but thanks to Pear's soap my complexion is only 17,"* the confident red letters claimed across her bosom.

"A bold-faced lie," Lucie admitted; "she does not look seventeen."

"Because she is near thrice that age, so it is her good right."

She turned her face into his neck, shamelessly indulging in his scent. "It appears the previous editors thought not everyone would be as partial to women of a certain age as you are."

He brushed a kiss across her forehead. "Allow me to hand you these weapons behind the back of the brotherhood: if only women knew the minds of boys trapped at Eton and men trapped in Her Majesty's army, they should never squander a thought on tapeworms in order to delight an admirer again."

"This simple, is it."

"It is. Most men will be glad just to win the favour of a willing woman."

"We should have you write the column on successful husband hunting."

"You are brimful of fantastic ideas this morning," he said, and kissed her mouth. A touching of tongues, and the contact became voluptuous and needy. Too needy. He had created a monster.

She drew back, breathing hard. "I had another grand idea. The St. Giles Fair begins on Monday."

"Yes?" Perhaps it was her imagination, but the glow in his eyes appeared to have dimmed.

"I thought, perhaps we could have another outing."

"To the fair . . . together?" There was an affected lightness in his tone, and she felt heavy with disappointment. He was not keen on the idea of going to the fair together.

He took her hand. "To hell with the absolute discretion about which you were so adamant, then?"

No, of course not. But in the milling crowds of the fair, their proximity could have appeared accidental. Or perhaps she had been telling herself so against better judgment. Her daydreams had been precarious for a while, revolving around outings with Tristan, on horseback, or in a closed carriage, headed to unknown destinations. She'd had warm visions of them smiling at each other over a sun-dappled breakfast table at a quaint seaside hotel, away from paperwork and paragraphs. Most unsettling were her fantasies of him sprawled in a wing chair, absorbed in his writing, his fingers absently scratching behind Boudicca's ears. . . .

She sighed ruefully. "You are right. It was just an idea."

His smile was vague. "It was a good idea," he said, and pressed a kiss into her palm. "We must go. Some other time."

Chapter 31

He would have taken great pleasure in attending the St. Giles Fair with Lucie. He would have won her a trinket at the shooting range, delighted in watching her devour chunks of hand-spun sugar floss, and made salacious comments about her riding a mechanical horse.

As it happened, it was Monday evening, the air smelled sweetly of candied fruit, and he was at the fair—but in the company of Lady Cecily, who clung to his arm with the tenacity of a barnacle. A fair had been the least intimate venue for an unacceptably short-notice outing he had been able to think of. Circus music blared from the street organs and clanking, steam-powered horse carousels; revelers moved about shoulder to shoulder. On the other hand, it also required cunning maneuvers to hold a long enough conversation with Lady Wycliffe to ferret out possible information about his mother. And it was a guess at best—just because the ladies had, until recently, exchanged letters and discussed betrothals, it did not mean any confidential clues about the situation at Ashdown had been shared. Either way, Lady Wycliffe appeared grimly determined to trail behind with her footman rather than engage, in any case.

"Oh, look." Cecily paused, and pointed. A little distance ahead, on a pedestal looming above the bobbing sea of hats and caps, a man was being readied to take flight, his harness attached to a thick wire running over their heads between two poles.

"Keep walking, Cecily," came Lady Wycliffe's low voice from behind. "Keep close to Lord Ballentine. There are scores of thieves present."

Impossibly, Cecily's grip on his arm tightened, her upturned face shadowed with worry beneath her elaborate hat.

Annoyance made his tone notably cool. "They are but the working classes enjoying an evening of revelry," he said. "Most are not intent on stealing genteel maidens tonight."

Thus reassured, she smiled. "Even if they tried, you would not let them, would you?"

"Aaaaaah!" The man on the pedestal had taken the plunge and was flying over their heads, both hands on his cap. Somewhere, a monkey shrieked, presumably one of those mangy creatures sitting atop a street organ in a little uniform. The only thing missing was a mad hatter popping up.

Cecily tugged at him. "May we go a little closer to the pedestal? I would like to see them jump."

He agreed because he had spotted the sign for a refreshment booth near the queue for the flight along the wire. He would demand his conversation with Lady Wycliffe over a lemonade.

Of course, they stopped dozens of yards away from the booth, because Cecily became fascinated by the shooting range, where a handful of chaps were manfully firing at tin cans. The proprietor was hollering at male passersby in a broad Irish accent, challenging them to try and win their sweethearts a trophy—bunches of dreary-looking wax flowers, by the looks of it.

Cecily put her free hand on top of his forearm. "Why are the rifles so quiet?"

"Because they are air rifles. Have you not been to a fair before?"

She shook her head. "Oh, I would so adore having such a bouquet." Her eyes grew larger. "It would forever remind me of our first visit to a fair."

Before he could rebuff her request, Lady Wycliffe was by his side. "Go ahead and enjoy yourselves," she said firmly. "I shall be watching from the lemonade booth, I'm terribly parched. Matthew?"

The footman cast a last, longing glance at the range. "Yes, ma'am."

Tristan watched her stiff back disappear into the fray with rapidly dwindling patience. But he should get nothing but monosyllables from the woman if he displeased her now.

"One round," he said to the Irish man.

"Yes, guv, great choice, guv." The man snatched the coins off the counter and turned to select a rifle off the wall.

Tristan shrugged out of his coat. As he made to place it on the counter, Cecily opened her arms with a solicitous smile, leaving him little choice but to hand her the garment.

Resigned, he hoisted the rifle up against his shoulder. A shudder ran down his back as his body recognized the long-practiced motion. And then he froze.

He felt her presence before he saw her. Felt her gaze burning a hole into his profile.

He could tell her slight form from the corner of his eye.

Lucie.

A sinking feeling gripped his innards.

She was still as a statue in the merry crowd, in her light blue dress. She had worn it during their outing on the Cherwell.

It had been a distinct possibility, her coming to the fair without him.

Stay where you are, his mind implored her. Having the two women in close proximity spelled disaster, he knew it in his gut.

She came directly toward him.

He lowered the rifle and turned to face her.

She was clutching a wad of pamphlets against her chest with a frozen fist. Her expression was frosty, too.

Grand, just grand.

She halted just out of his reach, her gray gaze sweeping over him in cool assessment.

"Lord Ballentine. What a coincidence to see you here." She nodded at Cecily. "And cousin Cecily. Another coincidence." She looked back at him, her eyebrows cynical arches.

Despite the absence of his coat, hot sweat broke over his back.

She was hurt. He had hurt her.

Cecily felt the disturbance in the air; she was leaning into the shelter of his body, pressing her whole length up against his side.

Worse and worse.

"Ho," cried the proprietor of the shooting booth. "Behold. A suffragist."

He must have noticed Lucie's pamphlets. Or the pin on the lapel of her jacket.

"I say, a suffragist at McMahon's shooting booth!"

Heads turned into their direction.

"Get a hold of yourself, man," said Tristan, his voice a growl.

"Of course, guv." The man bowed, and then he said to Lucie: "I reckon your aim is as sharp as your tongue, isn't it, miss? Here." He picked up a rifle and raised it over his head. "Here's your chance to prove it!" He was still excited and verging on yelling again, and a semicircle of curious faces began to form around them.

Lucie stared at the man.

"Come, miss, one round, on the house." McMahon, evidently tired of his life, placed the rifle before Lucie onto the counter.

She didn't spare the gun a glance. "Astonishing," she said, all her vowels sharpened to cut glass, "that you assume I was inclined to prove anything to anyone."

She looked back at Tristan, and the urge to pull her into his arms and hold tight was visceral. Pale and haughty, she was ethereal, easily dissolved into thin air by a breeze, and they were on the cusp of a storm.

"My lady," he said softly, and, because it was impossible to say anything: "Is the politicking going . . . well?"

She bared her small teeth at him. "Incredibly well," she said brightly. "How about you, my lord—are you enjoying the fair?"

"Oh yes," Cecily cut in, her voice sweet and glossy like a candied apple. "I've been feeling perfectly inspired—the vibrant colors, and the merry music, oh, and the levity of the crowd. Oh, my Lord Ballentine, what do you think of a themed ball to announce the betrothal?"

His heart stopped.

"We are engaged to be married, you see," Cecily told Lucie. "And I feel themed parties are going to become all the rage in London."

He looked down at Cecily with nightmarelike slowness, and she glanced back up at him.

The soft curve of her chin jutted mulishly. Her blue eyes were clear. He could see right down to the layer of steel at the bottom. He hadn't noticed it until now. Had overlooked it at his own peril. This woman was not a lamb at all.

Bloody hell.

A pang of dread hit his gut before he looked back at Lucie, the kind that had hit when he had been new to war, right before facing a tableau of carnage to search for vital signs.

It was grim. All color had drained from Lucie's face. Her lips were white as bone.

He took a step toward her, and she immediately stepped back.

"I see," she said quietly. "Congratulations." Her gaze became unfocused, began to stray into the crowd. "I . . . I am needed back on my post," she said. "Congratulations. Good evening."

He watched her walk away, holding herself terribly still.

"My lord?"

He shook off Cecily's grasping hands and glared down at her. "What possessed you to do this?" He barely recognized his voice. His heart was pounding. *Go after her. Go after her.*

Cecily's eyes were wide. "But . . . she's family. . . ." she stammered. "Surely, there's no harm in her knowing before it's official?"

"It won't be official," he said. Enough of this farce.

Cecily's chin quivered with alarm. "Whatever do you mean?"

"Is anyone going to shoot?" cried McMahon. "Half a penny for five shots!"

Lucie had vanished into the crowd; she would, she was short and she was fast.

No, she had not been fast just now. She had walked like a woman injured.

"My lord?" Cecily made it sound like a sob.

He shook his head and went after his heart.

Chapter 32

I t took her a quarter of an hour to reach home, and her breathing was still a distant, labored sawing noise in her ears. She knew she had a heartbeat, rattling around in the cavern of her chest, but she did not feel it; there was a disconnect, she was a cold, disembodied mind floating aimlessly from room to room.

Tristan had lied to her.

Tristan was engaged to Cecily.

Tristan had lied to her.

He broke into her kitchen not ten minutes later.

The familiar sight of him, his face handsome and guilty, when in truth she did not know him at all, slid sharp like a blade between her ribs. She realized she stood with her hands pressed over her heart.

He crossed the kitchen with three long strides and stood too close.

"Lucie—"

She slapped him so hard, the force of the blow turned his head to the side.

When he looked at her, his eyes glittered bright like fool's gold. "Allow me to explain."

Her hand had left a red mark on his cheekbone.

"I'd rather slap you again," she said.

He raised his hands in a shrug. "If you must."

She flexed her smarting fingers. "I want you to leave."

At least she wasn't railing and screeching. Her voice was as frozen as she felt inside.

He shook his head, making to say something, but she held up her hand.

"All I asked for was honesty. But honesty is an impossibly tall order for someone like you, isn't it? I might as well have asked a tiger not to kill—he can't help himself. More fool me."

He gritted his teeth. "You are not a fool, and I did not lie."

She crossed her arms. "Are you, or are you not, engaged to my cousin?"

"I am not," he said, his gaze so direct, so lucid, it felt genuine. A treacherous tendril of hope fluttered in her chest. She quashed it.

"Why would she make such claims if there were nothing to it?"

His eyes narrowed. "The little—" He shook his head. "It's not entirely her fault. It's Rochester."

A terrible fatigue came over her at his words, urging her to retreat, to go curl up in a black hole, safe from the sight of him.

"It's always someone else's fault, is it not." She turned away, because he wasn't leaving.

He followed her down the corridor, and she sensed his urgency on her skin like a touch.

"Leave," she said, her voice rising.

"Not as long as you are feeling like a fool," came his cold voice. "This is my fault entirely."

"So you admit it."

"Of course—but I hope you will accept mitigating circumstances." She gave a hollow laugh.

"Rochester is blackmailing me and holding my mother hostage." He said it quickly.

She stopped.

When she turned back, he met her gaze evenly, but he looked

unsettled and his hands were clenching by his side as though he were suffering a bout of nerves.

A crack ran through the icy shell holding her together; she could feel it. Still, she flinched when he made to take her arm, and he withdrew his hand with a scowl.

"Very well," she said. "You may explain yourself."

She guided him into the drawing room and settled on the old settee, hands folded, her back stiff as a board. He stood before her with the reluctance of an outlaw in the dock.

"Rochester is hell-bent on seeing the Ballentine line secured," he began. "He was alarmed when I made clear that I had no interest in marriage in the foreseeable future."

A sudden, leaden feeling pulled her back into her body. It should not have bothered her, his reluctance to marry, but hearing him say it with such certainty grated on some layer of her soul.

"Your main duty at this point in your life is to provide an heir," she said coolly. "Your father is hardly making unreasonable demands."

He inclined his head in agreement. "It is, however, unreasonable that he will stop at nothing short of murder to see the Ballentines hold on to the Rochester title. He was in the process of arranging a match with your cousin and gave me a few months to rehabilitate my reputation to allow her to accept me without causing talk about your family. To ensure my cooperation, he threatened to put my mother into an asylum. And one thing you must know about Rochester is that I have never seen him make an idle threat."

Gooseflesh rose on her arms. His tale was straight out of a gothic novel.

But his mother had always been deemed erratic and different. Inconvenient noblewomen *were* sometimes quietly locked away at private asylums . . . and she had seen the marks Rochester had left on Tristan's back—she wouldn't put such sordid behavior beyond him.

"This is why you need money," she said slowly. "The passive income from London Print."

He nodded. "I would have been cut off from any family accounts until my father's death. And life for two people in India requires deep pockets."

India.

She swallowed hard. "I see."

His eyes darkened with regret.

"My dear—"

She shook her head. "When were you going to leave?" Her voice was unsteady.

He ran a hand over his face. "In a few weeks."

"So soon," she said softly.

"I made a mistake, not to tell you sooner. I should have told you the moment I read all those letters—it was when I knew you would at least have understood the absurdity of the situation."

Sad, she felt so very sad. "Why didn't you—tell me?"

He was on his knees before her, looking up at her with a sincerity in his eyes that cut her to the bone. "Because at first, it was my own affair, and mine alone to solve. For what it's worth, I had not expected mutual feelings and esteem to grow between us. But they have, and fast, and I came to feel reluctant to share my failings as a man with you—it is shameful enough that I could not protect my mother while I still lived at Ashdown. As you might imagine, Rochester has always been a bully. Above all, I suspected if I told you it would come to precisely this."

Feelings and esteem. But evidently, no trust.

She glanced down into his flushed, handsome face. "So you were a coward."

He went very pale. "I was, yes."

How would he have told her in the end? To her face? In a letter, to be read when he was already on his way to the subcontinent, not to return for years and years? He *was* still going to leave her, in fact, and something vital splintered apart deep inside her chest.

"It's why you took the loan from Blackstone, isn't it," she said tonelessly. "An even greater criminal than your father."

He nodded. "Rochester cannot touch him. However, there is a twist in the plot: my mother recently disappeared, and Rochester is not behind it. And as long as I have no clue regarding her whereabouts, my hands are somewhat bound—I must find her before my father does."

Her mind whirled, from the feel of his hands clutching her skirts, from breathing in his warm scent. She shook her head in a bid for clarity. "All of this sounds . . . utterly outlandish."

His brows rose. "Does it? After everything you know about the plight of wives trapped behind closed doors?"

His tan had returned, and his features had softened. He looked like a man unburdened after carrying an impossible weight for too long, and it erased the last of her doubts—he was telling her the truth.

"And yet," she murmured, "and yet you came to my bed, when it threatened your solvency and thus your *plan*."

He gave her a dark look. "What can I say. You were naked."

She covered her eyes with her hand. As she had suspected all along, he hadn't meant to bed her. He had simply lost control over his urges.

She breathed through another jab of pain. "I understand your silence on the matter of your mother," she said. "I would have felt protective of such circumstances myself—it is hardly acceptable to speak about unpleasantness within one's own family. And yet, I still wish you had."

Because while her head understood, her nerves were still jangling, her pulse still spiking. *India.* He would have left, and he hadn't been truthful. The reality of it continued to ebb and flow through her veins, burning like acid. Images kept surging, of Cecily's face, the glimmer of triumph in her eyes, the guilt in Tristan's. Her foolish request of going to the fair with him; her dreams of going anywhere with him. It felt as though she were falling.

"My dear." His hands slid up from her hips and locked around her waist, the warm, possessive pressure unwelcome and devastating. Her instinct was to run from him, the source of her hurt and confusion. In a terrible paradox, it was his arms she wanted to run to.

She shook her head.

His eyes heated. He rose up on his knees and his face was close to hers.

"You feel very far away right now," he said.

She turned her face away, because he was near enough to kiss, and stupidly, she wanted to.

He leaned in and buried his face in her neck.

She was frozen in his embrace. But his lips moved up over her throat and the soft, familiar contact unleashed a warm wave of longing down through her legs, rendering them useless.

She took a fistful of his hair and pulled. He had cheapened something glorious, and she wanted him in pain for it.

"I never intended to hurt you," he murmured against her ear. "I ask your forgiveness. Forgive me."

"Sweet words won't absolve you."

He drew back, his eyes bright. "And this?"

She made an angry sound when his mouth covered hers, but her lips parted and let him in. His kiss was drenched in need, and her hand slid from his hair and curved around his nape to pull him closer, and she loathed herself for it. His arms circled her and pressed her to his chest, and she became soft and pliant in response, and she resented that, too. Her body was melting, wanting his, even without the honesty, without the trust. She wanted him inside her and resented him at the same time. How sordid, how grotesque.

His thighs were pinning her skirts to the settee, keeping her legs trapped. She could bite him, but she could smell the arousal on him, and felt the heat of his urgency, and knew the only thing stopping him now would be her asking him to stop. And the words did not come.

With an angry moan, she slid her hand down the flat plane of his stomach, over the front of his trousers, and found him hard. He made a guttural sound, and his weight crashed down on her, crowded her back into the upholstery. It was a tussle, a heated tangling of tongues and fingers dragging off clothes and untying laces, until fabric ripped, and she wrenched away. She gasped at the sight of the remnants of her chemise, torn like paper, clean from her collarbone to her navel.

She glared at Tristan, panting. "Get a hold on yourself!"

He gave her a thin smile. "This *is* me having a hold on myself."

His hands spread the ruined fabric, exposing her breasts, and his head lowered. A rush of heat swept over the surface of her skin as her body arched up.

She let her head fall back against the settee. There was no stopping either of them, now. He was in the grip of something stronger and older than reason, and she wanted one last time. One last time. She offered no resistance when he shoved up her skirts. She had taken a rogue into her bed, into her life, so a mad last tumble in a ripped bodice was a befitting good-bye.

He leaned over her, one hand on the back of the settee, his other hand working between them, unfastening his trousers, his expression so darkly determined, she barely knew him.

Her lids lowered, shutting him out.

When he did not move, her eyes slitted open.

Above her, his face was agony. "Lucie," he said hoarsely. "Say you will have me."

How tempting, to deny him his pleasure at the height of his pain.

Unfortunately, it would hurt her just as much.

One last time.

She slid her hands up his arms and held on to his shoulders. "I will have you."

He moved over her with the might of a storm, forcing the air from her lungs, and she clung to him, her mouth beneath his, as they tumbled through the dark. She knew he would not stop taking her until she would cry out. She would lose this battle gladly. How foolish of her, to once have thought holding back her voice would hold back her heart. How foolish of him to think wringing such bliss from her now would return her heart to him. She held out long enough to make him sweat, until he had to be hurting from it, and when the blaze consumed her, she screamed.

He was heavy on her until the beat of his heart against her ribs had slowed. He sank to the floor with her in his arms, cradling her close.

"Let me stay tonight." He was slurring the words.

She was too wrung out to send him away. "Draw the curtains and lock the door," she said, the leaden exhaustion after a shock already claiming her. By the time he had returned to her, she was asleep.

The sense of betrayal returned with the cold light of dawn creeping through the curtains. She lay staring up at the ceiling with tired eyes. The longer she looked, the more cobwebs she saw, flimsy torn veils graying with dust.

Tristan was still going to India, and she still felt like a fool. It weighed on her chest and leered at her as grotesquely as the gargoyles protruding from every roof in Oxford.

She should be rejoicing. With Tristan gone, she would have time for all the things that mattered again, and at least de facto she would have much more control over London Print. Free rein, had that not been her heart's desire a month or two ago?

How quickly things could change. The thought of him gone left her hollow.

What puzzled her most was that nothing had been missing from her life before him—how could he feel essential now?

She took a shuddering breath and rolled to her side, away from him, and dragged herself to a sitting position. He woke then; she could feel it.

A soft rustle of blanket, and then his fingers touched her bare spine. Her shoulders tensed in response.

The caress faded to nothing. "I gather you are still angry," he said.

The intimate scratchiness of his morning voice hurt her. The sooner he was gone, the better.

"I am," she said to the room. It had to be anger. The hollowness, the sickness in her chest.

There was a pause. More rustling, as Tristan was sitting up, too. "Will you look at me?" he asked gruffly.

She glanced back over her shoulder and blinked against the fresh pain the sight of his tousled hair and bare shoulders brought on.

"Funny, is it not," she said. "You told me not to trust you, but I did. I told you to be honest, and you were not. We have both broken the rules."

His eyes had a hard look to them. "No," he said. "It is not funny."

She looked away. At least he was not trying to deny his lack of honesty, or attempting to dress it up as mere secrecy. Dishonesty, secrecy, good reasons or not: at the end of the day, she had suspected nothing. She had been skin to skin with him, looked into his eyes while he was inside her, and she had suspected nothing. He was greatly skilled at guarding his secrets. He could hide anything he chose from her—until he couldn't, because the secret things always found a way to the light, and then they would pull the floor from underneath her feet.

"No," she agreed. "It is not funny."

She buried her face in her hands and ground her palms against her eyes. She had to look well put together for the celebratory lunch at the Randolph with the Investment Consortium today. The chance for this was slim. She was so fatigued, it felt as though her face were melting off her skull.

"I would be much obliged if you could take your leave," she said.

She looked away when he picked up his clothes and dressed, because this was the last time she would ever see him do so.

He let her herd him to the kitchen without protest or attempts to sway her, perhaps because he felt guilty still.

He turned to her a good few paces from the back door. "I wish to see you tonight."

She quickly shook her head. "I'd rather not."

His hands flexed by his side, as though he had to stop himself from reaching for her.

"Because of the broken trust," he said, calmly, but his body was a column of tension.

Because of everything.

She could only nod.

A dreadful emotion rose between them; they stood and watched helplessly while what they had created between them was changing as unstoppably as the tide was turning.

His eyes shuttered then, the amber glow gone. "I will find the countess," he said. "And then I will earn your forgiveness."

The sound of the kitchen door falling shut behind him came from a distance. Moments later, his head and shoulders darkened the kitchen window as he walked past. He was looking straight ahead.

Her back against the kitchen wall, she slid slowly to the floor, her legs sprawling on the cold flagstones.

The problem was not that she had not forgiven him. It was that she already had. She was an inch from bolting out the door to go after him, calling his name. She'd fling herself into his arms and bury her face against his neck. She'd breathe him in and ask him to stay; to forget everything that had happened and to ignore everything that was coming for them.

She was an inch from becoming his creature. So close to becoming someone who'd plead with their husband when he did not come home at night, who made excuses when they lied, who lied to themselves only so they could carry on orbiting around the fickle creature that was man. She was so close, when Tristan was neither the source of the food she ate, nor the roof that sheltered her, nor the name protecting her.

She had a choice. And here she was, on the floor.

Her nose burned. A hot tear leaked down her cheek. She swiped at it. How humiliating, to have secrets she hadn't known she kept laid bare to her, by Cecily no less—*we are engaged to be married.* The agony had been unexpected, like the cut of a razor blade hidden in treacle.

She had been so confident in her decision to never share her life with a man. So safe in her conviction that tender feelings and domesticity were for other people. The certainty had made it simple, had taken the sacrifice out of her work, which demanded that she remain alone, alone.

Her sobs came uncontrollably like hiccups, sounding silly in the silence, but she could not stop them. She had been deluding herself. There had simply never been someone to tempt her enough. Until now. And right away, she must have given whole chunks of her heart into Tristan's careless hands, because now the inside of her chest ached, felt torn up and bloody. She must have held a hope deep down that despite what the world told her every day, she was just as deserving to be handled with care as the next woman.

A dark smudge advanced on her, and then Boudicca crept onto her lap, comfortingly heavy and soft, and making low yowls of distress.

Lucie hugged the small furry body closer. "Don't worry. I shall get up in a moment. I always do, you know that. I'm just feeling very sorry for myself right now."

A black paw landed on her chest, right where it was hurting.

~⚶~

Tristan saw and heard nothing on his way to his lodgings, consumed by the emotional carnage raging back in Norham Garden. Raging in his own chest. His disgust with himself was a physical thing, it strained his nerves and every fibre of his muscles. Tender feelings and his deviant ways evidently made terrible bedfellows. But he had had a long life of deviance and only a month of loving a woman and thus he had made a mistake. Old habits. He would rectify it, and woo Lucie back, because damned if it didn't feel as though he had lost her today.

He pounded his door in Logic Lane with his fist.

A moment later, footfalls sounded. His eyes narrowed. Those were not the light steps of Avi.

His body was humming with tension when a moment later, the door opened.

His mind blanked.

He was face-to-face with the Earl of Wycliffe.

Chapter 33

The earl, of average height and build, had to tip back his head to meet Tristan's gaze, and his gray eyes briefly squinted with irritation.

He was not nearly as irritated as Tristan. This was the man who had banished his own daughter, and he was standing in his corridor, unannounced and uninvited.

"Good morning, Wycliffe," he drawled. "What an unexpected honor."

Chiefly, it was unexpected. Whyever this man was here, his unannounced presence did not bode well.

"Why don't we take this inside, shall we," Wycliffe suggested.

There was a crowd in his reception room: Avi was skulking in front of the cold fireplace, looking tight-lipped and affronted, and, at a markedly safe distance away from him, stood a bespectacled man with the grave air of a solicitor and Wycliffe's valet of twenty years. The valet was holding his crimson velvet topcoat. He must have left it at the fair last night.

"I beg your pardon, milord," Avi said, putting up his chin. "His lordship insisted." His eyes flickered balefully toward the earl.

"You did well." He sounded calm. He felt calm, too, alarmingly so.

He turned to the earl. "Pray, do tell how I may help you?"

Wycliffe tipped his cane at his own valet. "Is this your coat?"

"Given that my monogram and coat of arms are prominently displayed on the inner lining, I assume this is a rhetorical question. The question is, why do you ask?"

Wycliffe's face set in hard lines. "My ward, the Lady Cecily, returned to her hotel room wearing it," he said. "At close to midnight last night, after a search party had come up empty-handed."

The world turned cold as the meaning of the words sank in.

It was not yet nine o'clock. Whatever tale Cecily had told, it must have been cabled to Wycliffe Hall posthaste and spurred the earl to take the next train to Oxford.

"What exactly are you implying?" he said, his voice very soft.

Wycliffe raised a disbelieving brow at him. "That we have a situation."

"Actually, you and Lady Cecily have a situation."

"Of which you appear to be the cause."

"Is that what the lady claims?"

Wycliffe's expression was bemused. "She claims nothing, as one would expect in such a situation. What is clear is that you were seen together at a fair, just as you were seen leaving the fair together and so abruptly at that, it was impossible for Lady Wycliffe to follow her charge. What is also clear is that my niece was seen leaving the punt house at Lady Margaret Hall hours later, distraught, and wearing your coat, after a search party had been sent out for her."

The inside of his chest was ice. Circumstantial evidence would look crystal clear to the gossips. Who, at the end of the day, were the true judge and jury on such matters.

"My coat may have been in the boathouse with her ladyship, but I certainly was not," he said, to Avi rather than to Wycliffe, for his valet was regarding him with wide-eyed disappointment, and damned if that didn't sting.

"Then where were you between eight o'clock last night and midnight?" Wycliffe demanded.

In the corner, the man in gray had begun scribbling in his note-book.

And Tristan knew that he could not charm, or fight, or drink this away. It was coming at him with the unerring trajectory of a bullet, and he stood with his back against a wall.

He nodded, as if to himself. "Where I spend my nights is none of your business," he informed Wycliffe.

The earl's expression did not change; he had expected this. "Then I must ask you to accompany us to Wycliffe Hall."

"Of course," Tristan said pleasantly. "As soon as my lawyer is here. Avi, be so kind and send a cable to Beedle's St. James residence."

Wycliffe's face fell. "To London?"

"Yes." Tristan sat down in the wing chair and stretched his long legs before him. "It should take him three hours at the most to make his way here. Do you care for any refreshments?"

The bright, airy luncheon room of the Randolph smelled of summer, courtesy of the flowers spilling from the generous centerpieces on every table. Tiered silver platters were laden with tea sandwiches and lemon curd tarts, and tiny violet jam pots to complement the scoops of clotted cream for the freshly baked scones. It should have been a perfect feast for a woman with a sweet tooth, but Lucie might as well have been spooning sawdust into her mouth. A numbness dulled her senses. Again and again, her mind drifted back to Tristan's profile, looking so very pale, when he had walked past her kitchen window. *It is over*, she thought. She would never know his kisses again.

"Dear, if you were of a mind to leave, no one would take offense."

The soft murmur went through her very bones.

She slowly turned to Lady Salisbury, who occupied the chair to her right and had leaned in close. *How did she know?* Concern was writ plain on the countess's face.

She cleared her throat. "Apologies," she said carefully. "I have been a trifle absentminded."

Lady Salisbury nodded. "Well, it is a shame," she said. "Do keep in mind it is not your fault, though some of them may sneer at you. Personally, I have never been fond of placing a whole house in *Sippenhaft*, collective punishment, for the foolishness of one of its members—it strikes me as a rather socialist thing to do."

This did not make much sense after all.

She cast a furtive glance around the table, then the room. An undercurrent of tension hummed beneath the dazzling opulence, she now noticed; subtle, but oh, it was there. Gazes slid away when they met hers; heads that had been stuck together for some whispered gossip pulled apart.

She put down the teacup she had been holding up mindlessly for the past minute.

"Considering this is a celebratory luncheon, everyone seems vaguely nervous," she murmured.

Lady Salisbury shot her a poignant look. "Have you not heard?"

"Heard what?"

"Oh my, so you have not."

A prickle of alarm spread coldly down her back. "What happened?"

Lady Salisbury looked left, then right, and leaned in closer still. "About your cousin—Lady Cecily," she whispered. "Apparently, she did not come home after the fair last evening. There was a search party."

Lucie froze. "Has she been found?"

The countess tutted. "She returned by herself. All in one piece. Well, almost." Her left brow arched meaningfully. "Apparently, Lord Ballentine had disappeared with her. She was next seen late at dusk, wearing his coat."

Silence filled her head. The edges of her vision went white. Then the shapes and colors of the surroundings snapped sharply back into focus, and the murmur of voices swelled to a roar.

"Lady Lucinda?"

She stared back into Lady Salisbury's quizzing blue eyes. "Impossible," she whispered.

The countess shook her head. "What a shame. Such a lovely girl. Now her engagement will be marred by scandal. Though the silly geese her age will no doubt find it all terribly romantic. . . ."

She wanted to clap a hand over Lady Salisbury's moving lips, to stem the flow of poison pouring into the room.

All of this was a lie.

And no one knew but him and her.

Unless he had already told the truth, and she was now a social pariah.

"Are you not well?" Lady Salisbury's expression was genuinely concerned. "Deuce. I should not have broken the news so indelicately."

She shook her head. "Some fresh air is all I need."

Her stomach was churning with nausea.

When a gentleman compromised an innocent lady, he married her. When the rumors were already out in force, he hardly had a choice—if he refused, he signed the lady's social death warrant. And thus his own.

She hurried from the room, murmuring apologies, staunchly avoiding prying stares and glances. She had to speak to Tristan.

Oxford slipped by in a blur of noise and movements. Carriages rattling past. Passersby and students in black-and-white subfuscs dodging her with tuts and mutters. The Norman tower in Market Street loomed gray and crooked like a giant tombstone. At the clanging of the bells of St. Mary's, she tried to collect herself, knowing she was near Logic Lane.

She repeatedly jabbed her finger at the doorbell at number three.

After a long minute, the door swung back to reveal Avi, his dark eyes narrow with distrust.

Her heart sank. "Good morning, Avi."

"His lordship is not—"

"Please." She flattened her hand against the door. "I have important news for him."

Silence.

"Avi, the sooner he knows, the better."

Avi's face hardened as he deliberated. "Very well," he finally muttered, and stepped back. "Perhaps milady would leave him a card or a note . . ."

She pushed past him and made for the stairs.

He was not here—the whole place felt forsaken. She circled around the landing, into his bedchamber, where the bed was neatly made and the divan was yawningly empty, save a book lying face-down. A fuzzy layer of dust covered his desk and the shelves. He had not been home much. He had spent the past few weeks in London, or with her.

She raced down the stairs again, into the drawing room. Nothing, not even cold ash on the grate.

"Milady—"

She spun round and pinned the valet with a glare. "Is his disappearance related to an incident with Lady Cecily?"

His brows rose. "I can't possibly tell, milady."

"You can't, or you won't?"

His lips pressed together.

Lord, grant her patience. "Do you like his lordship?" she tried.

Avi tilted his head. "Milord is, in his own way, a good master. But now I learn he may have compromised a young lady."

He looked genuinely distressed. He did not want Tristan to be guilty, she surmised.

"I have reason to believe he did not compromise the lady," she said.

A ROGUE OF ONE'S OWN

Avi stilled. "He did not? Well, I am pleased. I found myself surprised his lordship would do such a thing."

"I am here to help," she said, which was a lie—she had come for help herself.

"May I bring milady tea?" Avi regarded her warmly now. "A sherry, perhaps?"

"Please just tell me what you know."

"Very well. They came here to wait for him—had I known, I would not have let them in. But I did, and so he went with them."

A terrible suspicion raised the hair on her nape. "Who were they?"

"The Earl of Wycliffe, and his entourage." He pursed his lips. "Unsavory fellows."

"Indeed," she said darkly.

"Very bad."

"What did they say? What did they want?"

"They said his lordship and the lady had been seen leaving the fair together, and she came back alone at night, wearing his coat. Lord Ballentine could not provide an alibi. Milady?"

She had sat down hard on a chair.

"No alibi," she repeated. "He did not tell them where he was last night?"

Avi shook his head, and she could tell that his nimble mind was working out its own story about the situation. "They went to Wycliffe Hall," he supplied. "Signing marriage contract papers, I believe."

"No." She shot to her feet. "He can't just marry someone based on an accusation. This is not the Middle Ages."

"But the lady's reputation would be all but destroyed if word got out. As would his, if he didn't confirm the betrothal."

"There is no betrothal," she snapped.

Avi bobbled his head. "There was an understanding, albeit an informal one."

He was right. She began to pace around the room. He had not provided an alibi. He was protecting her, and it unleashed a storm of hot emotions in her chest.

"I understand society may secretly adore a rogue," Avi said. "But they will cut one who turns against one of their innocents."

She gave a hollow laugh. "They will."

"And he cannot afford a soiled reputation, quite literally, can he now."

She paused the to-ing and fro-ing. "What do you mean?"

"Perhaps milady is aware that Lord Ballentine took a loan from a bad man?"

"Goodness, yes. Mr. Blackstone."

Avi gave her a grave look. "If he became known for ruining a debutante or breaching an engagement promise, who will buy his books? How could the ladies still find his romantic poetry appealing? And then how will he pay back the loan?"

With every question, she felt dizzier.

"The Prince of Wales will withdraw his endorsement for the other books." She met Avi's eyes. "One does not default on a Blackstone loan, I suppose."

"I suppose not," Avi said politely.

"I imagine doing so would entail more than a crippling interest rate."

"I imagine so, milady."

She sank back onto the chair. "It's worse," she said. "We had to purchase capacity from another publishing house. The production has begun, but customers will return their orders. And we had considerable costs for the refurbishment . . ." She caught herself. Avi's eyes had become huge, and she had no business distressing the man further.

She took a deep breath. "When did they leave?"

Avi's gaze shifted to the clock on the mantelpiece. "Around half an hour ago, milady."

Her pace slowed when she was back on High Street, because her legs were shaking. She paused next to a carved blue pillar of the Oxford Marmalade Shop. Behind the window, jam jars were artfully arranged in a pyramid.

Perhaps Tristan had named her as his alibi by now. Perhaps he would honorably take their secret to his grave. She couldn't tell which terrified her more. Terrified. She was that.

Because wedged between a marmalade pyramid and groups of students hasting past, she had a decision to make, and quick. On the other side of the street, the long arm of the clock on St. Mary's tower stood at nearly a quarter to twelve. The next train bound toward Wycliffe Hall left shortly past noon. Two minutes. She had two minutes to decide whether to board that train.

She couldn't breathe.

Tristan would know exactly what was at stake for him. He did not want Cecily but marrying her was now his most convenient option both socially and financially. Even if he opted to prove his innocence by throwing her, Lucie, to the wolves, they might well compel him to marry Cecily anyway, for her innocent reputation would require protection now while presumably no one cared about protecting Lucie's blackened one.

Tristan was not going to name her. It was in his blood to shield someone who could no longer defend himself and he bore the scars to prove it. He would never pull the trigger on a defenseless woman.

So she could just go back home. She could carry on with the life she had built. The day Tristan would have made another woman his countess had long been looming.

Or she could turn left toward Oxford Rawley Station and take a train.

The arm of the clock moved.

A cold calm came over her. Her heart knew before her mind dared putting it into words.

She could not go home. Not just because the vision of Tristan in

Cecily's arms made her sick. Day after day, she rose in the morning to do battle for more freedom and choice. Could she still do so, proudly, knowing she had been silent when Tristan's freedom and choice were falling victim to a great injustice? Hardly. It would eat away at her, like rot ate away at a badly done fundament.

But the Cause. If word got out, she might never be able to return to it. . . .

The heavy toll of the church bell announced it was a quarter to noon.

She glanced up at the tower.

Apparently, there was a part of her still separate from her work. She had lived and breathed the Cause for so long, she had assumed her principles and the movement were one and the same. It was not so.

The curious thing about causes is that they usually continue well without you. The question is whether you can continue well without them.

"Well, damn you, Melvin," she whispered.

She picked up her skirts and ran for a hackney.

Chapter 34

The town center around Newbury Station was mercifully unchanged since she had last passed through ten years ago. As she dashed from the main entrance, the redbrick façade of the coaching inn was already in view on the other side of the market square. She would never catch up with Wycliffe and Tristan, but she would well try.

The inn owner himself staffed the counter; it had to be him because he was reading the *Pall Mall Gazette* while on duty and did not deign to glance up when she swept through the door. Behind him in the left corner sat an older woman in a wicker chair, wrapped in a shawl and knitting.

"I need to hire a horse," she said to the *Pall Mall Gazette*, still trying to catch her breath.

The man's head appeared; he was squinting at her over the rim of the paper. "Where you going, milady?"

"Wycliffe Hall."

He nodded. "The stagecoach passing near Wycliffe Hall leaves in half an hour. It's three pence a ticket."

"Is there a horse for hire?"

Wycliffe Hall lay three miles south of Newbury straight across the fields. It was twice as far in a stagecoach.

The man was eyeing her skeptically. "A horse?"

"A horse," she confirmed. Her mouth was dry. Electricity crackled through her limbs. The long hand of the clock on the wall behind the man told her she was losing precious minutes—Tristan could be signing his marriage contract as they spoke.

The man turned to the woman knitting in the wicker chair. "Beth. Is there a horse?"

The woman glanced up, and contemplated. "Aye," she finally said. "The pony. But there is no sidesaddle."

The inn owner looked at Lucie and shrugged. "Afraid we don't have sidesaddles, milady. Are you taking the three-pence ticket?"

"No," she said. "I'm taking a regular saddle."

The man's eyes widened. "Ha ha," he then said. "A wee jest."

"I'm not jesting." Her dangerously calm tone should have warned him.

"Here, milady. It's a three-pence ticket, I'm afraid."

"I need the horse, with the regular saddle."

The man shook his head. "For yourself, milady? It's not safe."

And his newspaper made to rise.

Lucie's right hand slid into her skirt pocket.

The metallic click had the man looking up with a frown. Finding himself face-to-face with a derringer, he froze, his mouth slack with shocked surprise.

"I'm taking the horse," Lucie said. "With the regular saddle."

The man's hands were slowly rising over his head, his newspaper fluttering to the ground.

"Good Lord, man, this is not a robbery," Lucie said, exasperated. "Here is a shilling for the horse, and three pence for your shawl." She waved the pistol at the equally frozen woman as she slid the money across the counter with her left hand.

"See, none of this nonsense would be necessary if only women were allowed to wear trousers," she said not ten minutes later to the young woman, likely the innkeeper's daughter, who was holding a saddled and bridled New Forest pony in the stable aisle. The girl only stared as Lucie proceeded to roll up her fashionable narrow skirt and underskirt until it was a fabric sausage round her thighs and her legs were on display. When she had swung up into the saddle, she draped the swathes of fabric of the shawl around her to preserve some modesty. Her ankles and at least an inch of each her calves were still revealed, and she felt terribly naked the moment she rode from the stable.

They crossed the market square in a quick trot, drawing scandalized double takes from passersby. An eternity through cobblestoned streets followed until she reached the outskirts of town, where a mix of green and fallow fields stretched into the distance all the way to Wycliffe Hall. She maneuvered the pony off the road and loosened the reins. For all she knew, she was already too late.

Tristan had expected to find his father waiting in Wycliffe's library. Rochester stood in front of the desk, rigid as a fence post, next to a pinched-looking Tommy Tedbury and a man he recognized as Rochester's solicitor. Interestingly, Lady Wycliffe was also present, a little way apart, standing near the fireplace. The most important player in this quagmire, however, was missing.

He gave Rochester a hard look. "Where is she?"

"If you are referring to Lady Cecily, she is indisposed," the earl said coldly.

"Is she now," he said, his voice edged with such menace, Lady Wycliffe touched her throat.

"There's no need to expose the young woman to further distress," said Rochester. "You have done quite enough."

"Are you behind this?" The possibility had occurred to him on the long, silent train ride to Newbury.

"No." Rochester gave him a thin smile. "This is your reckoning. This is paying the piper for your sins."

Behind Tristan, Wycliffe cleared his throat. "I admit I am puzzled that marriage to a lady like my ward is presented as a punishment." He assumed position next to Rochester and Tommy Tedbury to create a united front. "It is a grand bargain for you, Ballentine, all things considered. I am therefore also puzzled why you would lead us all on such a chase—first you delay signing the papers, then you ruin the girl, now you refuse to do the right thing, when in truth it is all very simple."

"Simple," Tristan said, "and yet you came to fetch me with your lawyer in tow."

Wycliffe shrugged. "The betrothal is a necessity now and no papers have been signed yet."

Tristan turned to Beedle, who looked uncomfortable in the face of being outnumbered so vastly. "Beedle. I don't enjoy the coercion. What does the law say?"

Beedle shifted from one foot to the other. "An alibi for last night would help, my lord. It would not solve the lady's trouble with her reputation now, but it would restore your character in the eyes of the family and society."

Too bad, that. He had, of course, contemplated telling Wycliffe that he was sleeping with his daughter. Then the earl would think twice about who should marry whom.

While on the train, as the hazy beauty of the English countryside in summer was slipping by, every option for his life had passed before his mind's eye. And every option had run into a cold, black dead-end, for none of them led to Lucie. Lucie. His prickly fairy, his love. His body ached with the urge to go to her, even if it meant he had to walk a thousand miles. Now, on the brink of losing her, he faced the truth: he would marry her today. Not to save him from an existence with Cecily, or from the ruthless maneuvers required to avert such a thing; not for London Print; nor because their match was a good alliance between two earldoms. He would marry her because she was the constant, she was the light. If he gave her name away now, he could have her. She would hate him. But she would be his, and the dark, selfish part of him had murmured very seductively that it would be worth it. Shortly before the train had reached Newbury, he had known he'd never do it, and that he would rather be shot again than clip her wings. Icy fury had filled the emptiness inside his chest instead.

"An alibi," Wycliffe said impatiently. "Even if there were an alibi, the only correct course of action in this situation is to extend the protection of your name to my ward."

"He will," Rochester said. "He knows they would both be ruined otherwise."

Tristan gave him a caustic smile. "For the sake of truth and justice: has she actually claimed I took her into the punt house?"

Rochester made a face.

Wycliffe shrugged. "There was hardly a need for her to detail indignities. What matters is that circumstances are clear, and that she has been seen."

Hasty footsteps sounded in the hallway outside.

Behind him, the door flew open.

Everyone facing the door drew back, wearing expressions of disbelief. Which told him exactly who had made an appearance.

He turned slowly, trying to calm the sudden gallop of his heart.

Lucie's cheeks were flushed an angry red, her hair was flying loose around her face. She was a woman out to avenge.

Alas, as she strode into the room, her small chin raised with determination, he knew she was here to avenge—him.

He launched himself into her path. "Lucie, don't—"

She ignored him and squared up to Lord Wycliffe. "Lord Ballentine is innocent," she said. "I am his alibi. He spent the whole night with me."

Chapter 35

~⁂~

A deafening silence filled the library. The silence after an explosion, Lucie thought absently. Everyone looked as bloodless as if after a peppering by shrapnel. Time must have slowed to a crawl, too, for she had a long minute to take in the room. Tommy, her mother, men with notebooks who looked like lawyers, were all here, standing stiff like life-sized tin soldiers. There was Rochester, next to Wycliffe's wing chair, which was in the same place as years ago. There was the chesterfield behind which she had spent so many mornings, hiding, reading, playing chess, and it looked much less imposing than she remembered it. It was, in fact, just a regular sofa. And the ceiling appeared lower, the books lining the shelves were covered in dust. The carpet was worn even beyond the acceptable standards of a country home. This was where it all had started?

Facing her father left her astonishingly cold, too. Like his library, he was older and smaller than she recalled, the lines bracketing his mouth deep grooves now. He looked a little comical in his wide-eyed, frozen surprise. This was the man she had half-feared, half-resented, growing up?

Rochester stepped forward, and the present came rushing back at her. Tristan's father was still tall and imposing, and his green eyes were hostile. "What is the meaning of this?" he demanded.

"The meaning," she said loudly, "is that if Lord Ballentine spent the night in my bed, he cannot have spent it compromising my cousin."

A strangled noise sounded from the direction of her mother.

She felt Tristan staring at her, but she avoided his gaze. It would hurt to face him, and she could not afford chinks in her armor now.

"Stop scribbling," snarled Wycliffe. "If one word of this leaves this room, I shall see that each one of you loses his license." The three men who looked like lawyers froze with their fingers around their pens.

Rochester was staring at her. "You make an incredible claim. Can you prove it?"

"You are asking for a witness?" She inclined her head. "It is not usually commonplace to have a third person in the room during such encounters."

"Silence," her father barked. His face had gone from white to a worrying shade of crimson.

Her heart was racing, the thuds heavy in her ears. The dreamlike quality to the situation was wearing off; the urgency pounding through her out on the fields that had filled her with unnatural determination was draining from her.

"You may silence me here," she said. "But I won't hesitate to go to the papers to make my claim. Certainly not should I find it confirmed that there were *consequences*." She clasped a meaningful hand over her midriff.

The collective gasp sucked the air from the room.

Tristan took a step toward her before reining himself in, but it cost him; she sensed it from across the room that he was struggling. She took a tiny glimpse at him and found that his face was pale. *What have you done?* said the look in his eyes.

"Thomas," said her father, his dark stare still on her hand curving over her belly. "Fetch your cousin."

Tommy turned to his father with a look of shocked disapproval.

"Now," Wycliffe said. Lucie knew this tone. It was the one preceding fatherly discipline.

Tommy's lips pressed into a line, but he made for the door.

No one spoke a word until he returned.

Cecily certainly looked as though she had been debauched in a hedge and had lived to regret it. Her hair was tousled; her pretty face was blotchy and swollen from crying. Lucie was taken aback; it was no surprise that the men in this room were keen to protect her—she would have felt protective of her too, had she not known better.

When Cecily spotted Tristan standing next to the desk, her blue eyes widened with a measure of alarm. It turned to bewilderment when she recognized Lucie. Her face froze over entirely when Wycliffe informed her about Lucie's claims.

"So, Cecily, do you have anything to say?" Wycliffe asked her.

Cecily was not looking at anyone in particular; she stood with her shoulders drooping. When she spoke, her voice was high and soft. "It appears to me as though Cousin Lucie would like to claim Lord Ballentine for herself."

Wycliffe's brows rose in surprise, and a murmur rose among the lawyers. This had been an attack, rather than a defense of position.

Lucie made a face. "I would rather have my teeth pulled than marry, Cecily."

"And yet you are here," Cecily muttered. "And you say you and he . . ." She choked a little, as though she could not bring herself to say the words, and her nose wrinkled as if she were fighting back tears.

"Cecily," Wycliffe said, his tone notably cooler. "Again—is there anything helpful you have to say on the matter?"

Cecily's gaze met Lucie's directly for the first time since entering the library. "You never liked me," she said. "I daresay, you envied me."

"Envied you?" Lucie was genuinely surprised.

Cecily nodded. "For taking your place. Perhaps now, you wish to destroy my happiness in return."

Beyond Cecily's shoulder, Lucie saw her mother raise a hand to her mouth.

She slowly shook her head at her cousin. "I never *had* the place you occupy, Cecily, and I certainly was not happy here. As for your happiness—do you truly believe it is right, forcing Lord Ballentine's hand?"

Cecily's eyes narrowed at her, an angry glitter in their depths.

"Hold now," Tommy said, stepping forward with a scowl. "I do not like this—why, it reminds me of a cross-examination. And it is hardly necessary—Cecily never forced a thing."

"Then why am I here?" Tristan asked mildly. He had leaned back against the desk, his legs crossed over his ankles, looking deceptively idle. Lucie could feel his fury, tightly contained in his quiet form, and she had the disconcerting feeling that much of it was directed at her.

Tommy rounded on him. "Because a lady would not speak in detail on such a shameful matter, and she does not have to—she has been seen with you, and was gone for hours, unchaperoned. It suffices to ruin her, and by God, you will do right by her."

Tristan's smile held a hint of malice. "Your sister says I ruined her, too, and that I won't deny—do you propose I wed the both of them? Beedle?"

"Uhm," said Beedle.

"He has a tattoo," Cecily blurted. "Lord Ballentine has a tattoo on his chest."

Every head in the room whipped round to her again, and Lucie's heart stopped for a beat.

Her gaze flew to Tristan, and the look in his eyes said this had surprised him, too.

"Does he now," came Rochester's keen voice. "Why don't you describe it for us?"

Cecily was red as a beet, but when Rochester nodded encouragingly, she said: "It is on the right side of his chest."

Wycliffe turned to Tristan. "Is this true?"

Tristan gave a nod. "It is."

Tommy took a step toward him. "You," he ground out. "You dared to—"

"Hold now," Lucie said. "Cecily could have easily overheard this in the ladies' retiring room, rather than seeing it herself."

"Now, that is preposterous," Wycliffe said. "The girl hardly moves in circles that would discuss Lord Ballentine's tattoos in front of debutantes."

Clearly, her father had no idea what women were wont to discuss among each other in the secluded areas during wine-filled social gatherings.

Her gaze locked with Cecily's. Her cousin looked terribly out of her depth, but there was a recklessness in her eyes that said she was not going to relent.

"Why don't you describe it," Lucie said. "Because I dare you, you can't." It was a gamble, but there was nothing to lose now.

Voices swelled around them, protesting, lamenting, ordering—

"It is a . . . a nude woman dancing in a circle," Cecily said.

It was the flick of her eyes as she said it, furtively up to the right, that sent goose bumps prickling down Lucie's spine. "Are you certain?" she said quickly.

Cecily bared her small teeth. "You are terribly insistent, cousin."

"A woman, you say?"

"I just did, say so."

"And you found nothing unusual about her?"

Cecily leaned forward, almost a crouch. "She's very obviously in the nude."

"Obviously, you say—so you were close to see it?"

"Indeed."

It was very quiet in the library now, the moment where everyone in the room was picturing a situation that would have brought Tristan's bare chest close to Cecily's eyes. . . .

"And her four arms didn't strike you as peculiar?" Lucie said.

Cecily stared at her unblinking for a beat.

Then her eyes lit with a realization, as though she'd just solved a tricky puzzle. "Why must you try and trick me," she cried. "Of course she does not have four arms."

"This is enough now," Wycliffe said. "Enough of this. Gentlemen—"

"Actually," Tristan said, "there are four arms."

Everyone turned back to him. Only Cecily took a step back.

Tristan raised his hands to his cravat. "Does anyone care for a demonstration?"

"Hell, no," Wycliffe, Tommy, and Rochester said in unison, sounding appalled. And uncertain.

Despite the previous threat to their license, the lawyers had their pens at the ready and were following the exchange, riveted, as though watching a match of lawn tennis. Played with grenades.

Lady Wycliffe stepped forward. Pale and shiny, she could have been a waxwork as she moved toward her niece. "Cecily," she said quietly, one hand extended. "Say it isn't true."

Cecily was still backing away slowly.

"Oh, Christ," said Wycliffe.

Cecily's bottom lip quivered. "Arthur made me do it," she said, her gaze darting around the room. "It was all Arthur's idea—he said . . . the tattoo . . . he told me . . . I didn't mean to. I just got lost at the fair, running after you, after you just left me there." She directed a tearful stare at Tristan.

"Out," Wycliffe said to the lawyers, his voice flat. "Get out, now."

"I went to the boathouse to cry, because Lord Ballentine had spoken very harshly to me," Cecily said between sobs. "And I fell asleep on his coat with exhaustion. When I woke, the hour was late, dusk had fallen—was I to sleep in the boathouse? I had to walk unchaperoned—I had no choice."

"But there was a choice to clear my name," Tristan suggested in a gentle tone.

She gave him an incredulous look. "There was a search party, scandal was inevitable. You wouldn't have married me had there been a scandal that didn't involve you."

Tristan slowly shook his head. "I never meant to marry you at all, and I am sorry you were led to believe otherwise."

Cecily's hands balled into fists. "I shan't idly stand by and marry just any man they choose for me. . . ."

"Felicity," Wycliffe said quietly, "take her to her room."

Lady Wycliffe moved with difficulty, as though she were wading through glue.

Then the countess raised her chin and clasped Cecily's elbow. She did not grant the men in the room another glance as she led her charge outside.

When the door had fallen shut, Wycliffe slowly turned to Rochester. "Very well," he said. "It appears your son is going to marry my daughter, not my ward."

Rochester blanched. "The hell he will," he said. "My son is the heir of the House of Rochester and will marry in accordance with his position."

Lucie watched her father take a step toward Rochester, the movement so quick, it had to have been instinct. "Are you insinuating that a daughter from the House of Wycliffe is not fit for the position?"

"Come now, Wycliffe, a Ballentine can't marry a—"

"I advise you to treat this with consideration." Wycliffe cut him off icily. "When a Ballentine goes and ruins two Tedbury women in short succession, he will bloody well marry at least one of them."

"I'm not marrying anyone," Lucie said, and walked out.

She had expected Tristan to follow her. He reached her in the Great Hall when she was still a considerable distance from the exit.

"Wycliffe has a point," he said without preamble. She had expected this, too, and kept walking. Pray her pony was still there, at the ready.

"He has a point, and we must talk."

"Tristan, I will not marry you, so for the sake of our mutual dignity, please do not ask me."

His hand clamped around her upper arm and she was halted in her tracks and turned to face him.

Her stomach squirmed. She wasn't ready yet to be touched by him. To be close enough to smell him. She had little strength left right now to argue with him, not with his gaze boring into hers with such determination.

"You are aware that we have a situation." Despite his calm tone, she had never seen him look so serious. He probably didn't relish the prospect of marriage, either. He had told her so when she had interrogated him in her drawing room just yesterday. . . .

She shook her head. "I did not come here to make you choose between Cecily and me, but to give you a choice between Cecily and your freedom. I cannot marry. You should know this much about me at least."

She made to leave and was promptly snatched back by her arm.

His features were hard as if carved into rock. "How long do you think it will take until word gets out? What do you think it will do for your reputation, Lucie? For London Print? Your cause?"

For a beat, she couldn't breathe. The enormity of what she had done was presently kept at bay by a flimsy fence of temporary denial, and it would not withstand a battering now.

"My family will rather take this to their graves than allow word to get out, and nothing might happen at all."

"Possible, but hardly guaranteed, darling."

"It does not mean I have to be your wife," she said. "This was about justice."

"Justice?" His smile was deeply cynical.

"What else would it be?" Her voice was rising. She had to leave, leave this place, leave him.

The grip of his hand on her arm tightened. "What else?" he said.

"After last month, it is not too presumptious to assume you have an affection for me."

An affection?

What an innocuous, inadequate, ridiculous word.

"You seemed prepared to marry my cousin five minutes ago," she said instead, "so my affection would hardly matter."

His expression was plain incredulous. "The hell I was. And would you rather I had named you as my alibi? Very well, it crossed my mind—to name you. I did not, for how could I force you into it—but now you may have forced it upon yourself."

"No." She yanked her arm from his grip. "I'd rather be wrecked than enslaved."

He drew a sharp breath. "This is not the time or the place. Let us talk in private."

"Time and place have no effect on my decision."

"Christ, see reason, Lucie. You already have me in your bed every night and you like it; where would be the difference?"

She nearly kicked his shin. "Bedsport," she hissed. "Of course, that is all you see—oh, to have the luxury of male ignorance." She sprung into motion again, eyes on the door. "The difference between wife and lover is like night and day," she said, hating that he was following her again. "Name one married woman, just one, who advanced important causes outside the home."

He made a sound of great annoyance. "*That* is your worry?"

Easy for him to dismiss her, just like that. "Name a single one—you cannot, because it is nigh impossible for a woman to achieve anything when burdened with a husband, and the constant demands of wifely protocol, not to mention children. Why do you think it is that progressive women feel compelled to choose spinsterhood?"

"Stop," he said tightly, "stop running. Stop hiding behind your work."

"Hiding!"

"Yes, hiding." Again, he used his strength to stop her, and she hated him a little, then.

He must have seen it in her face, for his eyes lit with a combative glint. "Think," he murmured, and leaned in close. "If you truly were so opposed to a man in your life and all associated *consequences*, you would have never accepted the risks that came with taking me into your bed."

She felt his breath on her cheek. He was so near. The erratic beat of her heart jumbled her thoughts. *Run*, was all she heard. *Run*, more loudly, when his eyes softened and showed all the familiar flecks of green and gold.

"You are not a fool, Lucie," he said, his tone warmer, too. "You knew the risks. You wanted me anyway. Ask yourself why."

Her throat was horribly tight. "You are right," she managed. "I wanted you. But even if the laws were different, I would never marry you."

It stunned him for a beat, and she tore free.

"You think I am good enough to share your bed, but not to wed?" His voice was low, but fraught with outrage.

Many women must have cried those exact words at him in the not-so-distant past.

Wide-eyed footmen swung back the entrance door for them.

"We would not suit," she said, a few steps down.

"Ah," he snapped. "Care to explain why not?"

Relief crashed through her; her pony was still there next to the fountain, held by an alarmed-looking groom.

Bloody steps, infernally tight skirts, it was taking forever. "If I were to marry," she said, "I would need a faithful husband. And you could never be faithful."

"And how would you know I couldn't be?" he demanded.

She jumped the last step. "Because you are Tristan Ballentine."

He turned abruptly into her path, crushing gravel under his heels. "My reputation is half-based on rumors and you know it."

She glared up at him. "You don't even trust yourself—you told me not to trust you. I listen when people tell me what they are."

"God, I told you this because I believed it to be true at the time—and it was caused entirely by how I felt about myself as a man, not by how I feel about you. And if we talked calmly I would tell you that things have changed—"

"Words," she cried. "Words do not matter, and you are impulsive. Take our first night: the moment you saw I was naked, you fell on me, when you had much to lose."

He paled before her eyes. "Well yes," he said softly. "I *fell on you* that night because I had wanted you half my bloody life."

She raised her chin. "Step aside, please."

Instead, he stepped closer and leaned over her, an intensity in his gaze that stunned the screaming in her head into silence. "Then for your sake, I hope there won't be a child," he murmured. "Because if there is, I give you my word now: I shall drag you to the altar, bodily, if I must, and you shall say *I do*, and politics can go hang."

He might as well have gripped her by the throat.

For a moment, she feared she might be sick.

"And so the mask slips," she whispered. "Consider this, Ballentine—any child might be better cared for without you, lest you turn into a brute like your own father."

He blinked. He made to say something, but for once, he appeared to be lost for words.

At last he did not hinder her from leaving again. He moved not at all when she lurched past him, to the pony, and dragged up her skirts to scramble onto the saddle. From the corner of her eyes, she saw that he still stood as she had left him, rigid and with his back turned. When she galloped down the drive a moment later, she felt the tender bonds between them snap inside her chest.

Chapter 36

It was like the last time she had left Wycliffe Hall: she felt nothing at all. The pace back to Newbury was civilized; the pony was returned without further ado. On the train, her eyes were dry but saw nothing of the landscape flying past the windows.

Back home, she petted and fed Boudicca, then methodically went through the mail Mrs. Heath had left on her desk. Annabelle's card with a note, inquiring whether she was all right. Annabelle must have seen her hurry from the Randolph's luncheon room. Next, a missive from Lady Athena, reporting that people from the *Manchester Guardian* had visited Tristan's office yesterday. . . . She turned the letter facedown. The mere sight of his name stung.

While tidying up the desk, she decided to pack for Italy in the morning. No one knew about her, suffragists, or Lord Ballentine in Tuscany.

Lord Arthur stumbled into his dorm room at Merton College shortly before midnight. He fumbled with the light switch, muttering to himself and smelling of alcohol.

He was as embarrassingly easy to ambush as a lone gazelle.

The moment the door fell shut, Tristan moved.

In a second, Arthur was in a choke hold, his head forced sideways at an awkward angle.

The keys clattered to the floor.

Arthur was stiff as a salt pillar, with his back flush against Tristan's chest. Strong fingers had clamped over his mouth, making any sound die in his throat.

Tristan brought his lips close to his ear. "Do not move. I'm a hairsbreadth from breaking your neck. A pity if it snapped by accident."

It was not true—a neck did not snap quite so easily. But his lordship would not know this; all he presently felt was a mean pain and murderous intentions.

"I can make you more comfortable. But struggle or yell, and you shall regret it. Understood?"

A pause, then Arthur made a noise of acquiescence.

"Good." He spun the young man around and shoved him back against the wall, his hands coming down hard on either side of his head.

Arthur's eyes were frozen wide with confusion, but the sickly-sweet smell of fear was already pouring off him by the buckets. The anger roiling in Tristan's chest forbade him to commiserate.

He leaned in close. "My day was very, very unpleasant," he said, "and would have been worse if not for your poor eyesight."

Arthur pressed back into the wall. "What do you mean?"

"Or were you just too distracted to properly decipher my tattoo?"

Arthur turned white as chalk. "Cecily?"

"Cecily."

"God," he croaked. "I never—crikey, women. It was merely an idea. I never expected her . . ."

"She claims it was your master plan."

Arthur's mouth opened, but no words came.

Odd.

After the fierce displays of jealousy and the drunken nonsense in

Holywell Road, he had expected more of a struggle. But then, he had several inches of height and a few stone of muscle over the young man. Who *did* look rather young, with his blond fluff glinting above his lip. *Was he trying to grow a mustache?* The thought interfered inconveniently. Thinking of Arthur as a puppy was not conducive to strangling him.

He shook his head. "If you were me right now, what would you do?"

Arthur's throat moved convulsively in the silence.

He was staring straight ahead at Tristan's cravat, sweat dampening his brow.

"More interestingly," Tristan said, "are you planning to trouble me again?"

A moment passed, and then Arthur raised his pale face and looked him in the eye. "No."

He could smell whiskey on the boy's breath.

He realized he had shoved Arthur up against a map—a faded and battered map of Greece. In fact, the whole room was decorated with maps of all sizes, some colorful, some plain. He had no clue what subject Arthur was reading—archaeology, cartography, the Classics? Perhaps he just liked maps. He had never asked.

"Well." He stepped back. "Excellent."

Arthur sagged into himself and touched his throat.

A sour feeling spread through Tristan's gut. He suddenly could not leave fast enough.

"You don't know what it is like." The abject bitterness in Arthur's voice stayed his hand on the doorknob.

Arthur's eyes were bitter, too, but he had raised his chin. "You don't know what it is like, knowing beautiful people like you exist but shall never be mine. Not even for a moment."

Tristan gave him an incredulous look. His lordship only tipped his chin higher. Judging him.

He leaned against the doorjamb with one shoulder and contemplated Arthur's haughty face more closely. Defiance might have edged out the fear, but the misery beneath was plain as day to a keen eye.

"You are right," he said slowly. "I don't know what it is like."

Surprise flared in Arthur's eyes, then quickly darkened to suspicion.

"I have yet to meet the person who would not, eventually, have me, for an hour, or a night, if I set my mind to it," Tristan continued. "One could say Fortune has dealt me an appallingly favorable hand."

Arthur's jaw clenched with silent resentment.

"It may please you, then, that the only woman I ever loved rejected me," Tristan said coolly.

He made to finally take his leave, when Arthur bit out: "Why won't she?"

He glanced back. "I suppose because in order to share her life with me openly, she would have to marry me, thereby sentencing herself to life in a prison of sorts."

Arthur's lips twisted. "Not unlike me, then—prison, for but sharing my affections openly."

Tristan stilled. "Indeed," he then said softly. "Not unlike you."

"At least her jailor wouldn't thrash her on the daily," Arthur said, mockingly. He cocked his head, his gaze assessing. "Or perhaps he would."

Well, hell.

He had made the comment about prison without much thought, but it struck him now with the brilliant clarity of an epiphany that he was a fool. He had heard Lucie. But he had not understood her concerns, not truly—he would protect his wife with his life, could she not see? He understood now, as Arthur's antipathy washed over him in waves, and he imagined the boy dirty and hungry behind bars. A heavy feeling filled his chest. It all bled together in his mind now, the concepts of desire and prison and marriage.

His gaze locked with Arthur's. *You knew what I was and yet you took me along . . . you are a monster, you have no care. . . .* An emotion, hot like shame, rolled over him. Many developed an attraction to him, he could hardly help it, but the truth was, he hadn't cared either way.

He ran his hand over his face. "I apologize."

Arthur gave him a hard look. "What for, exactly?"

For not giving a damn. For these dire times, where the laws made it a bitter thing to be alive and in love, at least when one had not been born a man, and one who happened to love in accordance with the rules. He had not made the rules, but he had never set out to change them, either. He had wasted a lot of time fighting the wrong wars.

"For several things, I suppose," he told Arthur.

"I'm not in need of mollycoddling," Arthur said curtly. "In the end, I only wished for some respect."

"Do you prefer men exclusively?"

Arthur drew back. "What is it to you?"

"You are a younger son. It is not imperative that you marry. There are ways . . . a confirmed bachelor can keep another close. A valet—"

"Blimey." Arthur waved a slender hand, looking bemused and annoyed. "Of course there are ways. We have always found them, and we always will. However, there was precisely one reason why I would have desired for you to surprise me in my chambers at night, Ballentine, and assault or matchmaking gossip was not it. So, if you please, get out."

The hallways of Merton College drifted past in a blur on his way out. He had come to settle a score and left feeling humbled and distracted instead.

The morning sun filled Lucie's reception room with a cheerful brightness, as though it were a regular summer day. But today she was leaving. She had packed; she had her papers.

Catching Boudicca, however, was another matter. The cat hated the travel crate as if it were a portal to the underworld and had been in hiding all morning.

When Boudicca finally tried shooting past to reach her food bowl, Lucie lunged. She had a firm grip on the cat's middle, but the beast made herself impossibly long and she had to let go, unwilling to be left holding just a white-tipped tail.

The cat was already on top of the cherrywood cabinet in the drawing room. Her ears were completely flat.

Lucie moved the footstool and climbed on it.

"Give up," she said, rising onto her tiptoes. "I know all your tricks, and I always win—ouch!" She stared at the beads of blood blooming on the back of her right hand.

She glared. "Have you lost your mind?"

Boudicca's irreverent stare said she'd do it again, scratch her. Possibly bite her, too.

"Just you wait." She stomped to the washbasin to follow the burn of the scratch with the sting of soap. "Don't move, you mad beast." She kneeled by the carpetbag and rifled through it for her leather gloves.

She had found one when the doorbell rang.

She froze.

She hadn't imagined it—the bell was already ringing again, shrill and intrusive, and her nerves jangled in response. Whoever it was, she did not wish to see them.

The presence of the caller seeped through the walls like noxious smoke—they were still there, waiting, listening, holding their breath.

They would not go away.

She rose and strode down the corridor, glove in hand, and unlatched the locks.

A drawn, fine-boned face looked back at her—the last person on God's green earth she had expected. "Mother."

"Hush." The countess cast a nervous glance back over her shoulder.

A small hackney was waiting on the side of the road.

She hadn't heard it approach during her efforts to catch the cat.

Her mother's gaze swept over her travel dress and the glove, randomly held in her injured hand. "Well. Are you not going to ask me inside?"

She didn't open the door any wider. "What do you want?"

Her mother's lips thinned into a hyphen at the rudeness. "I would prefer to discuss it in private." Again she half-glanced over her shoulder, her brittle frame, if possible, stiffer than usual; quite possibly she was expecting a mob of nosy commoners to descend upon them at any moment. Her mother rarely ventured into residential parts of a town, unless, perhaps, to dispense charity. Whatever business had brought her here, she must consider it to be urgent. It was also, quite frankly, none of her concern and thus, she did not budge.

"Very well," said Lady Wycliffe, her blue eyes steely. "I need your help to make someone disappear."

Chapter 37

I need your help to make someone disappear.
   On the list of Least Likely Things her mother would utter, this came at the very top.

She stepped aside. "Whom have you killed, Mother?"

Lady Wycliffe strode past her, giving her a long-suffering look. "No one is dead. Yet."

The moment they had entered the reception room, the countess turned to her, her gaze pointedly fixed on Lucie's face. "You are not really with child, are you?"

She shook her head, because for all she knew, she was not. She wondered how her mother would have reacted had she said yes. But thus satisfied, Lady Wycliffe simply nodded. She cast a glance around the room, taking in the ink-stained printing press in the corner and the worn upholstery of the divan. She refrained from walking over to the fireplace to swipe a gloved finger over the mantelpiece, but it was obvious that she was tempted.

She did step closer to look at Aunt Honoria's portrait. "How cynical," she remarked, studying the Vinegar Valentine cards Lucie had tucked into the ebony frame. "Though I suppose Honoria would have found it amusing."

"If you don't mind, I must catch the train."

Her mother stiffened. "Of course." She turned and faced her. "It is about Lady Rochester."

The name hit her chest with the stunning force of a fist, and for a terrible moment, she couldn't breathe. Pain bloomed beneath her ribs as if the wound there were physical and had just begun to bleed again.

It would be very good to reach Tuscany, where no one had ever heard of the House of Rochester and wouldn't accidentally make her feel mortally injured by mentioning the name.

Her mother was watching her compose herself with far too knowing eyes.

"Go on," Lucie said hoarsely.

"There was a situation at Ashdown. The countess cannot stay there for the time being."

"I know."

"I suspected you knew, after yesterday's outrageous interlude. However, I would have sought your advice either way—she cannot stay hidden at Wycliffe Hall any longer. The house is vast, and Wycliffe is inattentive, but eventually the staff will talk."

She spoke with an utter lack of inflection, the tone saved for matters she found truly, deeply tedious. Admittedly, hiding a runaway noblewoman *was* highly scandalous. Why was her mother risking trouble by sheltering a vulnerable woman? A sense of duty toward an old friend? Wishing to spite her husband? Whatever the motivation, she, Lucie, had to help keep Tristan's mother safe. Tristan. It hurt. But she would have to let him know. At the very least, she would have to send him a cable.

"What do you have in mind?" she asked, trying to focus on the pressing task at hand rather than her aching chest.

"She needs to leave Britain posthaste," her mother said. "However, I prefer for her to stay in the familiar climes of Europe. Her son's death has left her . . . a little unwell. Any added stresses from living among, say, Americans, would be her undoing." Her eyes assumed a piercing quality. "Can you do this?"

Lucie shrugged. "Yes."

For every prostitute and her baby she'd sent to a halfway house, she had helped a noblewoman disappear: the pregnant, unwed relations of titled men, who wanted to keep their children; ladies who could not file for divorce.

"Well, I'm glad," her mother said, the stern set of her mouth relaxing.

"It costs," Lucie warned. "A lot."

"It should pose no problem."

"Oh?"

"Wycliffe has his faults," her mother said. "But tightfistedness is not one of them. A prudent woman may set aside a considerable fortune over the course of thirty years." She looked a little smug saying this.

"I see," Lucie said slowly. "Very well—I shall refer you to people who will assist you."

Her mother stilled, and then a worried furrow appeared between her brows. "You won't be involved in this . . . operation?" She sounded worried, too.

"My contacts are capable."

She stepped around her carpetbag and walked to her desk, which was already neatly tidied up for abandonment.

She opened the drawer and laid out a blank sheet of paper, pen, ink, and a lump of sealing wax.

Her mother had followed and hovered, watching intently as her pen scratched across the paper.

"Cecily confessed to scattering the pamphlets around Claremont," she said when Lucie was setting her signature.

Her pen slipped, adding an extra swirl to her name. "I know."

"Apparently, she feared you would come to replace her in my affections after we had conversed at Claremont in a friendly manner.

You are my daughter, after all. The thought of not being first anymore put her in a panic of sorts, and I understand she went to your room with the intention of causing you some mischief and saw the pamphlets."

Lucie sprinkled sand over the letter. This *confession* could simply be Cecily's latest manipulation, to flatter her aunt and make her think her affections were worth causing havoc in a ducal palace.

"She has shown an admirable combative spirit," she allowed. "Unfortunately, she applied it badly."

The countess shifted from one foot to the other. "Her conduct has been a great disappointment to us."

Lucie lit the candle to melt the sealing wax. "Will you send her to live with Aunt Clotilde in Switzerland? I remember you wanted to send me to her whenever I was a great disappointment to you." Which had been often.

"She is set to leave for Bern tomorrow," her mother admitted after a pause.

"Huh." Aunt Clotilde was a dragon. She could almost feel sorry for her cousin. Almost.

"Cecily never truly recovered from her parents' death," her mother said. "She has a potent fear of being alone in the world."

Lucie shook her head. Even confined, a woman could still make choices. "I had the impression you and Tommy adored her."

She poured the liquefied wax and pressed her seal into the splash of red.

She would visit the postal office on her way to the train station and have a message sent to Tristan. He wanted to find his mother, then work for her forgiveness, he had said. A dull ache filled her at the memory. After what she had said to him at Wycliffe Hall, he probably considered them even. She could safely assume that he would not work for a thing. She willed another burning surge of tears back down. It had crossed her mind to seek him out and have a conversation, like an adult woman in possession of all her rational faculties. But what would it change? The laws were what they were. And her fears would not simply dissolve into thin air. She would only prolong the inevitable: more heartache.

Distance. Distance would help.

She handed her mother the letter. "This will help you."

Her mother eyed the envelope with suspicion. "What precisely am I to do with it?"

"It contains my letter of recommendation. Furthermore, the addresses and code words for a woman who forges travel documents and a woman who shall select a suitable destination and take care of the logistics. I must ask you to treat this confidentially at all costs."

"Oh," Lady Wycliffe said weakly. "I must seek out two more people?"

The ignorance. "You wish to make someone disappear without a trace. Not just anyone, the wife of a horrid and powerful man. Believe me, this is as expedient as I can make it—years of work were required to make it so, in fact."

"Very well." Her mother slid the envelope into the inner pocket of her jacket, which was prudent. A reticule could be grabbed by a pickpocket. "Are you certain you can't be directly involved?"

"I would, but I must catch a train."

Her mother's gaze slid to the trunk and open carpetbag next to the door, then traveled back to Lucie.

"You surprise me," she said. "All things aside, I had not taken you for a woman who runs."

Lucie blinked. "Well. And I had not taken you for a woman who fights."

A slight intake of breath. Then her mother gave a tiny nod. "I suppose we all run and fight in our own way when the occasion requires it. Don't we." Again she looked at the bag. "You are planning to travel awhile, I suppose."

"Awhile, yes."

A pause.

"Would we be able to find you?"

"No." Why would they wish to find her?

An emotion flickered in her mother's gaze, erratic and fleeting like a candle flame fighting the draft. And then her gaze became distracted. "Oh, who have we here?"

Lucie glanced back over her shoulder. Boudicca, impudent traitress, had finally deigned to stroll from her hiding place. Ignoring Lucie entirely, she began circling the visitor's skirt, delicately sniffing the hem.

"How curious," said her mother. "So this is where you went." She bent to stroke Boudicca's glinting black fur with a familiar ease.

Ice spread through Lucie's chest. "What do you mean?"

"Hm?" Her mother glanced up, her gloved knuckles still rubbing behind Boudicca's ear.

"You said 'this is where you went.' As if . . . as if you knew her."

"But I do. I'm quite certain this is one of Lady Violet's offspring."

Lady Violet?

Her mother's hand gave an impatient flick. "The one who won second prize at the London Exhibition."

Her mind was blank. No, she had not paid attention to her mother's obscure preoccupation with cat shows, back in the day.

"I should have known he would give her to you," her mother said. "Lord knows why. You were nothing but prickly to him."

The whole world went quiet.

Foreboding ran coldly down her spine. "He?" she said. "Who is *he*?"

"Why, Lord Ballentine, of course."

For a beat, she was suspended in thin air, disoriented.

"You must be mistaken." Thoughts were clanging around in her head, not making sense. "It could be any cat."

Her mother looked affronted. "Any cat? Hardly. It took me years to have the breeder achieve such a look: black fur, a white-tipped tail. The long-legged build. I would know the line anywhere. How old is she?"

Her voice reached Lucie through a ringing noise.

"Ten," she managed. "Ten years old in autumn."

"Then this very much confirms what I said. I remember it clearly; Lord Ballentine took one of the kittens during his last summer at Wycliffe Hall—ten years ago. He claimed it was for a young lady who was in dire need of company—he reasoned very charmingly; I remember because I never give cats away lightly. But I indulged him because I owed his mother a debt, one I will consider settled in excess after this ghastly—child, are you all right?"

She was not. Her throat was tight. Her nose burned, her eyes pricked hotly. She had never been more wrong. She turned and staggered along the corridor, into the kitchen. She stood where she had slapped him, a hand clutched over her middle.

"Goodness." Her mother had followed, and her expression was concerned. "I confused you."

"No." She shook her head. "No. Everything is perfectly clear."

Tristan had left Boudicca on her doorstep. She was the young lady in need of company.

She watched her mother spin in a bewildered little circle, how she took in shabby cabinets and the cast-iron sink of a commoner's kitchen, foreign objects to her eyes, the kitchen an alien place.

All those years, she had despised him.

All those years had been kinder, warmer, more purpose-filled because of her four-legged friend. At some points, her only friend.

What if I always liked and admired you, Lucie. . . . I had wanted you for half my bloody life. . . .

She had brushed his words aside instantly, because her temper had been high, and besides, who could ever really know with Tristan?

And had she taken him seriously, what would it have done to her?

She had known she could resist a handsome, wicked, clever, unexpectedly tender rogue.

She had known she could *not* resist a handsome, wicked, clever, unexpectedly tender rogue who had quietly held her in his affections half his life.

"I'm such a fool," she said.

Her mother made a triumphant noise. She had discovered a wine bottle next to the ice chest, still half-full and recorked, and lunged for it.

"Here," she said, pouring wine into a tea mug. "You need a sip."

"Thank you, Mother." She meant it, and her mother heard it—she looked up midpour, wearing a startled expression.

"I don't have time," Lucie said. "I must catch a train."

Chapter 38

———◈———

Tristan was leaning over his desk, his hands braced on the tabletop, studying a paper spread.

Her knees went weak with sudden relief, and she greedily drank
in the sight of him. He looked handsome and beloved, as usual in
only his shirtsleeves, and his cravat was untied and hung on either
side of his neck. Her hopes to find him here had been fragile. During
the train ride to London, she had resolved that she would apologize,
but she had not dared to think any further. She only knew she needed
to apologize. And if he no longer cared for her, she would certainly
survive.

He looked up, and his neutral expression made her breathless
with dread. Mere survival was a low standard—she could have been
happy with this man.

There was a flicker of *something* in his eyes when she turned the
key in the lock.

"May I come in?"

This gained her an ironic glance. "By all means."

Her legs were uncooperative, as if made from lead, when she approached his desk.

Tristan's gaze swept from her stiff gray collar to her booted feet,
lingering briefly on her hands clutching in her skirts, and the corner

of his mouth twitched. "You don't look too wholesome, my lady. A rough night?"

"Dreadful," she blurted. "And yours?"

"Terrible," he said at once.

Her fingers gripped the edge of his desk, to prevent herself from crawling over said desk to burrow into his arms.

"You're wearing your earring again," she said instead.

He made to touch the sparkling stud, then dropped his hand and shrugged.

"Your mother is at Wycliffe Hall," she told him. "I assisted in her disappearance this morning."

He nodded. "I received a cable on behalf of my lady mother a few hours ago, informing me that she is well and planning to abscond to the Continent—I'm glad to hear it confirmed."

She shook her head. "It sounds as though they have had us both."

"Mothers," he said. "Terribly secretive creatures."

"Women become so, given the circumstances."

He inclined his head. "Without doubt. But something tells me our mothers' shenanigans are not the sole reason for your visit."

Her heart leapt against her ribs. She supposed it was courteous of him, giving her a prod. She took a deep breath to begin her piece when she caught the header of one of the papers on the desk.

Her mind blanked.

He was suspiciously quiet while she comprehended what she was seeing.

"This is our data," she said slowly. "The data for our report."

She glanced back at him, still confused, and he nodded. "It is."

She picked up one of the sheets. "Who gave you these?"

"A Mrs. Millicent Fawcett."

"Millicent Fawcett."

"Yes. You mentioned her once or twice."

How droll. She must have mentioned Millicent dozens of times. . . .

"I assumed she would have the same insights you have," Tristan continued. "In a fit of romantic ambition, I had meant to surprise you with a publishing opportunity—then a Shakespearean drama of my own making unfolded at Wycliffe Hall."

On the left side of his desk, he had arranged typewritten paragraphs, headlines, and report figures in the layout of a newspaper page.

She struggled for a calm tone. "I heard people from the *Manchester Guardian* were here?"

"The editor, yes."

The editor, who was also the owner of the paper, as she well knew.

"Why?" she said softly. "Why did he visit?"

His smile was an enigma. "I had made him an offer he could not resist."

Her heart sank. "Please do not tell me you forced the hand of a newspaper editor, a suffrage-friendly one at that."

"No." Amusement brightened his eyes. "On the contrary. I used to have a habit of, let us call it, collecting incriminating information about fellow gentlemen. It used to serve me well in case my funds ran low—they usually did. However, such a source needs to be tapped wisely and in moderation—"

"By *source*, you mean blackmail."

"Yes." He was not abashed in the slightest. "However, as I said, it may only be used in moderation, and it is also impractical when you reside abroad. Therefore, I had a potential wealth of secrets and debts owed left. I traded them."

Oh, her heart. "You have given your intelligence to the owner of the *Manchester Guardian* in exchange for him running our report?"

He nodded. "I believe headlines in a national newspaper will serve you even better than using the periodicals as Trojan horses. It has a wider reach; meanwhile, you can keep your periodicals."

Her pulse was spiking now. "Why did you? Why did you do this?"

"Because I could," he said. "My ledger contains a number of potential clues for troubling some high and mighty fellows, and they are worth their weight in gold for investigative journalists of liberal newspapers."

She must have been in a shock; she felt quite frozen. "I should be jumping up and down with joy," she said slowly, "and then again, I should feel put out, that it took you to masterfully solve our conundrum."

"Me—a man, you mean."

"Yes."

He chuckled. "You would have such reservations. But be assured, the ledger was yours the moment you stormed into Wycliffe's library like Joan of Arc on a quest to rescue me, as I would have used it up in some fashion when winding my way out of that trap."

She had a good idea what this must have cost him to let go of his potential income source, after everything she now knew about his situation, of his life lived striving for freedom from a tyrant's purse strings. Granted, their publisher was well on course to make them very comfortable in their own right, but old habits died hard. Old fears ran deep. And didn't she know it.

"I cannot believe you have given away all your leverage to the *Guardian*—for the Cause." She sounded amazed to her own ears.

"Most of it, I should have specified." He sounded vaguely apologetic.

Of course, he would not give away all his aces. Tristan would probably always have a last card up his sleeve. Part of her found it very reassuring.

"The report will make headlines—will they name me?"

He shook his head. "They will not name any names."

She had to lean against the desk for support. The truth would be out. And she needn't choose between a coup and a reform by stealth. And yet. The storm of exaltation did not come. Her chest was still as tight, her pulse as erratic, as when she had entered his office. Today, work was not her priority.

She met Tristan's gaze directly. "No more secrets."

His features sharpened with alertness. "Between you and me? I agree. My secrecy was unforgivable."

"Well," she said. "Not unforgivable under the circumstances—not entirely."

His eyes were reading her intently. "You have had a change of mind, then."

"I know about Boudicca."

He tensed as though he had been caught in the act entirely unexpected. Like a boy with his hand deep in the jar of sweets. Like a rakehell who had just been exposed as having a loyal heart beating away beneath his crimson waistcoat.

"Ah," he said, very low.

How she longed to touch him.

"You could have chosen any kitten," she said. "But you chose one from my mother's cat's litter—why?"

He considered it. "I suppose I felt your parents owed you some comfort after casting you out."

A lump formed in her throat. "She has been a tremendous comfort to me."

"I'm pleased to hear it."

"Why did you never tell me that you thought fondly of me?"

He laughed softly. "*Fondly* was not how I felt about you, Lucie. Frankly, I was too inexperienced to understand much of my feelings, then. I did know that I was eighteen years old and wholly under my father's thumb. I had nothing to offer a woman; certainly not a woman like you—my father would have never approved, as you can imagine."

She could imagine it all too well.

"I said a few ghastly things to you at Ashdown," she said. "And I apologize. I am awfully sorry. I was . . . afraid."

He inclined his head. "I know."

"You do?"

"Yes. You hiss and scratch when you are scared." He shrugged. "Cat behavior."

She had done more than scratch him. She had made a serious attempt at slicing his heart to ribbons, in the misplaced effort of protecting her own.

And yet. . . . Her gaze shifted back to the papers on his desk. "You are helping us publish our study. In the *Manchester Guardian*."

Tristan gave her a suspiciously sympathetic look. "Yes."

"Thank you," she said, and, on a shaky breath, "I think I love you."

He held himself very still then. As though he would shatter like cracked glass if touched.

"You think?" His voice was gravelly, and the light of a lifetime of riotous emotions shone in his eyes.

She could only nod. It had taken great courage to say the three words, and she hoped he knew this about her, too.

Gradually, a smile spread over his face. He pushed away from the desk and sauntered toward her. "I'm glad to hear it. Because I was going to come for you."

She swallowed. "You were?"

His eyes shimmered in mesmerizing shades of gold. He cradled her face in his hands, his palms warm against her clammy skin. He had held her like this the first time he had kissed her. She understood now that the first time his lips had touched hers had marked the beginning of the end of her old world. And she would never be able to go back to it. The only way was forward, into vaguely chartered territory where kissing Tristan was necessary and good. And where her own place was largely a white patch on the map.

"You have not really thought I would simply leave it at that." He was studying her with mild reproach edging his lips.

She had. Before she had known about the cat.

"Silly," he said. "I would have tracked and found you. To grovel," he added hastily, "for keeping secrets, and for proposing to you with the grace of a wildebeest."

"Oh."

His head lowered, and her lips already parted in response. A wicked gleam kindled in his eyes. "I was going to kiss you." His mouth brushed against hers, the velvet of his lips light like a whisper. "And then," he said, "I would have shown you a list."

She drew back. "A list."

"I know you like a good list." His fingers slid into the chest pocket of his waistcoat and extracted a slip of paper. "Voilà."

The list contained names:

Mary Wollstonecraft
Mary Shelley
Ada Lovelace
Mary Somerville
Harriet Taylor Mill
Elizabeth Garrett Anderson
Millicent Fawcett

Mary Shelley, the author of *Frankenstein*. Elizabeth Garrett Anderson, Millicent's sister and the first woman to obtain a medical degree in London. Ada Lovelace, known for her excellent mathematical work on a difference engine. All women who were pioneers or outstanding contributors to a particular field. But if that was the criterion, the list was hardly exhaustive, and so her mind scrambled, trying to find the common denominator linking the names. . . .

"Women who advanced worthy causes outside the home," said Tristan, "despite being *burdened* with a husband, protocol, and often-times, children. Mary Somerville had six, I think. I am sure there are many more, it is my knowledge about them which is limited."

Her gaze locked with his. Heat ignited in her belly, her cheeks were hot. He had listened. During their argument at Wycliffe Hall, at the height of his own emotions, he had listened. And he was addressing her worries, rather than judging her bitterly, as was the common, if not only, reaction when a woman questioned her ordained role as mother and wife.

She was rather certain she loved him then.

"I knew of these women," she said hoarsely.

"I assumed as much," he said. "I wondered why you chose not to remember them."

She blew out a breath, crumpling the list in her fist. "What if I am not like them?"

His brows pulled together. "No one could deny that you are equal to them in terms of determination."

As observed from the outside, perhaps. Her fist holding the list was shaking. "I'm not good at doing things half-measure."

"I never guessed." He noticed the shaking, and his hand closed protectively over her fist. "What is it?"

She held his gaze with some difficulty. "What if I love you too much," she said. "What then?"

"Love me . . . too much?"

"Yes. And what if our connection resulted in a child, and what if I loved the child too much. And it made me stop fighting for the Cause with all that I have." Her mouth was trembling, too. "You saw what happened, how I began to neglect my duties—missing appointments, lacking attention. The truth is, I hardly felt sorry for it, in the moment. What if I stop fighting because I stop *caring*, whether I want to or not?"

His features gentled with dawning understanding. "I see," he said. "It is not only the constraints and loss of credibility you fear."

She gave a helpless little shrug. "Being at the front line is exhausting."

"Oh, I know."

"I do not need an excuse *not* to do battle, day after day. What if having people to love makes me weak."

"My sweet." He raised her hand to his lips and pressed a kiss against her fluttering pulse. "Is it possible you were simply caught in the whirlwind of something unfamiliar and exhilarating when you took up with me?"

"Well," she murmured. "Perhaps, yes."

"Also, do not confuse weakness and vulnerability. The two are hardly the same."

"They are not?" She sounded weepy.

His smile was infinitely tender. "No. I was vulnerable at the front line. Never weak."

"I suppose. I suppose there is indeed a difference."

"Then consider, perhaps, that you needn't have to choose," he said carefully. "What if love makes you want to fight harder? What if you look at your daughters and see the best reason to keep campaigning for women's liberty? Or, think of the sons who might raise hell in Parliament as long as women cannot."

What a picture he painted. Fierce red-haired daughters by her side. Lanky sons towering over her. Unfamiliar scenes she had rarely allowed herself to imagine, but well, she supposed she could consider it.

She gave a shake. "You are too good with words."

"I am." His fingertip swiped an indecisive tear from the corner of her eye. "Furthermore, I spent half my life ambitiously disregarding protocol. We shall make our own rules, always."

"But we would, wouldn't we? Alas, you would still own me!"

"How fortunate then, that I have not asked for your hand in marriage again."

Her mind blanked so utterly, she failed to surmise a reply.

Tristan grinned. "I was, however, going to go down on one knee and ask you to live in sin with me until the Married Property Act is amended."

And before her rounding eyes, he was, slowly, going down on one knee.

"I must be frank," he said, his upturned face deeply serious, "I loathe offering the woman I love less than my name. But given your objections, I understand. An official engagement, however, no matter how long, would defuse any scandal that might be about to descend upon us, while still allowing you to retain your money and independence."

She stared down at him, feeling dizzy, her heart racing.

Uncertainty flickered in his eyes at her silence, and she wanted to throw her arms around his neck.

"What about heirs," she managed. "You need an heir—and the Act might never be amended."

"I have an heir," he said. "Cousin Winterbourne. He is welcome to brick and mortar after I die. What I want is a life with you, Lucie."

She sank to the floor before him, her skirts against his knee. "Why?" she whispered.

"Why?" He sounded nonplussed.

She closed her eyes. "Why do you love me?" He had said it so easily: *the woman I love.*

"Why does one love?" There was a frown in his voice. "Why, one just loves, Lucie."

Perhaps I have always liked you, Lucie, . . . I had wanted you half my bloody life.

A part of her, still fledgling, tentatively unfolding, understood. And she had an inkling it was her own lack of trust that compelled her to doubt. And yet . . . "Reasons would help."

Because there was also a vast, hardened part of her upon which all the reasons why she was not lovable at all stood engraved. Clearly stated, measurable, numerous reasons: too demanding, too direct, too angular, too impatient. Too much, too little, too unnatural. But one by one, those faults could have been modified. Controlled. The diffuse magic of romantic love, however, seemed prone to slipping through her fingers like wafts of fog, beyond reason, beyond control. *One just loves.* She never wanted to lose him.

"Well," Tristan said. "For one, I have a favorable influence on you. You laugh more and you work less when I am with you."

Her eyes opened. "These things give *me* happiness."

He shrugged. "I discovered it is one and the same to me. There is great pleasure in pleasing a woman knowing she does not depend on my attention. You allowed me into your life because you desired me, not because you needed me. Very flattering. I consider you thoroughly seduced."

But she did need him. Love, she was learning, was needing someone even when he offered nothing but himself.

"It takes a brave man to want a woman who wants rather than needs him," she said instead.

"Fortunately, I can be brave. Shall I show you my Victoria Cross?"

"Now, be serious."

"I am. From the moment you galloped at me on an oversized horse when you were thirteen years old, you have been the bravest woman I have ever met. I thought I knew you, but it was at best a long-enduring, boyish obsession, fraught with stung pride and fantasy. The last months have opened my eyes to the woman behind the warrior, and you exceed what my imagination pictured, and I laugh at my stupidity. Your stubborn courage humbles me. Your rage inspires me. You are like a storm moving through, rearranging whomever you touch in your wake—imagine the trouble we could cause if we joined forces. But I digress. When you look at me, I know you look right into me, because it is what you do—you look deeply. You prefer truth over comfort. And believe me, I'm in need of a woman who laughs in the face of ugly, for there is some darkness in my soul. But my heart, blackened as it is, is yours, and only yours, until you stop desiring it. And it shall be yours even then."

When she didn't speak, he cocked his head. "Too purple?"

"No," she said thickly. "No. You feel seen by me."

"I do."

"Despite all the shrewish things I said."

"My love, I trust you because of all the shrewish things you say."

"I feel the same when I am with you," she said, her eyes swimming. "Seen."

He had seen the vulnerable girl in need of a friend ten years ago where everyone else had seen a scandalous shrew. He had seen her need to dance, to be held, to be challenged and pleasured and teased, and he had provided it. He had never been afraid of her. He had been afraid for his own heart, and for that, she could hardly blame him.

"Yes," she whispered. "I see you and you see me. So my answer is yes."

"Yes?" He sounded wary.

Her hands framed his face. "I agree to a betrothal until I can be your equal before the law." And before he could reply: "I must warn you now, married or not, I shall never have the disposition to be an Angel of the House."

His hands were on her waist, his smile dark. "You are looking at a man who prefers shieldmaidens over angels."

Shieldmaidens.

Surely not.

"The poems," she murmured. "Were they . . . ?"

He looked resigned. "I suppose, in some shape or form, it has always been you."

"I must say," she said after a breathless pause, "you are a terrible rake—a pretend rake. Next, you tell me you have been saving yourself for me all along."

He laughed, and she leaned in. His face blurred and their lips met in a kiss, finally, at last.

Yes.

They were kissing still when he moved, and she was floating, literally, her feet lifting off the floor, and she was up high in his arms cradled against his hard chest. His delicious scent curled around her, and it felt so very good to breathe deeply again.

He looked her in the eye. "Contra mundum?"

She smiled. "Contra mundum." *Against the world.*

She pressed her nose to the strong warm column of his neck.

"I should add what a lovely, pocket-sized thing you are," came his voice, "with very lickable breasts and an arse that fits my hands perfectly, all of which I find greatly arousing."

"I see. In the absence of male authority you could lawfully lord over me, you will just shamelessly try and seduce me into whatever it is you want with lewd talk."

"I'm afraid so."

She burrowed closer. "Where are we going?"

He was striding with great confidence toward the side entrance door.

"Do you know the director's apartment on the upper floor?" he said. "I suggest we make it a discreet second home for the duration of our betrothal."

"Discreet—I gather we are keeping our living in sin a secret?"

"Yes. I believe Mary Wollstonecraft's first child was born out of wedlock, but it is also true that the world is not ready for it yet, my love."

"An open-ended betrothal, and a secret love nest in our London office building. Blimey, we shall be spending a lot of time in our office."

"I hope it is sufficiently unromantic for your taste."

"I do like it."

He opened the door with his elbow. "The director's apartment," he said as he carefully maneuvered the spiral staircase with his arm full of woman. "It has a large settee. I'll ravish you on it."

"Oh," she said faintly. "Yes, please."

"And afterward, when you are soft and in a good mood, I shall

try and convince you to let me blackmail a peer or two into supporting the amendment of the Property Act."

She sighed with delight. "I insist you do it."

Because when a woman happened to acquire a rogue of her own,
she might as well make good use of him.

Epilogue

───────❧───────

The warm, golden glow of the first August afternoon filled Hattie's drawing room in the Randolph, inspiring a drowsy languidness in the four occupants lolling on various settees and fainting couches.

"I confess my legs do not feel healthfully exercised," said Annabelle, her half-lidded gaze idly following the cherubs dancing across the painted ceiling.

On the divan opposite, Hattie's head lifted a fraction. "They do not?"

"No," came the dark reply. "They feel veritably destroyed."

"Ah." Hattie slumped back into the silken pillow. "I'm relieved to hear it. For a moment, I worried I was the only one whose limbs feel like gelatin."

"You are not," Catriona assured her from the plush depths of her armchair.

"Still," Hattie said after a moment, "I'd quite like to ride one again, and soon. A proper Ordinary like Lucie's, even, not just a tricycle."

Lucie grinned. Today marked their very first outing on bicycles, or, in the case of Annabelle, Catriona, and Hattie, female-friendly Victor tricycles. It took a formidable effort to capsize these tricycles and Hattie had almost managed it twice—Lord knew how she would fare on a two-wheeled contraption.

She probingly rotated her right foot, then her left. *Her* legs felt fine. Surprising, considering she had taken up horseback riding again after Tristan had urged her to set a few hours a week aside for *pleasurable activities*, not counting those behind closed doors. He rented horses in a stable in Binsey, hardly fiery thoroughbreds, but the stables were sufficiently far from the university crowd and still reachable on foot from Norham Gardens. Every Tuesday night, they took a walk across Port Meadow and then went for a deliciously long ride along the Thames at dusk. *Astride*.

"You will need to wear breeches to ride an Ordinary," she told Hattie. A woman's split pantalets would cause the scandal of scandals if exposed to the world from the lofty heights of a bicycle.

"Gladly," said Hattie, "as long as they go *under* my skirts instead of replacing them."

"I wonder," said Catriona, "will our morals and fashion have to become more accommodating of bicycles before we are allowed to ride them or will the new technologies force a change in our minds and clothes?"

"Fashion follows practicality," Lucie said lazily. "Unless you are wealthy. Then it serves to display wealth."

"I dread to say it, but I am beginning to share your cynical views," Hattie said. "I have been corresponding with Lady Harberton on the matter of my Rational Dress Society article for the *Discerning Ladies'*, and it appears she harbors quite a rage against the current fashion of trains in female dress. In her last letter, she detailed the relics she found in her niece's train after a London outing. I don't recall all the items, but they included"—and there she squinted—"they included two cigar ends, a portion of pork pie, an orange peel, half a sole of a boot, chewed tobacco, hairpins, and toothpicks. Rather unattractive, seeing it spelled out."

Her friends' horrified groans were still ongoing when she stretched out her arm to angle for the last éclair on the table.

"You should write a regular column about fashion hazards for the *Discerning Ladies'*, and how to remedy them," Lucie suggested. "Officially make a name for yourself as an expert."

"I should," Hattie said, and raised the pastry to her lips. "Harriet Greenfield, discerning art and fashion fiend."

"Speaking of which, how was your excursion to London last week, Hattie? Pre-Raphaelites, was it not?" asked Catriona.

The éclair abruptly stopped its descent into Hattie's mouth and quivered suspended in midair.

"It was excellent, thanks." Hattie's voice was close to a squeak. "Very . . . educational."

Lucie watched her friend's alabaster throat and cheeks flush a nervous red. Interesting. "What excursion?" she probed.

Hattie avoided her eyes. "A private art exhibition in Chelsea. About the Pre-Raphaelites."

"So I gathered," Lucie said wryly. "I assume you escaped Mr. Graves to go?"

"Yes?" Definitely a squeak.

"How did Mr. Graves cope?" asked Annabelle, possibly planning to escape her own protection officer for an excursion or two.

Hattie's answer was to sink her pearly teeth into the pastry with a shrug, a wealthy girl unconcerned about what the staff might think.

Oh, she was hiding something outrageous.

But Hattie could never keep her secrets for long. When she was ready, she would summon them and spill it all to the last detail.

Her own secret, that she was presently sharing her life with Tristan behind closed doors, had been received surprisingly well by her friends. Much more readily, in fact, than the news that she might—one day—marry him, which they deemed worryingly out of character. It had taken a very large engagement ring on Lucie's finger—courtesy of Lady Rochester's heirloom chest—for Hattie to approve of the idea. It had taken every ounce of Tristan's charm to win over the coolly appraising Catriona. Annabelle, still the only one who knew of the clandestine affair preceding the betrothal, had left it at a knowing smirk and a "You do not like him at all, hm?"

She was besotted with him. Every morning, she woke up feeling light and warm, knowing he was hers. In time, she might even become used to the presence of someone in her life who cared about her needs more than she did. It was also very nice to have his unruffled presence by her side when their report broke. Powerful men were closing ranks behind the editor of the *Guardian* to defend his choice to publish the findings, but they were outnumbered by other powerful men who accused the paper of waging war on the sanctity of the family. The main point of contention was not the widespread maltreatment of wives in their own homes, but the revelation that middle- and upper-class wives were being maltreated, too. Well. It was to be expected that a tyrant who saw power slipping from his grip would double his efforts to hold on. The rage they now witnessed was proof that they had done more than pull the beast's tail. They had fired a shot at its very heart: every man's prerogative to be the unaccountable rule in his home. While the *Manchester Guardian* hadn't named names, for the time being, the suffragist chapters across Britain had decided to lay low, and, as usual, had to wait until the dust had settled. Resorting to bicycle rides for diversion was the least a woman could do under the circumstances.

One welcome effect of the outcry surrounding the report was the distraction from the betrothal. There had been a headline in the *Pall Mall Gazette* after the announcement: *Who Tamed Who? The London Lothario vs The Suffragist Shrew!* But since the long-standing connection of their houses was well known, as was their new business relationship, and since Wycliffe and Rochester had issued the announcement in the *Times* in accordance with the custom, the rumors were not boiling beyond the ordinary. Rochester had resigned himself to keeping mum on all matters for the time being. Since his heir had only barely escaped a full-blown scandal he was not keen to pour water onto the rumor mills.

The only one besmirched had been Cecily, and, by extension, the House of Wycliffe. And there, too, had been a development to remedy the situation.

Lucie propped herself up on her elbows. "I forgot to share the latest news."

Three drowsy faces turned toward her.

"My brother is engaged to be married."

Three brows creased with confusion. She had not the habit of talking about her family nor of being interested in weddings.

"To our cousin, the Lady Cecily." She grinned at the collective gasp. "Who would have thought Tommy had it in him. He's a prig, but at least he is a proper prig—denting his own reputation and pride to restore the family's standing. I do salute him, truly I do."

"Oh, but it was sly of him," Hattie said. "He was plainly pining for her at the house party and now Lady Cecily will forever be in his debt and devotedly adore him."

"That, too," Lucie said after a small pause. "Hattie, are you certain you don't wish to tell us about the Pre-Raphaelite Art Exhibition in Chelsea?"

"Very," Hattie said promptly, and Lucie knew the next scandal was already waiting in the wings.

Author's Note

Lucie's story was inspired by a Victorian verse and a letter I had come across during my research for *Bringing Down the Duke*, the first book in this series.

Below, some of the stanzas of the verse:

Woman's Rights

The right to be a comforter
Where other comforts fail
The right to cheer the drooping heart
When troubles most assail.

The right to train the infant mind,
To think of Heaven and God;
The right to guide the tiny feet
The path our Saviour trod

The right to be a bright sunbeam,
In high or lowly home
The right to smile with loving gleam,
And point to joys to come

Such are the noblest woman's rights,
The rights which God hath given,
The right to comfort man on earth,
And smooth his path to heaven.

By M.C.M.R.

The following excerpts are from a letter by Mrs. Anne Brown Adams, daughter of U.S. American abolitionist John Brown. It was addressed to Canadian abolitionist Mr. Alexander Ross, sometime between 1870 and 1880. For *A Rogue of One's Own*, I took the liberty to repackage it into two letters that had been sent to Lucie by British women:

"*. . . The struggle for a married woman's rights will be a longer and a harder fought battle than any other that the world has [inserted: ever] known. Men have been taught that they are absolute monarchs in their families, (even in a republican country,) ever since the world began, and that to kill a wife by inches, is not murder, women are taught from infancy that to betray [inserted: by look or word] or even to mention to an intimate friend the secrets of their married life, is worse than disgraceful, There in lies the power of the man, He knows that no matter what he does, the woman will keep silent as the grave [2]*
I could tell you things that have come under my observation, that would make the blood boil in your veins (. . .)
Women are taught that their only hope of heaven, is to 'endure to the end,' (. . .) I know a man who tells his wife 'I own you, I have got a deed (marriage license and certificate) to you and got it recorded, I have a right to do what I please to you,'. . . ."

I found the contrast between the poem and a real woman's private thoughts rather startling. Clearly, the Victorian cult of domesticity had a dark underbelly—behind closed doors, it was the luck of the draw for the Angels in the House: wives had very little legal recourse if their husbands mistreated them, and they could not just discuss matters with their friends, either.

I wondered how a woman like Lucie who had her eyes wide open would fall in love under such circumstances. What would make her say "I do" to effectively being owned?

I took a closer look at real-life Victorian couples, such as Millicent Fawcett, who led the British suffrage movement, and Harriet Taylor Mill, who influenced John Stuart Mill's famous essay "The Subjection of Women." Both women were proponents of women's suffrage before they got married, neither had acute financial pressures, and both decided to give their few rights away anyway. I made the wild guess that they had fallen in love and wanted to be with their husbands, come what may. It is well documented, however, that their husbands were at the forefront in the fight for women's rights in Parliament.

Lucie would have married Tristan in 1882, when the Married Women's Property Act was amended, though women in Britain were not allowed to vote until 1918. The Property Act still exists in British legislation; it was last amended in 2016 to allow a widow in her own right to enforce her late husband's life assurance policy.

All policies mentioned in this novel existed at the time. Unfortunately, so did the collection of debris that Lady F. W. Harberton, head of the Rational Dress Society, detailed in her battle against the train in female dress.

Tristan's character was inspired by the artists who were part of the British Decadent Movement, which was led by Irish writer Oscar Wilde.

I took artistic license with some timings: the poem "When You Are Old" by Yeats was first published in 1889. The excerpt from Millicent Fawcett's lecture at the LSE dates to the 1870s. Ruth Symthers's advice for new brides was not published until 1894 and is widely considered a hoax in any case.

Acknowledgments

Finishing any book is a challenge, but second books are special beasts. I'm lucky—a whole crowd of wonderful people supported me during *A Rogue of One's Own*. A huge thank-you to:

Matt—my love.

Mum and Oma—so endlessly supportive.

Bernie—what badassery, to do a one-day round trip to NYC in a three-piece suit. From PA. In July.

All my friends who picked up a romance novel for the first time—special thanks to Anna, Rob, and Nils.

All my fantastic cousins, from Beirut to Niagara Falls. *Merci.*

My sensitivity readers.

Kate and Montse—what would I do without a daily dose of Lilac Wine?

A battalion of historical fiction and romance authors who took the time to support my work—in particular Renée Rosen, Chanel Cleeton, Gaelen Foley, Eva Leigh, Anna Campbell, Megan McCrane, Amy E. Reichert, and Stephanie Thornton.

I wouldn't be where I am without their endorsement and encouragement.

Jennifer Probst, Rachel Van Dyken, Lauren Layne—the Tree of Trust is a gem and I love being part of it.

A special thank-you to my marvelous agent, Kevan Lyon, who is always a step ahead of things, and to my formidably patient, eagle-eyed editor, Sarah Blumenstock. Working with you is pure joy.

A Rogue
of
One's Own

EVIE DUNMORE

Discussion Questions

1. Throughout the course of the novel, Lucie discovers her sexuality. How would you describe this journey? What do you think were the main drivers behind Lucie's risky decision to accept Tristan's offer, knowing that a sexual relationship outside of marriage would be socially unacceptable?

2. Can you relate to Lucie's concerns that working hard on a cause will automatically pose a conflict with married life or a romantic relationship? Do you agree or disagree? Be specific.

3. How would you describe the conflict between Lucie and her mother? Did your opinion of Lucie's mother change throughout the story? Why or why not?

4. Tristan does not immediately turn into a suffrage activist, despite witnessing how little protection the law provides his mother from the abuses of her husband. Why do you think that is?

5. What role does Annabelle play in this story? How is her approach to the Cause different from Lucie's?

6. Fashion is a frequent topic of discussion among Hattie, Lucie, Annabelle, and Catriona. In the Victorian era, women of means were expected to present themselves fashionably and dress immaculately at all times. Fashion was also one of the few ways through which a woman could express her personality. How is fashion used in this story? Do you think fashion is political for Lucie and her friends? Why or why not? Do you feel fashion is still more than *just fashion* today?

7. Women's magazines in the Victorian era were frequently edited by men, and usually aimed to inform and facilitate women's correct conduct in society and in the home. How has this changed?

8. While we do not see Lucie tackling an overarching political event in the course of her story, she is regularly confronted—due to her political work—with what we today would call microaggression. Do you recall any of those instances, and how do you think these experiences would shape an activist like Lucie over time?

9. Lucie tells Tristan women have been explicitly fighting for equality for nearly a hundred years—ever since Mary Wollstonecraft wrote *The Vindication on the Rights of Women*—yet *here we are, still fighting*—another 140 years on. Do you feel this is still applicable, why or why not?

Don't miss Hattie and Lucian's story,
now available from Berkley Romance!

London, July 1880

All the best adventures began with escaping Mr. Graves. All the most perilous ones, too, admittedly—as she hovered on the rain-soaked pavement in front of the Chelsea town-house she was about to infiltrate, feeling hot and damp beneath her woollen cloak. Hattie Greenfield's mind inexorably wandered back to the last time she had run from her protection officer. It had resulted in an altercation with a toad of a policeman, and a dear friend being held in Milbank penitentiary.

She raised her chin at the lacquered front door atop the steps. Unlike the last time, she was not partaking in an inherently risky women's rights march but in a private art gallery tour. Perfectly harmless. Granted, her friends would point out that both the art and the gallery were owned by a man society had nicknamed Beelzebub, and that he furthermore happened to be her father's business rival, and no, she should not be found admiring the man's Pre-Raphaelites unchaperoned.

She lifted her skirts and began the ascent, because first of all, Mr. Blackstone—Beelzebub—would not be present; in fact, very few people had ever seen him in the flesh. Second, she had registered for the tour as a Miss Jones, Classics student at Cambridge, rather than as Harriet Greenfield, Oxford art student and banking heiress. And lastly, she would not be unchaperoned—the full tour through the

Sorcha Gallery of Arts and Antiques comprised a handful of other young art connoisseurs and likely *their* chaperones, and the invite in her reticule said she was keeping them waiting. The tour had begun at two o'clock sharp.

The iron-cast lion's head on the door had large, pointy teeth. The warning that she was about to enter the lion's den was almost too shrill to ignore for someone selectively superstitious. However, the advanced hour on her small pocket watch was all but burning a hole through her bodice.

The repeated thuds of the door knocker appeared to fade away unnoticed into the entrance hall beyond.

She rang the bell.

Silence.

Beneath the hem of her camouflage cloak, her wet foot began to tap. They must have begun the tour without her, unwilling to wait past the acceptable fifteen minutes. She had climbed from the hackney, hopelessly stuck in traffic and a downpour soon after leaving Victoria Station to walk the last quarter mile, and now she felt like a drowned mouse all for naught? The pounding of iron on oak became a little frantic.

The heavy door swung back unexpectedly.

The man facing her was not a butler. His thinning gray hair was disheveled, he wore a paint-stained apron, and he smelled pungently of turpentine and . . . antique wax polish?

She tried to assess without staring whether his face, long and lined, was familiar to her from the artistic circles.

His assessment of her person was not subtle at all: his gaze searched the empty space to her right where a chaperone should have been—then roamed from the tips of her sodden shoes up over her cloak to linger on her undoubtedly frizzy red hair.

"And you'll be?" he drawled.

She cleared her throat. "I am here for the tour."

"The tour?" Comprehension dawned in the man's eyes. "The tour."

"Yes."

His thin lips curled with derision. "I see."

She shifted from one foot to the other. "I'm afraid I was delayed on my journey. I have come all the way from outside London, you see, and then there was such dreadful traffic on Lyall Street because of the heavy rain; the roads are—"

"Come on then," he said, and abruptly stepped aside with a wave of his hand.

He had to be an artist, and he was cross, likely because she had interrupted his work; male artists had this prerogative, to let it be known that they were cross.

No maid or footman was in sight to take her cloak and hat, in fact the entrance hall was yawningly empty. A nervous flutter tickled her neck. But the turpentine man was already several paces ahead, his hasty footsteps echoing on the black-and-white marble tiles.

"Sir." She hurried after him, water squelching between her toes.

He turned into a shadowed hallway. To her left and right, the intriguing lines and curves of statues and vases beckoned, but it was impossible to take a closer look; not slipping on the polished floor at this pace was a balancing act. Ahead of her, the man had stopped and opened a door.

He motioned for her to enter, but she hesitated on the doorstep, for while the room was brightly lit and spacious, there was no group of art students waiting for her here. There was no one here at all.

She glanced up at the painter, and he flicked his fingers impatiently at the nearest settee. "Go on, take a seat."

She gave a small shake. She could hardly sit down on the butter yellow silk in her damp cloak; even from here she could tell the settee was from the days of Louis XIV.

"Will you send someone to take my coat, please, Mr. . . . ?"

The man inclined his head in a mock bow. "You shall be seen to shortly."

"Sir, I must ask you to—"

The door was firmly closed in her face, and she stood blinking at the white wood paneling.

"Right," she muttered.

She blew out a breath. In the silence, the beat of her heart was loud in her ears. Warm sweat trickled down her back. Her toes felt . . . wrinkled in her soaked cotton stockings.

She tried a smile. "Adventurous," she said. "This is fabulous, and adventurous."

She turned back to the room, and briefly forgot about her sorry feet altogether.

This was a pirate's lair. And the treasures were piling up high. Every shelf and table surface coming into focus was crowded with splendor: glossy, whirling porcelain couples—Meissen, at a second glance; filigree ivory-and-gold statuettes; ornately carved boxes with softly rounded edges in all shades of jade green. Select pieces were illuminated by small table lamps with ceramic shades so fine, the gaslight shone through them as if they were made of silk. The wall opposite was papered in a riotously floral Morris wallpaper—a waste, considering it was covered from floor to ceiling in paintings, their gilded frames nearly touching.

"Oh my."

She laughed softly. On the Morris wall, a Cranach the Elder was on display, in between a picnic scene that looked like a Monet, and a smaller painting in the brown tones of a Dutch Renaissance work. Most people would have considered those considerably more intriguing than the Pre-Raphaelites. But in the fireplace to her right, a few embers were still aglow, and presently they held the greatest appeal of all.

She carefully picked her way through the array of decorated side tables, but her cloak still jostled one of them and sent a porcelain ballerina swaying precariously on her pointy toes. Goodness. Mr. Blackstone had a lot to answer for—each one of these pieces deserved its own secure display case. What had possessed him or his curator to jumble them together like guests of a carelessly composed, over-crowded dinner party, and in a room open to the public no less?

The heat coming from the grate of the fireplace was feeble; she stood as close as was safely possible in billowing garments and she was still shivering. Her reflection in the wide mirror above the mantelshelf confirmed she looked a fright: the purple feather on her hat was thin as a rat's tail, her usually silky curls were a fuzzy riot, her upturned nose glowed pink.

If this was what her little walk had done to her face, she shuddered to think what havoc it had wreaked upon her slippers. She stuck out a foot from beneath her hem. Dainty heels, white silk, embroidered with the tiniest pearls. Clearly damaged beyond repair. Her stomach dipped. There went another of her favorites.

It was, by some stretch of imagination, Professor Ruskin's fault. If he had not called her *Abduction of Persephone* "lovely" the other week, she probably would not have boarded the train this morning. It had been one such *lovely* too many since she had enrolled at Oxford last year. He had said it in passing, with a friendly nod; then he had lingered next to Lord Clotworthy's isle and had critiqued his work for a full ten minutes, and she had stood with her ears straining to catch his advice on how to strengthen the Gothicness in the painting. Somehow, the idea to take a good long look at Millais's *Ophelia*, which Blackstone had miraculously secured for his gallery, had taken root during that class. And yes, there might have also been a tiny, tantalizing temptation in the prospect of setting foot onto property owned by Mr. Blackstone, the one man in Britain who let her father's luncheon invitations pass unanswered. . . .

Her attention, of its own volition, shifted to the pair of green-glazed, round-bellied vases flanking the mantelshelf clock. They were easily overlooked at first glance as they hid in plain sight, unremarkable in their earthy simplicity like the poor relation in a ball-room filled with opulence. And yet . . . their shape . . . her eyes narrowed at the relief on the nearer vase. After a moment's hesitation, she tugged the glove off her left hand, stuffed it into her cloak pocket, and lightly skimmed her index finger over the simple pattern on the vase's rim. A keen sensation prickled down her back. She was looking at something extraordinary indeed. With some luck, there was a mark to confirm her suspicions—if she dared to check for it.

Her deliberation was brief.

She took the vase in both hands, handling it with the anxious care she would afford a raw egg, and turned it bottom-up. She sucked in a breath—there was a mark. All the fine hairs on her arms stood erect. This unassuming piece was almost certainly a Han vase. Or an excellent counterfeit of one. *If* it was real, it was two thousand years old. Her palms turned hot and damp.

"I'd rather you not touch that," came a gravelly male voice.

She jumped and shrieked, pressing the vase to her breast.

What she saw in the mirror made her freeze.

The pirate had returned to his lair.

He must have very quietly opened the door while she had been engrossed. He was watching her, with his arms folded across his broad chest and a brawny shoulder leaning against the door frame.

She turned slowly, her stomach hollowing. While he was of course not a pirate, this man was no improvement over the ill-mannered artist earlier. He was not decent—he was missing both his jacket and his cravat, and his sleeves were rolled up and exposed muscular fore-arms. His coal black hair looked rough to the touch. Stubble dark-ened his square jaw. But the most uncivilized part of him were his eyes—they were trained on her with a singular intensity that curled her toes in her wet slippers.

"I just . . ." her voice faltered.

He closed the door. Her grip on the vase tightened. Obviously, he had been sent to fetch her, but her instincts were alarmed and urged her to retreat. He moved in on her smoothly, too smoothly, rattling precisely nothing on his prowl through the delicate art pieces. She was motionless like a rabbit arrested by a predator's stare until he was right in front of her.

He *was* arresting. His eyes were cool and gray as slate. Impossible to tell his age; he radiated a compelling vitality, but he had the look of a man who had lived too much, too soon. His features were all contrasts: coarse but well-proportioned; his inky lashes and dark brows stark against his pale skin. His nose might have been noble once, but it had been broken and now the bump vaguely disturbed the symmetry of his face.

He held her in his gaze while he slid two fingers of his right hand into the mouth of the vase. Which she was still clutching like a thief caught in the act.

"Why don't you give this to me," he said.

Her skin pulsed hot red with embarrassment as she released the precious ceramic. Words were hopelessly jammed in her throat. She had brothers, and she studied alongside men, daily. She was never tongue-tied in their presence—she was never *tongue-tied*. But as the man placed the vase back onto the mantelshelf, she was preternaturally aware of his scent, an attractive blend of pine soap and starch, incongruently clean with his piratical appearance. She was altogether too aware of this man being a *man*. He was of average height, but so very . . . broad. Shirtsleeves of finest cotton clung snugly to his biceps and the balls of his shoulders, hinting at swells and ridges of muscle no gentleman would possess.

She glanced back up at him just as he inclined his head, and their eyes met in another mutual inspection. Her mouth turned dry. Perhaps it was a trick of the light, but his irises had darkened by a shade or two.

"I had not meant to touch it," she said, sounding prim.

A faintly ironic expression passed over his face. It failed to soften the hard set of his mouth. "And with whom do I have the pleasure, miss?"

The heat emanating from his body was warmer than the embers on the grate. She knew because he stood too close. His right hand was still braced on the mantelshelf next to her shoulder, his arm subtly cutting off any escape route to the left.

"My name is Miss Jones." It came out on an unnatural pitch.

A flash of silver lit his eyes as he registered the lie. "And what is the purpose of your visit, Miss Jones?"

He was a Scotsman. His *R*s were emerging as softly rolling growls. This certainly explained the Celtic dark locks and fair skin. . . .

She licked her lips nervously. The purpose of her visit? "The full tour?"

There was a subtle tension in him, and a flare of contempt in the depth of his gaze. "And are you certain of that?"

"Of course, and I would be much obliged if you could—"

He raised a hand to her face, and a rough fingertip lightly touched her cheekbone.

The man was touching her. A man was touching her.

Everything slowed.

The gray of his eyes was as soft and menacing as smoke.

She should scream. Slap him. Her body did not obey, it stood hot and useless as the air between them crackled with a knowing, that she was on the cusp of something vast.

"Aye," came his voice as if from a distance. "Then I shall give you the tour, Miss Jones."

His fingers curved around the soft nape of her neck, and then his mouth was on hers.

Photograph by the author

Evie Dunmore is the acclaimed author of *Bringing Down the Duke*. Her League of Extraordinary Women series is inspired by her passion for romance, women pioneers, and all things Victorian. In her civilian life, she is a consultant with an M.Sc. in Diplomacy from Oxford. Evie lives in Berlin and pours her fascination with nineteenth-century Britain into her writing. She is a member of the British Romantic Novelists' Association (RNA).

VISIT THE AUTHOR ONLINE

EvieDunmore.com

EvieDunmoreAuthor

Evie_Dunmore

EvietheAuthor